FUGITIVE FROM ASTERON

GEN LAGRECA

Winged Victory Press
www.wingedvictorypress.com

Available in print and ebook editions

Fugitive From Asteron
ISBN paperback: 978-0-97445792-5
Library of Congress Control Number: 2015907926

Published by Winged Victory Press
www.wingedvictorypress.com

Cover by Elizabeth Watson, graphic designer
emwatson@earthlink.net

Printed in the United States of America
First edition 2016

Quality discounts are available for bulk purchases of this book. For information, please contact Winged Victory Press.
Email: service@wingedvictorypress.com

OTHER NOVELS BY GEN LAGRECA
available in print and ebook editions
NOBLE VISION
A DREAM OF DARING

AUTHOR'S NOTE

Fugitive From Asteron is actually my first work of fiction, completed before my two previously published novels, *Noble Vision* (2005) and *A Dream of Daring* (2013). Now updated to reflect today's technological advances and tomorrow's possibilities, it's my third novel to be published.

I want to thank Sara Pentz and Randy Saunders for reading an early draft of this novel and offering valuable comments.

CHAPTER 1

This was to be the day I ended my life.

The thought jolted me as a cold draft hit my face and brought me back to consciousness. How long had I been out? I wondered. Was there still time to act before the sun rose?

I knew by the familiar odor of stale vomit that the guards had thrown me into the room for attitude adjustment, a small cell in the men's section of the space workers' quarters where I lived. No one had bothered taking me to the detention center, with its tighter security, since I would only have to be moved again in the morning and not much was left of me anyway.

I lay curled on the concrete floor. When I tried to move, a mass of raw wounds throbbed in protest. Gashes on my back burned against the cement, and my fingers rested on a sticky curd of my blood. A thick metal ring around my neck chained me to a pipe that was supposed to bring heat, but none was wasted on me.

With effort I pried my eyelids open. Seeping through the bars of the cell's small window was a yellow tinge of moonlight. There was still time! If I could execute the plan I had devised before I lost consciousness, I would not have to face another day.

Outside the barred door of my cell, the hallway was dark. The lack of lighting told me that it was the nightly blackout period, a measure taken to save power in the building—and one that would aid my escape. I needed to wait until the guard walked past my cell on his patrol. That would give me the time between his rounds to get away. I remained lying down so that he would think I was still unconscious.

In the moonlight I could see a pair of eyes staring at me from the room's only ornament, a poster of our leader, Feran. He wore his kind public face, one that he never bothered to display when dealing with just me. "One People, One Will," read the slogan above Feran's head. One will did indeed run things here on the planet of Asteron, and it was not mine.

In fact, I had no will left to go on. It felt strange to lose everything and have only a vacant space inside me where my dreams had once lived. But there was still one thing I cared about: the place where I would die. That would be of *my* choosing.

As I waited in the gloom for the guard to pass, the fog of unconsciousness lifted. For me, to be awake was to be angry, so I felt my fury gaining steam, despite my effort to cool it.

When someone died on Asteron, people noted the occasion with nothing more than indifference. Could I not feel that way about my own end? Could I not find peaceful acceptance in my final moments? Or would I meet my end without relief from the hot pain of having the things I had lived for ripped from my life?

I had heard elders talk about another time, forgotten now, when a death brought great sorrow. The elders said that people would gather to recollect the life of the deceased, and that this was called paying one's respects.

Memories from my own life were running loose in my mind despite my resolve to lock them down. Was this my way of paying my respects . . . to myself? I wondered. Lying there in the darkness, I thought of the things that had fueled my life and how those very things had also sealed my doom. I thought of that night of the four moons several months ago, when my troubles had begun. . . .

CHAPTER 2

That night, I was in my aircraft on a mission. I saw the four moons of Asteron through the canopy of my plane. Only occasionally were all four of the planet's satellites visible at once, so they captured my attention.

During past flights, I would gaze in wonder at the stars and dare to imagine a day when I would be assigned to pilot a craft to a world beyond my homeland. But on this particular night there were other matters on my mind. I had to execute a task new to me, and I could not let anything go wrong.

I had an important assignment to perform, but my body was rebelling against the job. Dank sweat formed under my flight suit. My right hand tensed in a vise grip over the control stick, even though I was some distance from my target in the calm, pre-dawn sky. My mind was also playing tricks. The spectacular array of glowing instruments surrounding my lone seat in the cockpit seemed ready to close in and swallow me.

Ahead I could see the deep blue of dawn and the red tint of the sun rising. Below, a thick layer of clouds blanketed the ground in gloom, sparing me the sight of the approaching city that was my destination.

Interrupting the silence of the sky and the hypnotic hum of the engines, a voice suddenly blared from my headset. *The Daily Word* was beginning its regular broadcast, a steady stream of messages throughout the day to provide Asteronians with the latest news, along with what our leaders called inspirational thoughts to bolster our morale. These broadcasts were so pervasive—in the streets and buildings of every town and in the fields of every countryside—that people found them unavoidable. Even pilots when not engaged in combat were obliged to listen, so there was no way to shut off the sound. Because I was in no mood for such enlightenment, I turned the volume down to a whisper.

The narrator began with his usual forced vigor. "People of Asteron, we begin another day of dedication to the ideals that make us the best planet to live on in the galaxy."

I had idle time before I would need to descend, too much time in which I could do nothing but agonize. If I failed in my mission, I would never fly again, perhaps never breathe again. To me the two activities—flying and breathing—had become one. How had it happened, I wondered, that flying became the whole of my universe? I could not remember how it started, because it had always been that way. Soaring across the moonlit sky, I thought of the risks I had taken to sit in a cockpit, to grasp a control stick, and to feel the thrill of an aircraft yielding to my command.

Since childhood, I had wanted to fly to other worlds the way a bird flies to trees. I had observed the curious aliens who came here to mine our gold, wondering where they lived and what life was like beyond Asteron. But although those humanoid figures looked like us, we were told they were different inside. The aliens were primitive, whereas we Asteronians had advanced beyond them.

Our officials prohibited us from having contact with the aliens for fear they might corrupt our ideals, so they remained a mystery to me. Of the educational materials, books, and news sources approved for us, none answered the question that absorbed me: What people and worlds existed beyond Asteron?

"The first pillar of our society is *equality*," droned the narrator of *The Daily Word*. "There are no winners and losers here, no exploiters and exploited, no rich and poor. We are *all* winners, *all* rich in mind and body, *all* living the same as everybody else in a state of supreme fairness."

Why was there no fairness for me, I wondered, when I had finished school and passed the examinations to become a flier? I had scored too high on the tests, so I was disqualified. Fliers were supposed to obey orders without question, like robots in the sky, and high grades made such compliance doubtful.

I remembered how Feran had yearned to create a robotic fleet of aircraft by buying alien technology unavailable on Asteron. But this was unaffordable because of an issue our rulers did not like to discuss, the growing, unrelenting menace we faced daily: the famine. With resources strained by warding off hunger, Feran's robotic fleet never came to be, so instead he sought human pilots who best matched his ideal.

"The second pillar that defines us is *unity*. The debate about our direction was resolved long ago. Now everyone accepts what we have shown to be the best course for all and rejects the regressive notions of those who try to stir up unrest," said the narrator. "We are one people with one united will to do good for all Asteronians."

One will directed my mission, and I warned myself that I must obey it. Tonight, more than ever before, I must follow orders. My past record on this matter was not very good at all. In fact, my missteps had almost cost me my job as a pilot, but I was given one final chance to redeem myself, and tonight's mission was it.

"Our third pillar is *security*. We defend our homeland against those troublesome aliens who spread doubts, disloyalty, and corruption among us."

Had I been corrupted? Even without help from the aliens, I knew I had been. My corruption had started early and was already hard to control by the time I finished school, when the teachers who gave us our work assignments designated me as a train dispatcher. I found in our group a boy of my height and similar appearance named Arial, who wanted a ground job but was assigned to pilot training. Although we were supposed to accept the work given to us without question, Arial was so frightened of flying—and dying—that I persuaded him to switch places with me. Then with the technical skills I had carefully honed, I caused something unexpected to happen. Right after we had received our job assignments, there was a terrible crash of the computer system that recorded them, and in the confusion that followed, no one noticed the change of two boys among hundreds. That was how I got the name Arial and learned to fly.

"The topic of this morning's broadcast is 'character,' and here to discuss it is our leader, Feran," continued the narrator.

Character? Why that *of all topics?* I wondered. According to my superiors, character was the thing I sorely lacked. They observed that as my flying skills progressed, my attitude regressed. My job became testing aircraft because my commanders could send me out in anything, including the slipshod products manufactured on Asteron, and I somehow always managed to bring my plane back. But I did things that were unacceptable. Recently, when my commander instructed me to test a new plane, I did so, but not according to his protocol. That time my plane was an advanced, alien-made ship, the best craft I had ever seen, an engineering masterpiece equipped to do my bidding. I tested it beyond the commander's modest protocol and to the limits of its performance and my imagination. I turned, I rolled, I looped, I dived in every possible way. I stalled, dropping from the sky in a whirling spiral, then managing to stabilize as the ground closed in. I flew into the mountains and charged through the canyons at high speed. When I returned, I jumped out, threw my arms up to embrace the fuselage, and kissed the plane that had given me the greatest thrill of my life. I had never before kissed anything or anyone.

Then I saw the icy eyes of my commander staring at me. I was not surprised that he then had me beaten, only that he spared my life—not because of the value of my life but because of a sudden crisis in a city of Asteron, a crisis requiring the deployment of every skilled pilot. That was why my commander had given me one final chance—today.

The next voice to filter through my earphones was one of strained calm, but I could sense the anger beneath it.

"My fellow Asteronians," said Feran, "*The Daily Word* today is about character. All of us, especially the citizens of Nubel, need to remember that our security rests on maintaining a peaceful, law-abiding society. I regret that a band of insurgents has poisoned so many in the city of Nubel. Traitors have infected the people there with outmoded, wrongheaded, and dangerous ideas. Poisoned by seditious alien writings smuggled into Nubel, the insurgents have attacked the government. They have reopened debates settled long ago and caused an uprising. Those taking to the streets have been ordered to disband, but they have refused. They show a deplorable lack of character, and they shall be punished. I want to assure you, I will protect your safety. The anarchists of Nubel will be dealt with as the law requires."

I flew into the breaking dawn and descended through the clouds. I could now see Nubel clearly. I glanced at a monitor showing an aerial photograph of my target. It was the stretch of road between the clock tower and the bridge.

Nubel, I knew, was doomed. The people were armed only with their dreams, but Feran had the military. The rebellion in Nubel would be crushed just as all the others like it had been. I told myself that if I failed, Feran would simply order another from his fleet to execute the task. But if I performed the unspeakable deed, I would still have a chance to fly . . . and maybe one day to do the unimaginable . . . to reach another world. The people of Nubel were finished. But was I?

Feran's battle cry rang from my headset: "Our spirit is unbreakable. We are one people with one harmonious will! Asteron!"

I spotted the clock tower. I descended further and located the bridge. My mission was to blanket everything in between. What was in between? A sea of humanity crowded every space in the roadway between the clock tower and the bridge, a sea of placard-waving, fist-raising, shouting people committing the first—and last—unbridled act of their lives. Defying Feran's demand that they return to their quarters, the protesters of Nubel had increased in numbers overnight, flooding the streets to continue their defiance.

A knot contracted in my stomach like a fist. I was unbearably warm and sweating feverishly. Would I black out and never have to face the dreaded moment?

After Feran's statement, *The Daily Word* broadcasted comments from what it said were random people gathered outside the studio. They spoke in the monotonous tones of those reciting rehearsed lines. First I heard a female voice. "Our loyalty to Asteron is unshakable. We stand by Feran."

Would I smell the burning flesh from here? Would I hear the final screams?

Next I heard a male voice. "We will defend our homeland against terrorists and anarchists."

I descended. There was no resistance of any kind. I descended further until I almost scraped the buildings. The deafening roar of my engines startled the people below. The brown streak of hats I had seen from a distance between the clock tower and the bridge became an unbroken ribbon of ashen faces looking up at my plane. My hand fidgeted on the control stick as I placed my thumb on the weapon-release button.

The next voice I heard through my headset belonged to a child. "Feran takes care of the children. He will protect us from our enemies."

The starving, desperate people of Nubel stood their ground. They did not flinch. The thousands of faces between the clock tower and the bridge stared up at me, their bodies fixed in place. They would not run away. They would die standing tall.

"Press it! Press it!" I screamed to my thumb on the trigger, trying to force it to comply.

Suddenly I veered right until the haunting faces in the city were replaced by a sea of blue. It seemed that my craft had malfunctioned. My bombs released late, very late, and fell into the Asteronian Sea.

The Daily Word was abruptly interrupted by the outraged howling of my commander through the headset: "Coward! Traitor! Pig! I will scrape the streets of Nubel with your face!"

Two aircraft flanked my ship and escorted me back to the base.

CHAPTER 3

The reception I received from my commander left me unable to walk. He discharged me from my pilot's post for insubordination, cowardice in battle, sabotage, and other crimes—and he argued forcefully for my execution.

But Feran decided to spare my life. I could only wonder at his reason. His untold acts of violence against real and imagined insurrections had depleted the population, especially the young men like me, causing a scarcity of Asteron's strongest laborers. Was this why he let me live, I wondered, or was it due to the peculiar interest he seemed to take in breaking my stubborn resistance to his will? In any case, I was given the new job of cargo carrier at the space center, and my specific assignment was to service Feran's ship.

I was transferred to the space workers' quarters and spent my first days in the room for attitude adjustment, where I became a frequent visitor. When I had recovered enough to function, I was released from my cell and assigned a pallet to sleep on in the great room of the men's section. There I took my place on the straw-covered floor among three hundred others. Keeping us all together in one room promoted equality and fairness, we were told. It also made it easier for the guards to watch us.

Gone was the comfort in which I had previously lived. Even though everyone on Asteron was supposed to have the same living conditions, Feran favored certain groups—like the pilots essential to his government—and provided them with real beds, heating, hot water, and other luxuries unavailable to most other citizens.

I adjusted to the squalor of my new living conditions, but the loss of flying was harder to accept. Instead of soaring across the sky, I now crept along the ground. I serviced Feran's ship, delivered items around the city on errands for my superiors, appeared at meetings to discuss *The Daily Word*, and ate the dried morsels once used for animal feed but now given to us to stave off starvation.

My dream of space travel refused to die. In fact, it was constantly stoked by the sleek feat of alien engineering that was Feran's spacecraft. I learned everything I could about the spacecraft, a gateway to mysteries outside the tight perimeter of my life. I furtively observed the engineers testing the systems, and I memorized their access codes whenever I had the opportunity.

My yearning to explore other worlds was especially aroused when Feran returned from one of his trips to planets unknown to us. On that journey he brought back two heavy crates. As I was about to remove one from the cargo bay, it talked to me—and in my own language.

"Water, water," the crate whispered in a weak male voice.

I looked between the wooden slats of the box to see the silhouette of a male humanoid, his face hidden in the darkness. When I brought water in a paper cup, five shaking fingers emerged from the dark crate to accept my offering through one of the slits. I heard him gulp down the water, and then his hand reappeared, giving me—of all things!—a gold coin.

"Thank you, son," the faltering voice said.

I hesitated.

"Here, take it." He moved his hand insistently until I accepted the coin. I quickly concealed it in my pocket before anyone noticed. I was still kneeling at the crate, trying to get a better look at the peculiar alien, when Feran entered.

The calm, smiling countenance he liked to display in public had vanished. A sneer and wild eyes edged by jagged eyebrows revealed his inner fury. His shiny black hair looked like a military helmet above his gaunt face. He leaped toward me and grabbed my throat, then banged my head against the floor. "Get away from there!" he bellowed. "How dare you meddle in my affairs, animal!"

Although it was against the law for us to talk to aliens, Feran's anger over my contact with his boxed captive seemed excessive. He towered over me, punctuating his message with kicks to my ribs. "One day, I will send you for treatment with the calming probe!"

I gasped in horror, for many rumors were whispered about the calming probe, but because I had delivered medical supplies to the Mental Health Caring Center and done my own probing, I knew what occurred beyond the creaking doors that rebellious citizens disappeared behind.

The calming probe, I had discovered, was a surgical instrument that removed pieces from the front of a citizen's brain, troublesome chunks of tissue that made the person defiant. When the doctors inserted the instrument at a specific angle and depth, they could avoid death by hemorrhage—usually. At best, the probe produced a tranquil citizen who followed orders and performed useful work. At worst, the probe produced an imbecile that officials had to dispose of quietly. In either case the patient was deemed cured because the disobedience, rage, and violence were no longer a menace to society.

As I faced Feran and his unspeakable threat, my mouth hung open and my eyes widened in unveiled panic. I had never before displayed this abject terror when Feran had threatened me. Like an animal smelling a scent that pleased it, Feran smiled at my unguarded moment of horror. "*Now* I know how to make you obey," he said, quite satisfied with his discovery. "You show no fear of beatings or dying, but now I know! One more misstep, and you will be brought to the health center for your curative treatment."

For that particular misstep, Feran summoned the guards to school me, so I supposed the beating I received was the only skill they had learned in school. After my lesson, I spent yet another night in the room for attitude adjustment. Lying on my face and shivering that night in the cell, my body swollen with wounds, I wondered about many things. What was a human doing in a crate? Why did he utter useless words like *thank you?* Elders on Asteron occasionally used that expression, but it must have become obsolete, because no one had ever thanked me for anything, nor had I thanked anyone.

And why did the alien call me *son?* I knew of the old custom in which a couple lived separately from others and raised their children themselves. But that practice was outdated on Asteron. Because our leaders provided the children with nourishment, schooling, and other necessities, it seemed that raising them in the public compound they called Children's World was a better way to ensure their proper upbringing, as well as to foster equality. Was the boxed alien from a primitive culture that had not yet advanced to our stage? Why did he speak our language? And why did he give me a coin?

I knew that coins had once served as money and that primitive people used money to buy things that they called possessions. But I had no need to buy anything because everything on Asteron was free, and, besides, there was nothing to buy. Why was I so interested in keeping a coin that was of no use to me?

And if money was a corruption, why did our leaders covet it and seek it from the aliens they despised? I wondered why aliens were allowed to come here to mine the gold on Asteron, which our leaders seemed unable to extract themselves. The money our rulers received from the aliens' mining operations had built the space center and fed our people. But now the once-plentiful mines were on the brink of depletion—and Asteron was on the verge of starvation. Were our spirits on the brink of depletion too? I had many questions but no answers.

As soon as I was able to sit up that night, I hid the coin underneath the inner sole of my shoe, where it formed a shiny circle nearly as large as my heel. I had been punished for my misdeed, but the coin was worth it! I now had a curious object from another world. What was this world like? Would I ever know?

When I returned to work, I warned myself that I could not sway in the slightest from Feran's commands for fear of the calming probe. But even before he made his vile threat, one magnetic presence was gripping my life, pulling me out of alignment.

It was someone I had encountered: an exceedingly ugly, traitorous, and irreplaceable female named Reevah. Being different from others merited official disapproval on Asteron. In practice, though, we excused many for being different, such as those who lacked brains or sense. But Reevah's manner of being different was inexcusable. Whereas most Asteronian females had brown hair, Reevah's was the color of the newly minted gold from the alien mines, and it plunged down her back in a liquid flow of curls. Whereas the features of other females lacked symmetry, Reevah's seemed designed by an engineer: Her full lips, straight nose, and giant piercing eyes were in perfect balance. And Reevah was taller and thinner than the others, with longer legs and fuller breasts than they had. By the standards of our world, Reevah was ugly.

To make matters worse, she seemed to revel in her ugliness, resisting attempts to make her blend in. Reevah would forget the scarf she was supposed to wear on her head; she would forget to confine her hair with clips; she would become sick on hair-cutting days and miss her assigned time; and she always seemed to have problems locating the larger sizes of clothing that masked her exceedingly female form. Besides these flaws, Reevah had an odd manner of staring straight into people's eyes. Such was not the way on Asteron, where we were taught to look down.

I had seen Reevah at meetings we attended to discuss *The Daily Word*, but we had never spoken until the day I delivered cargo to the foreign agents' quarters, which housed the elite group of spies who traveled to planets beyond our homeland. I knew nothing of the spies' activities, only that Feran favored their group above all others.

I had arrived during the janitors' cleaning period, so some of the doors were open. I peered into the rooms to find only one bed and—shockingly—a bath. After delivering my goods to a supply room, I was startled to find Reevah, in a janitor's gray uniform, staring at me from the hallway.

Although the spies' work areas were cleaned by robots as a security measure, such a luxury was unaffordable in their living quarters. Their residences were cleaned by human janitors, and Reevah was one of those workers. Brushing past her in the hallway on my way out, I felt the whisper of her breath in my ear.

"I saw a sight from an alien world," she said.

I stared at her, astonished.

"I peeked inside an open door and saw a spy watching a most unusual movie on her monitor. I had never seen anything like it. When the spy noticed me staring, she ordered me back to work and closed the door."

I listened intently.

"I must meet you to tell you what I saw."

"Why do you want to tell *me*?"

"Because you are one of the ugly ones."

I had avoided Reevah because to look at her was to think thoughts that could be dangerous. But at that moment in the hallway, Reevah and I warmed the column of air between us until it rose above our heads, and we were pulled together in its place.

I arranged to meet her at a window of her quarters during the nightly blackout, a time when we could avoid the security systems and slip away for a while unnoticed.

That night I propped a bundle of straw under my blanket to make it look like my body was still lying on my pallet, and I secretly exited a window of my domicile. The task went smoothly, for it was not the first time I had performed it. I walked to the dark gray building with smudged windows that was the janitors' quarters. In a little spot along the colorless wall, I saw a band of gold hair radiating around a gray kerchief. Reevah was waiting by a window for me.

I did not want to involve her in my misdeeds, I told myself, but this was the only way we could talk. Seeing each other alone required permissions that were not granted to citizens like us who were troublesome to their superiors. As I walked toward Reevah, the thought of punishment haunted me. Every rustle of a leaf or movement of a ground animal filled me with fear. But that was before I pulled her slim body down from the window and brought her along a dirt path through the trees to a nearby lake. There we were alone.

The spot I chose was a grassy clearing near the water, where a line of dense shrubbery blocked us from view of the town. On past occasions when I could get away from the eyes that constantly watched me, I had gone to this spot alone to gaze at the stars and wonder what secrets they held.

On that warm night, the moons of Asteron bathed Reevah's face in soft light. She eagerly explained that she had seen on the spy's monitor two alien humanoids, a man and a woman, and they were dancing. A narrator was describing the movie as a study in primitive cultures. Reevah said she tried to ignore the narrator's voice because under it she heard music playing in the movie.

"Yes," she insisted, "aliens who resembled us danced to music."

I was astonished.

"There were no soldiers marching," she continued. "Why do we play music only on military occasions? The aliens found another use for their music. It was soft and light, and it lifted their steps as the wind lifts the leaves."

In a sweet voice that seemed to enfold me, Reevah hummed the alien music and began to dance on the grass. Her soft voice and graceful movements strangely gripped me.

"And the aliens not only resembled us but also spoke our language. Can you imagine that?" She gasped. "But they closed the space between their words. They said *eim* instead of *I am*, and *weer* instead of *we are*. Their words flowed so easily, like the notes of a song. They made our words seemed stilted, as if we speak the way we do to avoid talking to each other."

"Maybe the aliens talk more than we do, so they have to shorten their words to get them all in," I suggested.

"Maybe if we talk more to each other, we will sound like them," she said hopefully.

"We will try that and see." I nodded.

Reevah continued with her revelations. "And when the aliens danced, they closed the space between their bodies." She smiled at my surprise. "Yes, most incredibly, the couple danced together. The female wore a remarkable red uniform with a long tear in it that exposed her entire leg, and the clothing was covered with a thousand tiny metal circles that shimmered in the light. And the uniform clung to her body like a second skin."

She pulled her loose gray trousers and shirt tightly against herself in demonstration. She continued to hum the alien music and swirl around me, her body rustling against the shrubs.

"Did the female alien wear a kerchief?" I asked, pointing to the covering on Reevah's head.

"Oh, no!"

She stopped dancing to face me. I untied the kerchief and let it fall to the ground.

"Did the alien confine her hair?"

"Oh, no! Her hair was loose and free. It swayed and rippled with every turn of her face. The shiny strands rose and fell like ocean waves in a flowing dance with the breeze."

I unfastened a clip, and hair that was hidden in a tight ball suddenly tumbled down Reevah's back in a glowing tangle of curls.

"The female wore a flower in her hair. Can you imagine? A flower! It was as red as the sunset. And there were flowers on all the tables that circled the shiny wooden dancing floor. Why do we plant flowers only in the neighborhoods of the rulers? Why do we have only dirt and weeds on our soil, except for a few wild flowers that have the courage to defy the rulers and open their petals to the sun?" she asked.

I did not know why the common people of Asteron had no flowers and why we saw them displayed only at military marches. I just knew that I had a sudden urge to find some wild blossoms for Reevah. "Wait," I told her.

I searched on a nearby ridge of rich soil, where on past occasions I had seen wild flowers, and I soon came upon a cluster of new pink blossoms. I tore them at the stem, being careful not to disturb their roots so more would grow, and I brought the little patch of color to Reevah. She eagerly brushed the blooms against her cheek and inhaled their fragrance. She placed one flower in her hair, another in mine, and the rest in the buttonholes of our shirts.

"The male alien in the movie was named *Honey*. Beneath the voice of the narrator, I could hear the woman call the man this name. Is that not curious? The aliens must have bees, the way our rulers do here in their secret fields. Surely you have been called to labor there on occasion."

I nodded, for I had glimpsed some of the animals and lush vegetation, including flowers, that were cultivated by the rulers for their use and not shared with the people.

Reevah's eyes widened with excitement. "Honey had dark hair and giant eyes the color of the lake, just like you. And he was tall and strong and amazingly ugly, just like you. I want to call you Honey."

"You mean the man was named after a sticky substance oozing from an insect?"

"Yes, and he liked his name."

My mind warned me, but my arms rebelled. I slipped them around her thin waist and drew her closer, imitating the way the aliens danced, until the flowers on my shirt lightly touched their counterparts on hers. I began humming Reevah's melody too. As we swayed to the rhythm, the flowers on our shirts slowly crushed together.

While we danced, Reevah whispered more of her story: "The humans fed at an exceedingly small table that sat only two. And the table was covered with white linen so crisp and clean that I almost smelled the fresh scent and wanted to sneeze. The aliens drank from glasses with long, thin handles that held their drinks the way a stem holds a flower. They touched their glasses together before they drank. It was like a kiss. Then the man smiled at the woman, and he closed one eye."

"He closed one eye?"

"Yes, he blinked with one eye."

"And what did she do?"

"She laughed, because the blink with one eye meant something to them, like the kiss of the glasses."

I looked at Reevah's glowing face and blinked with one eye. Then she threw her head back and did something we adults on Asteron did not do— she laughed, easily, freely, abundantly. Often people snickered bitterly, to be sure, but Reevah's laughter sounded more like the call of a lively bird.

Then my mouth landed on hers with an urgency that surprised the both of us. I tugged at her slim hips until her thighs pressed against me. I pulled her down on the cool grass. I set about the remarkable new task of discovering Reevah's willing body. She answered my sudden need by pulling me close, tugging at my clothes, and opening her warm mouth to mine. I explored the exciting mystery of soft breasts and taut legs and tasted the sweetness of her skin. Then I tore myself away abruptly and sat up.

"We have to go."

"Honey, we can stay a little longer." She reached up to me.

"No."

She knew what was bothering me. "Honey, listen to me. Nothing bad can happen. I took the tablet."

I urgently reminded myself of rules I must not ignore! Couples had to be approved by our superiors, and the disobedient did not receive permission, for fear they would produce more citizens of their own kind. Because the state expended great resources on children, the rulers thought they should intervene in the affairs that produced them.

"Honey—"

"No!"

"Honey, I tell the truth. I stole a tablet from the room of a commander of female spies who had a supply of them for her fleet. I have taken the treatment and am most securely protected from any danger."

I looked at her suspiciously because no medicines were available to us outside of the supervisors' dispensaries.

"The female spies engage in relations with aliens. That must be how they gain secret information. They keep a stash of supplies for such purposes. I tell you, I found them and took what I needed."

I wanted to believe her.

"And I was not approved to be matched, because my supervisor declared me unsuitable to bear offspring due to my ugliness and lack of character. So I am free and safe."

Had I not also been left out when my co-workers were matched? And would Reevah not snoop? Would she not discover and steal things useful to her, like the tablets that the female spies took? Had I not broken the rules more times than I could count?

"Honey, there is no danger."

Finally, she convinced me. I reached down to find her mouth, to tangle my body with hers, and to feel her warm flesh trembling under me in what was a new experience for both of us.

We met many times by the lake during the nightly blackouts. We hummed the alien music, danced, searched for flowers, and on warm nights swam naked in the moonlit water. We discovered the base world of primitive humans who cared nothing about the leaders' rules but only about the thrill of seeking their own satisfaction. Reevah laughed so effortlessly that I wondered if she too were an alien. I tasted the laughter that she sprinkled on my lips, and it soon became the supreme nourishment of my life.

Then on the second night of no moons, Reevah stopped meeting me. I waited at the window of her residence where I had often helped her slip out, but she no longer appeared. I searched for her at the meeting hall, but to no avail. When I made deliveries to the foreign agents' quarters, I did not see her. With the planting season approaching, I wondered if she had been sent to the fields. But another thought gripped me with terror. Had someone discovered her absence during the night? Had she been caught?

CHAPTER 4

As I lay on the floor of my cell, I listened for footfalls, but the hallway remained quiet. While I waited for the guard to make his rounds, I remembered how desolate I had felt after Reevah's disappearance. Without the lively notes of her laughter, my life was muted. I became preoccupied with finding her—until the day that had just passed, the unspeakable day that ended with my being thrown into this cell. It seemed long ago, but it was just the past afternoon when the music stopped forever.

The sunny morning sky bore no hint of the storm clouds to come. The past day began with events that recharged my stubborn interest in space travel. Feran was planning a journey to another world—more important than any other I had ever known him to take. I arrived at the space center to find the entire fleet of ships being readied for a mission. Workers in uniform swarmed around a cluster of spaceships parked on a concrete ramp, forming a landscape of gray tones. I walked past this area to a vehicle set apart from the others by its black exterior glistening in the sun. The small, striking jewel of a vessel was Feran's.

I boarded the ship, about to begin my tasks, and I noticed a technician in the cockpit starting a computer. Absorbed in her work, she paid no attention to me as I observed the access code she used for entry. The computer she engaged was on an auxiliary system, which was used not to operate the ship but rather to provide Feran with short video clips as diversions. Evidently these clips brought temporary rest to his perpetual nervous state and matched the brevity of his attention span. On previous occasions I had seen the technician queue this computer with highlights from Asteronian plays, official celebrations, and speeches that Feran favored. But this time she engaged a new icon, and a video clip the likes of which I had never seen appeared on a monitor. I furtively observed her as she rose from her console to perform other tasks, leaving the video running. Although no sound was playing, I watched the screen, and what I saw next amazed me.

The monitor showed an arena from an alien world where tens of thousands of people watched an event. Men in white uniforms were positioned on a grassy field. I assumed they were the military, because I knew of no other humans in uniform who performed before large crowds. One of them threw a ball to another. The second one carried a club, a crude weapon for warfare, but one I feared could kill the others on the field. However, the clubsman did not strike anyone. He aimed only at the little ball spinning toward him. With a powerful swipe, he hit the ball, sending it high in the air and completely out of the arena. The crowd rose to their feet, clapping and jumping wildly. They looked like Asteronians but must have been a different human species, because on my planet only babies behaved in such an unseemly manner. To my astonishment, a large sign flashed words in my very own language, but in a phrase I had never seen: HOME RUN. The clubsman dropped his cudgel and ran around the field, stepping on what looked like sandbags and skipping and jumping in a most undignified way.

A squadron of other officers ran toward him. I wondered if a home run were something bad and the stampeding officers would attack him. However, when they reached the clubsman, the officers embraced and even kissed him! They lifted him onto their shoulders and whirled him around. The aliens displayed behavior I had seen only from the youngest children on Asteron—unbridled merriment and laughter.

Fireworks burst in the sky above the arena. They resembled the ones our military used to celebrate their victories, but this display appeared to honor only the humanoid who executed the home run. Letters across the back of the clubsman's uniform spelled ALEXANDER, which I assumed was his name.

A wave of questions flooded my mind about the peculiar alien who hit a little ball into space, inducing thousands to cheer wildly. I was so engrossed by this scene that I leaned closer to the screen for a better look. My movement attracted the attention of the technician, who was returning to her seat. She turned to glare at me, so I had to walk away and attend to my tasks.

I heard snippets of conversation as I worked. Feran was taking unprecedented steps for this particular mission. He was planning for his entire fleet of ships to follow him, and he wanted to supervise every detail of the preparations. Curiously, Feran's ship was to leave first, the next morning, with the rest of the fleet deployed two days later. Why the delay? I wondered. Where was Feran going? What was he planning? These questions joined unanswered others in my mind, because Feran did not mention this mission to the people.

Our leader was so concerned with his journey that he summoned the workers servicing his craft for a meeting. "No one is to make any mistakes under any circumstances!" he ordered. "Be sure your work is correct and complete. If any one of you delays my mission, I will deal with you firmly!"

He displayed unusual interest in a particular cargo that I loaded onto his ship, a curious metal box that came up to my knees and was the weight of a small child. "Be careful with that, idiot!" he barked, while I carried the box to a support in the cargo bay specially designed to secure it for the voyage.

Why did he not use robots to carry things the way he wanted? I thought as I fastened the odd box in its brace. But why would he, when humans were so much cheaper and just as compliant?

On the craft's main computer Feran called up maps of places I had never seen, with areas marked *food production*, *aircraft*, *power supply*, *communications*, and *military headquarters*, displaying the names of Asteronian commanders under the items. I understood nothing of what I saw.

After the preparations were completed, Feran seemed satisfied. He laughed maliciously, then said: "When the sunbeam stings, Asteron sings." I wondered what he meant, because our pleasing sun did not sting, and the people of Asteron did not sing.

By midafternoon our shift ended. The security gates of the space center opened to allow a stream of people to flow out. The usually listless workers walked with haste that day to attend a special event.

Under a sky growing gloomy with the threat of a storm, thousands of people gathered in a crescent-shaped outdoor arena called the Theater of Justice. Every city of Asteron had its own theater, with similar dramas performed there during the Days of Justice that were frequently observed. On this afternoon, before Feran's great mission, our city was holding such an event.

Because citizens who missed these gatherings were assigned to work extra hours and perform undesirable tasks, large crowds attended. Some people, caught up in a peculiar excitement for the affair, completed their work early to arrive first and obtain the best seats. After loading Feran's spacecraft, I found excuses to linger, arriving after the seats were filled. I made sure that the leader of my quarters saw me and that my attendance was recorded, and then I found a place to stand far behind the seated spectators, trying to lose myself among the thousands of people standing.

Guards were present in large numbers during these occasions, their dark-gray uniforms speckling the mass of light-gray workers' uniforms. The mayor of our city and other officials took their reserved seats in a viewing gallery on the stage.

I watched three people step up to the stage. Two wore long judges' gowns: the counselor, a woman who provided guidance, and the commissioner, a man who pronounced sentence. The third person on the stage, a large, shirtless man with a vacuous face and wooden movements, did not wear a robe.

19

Instead, he wore a leather apron covering his thighs and bare chest. We called him the Arm of Justice.

As the Arm set up the stage, the counselor stepped to the front, opened a book, and read to us from Feran's teachings: "Our lesson today is about compassion. Our state has created a culture of helping and caring for its citizens that is the envy of the galaxy."

The Arm brought to the stage two vertical posts, each with a metal ring for locking to a wrist, and spaced them so a person could be strung between them. Then he placed a whip beside them.

"Our state protects its people from fear and want," continued the counselor.

Next to the posts the Arm placed a scaffold with a noose hanging from its crossbeams.

"No one is left to stumble through life on his own."

The Arm hoisted the last of his equipment onto the stage—several coffins piled one upon another. The stage had a roof so there would be no discomfort to the players in the rain.

During the preparations, the youngsters from Children's World arrived and sat on the grass alongside the main crowd. I caught glimpses of them. Some stared at the stage with already hardened eyes. Others buried their heads in their schoolbooks in what seemed like an attempt either to block out the spectacle or merely to get a start on their homework, until their teachers admonished them to pay closer attention.

"Asteron is the planet that puts compassion on the highest pedestal," the counselor concluded. Then she closed her book and turned to a door on the stage.

The door opened and Feran appeared. Our supreme leader wore an imposing black cape ornamented with military medals. The cape rustled like a black sail in a storm, filling with wind fore and aft of the rigid mast called Feran. Thick black hair, a restless face, and impatient movements added to his intimidating presence. He took his place in the center of the gallery, towering over the mayor and other officials. In one sweeping motion the crowd in the seats rose to attention. We all saluted our leader with his favorite slogan, "One people, one will! Asteron!" And the proceedings began.

Feran greeted the crowd: "My fellow Asteronians, we meet today to reaffirm our great tradition of the rule of law and to deal with the Unteachables in a just way."

The counselor announced the arrival of the Unteachables' cart, an open wagon transporting prisoners through the streets to the Theater of Justice. The crowd was sufficiently dense to block my view of the cart, sparing me the sight of the prisoners' faces, at least until they stepped up to the stage. I did, however, see the faces of those who turned to gape at the arriving cart, barren ovals that watched the doomed without pity or protest.

The commissioner announced the first case: "Hoarding food."

"The Arm takes no coffin from the stack," someone behind me whispered in a tone of disappointment.

"And he has not been wrong in the last three single moons," someone else replied.

It was the Arm's habit to prepare in advance for each case, and this male giant seemed to have an uncanny premonition about the outcome.

The prisoner rose to the stage. He looked a generation older than I was, with the tanned skin and muscular arms of a farmer.

"You are accused of growing crops in a secret field that you kept hidden so you would not have to contribute your fair share," the commissioner charged. "With a famine going on, do you realize how unpatriotic your actions are and how serious a crime this is?"

"But sir, I already contribute the highest crop yield of any farmer in my group. I worked substantial overtime during my scheduled time off to produce those extra crops. I cannot eat the dried nutrient cakes we receive in our rations. They make me sick to my stomach."

The commissioner's tone became more heated. "In our challenging times, we are concerned with spreading the food around so there is enough for everyone, and not with letting one person feast while others go hungry!"

"But, sir, I found a way to increase my yield so that my fields would produce a surplus unheard of on that land. I proposed my methods to the community supervisors. They said they would discuss the matter with the town supervisors, who would discuss the matter with the county supervisors, who would discuss the matter with the state supervisors, and so on, and that I should receive an answer in five years. Instead of waiting and starving, I put my methods into practice in what you call my secret field, which was land thought to be barren and discarded by my community, and my crop yield was fantastic."

"So why did you not share it?"

There was no reply.

"Who put you through school? Who nurtured you through your childhood? Who built the plows you use? Who wove the clothing you wear? Whatever you did, you did not accomplish it alone, without the help of everybody else. You owe us. It is only fair to spread the food around."

"Fair? Is that not for the judges to decide?" said the farmer, now hot with anger. "You wear the robes of judges, but you are not them. Where are the real judges the elders whisper about, who once existed in another age? And where is the legislature the elders remember, which used to be elected by the people to give them a say in their affairs?"

Even from my distance, I could see Feran bristle at the mention of treasonous topics.

The Arm reached for a coffin from the stack and placed it near the accused, a more encouraging sign to the eager faces around me.

"Ten people in your community starved to death while you were gorging yourself. You profited while they died. You killed them!" The commissioner fired back. "Now, how do you plead?"

"But I only ate the way our rulers eat. There are no dried nutrient cakes found in their residences!"

The crowd snickered. The counselor looked shocked by the farmer's impertinence. Feran nodded to the commissioner.

"The prisoner pleads guilty," said the commissioner.

The farmer paled. He fell to his knees, stunned, all life draining from him. The Arm of Justice nudged him, but he did not rise. Then the Arm lifted him like a sack and carried him to the scaffold, propped him up, tied his legs, and curled the noose around his neck. With the hint of a flourish, the Arm pulled the bolt from the trapdoor under the farmer's feet, and the matter ended.

The counselor said, "Justice has been done."

The crowd applauded. I remained motionless. A guard stared pointedly at me until I raised my hands and clapped.

The commissioner called the next prisoner, a reporter accused of writing and distributing political essays that contradicted the principles of the regime. The charge was treason. The Arm reached for a coffin.

The counselor complained, as if she were the injured party. "Our laws let you write and publish anything you wish—and all we ask is that you not spread creeds that threaten the public safety. Is that too much to ask? You violated these simple rules."

"But if I can publish anything I wish, as you say, then what is the problem?" asked the writer.

"When your writing runs counter to the interests of the public, then the harm done to society outweighs your personal privileges. Now, we know you had an accomplice. Name this person, so you can clear your conscience and do some good."

The accused, a young man with a face as unmoving as marble, stared at the counselor. She waited for a reply. Then as if resigned to his doom, the prisoner smirked. "Why not?" He pointed his bound hands at the person sitting next to Feran. "The mayor!" he shouted. "The mayor of this city is my accomplice!"

The crowd gasped, the mayor cursed the accused, the guards moved in on the mayor, and a great commotion followed. The writer called witnesses from among the spectators. They testified to the mayor's traitorous statements and suspicious actions, but the official furiously denied the charges. Finally, the matter was settled. The Arm removed an extra coffin from the stack and dispatched both the writer and the mayor on the scaffold. The faces of the people near me were wild with excitement, for the day's performance was exceeding their expectations.

Then the commissioner announced the next case: "Stabbing an official and attempted murder."

The Arm of Justice brought the next coffin down from the stack.

The commissioner continued: "A guard took someone who needed medical attention to the hospital. When the doctor attempted to treat the patient, the rebellious citizen grabbed a scalpel and threatened to kill both the guard and the doctor. When the guard tried to disarm the anarchist, the accused stabbed him and fled. A short time later, the citizen was apprehended."

As the prisoner took the first step to the stage, I glimpsed a gray kerchief with a band of gold hair around the rim. On the next step, my incredulous eyes froze on Reevah's childlike face.

"I do not need what you call medical attention," she shouted.

A desperate voice that I did not recognize tore out of me. "No! No!" I screamed. "No!"

My cries were smothered in the crowd. I pushed and shoved to fight my way to the front.

"My dear citizen, when you needed medical attention, you should have complied with those trying to help you." The counselor spoke kindly, as if her words' soft tone could make their content seem reasonable. "We set the highest standards for your health, so there was no cause to object, much less to kill anyone."

I had to avoid the guards on the sides, so I furiously pushed forward from the center of the standing throng of thousands, struggling to reach the stage before the officials could seize me. All the time my mind frantically searched for the answer to a question that had none: How could I rescue Reevah?

The commissioner spoke next: "First, citizen, you behaved irresponsibly, which led to an unlicensed pregnancy. You acted with no regard for the community that has to feed and rear the product of your indiscretion. Nonetheless, we showed leniency in your case by giving you a job in the fields. With the planting season approaching, and you so young and strong, you still had a chance to start over and learn better ways."

The counselor added: "The people asked only that you undergo a minor medical procedure to aid with your rehabilitation. And what did you do? Not only did you defy the order for your abortion and sterilization but you showed yourself quite capable of committing violence to thwart these measures."

"I want to have my child!" Reevah shouted.

"Why? To bring another miscreant like yourself into society? You need a license to have a child," said the commissioner.

"Then give me the license I need, and let me have it."

"And how would you feed it? We cannot give ration cards for unauthorized children. What if everyone acted like you, and people bore children whenever they wished? How would we ever feed them?" added the counselor.

"I will feed my baby from my own rations."

"As you well know, that would not be enough. You would have to bring your child to Children's World, and they could not accept it without the proper registration," said the commissioner. "So you were ready to bear a child that would have starved. That is the kind of mother you want to be!"

"I will see that it lives! I want to have it."

"Then you should not have stabbed a guard," the counselor admonished.

"In view of the circumstances," said the commissioner, "any plea for leniency is out of the question."

There was a rumble in the audience as I shoved my way to the front. People turned to see what was happening.

"You have sealed your fate," said the counselor. "Now name the accomplice in the deed."

Reevah said nothing.

The counselor prodded. "Well, citizen? . . . Well?"

"The Devil!" Reevah shouted, as I reached the seating area and raced down the center aisle. "My mate is Satan! Yes, the monster from the elders' old fables. I met Satan, and I wanted him!"

The crowd whispered. They sensed the presence of a great evil in their lives, and the name Reevah uttered struck fear in them.

"If anyone touches me or my baby, Satan himself will put a curse on all of you! He will extinguish the light of the sun, and you will all rot in darkness, as you deserve!"

Reevah's threat agitated the crowd. Some people screamed. Others shouted, "Witch! Kill her! Kill the witch!"

"Let her go!" I demanded as I tore away from the guards trying to grab me. "She is innocent," I cried, jumping onto the stage. "Release her at once! I am the one you want."

The guards were about to follow me onto the stage and seize me, but Feran intervened, signaling them to wait. Then he gestured to the commissioner to proceed.

"Are you responsible for her condition?" asked the commissioner.

"I never saw him before! You must not let him speak!" Reevah screamed.

"Quiet!" the commissioner ordered.

"I am the one who violated the law," I cried. "I entrapped her. I committed this vile deed because I have no noble desires to serve any of you, but only wicked desires to serve myself. I am responsible. Let her go."

"I never saw him before! You must believe me!" cried Reevah.

The commissioner and the counselor looked confused. They left us for a moment to confer with Feran.

"So you did not take the tablet," I said to Reevah.

"No."

"You lied to me."

"Yes."

"Why, Reevah? Why?"

"Because once, just once, I wanted something that was mine. And Honey, you were mine. The little thing I feel living inside me is mine." She moved her bound hands over her stomach, tightening her clothing so that I could see an impression of the growing object. "Do not be angry with me. Now we must not involve you. I beg you, Honey!"

"Reevah," I whispered as I scanned the guards, my voice shaking with terror, "I do not know how to save you."

"I cannot be saved. But *you* can. Listen to me. You must stay out of this!"

The commissioner returned to address me. "Your name is Arial, and you have been in trouble with the law before. You have been discharged from the military for crimes against the people. Now you continue your unlawful ways. As your punishment . . ."

The Arm removed a second coffin from the stack.

". . . for the deed you have just confessed to—"

"You will be treated with the calming probe in the morning," Feran said, interrupting from the gallery.

The crowd gasped. The Arm put my coffin back in the stack.

"Very well." The commissioner nodded at Feran, then turned to me. "Tomorrow you will receive the calming probe, and now you will be whipped until you recant your evil ways."

"No!" Reevah shouted. "You will set him free. He is innocent!"

"Quiet!" ordered the commissioner.

Reevah closed her eyes and bent her head. The tears that dropped made dark streaks down her shirt.

"You, Arial, will be dismissed from the space workers' quarters and transferred to the Mental Health Caring Center, where you will receive your therapeutic treatment," instructed the commissioner. "When you recover from the procedure, you will be moved to the farms, where you will labor in the fields for the planting season, and then we will decide from there what is to become of you."

The counselor added, "Dear citizen, Feran is giving you another chance. Once cured of your disruptive tendencies, you will be able to serve your community with a willing heart and a tranquil spirit."

I shut my eyes in horror at the thought of my future, and then I turned to Feran. "I accept my punishment. Now let the female go free."

Feran did not deign to answer but pointed his finger at the commissioner to proceed.

"I think not, citizen," said the commissioner.

With a nod of Feran's head, three guards leaped onto the stage and encircled me.

"Justice will be dispatched." The commissioner nodded to the Arm.

"No!" I screamed. I grabbed Reevah and pulled her toward me. The Arm also grabbed her and pulled her toward him. With her hands tied, Reevah stood helplessly between us. The guards seized me. "No!" I screamed, my arms in an iron grip around her waist, my head pressed against her abdomen, my body raised like a rope tugged by the guards. I thought I heard the thing growing inside her crying out too. My grip was so tight that the guards could not pry me loose.

Then there was a terrible blow to my head, fists in my eyes, and kicks in my stomach. The guards pulled off my shirt, spread my arms between the whipping posts, and chained my wrists. I twisted savagely to break the chains, but they held firm.

"You cannot do this!" I screamed so loud that my voice reverberated through the crowd, echoing to sound my alarm again and again. "This is murder! *Murder!* You vile *murderers*—"

The Arm threw a gag over my mouth, tying it tightly around my head. He then picked up his whip and repeatedly lashed my back until my feet gave way and I hung limply by my arms. Then the Arm took care of his other chore. He brought Reevah to the scaffold, tied her legs, and placed the rope around her neck.

Her much smaller female form beside the monstrous Arm and her long, fragile neck inside the coarse noose moved the crowd to silence.

"I have a request," Reevah said. I turned my head to the side to see her.

The Arm stopped.

"I would like the kerchief removed from my head."

The Arm looked at the commissioner. The commissioner looked at the counselor. The counselor looked at Feran. No one had ever made such a request. Feran looked out at the spectators, studying their mood. Our leader dispensed his medicine carefully, never exceeding the dosage he thought the people could take. The sudden somber turn of the crowd seemed to weigh on him, because he nodded to the officials on stage.

The counselor stepped forward. "Of course," she said, removing Reevah's kerchief.

"And I would like my hair unfastened."

"As you wish." The counselor unfastened the clasps.

The wind, stirring with the threat of a storm, blew Reevah's golden hair in wisps, like hot flames dancing in the cool gray sky. She turned to the side so that she could see me. With the cloth gagging my mouth, I could not say the things I had never said but urgently wished to say at that moment. I could not tell Reevah how the sweet drink of her laughter poured life into me.

"Honey, when I lied to you, I never intended you to be punished. Never! Only me."

I nodded, wondering how I could accomplish the only act now left to me, that of wiping the torture from her face.

"Do not let them hurt you. Find a way to . . . to prevent. . . . You are clever. Surely you can find a way—"

A fury of tears choked her trembling voice. She looked at me helplessly. I wanted to reach out to her, but I could not. I wanted to cry out to her, but I could not. Then I thought of the only thing I could do: I blinked at her with one eye.

She emitted a tiny laugh, a mere puff of air expelled from her lips. She lowered her head, seeming to struggle against a great turmoil within her. Then Reevah slowly raised her head for the last time, her eyes choosing me for their final sight. The serene glow I knew so well had returned to her face. She held herself in that familiar way that was Reevah. No word in Asteron's language could describe the way she lifted her head. I could only say what it was not: It was not repenting or guilty or meek or broken. Indeed, it made a mockery of all those things.

"Honey, the place where the flowers grow is out there somewhere."

Her voice was strong now. The giant blue pools that were her eyes looked across the skyline, and what I saw pouring from them was hope.

"Go and find it. Find the place with the flowers for both of us!"

Then the Arm of Justice pulled the bolt from the trapdoor and Reevah's legs fell through it. Her slim body sagged, while her hair rose defiantly in the wind like a banner of sunshine against the dark sky.

CHAPTER 5

I was grateful that the lashes across my back had resumed quickly, because the sting of them forced my eyes shut. I did not recant, so I was beaten until I lost consciousness. When I awoke in my cell, I knew by the fury pounding in my head that I had not yet undergone any calming treatment. Feran had torn from my life the things that mattered to me—first flying, then Reevah—but I was *not* going to let him take my will. I would die with it, and in the place of *my* choosing.

As I lay in the darkness, the events of the prior afternoon scorched my memory. I wanted to squeeze Feran's throat and watch him turn blue as I wrung the life out of him. But to attack Feran directly was to risk torture by the only device of advanced technology made on Asteron, an electronic gun that was Feran's exclusive weapon. Its agonizing rays could be adjusted to inflict any level of pain without quite killing the victim, unless Feran gave the ultimate signal. He called this perverted device Coquet. The only genuine softness I had ever seen him display was when he stroked Coquet at his side. For Feran, Coquet was a living presence—an animal, a female, perhaps even a master.

I remembered how he had conveyed threats to me from the device while I worked: "Coquet is displeased with you. . . . Coquet will want to know about your blunder. . . . Coquet grows impatient with your slowness."

The thought of being tortured by Feran and Coquet made me rule out a direct attack on him. I would have to die knowing that Feran lived. I would die without *my* theater of justice!

All of these factors had flashed before me while the Arm was lashing my back. With my body strung between the posts and my arms throbbing each time my legs gave way, I knew I would rather face my end than face the calming probe, and I decided right then how I would do it.

Feran forbade willful dying, which he interpreted as a person's lack of appreciation for all the things our leader provided. Many ungrateful citizens, however, did take their own lives. Some jumped off buildings, some plunged in front of moving vehicles, and some just dived into the lake and floated back head-down. But I wanted none of that. I resolved to die in one place only: in Feran's spacecraft.

I hoped to resist the guards' guns long enough to see what *I* chose for my final scene. I wanted to see the alien Alexander execute his home run and to know that somewhere in the universe human creatures were laughing and, remarkably, unafraid.

Lying in my cell, I was reviewing my plan when—finally—I heard the thump of the guard's steps down the corridor. I closed my eyes and feigned unconsciousness. As he walked toward me, the air thickened with the odor of a substance forbidden to citizens but somehow obtainable by guards: whiskey. He stopped at my cell, and the heavy stench from his beverage descended on me. I felt the beam of his flashlight moving over my face. I heard his wheezing. Then he walked on.

When he left my corridor, I sat up and reached into a crack in the floor, where I located a small piece of metal that I had kept hidden in this room. It was once a paper clip, but I had carefully molded it into something useful to me. With this tool I unlocked the collar around my neck. I could work quickly, because this task was not new to me.

On previous occasions I had taken great care to arrange the room's only furnishings, a torn shawl for a blanket and a clump of straw for bedding, so that it looked as if my body were sleeping under the fabric with the chain at the neck. That way I could slip out for a while undetected, and then return before daybreak. This time I performed the task indifferently. I would not be coming back.

I forced my stiff, aching arms through the sleeves of my worker's shirt, which had been thrown on the floor next to me. Then I made a shaky attempt to stand, but everything in the room swirled around like water down a funnel, unsettling my stomach. I collapsed against the wall and grabbed the bars of the window until the sickening nausea passed and I could finally steady my legs.

When everything stopped swirling, my eyes met those staring at me from Feran's poster. In unrepeatable words, I said my farewell.

I planned to follow the escape route that had worked for me previously. Because the window in the room for attitude adjustment was barred, I would leave through another one.

With my small metal tool, I manipulated the door lock. It was a temporary one, which I easily picked. I knew of this lapse in security because I had damaged the other lock some time ago. No parts had yet arrived for making the repairs. Even security, with its priority over all else, now waited while scarce resources were summoned to ward off the famine and, of course, to keep Feran's favorite place—the space center—running.

The lights were off in the hallway, which meant it was still the blackout period. This aided me as I made my way out.

Cool air hit my face as I jumped out a window at the end of the corridor. I felt a brief satisfaction in knowing it was the last time I would have to pass the billboards lining the streets, which I could read in the moonlight: *Let us eat two meals a day. Fill your bucket before the water pump shuts at night. Our coats make excellent blankets. If Feran decides, we do.*

Beginning my half-mile walk to the space center, I saw up ahead the imposing glow it made in the night sky. It looked like a mythical kingdom from books long forbidden called fairy tales, which the elders still related. The lights from the space center were the only break in the darkness caused by the scarcity of power that turned our city into a graveyard every night. The power station, a marvel of advanced foreign technology, had been run by the aliens when they conducted their mining operations. With the mines near depletion and the aliens leaving, the resources to run the power were also vanishing. I walked on, reminding myself that the many questions these facts provoked would never be answered, and it was no longer necessary for me to wonder about them.

Feran's spacecraft, scheduled to take off at dawn, would be on the airfield. My goal was to reach the ship before I was killed. Once inside, I was sure the guards would seize me, but I hoped not until after I had started the auxiliary computer and played the video of Alexander.

I had gone a few blocks when a small vehicle came to a stop alongside me. Expecting this, I forced a calm turn of my head to face a guard getting out of his car and walking toward me. He looked annoyed at my intrusion on his routine. With a small flashlight he read the identification card clipped to my shirt.

"What are you doing out at this hour?"

With factories and plants affected by the power shutoffs, there was a shortage of manufactured parts for the communication and transportation systems. So supervisors resorted to sending workers out on foot to deliver messages or perform other errands at all hours. I gave the guard an excuse about being on such an errand.

He eyed me suspiciously. Then he pulled an electronic device from his pocket and scanned my card to learn more about me. But the device did not pull up any data; its screen remained blank. The official scanned my badge again. Then again. He swore at the object in his hand and almost flung it on the ground. Then he returned to his vehicle and sped off. Like so much on Asteron, his device had stopped sensing anything.

I continued walking until the dilapidated old buildings of my city were behind me and the modern space center loomed ahead. It felt as if I were on a plank between two opposite worlds: an archaic land of torture and a shining new land of interplanetary travel. The first world was Asteronian-made, but the other was built with foreign technology and money from the mining operations. What was the force driving these two worlds? What would happen if they collided? I wondered, but I reminded myself that it was no longer of any concern to me.

As I approached the space center I saw the dense pattern of dots and shadows formed by the lights, people, and vehicles beyond its fence. Although my identification card had not been programmed for entry that night, I was determined to get in. The combined power of sentries, gates, badges, barbed wire, motion detectors, search lights, alarms, face scans, and other security measures was said to make the space center impenetrable. My task was to cut through all of it.

My plan was simple. It involved one of the vehicles called frogs that serviced the spacecraft. The frogs moved along the ground. Then when they reached an impediment, they leaped into the air to continue aloft. The size of a truck but with an oblong shape, these vehicles transported supplies, equipment, and personnel in a car behind the driver's cab. Security prohibited the frogs from leaving the confines of the space center. However, one did.

A security commander himself broke the rules, I had one day discovered. He used a frog as his personal car, and he left the space complex with it several times a day. Because his frog bore the red stripes of a commander's vehicle, it could leap into or out of the complex at will. Who would challenge his movements? His subordinates at the gates? No, only those eager to appear at the Theater of Justice, because on Asteron, people never questioned their superiors. The commander, I had learned, left the space center to visit a tree, a dead one, a leafless mass of rotting black bark in a nearby empty field. One night I had investigated and found that the hollow trunk of the tree was not empty at all but filled with bottles of Asteron's favorite contraband: whiskey. My plan was to hide near the commander's beverage, await a visit by his frog, then climb inside the car in the rear for the ride back into the complex.

I walked to the dead tree just off the road and picked my hiding spot in the shrubs. Soon the squatty, six-wheeled frog came clanging down from the sky.

The commander, a short, rotund, neckless man, shaped remarkably similar to the frog he piloted, exited the driver's cab along with a fellow officer.

"I've never worked such long shifts or saw so many spacecraft readied at one time," said the commander, reaching into the bark for a bottle, then taking a long draft.

"Nor I," said the other, joining him.

"I wonder what Feran is up to."

"Something that brings food, I hope."

"Or that takes away bodies to feed. Thousands of troops are leaving in two days."

"Maybe they will die in battle."

"We can hope."

While the two commanders sat on the grass in front of the frog, I waited for them to imbibe enough to dull their senses. Then I quietly slipped through the back door and into the car. From among a few implements strapped down in the car, I grabbed a wrench to use as a weapon. Then I stayed clear of the windows and waited. Finally, the stench of alcohol floated over me from an open window, marking the commanders' return to the driver's cab in the front.

All I had to do now was protect myself from injury as the commander made the frog rise from the ground, then hit it again with a thump, rise again, and then swerve dangerously. We finally descended from this brief but treacherous journey, my head banging on the floor of the car during the commander's wobbly landing. The two officers dismounted from the cab and walked away. A glance out the window showed that I was inside the gate, past security, and near Feran's ship. I had to act quickly before the commander made another visit to the tree.

I slid out the back door with the wrench hidden up my shirt sleeve. I saw the engineering wonder that was Feran's spacecraft. Its smooth, black body shined in the moonlight. Its nose curved down and tapered to a point. Its sleek wings drew back in sharp lines that fanned out into sweeping curves. Its tail rose up and arched back. The vessel look like a bird of prey poised to face a strong head wind.

Keeping my head low and the hidden wrench close to my body, I walked toward Feran's craft. In preparation for his arrival, the ship's door was ajar and a stairway with a platform was positioned outside of it. Just as I was about to jump up the steps, an officer patrolling Feran's ship blocked me. I knew him.

"Arial!"

I stopped.

"What are you doing here? You have no orders to work tonight."

"I respectfully suggest, captain, that I do have such orders."

The guard's face reddened, because we were not allowed to contradict a superior. "We will see about that!" He reached for his pocket device to check the schedule.

I startled him with a move unthinkable by anyone planning to live past the hour. I slid the wrench out of my sleeve, and with one decisive swing I pounded his skull. His eyes closed and his body fell to the ground. In two leaps I ascended the six steps to the door of the spacecraft. Within a moment, I was inside!

To the back of the metal entryway were the living quarters and cargo bay. To the front, beyond an open sliding door, was the moonlit sparkle of instruments that formed the flight deck. I would go to the deck and watch the alien perform the home run, then wait for the guards to shoot me. That was the plan.

But once inside the shining electronic world that had always held me spellbound, a different vision suddenly pulled my thoughts from the craft, and from the planet itself, carrying me into the vast, mysterious sky. A composed figure on a scaffold looked at me with hope. A soft voice whispered about a place with flowers. A sweet presence I could not resist dissolved my bitter despair.

Suddenly I realized what I had subconsciously wanted to do all along— what I had dreamed of doing every time I had ever been in this spaceship. I would *not* sit and wait to die. I would start the engines and blast my way out!

CHAPTER 6

Escaping air hissed as I clamped the hatch shut like a tomb. I rushed to the front of the plane, the clanging of my steps amplified in the metallic passageway. Then I stood in awe before the dense electronic network of the flight deck.

A dizzying pattern of instruments encircled me, framing the windows, paneling the walls, and arching overhead. A rush of blood heated my face as I slid into the commander's seat and felt my fingers on the controls. I forgot about engaging the auxiliary computer and watching the video of Alexander. Instead I called to mind the engineer's access codes for the main computer, which I had gone to great lengths to capture on past occasions when I had serviced the craft. Now I entered those codes in the system, compressing my life into one final, desperate act.

Suddenly the spaceship pulsed with electronic sounds and flashing monitors. Charged with a new energy, I raced through the computer's menus, searching for the start-up procedure.

The main screen responded, displaying a series of steps to start the engines. Did I have enough time? At any moment the fallen captain outside would attract the attention of others, and the pink tinge of dawn on the horizon beyond the windshield warned me that Feran would soon arrive for his departure.

I heard banging on the ship's door. I slipped on my headset and turned on a control to hear what was going on outside the craft and to communicate if I chose. A familiar voice came through the earphones. "Who is in there? Answer at once!"

It was my superior, the supervisor of the cargo carriers.

"Who are you?" He continued. "I order you to answer!"

I said nothing.

"Very well, I will call the commander."

"And let him think . . . I cannot handle . . . one idiot worker . . . who thinks he is an astronaut?" I recognized the voice of the officer I had struck, his words coming in short breaths as if he was just regaining consciousness.

"Captain, are you okay? Let me help you to your feet." My supervisor softened his voice to the fawning tone he used to address those who outranked him. I heard him rushing down the stairs to assist the guard. "You have a head wound. Here is a handkerchief."

"Forget about me!" The captain's voice was stronger now. His angry tone told me that he was shaking off the effects of my attack.

"Someone has sealed himself in the ship, captain. I was about to call—"

"You will not bother the commander with this trifle, unless you want to explain how *your* worker locked himself inside!"

"*My* worker?"

"Arial."

"Arial? He has no permission to be here now."

I heard the captain climb the stairs to the hatch. I recognized the electronic buzz that his weapon made when he cocked it, and I felt a familiar knot form in my chest.

"Can you hear me in there?" said the captain. "Open this door, pig, or watch me blast in and wash the floor with your guts!"

"Wait!" I spoke into the headset's microphone. "If you damage Feran's ship, you will delay his mission. He said that anyone who interferes with his journey will be dealt with *firmly*."

The pause that followed told me that the captain was reconsidering the matter. "This is an outrage! The insurgent is *your* charge," he finally said to my supervisor. "You have allowed a common laborer to threaten the security of the planet. Now seize him or face arrest!"

"But captain, sir—"

"You will force this door open and serve me the traitor's head."

"Of course, captain. No need to point your gun at me, sir, really." My supervisor's smooth voice began to trembled. "I am honored to have the privilege. However, with you being such a superb patriot, perhaps you should have the opportunity yourself of rescuing the ship. There might be a reward—"

"Hold your tongue and force the door."

"Why, certainly, captain. My only concern is for you. Feran's craft will be damaged, and he has demanded that no one disturb his mission. The record will show that I gave no order to the idiot Arial to work this shift. Indeed, he was to be transferred out of my department today. The record will also show that he . . . well, slipped by you, sir. Now, if you add this incident to the one last week when you left your post and the commander reprimanded you . . . well, I assure you, captain, I will speak in your favor when you are tried at the Theater of Justice."

As I worked feverishly to complete the start-up procedure, I heard the captain swear furiously.

"And none of the other spacecraft are ready to launch today," I added, "so you will delay Feran's mission if you damage his prized ship to spill my worthless guts."

"The idiot is *your* worker!" The captain screamed at my supervisor. "He is *your* charge. You must seize him before he starts the engines, which he is surely attempting to do."

"If I am an idiot, as everyone claims, then I lack the brains to start the ship," I said, "so you have time to open the door with the combination." An electronic keypad on the outside would release the lock if they knew the code to use, which they apparently did not. I hoped my suggestion would buy time.

"Captain, sir"—my supervisor pleaded—"the commander can get us that combination from the flight director. Then we will not have to damage—"

"Shut up!" the captain replied. "I will not have you call my superior and have him think a rebel got by me! Get the engineer. He knows the combination."

With Feran's policy of giving no one person too much information, I was not surprised that the guard was ignorant of the door's locking combination. By Feran's design, the security force had access to the exterior of the ship but lacked knowledge of its controls, whereas the engineers could enter and operate the ship but had no access to it without the guards' authorization.

Meanwhile, I was still tackling the computer's checklist for starting the engines. I knew Feran's ship could be flown in two different modes, as a spacecraft or as a plane. I had observed occasions when he used the aircraft engines for takeoff so that he could do an aerial survey of sites of interest to him before engaging the rockets for propulsion into space. I found that for his pending flight the ship was set to take off in aircraft mode. This meant I could block out all the rocket gadgetry, which I did not understand, and focus on the plane's aircraft controls, which were familiar from my training.

The activities continued on the platform outside as the engineer, Dakir, arrived.

"Dakir, there is an insurgent in Feran's spacecraft," shouted the captain. "Open the door at once with the combination!"

"Captain, the rules prohibit me from opening the door without my superior's authorization. Let me call her—"

"No!" screamed the captain. "No superiors need to know what we are doing here! I will not risk my standing when we can settle the matter simply with you opening the door. Now!"

"But . . . but captain—"

I heard another familiar sound: the smack of a fist striking a face. A cry of pain followed, then kicks, then more punches.

I completed the checklist and waited to hear the power charge. Nothing happened. A snag! Sweat from my face dripped onto the instrument panel.

Dakir gasped. "I have my orders."

"Your orders are no good now. There is an insurgent inside who must be captured!"

"My rules say nothing about an insurgent."

"Forget your rules and open this door!"

"But captain—" Dakir's voice was barely audible. I heard the low pounding of more blows, then a violent spasm of coughing.

I wondered what step I had missed in my haste. I reviewed the opening checklist, matching its instructions to my instrument settings. I suddenly realized something. I found a control that was set for the ultra-high speed used for space travel. Because the aircraft engines operated at a minute fraction of that speed, I corrected the setting and again started the fuel flow to the engines. This time they whined in answer.

"Now get up and open this door or be shot!" shrieked the captain.

I heard a terrible moan, then a helpless voice reduced to a whimper. "Yes, captain."

I felt my hair growing strand by strand while I waited for the ship to gain sufficient power for takeoff.

The voices and sounds I heard next told me that Dakir was having difficulty rising to his feet after the beating, so the captain pulled him up and shoved him against the door.

My supervisor shouted at Dakir. "Hurry, you imbecile, or we will all go to the Theater of Justice!"

The beep of the first number Dakir entered on the keypad shot through my headset like a bullet.

But it was I who spoke next. "None of you will go to the Theater of Justice."

"Because in three seconds I will kill you!" said the captain.

"Because in two seconds you will be burned to death by the engines. Good-bye!" I yelled, fastening the buckles of my harness.

Only Dakir had the quick reflexes to heed the warning I gave them. He stopped entering the code, and from my window I saw him jump off the platform and land clear of the explosion. The others remained, forming two columns of burning flesh in the exhaust of the engines as I lifted straight up in a vertical takeoff. I looked down on the space center for the last time. I took the ship higher, and I caught sight of the crescent shape of an outdoor theater.

"Good-bye, Reevah," I said to the silver tinge of the stage in the last gray moment before the dawn.

I pitched the nose of the craft high and climbed into the new day's sky. Suddenly a sleek projectile was ripping upward through the sky, closing the distance between us. From my military training, I knew it was a missile launched at my craft. Like a hungry beast, it would stalk me, find me, and devour me—unless I could activate my ship's rockets. I called up directions, turned switches, flicked controls, pressed buttons, talked to the computer, ordered it, begged it. But no rockets fired.

A flashing light and a high-pitched whine from the instrument panel signaled that the missile had locked onto my ship. Without rocket power to propel me out of the weapon's range, my only chance was to outmaneuver it. I needed to change direction suddenly to try to lose the missile. But I had to wait until it was close, very close, so it would not have time to correct.

I waited, staring at its dark streak of exhaust cutting across thin pink clouds of dawn. I waited, clutching the stick so tightly that my arm became a network of pulsing veins. I waited, my predator growing from a small object in the distance to a menacing presence closing in on me. Now!

I turned, I dived. I saw the missile pass me overhead. Flying too fast to correct in time, the weapon overshot me. But the audible alarm persisted because another projectile was coming at me, and another behind it. I tried to adjust to the capabilities of the new craft while fighting off these weapons.

I turned hard again, pushing the blood into my legs and the gravity meter into the danger zone. I veered, and the missiles veered. I looped. They looped, staying with me. I made a series of tight turns, and one weapon finally passed to the side of me and vanished in the distance. But the one behind it corrected. I took the ship into a dive to gain speed, then turned again. Suddenly the dawn began reversing into a fuzzy night sky on the edges of my vision. I tried to focus the missile in the center of a shrinking field of sight.

"No!" I cried aloud.

My violent maneuvering was taking its toll on me, and my vanishing sight was a signal I could not ignore. I had tunnel vision.

I was about to lose my sight, and then consciousness, from pulling gravity forces that were too high. I urgently needed to stop my insane maneuvering, but I had no choice with the missile about to strike. I turned again. My vision shrunk further as gravity sucked the blood from my head with a pull of many times my normal weight. The high-pitched alarm still buzzed in my ears as the missile tenaciously stayed on me. I turned again.

Then my head dropped and my eyes closed. A moment later, I awoke to find myself spinning out of control, with the ground closing in fast. I grabbed the controls and struggled to recover. Finally, I managed to stop the rotations and level the craft before it hit the pavement. I climbed quickly and at last reached a point of peace. The trailing missile had failed to intercept. The alarm was silenced at last! I loosened my grip on the stick. I felt my first moment of peace. But not for long.

The alarm shrilled once again as another missile raced toward me. I turned hard, but the stubborn rocket stayed with me. I could see it at the center of a tunnel that was closing. My shrinking vision was about to be swallowed by eternity. To lose this missile meant pulling more *g*'s and blacking out. To stay conscious meant flying steady and waiting for the weapon to strike. How did I want to die? Crashing to the ground in a fireball or blasted to smithereens by a missile? More warning lights flashed on the flight deck, and a voice inside the computer addressed me.

"Four seconds to impact," the female voice said tonelessly. "Three seconds to impact."

I could maneuver no longer. Instead I had to increase my speed to outrace the weapon, but the craft would not oblige. I tried to manipulate the controls to ignite the rockets, but I heard nothing except the high-pitched whine of the missile alarm.

"Two seconds to—"

Just then a tremendous explosion jolted the ship. It no longer responded to my controls. Its nose turned straight away from Asteron as the sky behind me ignited with flames. A most amazing force had suddenly seized the craft and catapulted me away. The rocket engines had ignited! The missile, which moments ago had almost touched my craft, now trailed farther and farther behind. The computer informed me that I was on an automatic, pre-programmed flight route, and yes, I was indeed in rocket mode. Feran's ship had been set to fire its rockets and to begin an automatic flight route just after takeoff—none too soon for me.

As the ship blasted through the Asteronian atmosphere and journeyed beyond its grip, I turned to the computer that contained the video I had watched at a point that seemed long ago but had only been the previous morning. Repeating the steps I had observed the technician use, I started the device, and the monitor came alive. I engaged the icon that was of interest to me, and soon the alien Alexander, in his white uniform, appeared before me, holding his club.

Sitting in the commander's chair of Feran's spacecraft, I watched the amazing performance. As a ball was thrown to him, Alexander's body twisted with all his strength, and he struck it. The little white sphere whirled high in the sky, almost out into space. Alexander leaped into the air. He threw his head back. And in surrender to a moment that meant something great to him, he laughed.

I glanced out the window in time to see Asteron shrink to the size of a small ball, leaving only a serene black void to embrace me. The clutch of gravity had already eased its grip when Alexander's ball left the arena on screen. With the alien laughing under a shower of fireworks, I unstrapped my harness and set myself free.

I was not living my final minutes as I had expected, but in fact the moment felt strangely like my first. Where was I going? I had no idea. At that moment, I also had no cares. I tumbled and bounced around, more unruly than Alexander, in the supreme buoyancy of space.

CHAPTER 7

I glided around my new dwelling like a ripple in water, drifting from the flight deck to the living quarters to the cargo bay of the sleek ship. I was intrigued by the new motion that no longer distinguished top and bottom from side to side. Not only was my body now free of gravity's pull, but my spirit was also free of Feran and his guards, making it too seem lighter. This produced a calmness that I had never experienced.

The steady hum of the ship's instruments and the black void outside the windows were like new companions accompanying me as I examined the interior of the craft, with its rounded, blue-tinged walls, bright lights, and compact living quarters. The ship was equipped with a desk bolted to the floor, a sleeping bag strapped to the wall, a treadmill, a small bathroom, and an array of cabinets and packs for supplies. There were numerous magnetic strips and other fasteners to anchor the items needed for showering, dressing, eating, and working in zero gravity. In contrast to the cramped living area, the cargo bay behind it seemed like a hollow barrel, except for a couple of curious objects loaded for Feran's journey: the mysterious metal box that I had carried onto the ship and an odd protective suit, each fastened securely and intact. I was eager to examine these items and explore the rest of the ship, but first I had a more pressing matter to address.

I had entered Feran's spacecraft certain my life would end, but now I urgently wanted to begin it anew. Remaining alive required that I accomplish one thing. I had to alter the course that was taking me to the one place in the universe where I must not go: to Feran's intended destination. I had to disengage his automatic flight plan, find a suitable new location, and navigate a course to get there.

I returned to the flight deck to bring my case before the ship's computer. But to my dismay, I was unable to change my course even after exhaustive attempts over many hours. Although I could use many of the ship's systems and functions, I could not alter its flight plan and navigate a new one. Programming a flight plan required a higher level of clearance with an additional access code, which I did not have. That left me no choice but to continue on Feran's flight plan. Would his spies be at my destination to open the hatch when I landed?

I pondered this situation until I could no longer stay awake. Exhausted, I finally dimmed the lights and crawled into the sleeping bag. I looked contentedly at the dark serenity of space outside my window, then closed my eyes for a much-needed sleep.

I awoke hours later in the same peaceful state. I lay cocooned in the warm bag, pleased with the new experience of being able to linger in my bed. I yawned and stretched like an animal awakening in its den, feeling calm and secure in a place free of predators. A new thought struck me: I could either open my eyes or shut them, arise or continue to rest, explore the ship or gaze at the stars. I realized that *I* could decide what to do, and I felt a strange eagerness to begin something that seemed almost solemn: a new day of my life.

While I was in space, my life was my own, I thought contentedly. But then as I became more awake, the worries seeped in. I feared that Feran's guards could be at my destination, ready to uproot my sprouting new life.

I floated out of the sleeping bag to clean up and get to work. A need for fresh clothing brought me to Feran's dressing cabinet. I was about to grab a pair of pants and a shirt when I recoiled at the thought of wearing clothes that had touched his repulsive body. But this matter was trivial, because I could have a far more disturbing bond to him.

For the generation of Feran's rule, many women had conceived offspring with him, or if they were more fortunate, merely with test tubes of his vile protoplasm. He was obsessed with improving our gene pool, a goal he claimed was best achieved by his own contribution. The females assigned to assist with Feran's progeny were given extra rations and better living conditions than the rest of us, which made selection for such a revolting job a prime way to ward off misery and starvation.

This matter sometimes troubled me because I did not know who my father was. In Children's World, where I had been raised, parents could see their offspring on visiting days. I remembered being with my mother, who died in my early school years, but I did not recall any father coming to visit. I sometimes ruminated on the identity of the father I had never known—because I did not want him to be the man I loathed.

Many of Asteron's children looked like Feran and surely were his offspring. Did I too have his contemptible genes? I reminded myself that my features were proportional, so I was considered ugly, whereas Feran's large nose, feeble eyes, and thick lips were disproportional, so he was considered beautiful. At least he had been beautiful until he sustained what appeared to be an accident that injured his face. After his alien-trained surgeons operated, Feran's face became ugly, like those of the aliens who mined our gold and who somehow had more of everything than we did. Although Feran ceaselessly condemned them, he just as zealously courted them for aid and assistance. We citizens wondered if Feran had used the occasion of his accident to change his looks in order to promote better relations with the aliens through his resemblance to them. People whispered hopefully that the change in Feran would somehow bring more food. But this did not come to pass, and our flesh continued to wither away because of the famine.

With a shrug of my shoulders, I dismissed my preoccupation with Feran's genes and took his clothes. Then I showered and shaved. I checked my bruises in a mirror and applied fresh ointments, something I had begun doing the day before. With the aid of an alien medicine kit unknown to me on Asteron, my wounds were healing remarkably fast. Patches of healthy new skin were already growing over the lashes on my back. For the first time since my punishment at the Theater of Justice, I could open my eyes completely, because the swelling was receding. My face was changing too, I noticed. The hard cast of anger that had pulled my features tight seemed to have loosened a little into a look of cautious calm.

Although food had not yet been loaded when I seized the craft, I found potable water and an ample supply of powdered fruit drinks and milk, beverages available to me only rarely on Asteron. I rehydrated some for a satisfying meal. On this new day in space, I was now in the rare state of being well rested, clean, and fed.

I wished I did not have to be concerned with Feran's affairs, because outside my window I noticed a bright star, one I had not seen before. I went to the flight deck to take a closer look through the ship's telescope. With remote controls, I adjusted the telescope's lens outside the craft, searching on its monitor for the star. It was behind the ship. I marveled at the power of the instrument to reveal so many secrets of the universe and wished I could spend the rest of my life on this ship peering at the stars, so content was I at this task. I adjusted the telescope until the bright little image came into view. Then I gasped. The object I saw was no star. It was a spacecraft pursuing me.

Suddenly a blast from the radio receiver overpowered the ship's serene hum, confirming my fears.

"Animal!" It was Feran. "I demand an account of my ship and cargo. Speak!"

I did not reply.

"I order you to respond!"

Again I said nothing.

Feran unleashed a string of Asteronian curses before he was coherent again. "If you *dare* touch my cargo, you will rue the day! I am not far behind, and when I get you—as I will, pig!—I will turn your punishment over to Coquet. She will want to try all her tricks, to linger with you, to watch you die . . . slowly . . . very slowly."

Feran had brought with him his favorite companion, the weapon notorious on Asteron for its beams of torture. My moment of calm had ended, and I listened with dread to the plan he and Coquet had for me.

"We will meet again soon, because I know something you do not." He laughed viciously. "I know where you are going and how to catch you."

CHAPTER 8

With Feran's threats grating on my nerves like a missile alarm I could not turn off, I headed to the cargo bay to take a closer look at the object of his concern, the mysterious cargo I had hauled onto the spacecraft.

I released the object from the brace that had kept it intact during the violent maneuverings of my takeoff. I ran my hand along the smooth gray metal that covered all six sides of the rectangular box. It measured up to my knees in height and also in width, and half that distance in depth. The object stood on four small feet of the same metal. Each of the four sides consisted of a solid plate of metal. On the bottom there was an impression in the plate, and within it there was a tightly fitting black metal cone, as long as an index finger, two fingers thick at its base, and tapering to a sharp point. I had never seen such an object before and had not a clue to its identity.

The top of the box had a circular piece of the metal cut into it about the size of a person's face, with more of the same metal around the rim. Figuring this circular piece was where the box opened, I gently pressed on it, but it was tightly sealed. A large steel pin jutted out from a slot in the side of the box. This pin was loop-shaped and looked as if it had to be pulled to activate the device. A protective cover of hard plastic prevented the pin from being pulled accidentally. When I moved the box, I heard nothing rattle; it felt solidly packed. The box resembled nothing I had ever seen.

I secured the cargo back in its frame, then examined the other item in the bay, which was strapped down near the box. It was an unusual kind of protective suit, bright purple in color. I unfastened it for a closer examination. It was made of a shiny, flexible, metallic purple material that was a bit thicker than a thumbnail, making the suit not very bulky. The entire suit was made of this material, from the bottom of the feet to the tips of the fingers and to the top of the head. It had a transparent face visor, also tinted purple, that flipped up or down. The one-piece outfit contained fasteners and zippers, all purple, apparently made of the same substance. The suit had no life-support system in it, only various filters of a finely graded metal mesh, also purple colored, under the mouth. I wondered if the air at my destination needed refining through these filters. But why was the rest of the suit necessary? It was not pressurized or powered, and it contained no heating or cooling coils. The suit resembled nothing I had ever seen.

I drifted back to the living quarters and took a look around. I examined the cabinet over Feran's desk. Reflecting the mental capacity of its user, the compartment was almost bare. It contained a leather folder with a pen and blank notepad inside. These three items were imprinted with the capital letters *MAS*. The bold black letters were slanted, and they appeared on the image of a sleek silver rocket. This small imprint—the letters and their design on the body of the rocket—meant nothing to me. Another mystery, I thought, rubbing my fingers over the curious design on the folder, pad, and pen.

I found no weapons on the ship. Why was Feran traveling alone and unarmed? Where was he going? What was he planning? Why was he preparing his entire fleet of spacecraft to take off, and why would the fleet be launched two days *after* he had left? Was the fleet going on another mission, or would it follow Feran? Where were the maps I had seen Feran call up on the ship's computer? They must be accessible only with his password, because I could not locate them in any database open to me.

Next, I moved to the ship's airlock, where I found a device called a camper. This was a small, bubble-shaped vehicle used for travel away from the mother ship. With some investigating, I discovered that I could activate it and use its communication system to send a signal to another ship in the Asteronian fleet. Could this device help me throw Feran off my trail? I set to work on a plan.

After another day in space, a planet that had been merely a bright point in the distance grew to a large sphere filling the windows of my craft. I had passed other planets along my journey, which I had studied through the telescope, but the one I was fast approaching was different. Though the dusty rocks, frozen gases, and spewing volcanoes of the others looked forbidding, the planet looming ahead was a lively swirl of blue, brown, and green patches dappled with wispy white clouds. As I sat on the flight deck, I looked from the telescope's screen to the ship's window, observing the curious sphere. It possessed a life-giving mix of sea and land, with green fields and sunlit skies. The sight of this planet alarmed me because it looked remarkably like Asteron.

The presence of only one moon reassured me that I had not reversed course. It did not soothe me very much, however, because this colorful planet was Feran's chosen destination—the one place in the universe where I most profoundly did not want to go.

The spacecraft began firing directional rockets, slowing down, descending. A spectacular pink glow surrounded my craft as I left the black void of space and entered the planet's atmosphere. While I descended, the automatic flight plan remained engaged. When would it disengage? Feran would probably have programmed his ship to carry him as close to the ground as possible and perhaps even to land for him. He had no desire to curl his hand around the stick and feel the thrill of harnessing the craft's power himself. The only thrill I had ever seen him display was when he harnessed people. I instinctively touched the scar made by the chain I had so often worn around my neck. Fearing I would have little or no time or fuel to alter the ship's destination, I had devised a plan to throw Feran off track. I might be forced to land at or near his programmed spot, but I could make him think I came down elsewhere.

While the craft brought me to the alien world, I waited for the right moment. Outside my window I observed a clear moonlit night on the planet. I saw signs of intelligent life in the lighted clusters that signified cities and the roads emanating from them. Then a fortuitous thing occurred. I saw that I was heading over a mass of water, a gulf, curled inside a crescent of lights from the land masses on its sides. This was the perfect place to set in motion my plan.

I was now flying at the reduced speed of aircraft travel, and I could feel the new tug of gravity as I walked to the airlock. I slid inside the camper and activated its systems.

"Help me. Help me. Can anyone hear?" I said through a communication channel set to reach other craft in the same fleet. "Help me."

"Is that you, pig?" Feran had indeed picked up the signal. "But wait! You are transmitting from the *camper*." A touch of fear heated his voice. "What are you doing in the camper?"

"There is a fire onboard. The ship is going to crash."

"What? Impossible!"

"I sealed myself in the camper, where I have life support. Maybe the aliens will rescue me when I eject."

"You worthless blockhead! Go back to the craft at once! By my calculations you should now be passing over a gulf. *You must not lose the ship!* I will have Asteron flight control tell you how to save it."

"If you can get me off auto-flight, I will head for solid ground and attempt to land before the ship crashes into the sea. That way I can save your cargo. What is your password to disengage auto-flight?"

He paused, suspicious. "Flight control will tell you what is necessary for you to know and nothing more."

"It is too late anyway. The fire is out of control."

"What is this fire, and where is it?"

I did not reply.

"You have three orders, you miserable swine: You must not let the cargo sink into the sea. You must not let it catch fire. And you must not let it crash."

"Maybe you should order the fire not to burn."

"Go back to the ship and put the cargo in the camper to protect it!"

"What exactly is this cargo, Feran? What is it you are asking me to place in a safe container while I go back into the flames?"

"It is something that is *mine* and that you had no right to take. Do you understand that?"

"Fully. There was something that was *mine* and that *you* had no right to take. *No right at all!*" I did not recognize the savage cry that was my voice. "For that, I will watch your cargo sink to the bottom of the sea!"

"Shut up! You have no idea what you are saying. You must save Asteron!"

"What is this cargo? How will it save Asteron?"

"Get to the deck for your commands."

"There is no time to save my ship. Oh, I mean *your* ship, Feran."

He moaned in fury and frustration. "You must save the ship! I command it!"

"I am too weak to save the ship, Feran. My rations of animal feed have not fortified me enough for my journey. I will eject in the camper and save myself."

"The camper does not have engines for a power landing on the planet. It could break up on impact. Your despicable traitor bones are safer if you follow flight control's orders and save the ship."

"I will follow my own orders and take my chances."

I shut down the communicator and jumped out of the camper. Then I sealed the airlock behind me and returned to the flight deck. I figured that if Feran found evidence of the camper in the sea, it would lend credence to my story about the fire and make him think that the mother ship and cargo also crashed there. So I ejected the device. From my window I watched it fall. My ruse, I hoped, would stall him.

I harnessed myself into the captain's seat, waiting for the autopilot to disengage. Why was I not dead yet? Where were the missiles from the alien planet? Did it not protect itself from alien spacecraft entering its territory? If this were Asteron, I would have already been tracked. And why had no alien tried to reach me by radio?

The fuel indicator was approaching empty. When the autopilot disengaged, I would not have enough fuel to fly any significant distance from Feran's destination. My fingers moved restlessly over the stick, waiting for it to respond.

I was now flying up the coastline of what appeared to be an ocean, with waves breaking on the beach. The shoreline glimmered with the lights of cities and with roads flowing into and out of them like arteries. I was descending rapidly now, flying above one cluster of lights, then over an area with more scattered lighting. My craft was set to land near the coast, in a less-populated region on the outskirts of a city.

With the glow from the lights below adding to the moonlight, I could see objects. I spotted an expansive wooded field that appeared to be deserted. It had areas that were sufficiently open for a vertical landing of my ship, yet surrounded by thickets of trees and shrubs for concealment. This was where I would touch down if I got the chance to maneuver. Just when I had given up hope of exerting any control over where I would land, the computer announced that auto-flight was disengaging.

Suddenly, the stick came alive in my hand! I quickly turned the ship and headed straight for the field behind me. Just to be safe, I turned off a sensor that transmitted the craft's location, although I did not think it was operable outside of the home planet's satellite network.

I maneuvered the ship over what I judged to be the optimum place in the field for a landing. For a few tense seconds the craft bumped and scraped against the foliage as I brought it down. It hit the ground with a thump. I cautiously moved my neck and limbs, and then I checked the flight deck. My body and the ship seemed intact.

I observed my new planet from the windows. The shrubbery brushing against my craft seemed astonishingly similar to that on Asteron, as if someone had transplanted the vegetation from one place to the other. An instrument onboard registered a benign atmosphere containing oxygen, so I carefully opened the hatch and took a breath. Warm air, scented with sea and grass, filled my lungs. I saw no need for the curious purple suit in the cargo bay because the fresh air felt remarkably similar to that on Asteron.

To my great relief, no one seemed to be waiting. My arrival, apparently, was of no interest to anyone. I slid down from the ship to the ground.

Like the military craft I had flown, the ship was coated with a substance to prevent detection by thermal and infrared instruments. Nevertheless, I still had to protect the spacecraft from detection by the naked eye. Although my landing spot provided good camouflage, I gathered leafy branches from the shrubs around me and worked diligently to cover the top and any remaining exposed areas of the craft with foliage so that it would not be easily seen by anyone.

After completing this arduous task, I sat in a nearby grassy area to watch fire-red spears strike a cool blue sky. Opposite the vast sea there was a mountain range, and over it the sun was rising in my new world.

As daylight arrived, my worries subsided. I could find nothing to fear. The alien sun was not harsh but warm and nourishing. The alien winds were not severe but cool and gentle. The alien sky was clear and bright blue. The alien land was rich with trees, shrubs, and grass growing abundantly. The alien creatures, birds busy with morning rituals and little ground animals sniffing around me for food, were not frightening but harmless and engaging. My new refuge was like a potent drug that numbed my fears. I lay down on the grass with the sun flushing my face. Instead of watching for dangers, I closed my eyes for a moment of untroubled rest. Then I sprang up at the buzz of a plane's engine. A small aircraft of the most unusual color—bright red—glistened in the sky.

Startled, I dived into the bushes. The plane was directly overhead! It was searching for me, I feared. My heart was pounding to match the motor's roar. What was I to do? If I tried to flee, the plane could shoot me down. If I remained where I was, it could land and deploy guards to catch me. I waited for the plane to hover, to land, to shoot, to be joined by other aircraft, but none of these things occurred. Instead, the little red ship did something most unexpected.

It flew upright, then inverted. It rolled like a leaf tumbling in the wind. It looped to form vertical rings, then it carved a perfect figure eight, executing smooth rolls and quick spins along its path. The pilot raised the nose, climbing straight up to a point of zero airspeed, and then he began spinning in a spectacular vertical descent. At an altitude that seemed too low for recovery, he suddenly stopped the rotations, coming out of the spin in time to avoid the ground. The pilot performed these maneuvers with such balance and grace that I thought of the alien music Reevah had sung to me. I hummed the melody while I traced the aircraft's flowing loops, rolls, and spins. The pattern of the flight matched the rhythm of the music so well that the craft seemed to be dancing through the sky.

I realized that the plane was not looking for me or anyone else but merely for an open field over which to perform. The graceful ship seemed concerned with nothing beyond its own exciting movements. Watching it fly with ease through its skillful sequence, I remembered the time I had performed similar maneuvers in my plane, the day I was caught and . . . A sudden fear stopped my humming. Had this pilot swayed from his regimen? Would he be punished for his behavior? Would he be beaten—or meet a worse fate—for the superb patterns he traced in the air? "No!" I cried. "No!"

The plane began a vertical descent, a graceful red object hovering in a blue sky, slowly falling to the ground. I ran to the edge of my field, crossed a paved road, and climbed up a grassy hill to the nearby area where the plane was touching down. It landed in front of a domicile of some kind, but one that did not look large enough to house a multitude of people. I wondered about the security problems posed by its glass doors, large windows, and outdoor porches. It looked like a place too easy for inhabitants to escape.

Concealing myself in the bushes surrounding the small building, I watched to be sure that the skillful pilot was safe. I vowed to smash anyone who would punish him. Just as the door of the small craft opened, a stout male humanoid who looked like an Asteronian approached the plane. He wore a brown uniform and carried a large shovel, its scoop raised high and ready to strike. It was a primitive weapon indeed for a commander, but one that could crush the pilot's skull in one blow.

The pilot emerged wearing a short, zippered jacket over pants. To my surprise, the flier's slim lines and gracefulness in jumping to the ground were unmistakably female. She removed a hair band, and a rush of brown hair tumbled around her shoulders. In the morning sun, her hair glistened with streaks of red like burnished wood. The pilot shook her head briskly, as if to remove the tangles of her hair's confinement. Then she smiled, an effortless gesture that seemed as buoyant as the loops of her plane. I guessed her to be a bit younger than I was.

Was she in the military as I had been? Had she stolen the plane? I eyed the commander brandishing the shovel. He was a full head taller than the flier and about three times her weight, and his neck was of gargantuan thickness. His big steps quickly advanced him to within striking distance. Jumping out of the bushes, I lunged in front of her to face the monster that I could match in height but did in no way equal in bulk. I grabbed the shovel from his hand and gestured to the pilot. Although I did not expect aliens to understand me, my words spilled involuntarily.

"You will not strike this female! You will not hurt her!"

The commander raised his eyebrows.

"Just what do you think you're doing?" said the female.

"You speak my language!" I gasped incredulously.

"You speak *ours*." She grabbed the shovel from my hands and gave it back to the commander! However, he did not move to strike either of us.

"Now, who are you, and what do you think you're doing, kid?" said the commander. He dug the blade of the shovel into the ground, clearly not intending to hit anyone.

"I think I was mistaken," I said.

"What business do you have coming here?" the pilot asked.

"I am lost."

"Where are you from?"

"Another place. Where am I now?"

"You're trespassing on private property," she said.

"What is that?"

"My father owns this land."

"You *know* who your father is?"

"Who are you? What's your name?"

I hesitated. With Feran in pursuit, I did not want to give any Asteronian name or hint of my origin. I knew only two alien names, and, although I had favored Reevah using the title, I did not want to be addressed publicly as Honey.

The female persisted. "Well? What's your name?"

"Alexander. My name is Alexander."

"Is that your first or last name?"

I had no reply.

"Or do you have only one name, like some of the aliens?"

"My name is Alexander."

"Why are you trying to rescue me from my gardener, Alexander?"

"What did you say he was?"

She gestured around us, pointing to mounds of freshly turned soil along a pathway up the hill and to two robots working the ground. The man in the brown shirt and pants was apparently the commander of a robotic grounds crew. "He's a gardener, someone who plants flowers, Alexander."

"You plant flowers?"

"Excuse us," said the oversized alien.

He grabbed the pilot's arm. My fingers instinctively seized his wrist before I could stop myself.

He gently removed my hand and then held up both of his to show he was not dangerous, and he spoke to me softly, the way one addresses a child. "Now, nobody's going to hurt anybody. You just wait here a minute while the lady and I have a little chat." He smiled, moving a few steps away from me with the pilot.

I heard a smattering of words, sufficient to understand. The gardener said something about my needing medical attention. He reached for a pocket phone and uttered the word *police*. Knowing that word's meaning quite well, I prepared to race down the hill and vanish from their sight forever. But the pilot stopped him, presenting a different theory about me. She thought I was an alien from Cosmona, a place from which a spacecraft apparently had just landed with refugees looking for work. Because I could not pretend to be from this bizarre new place, could not divulge I was from Asteron while Feran lurked, and did not intend to deal with the police, I thought I would encourage the pilot's hypothesis.

"I mean no harm," I called to them. "I am a stranger here and unfamiliar with your customs. I am in possession of my faculties, but I know nothing of my whereabouts. I am lost, so perhaps I can ask a few questions and then leave."

The pilot turned to the commander of flowers. "It's okay, Jack. I'll handle this."

"If you're sure, Kristin." He eyed me suspiciously as they stepped toward me. "We don't get around much to the primitive planets—no offense. So we don't know how things work where you come from, but if you want to live here, you should know one thing."

He paused, still staring at me.

"We don't stick our noses in other people's business."

"Yes, sir."

He turned to go, then stopped. "Oh, Kristin, I almost forgot what I was going to ask you." He glanced at me as the cause of the interruption of his thoughts. "I was wondering how much your father wants me to trim back the shrub roses on the east border. Did he leave for work yet?"

"He's away on business, Jack." I detected a touch of sadness in her voice. "He doesn't seem to have time for the garden, so why don't we decide?"

"You know how particular he is about his roses. Maybe I should wait till he gets back."

"Lately he's had business matters on his mind, so it's hard to get his attention," she said with disappointment. "I'd say to trim them down to four feet."

"Okay," said the gardener.

He glanced at me suspiciously once again, then took his shovel and walked away.

Incredulously, I eyed dozens of trays filled with tiny blossoms sprawled along the hilly path from the street to the domicile. The short, headless robotic gardeners had rectangular bodies with various pockets to hold small tools. They seemed well suited to working the ground. Each robot's four arms were engaged in digging holes with their trowels, lifting tiny plantings from their trays, and settling them into the ground. I breathed in the sweet scents that the wind tossed at me. A sudden aching made my mind wander to a place by a lake where a tall, delicate figure with golden curls placed a flower in her hair, a rare blossom that I had to search to find. I imagined her seeing the spectacle of color and fragrance before me, and her laughter became almost audible—

"Alexander . . . Alexander."

I realized the young female named Kristin had called me several times. "Yes?"

"I've got to grab breakfast." She pointed to the curiously small quarters near us. "Then I'm going to work. If you're just arriving from Cosmona, there's a place a little north of here called the Center for Alien Orientation. Take the road outside my house to Evergreen Avenue, then east on Evergreen to Sanders. The center helps aliens find work here, and they put you up temporarily in housing and feed you."

"Is that where I am required to report?"

"You're not *required* to go there, no."

"But how does a person receive food and other rations?"

She cocked her head, looking puzzled by my questions. "You *buy* them, so you need money."

"You mean they are not provided for free?"

"Why, no." She looked surprised by my question.

"How do I obtain money?"

"You take a job and get paid for your work. The Center for Aliens is run by a group of local employers. They can help you find work with their companies, or you can get a job on your own. Whatever you choose."

"You mean I can . . . choose . . . my work?"

"Of course." Kristin looked at me curiously.

"Where am I?"

"In Rising Tide."

"Where is that?"

"It's a city in California."

"Is California the name of the planet?"

She smiled. "No. You're on Earth. Planet Earth."

The name sounded familiar, but I was sure that I had learned nothing about Earth, or Cosmona, in school. I figured from my education that I was on a primitive planet where people were still in the grip of what my teachers called the idolatry of money.

"What kind of humans live here?"

"Earthlings." She smiled. "By the way, you never answered my question, Alexander."

"What question?"

"Why did you try to rescue me from the gardener?"

"I saw you perform the most skillful maneuvers in your plane. I thought you had stolen it from the military, and you would be punished. I thought the gardener was a commander."

"Hmm, I see. I think I see. That plane doesn't belong to the military."

"Who else could it belong to?"

"It belongs to *me*. And as long as I'm not endangering folks—say, by practicing my aerobatics over populated areas—I can do what I want in my plane. No one can stop me—least of all the gardener." She tried to suppress a laugh. "I'm sorry. I don't mean to make fun of you."

"I am relieved you were not in danger."

"Actually, my life's never been in danger."

An astonishing state of existence that I could hardly imagine.

"No one ever tried to save my life before." She looked up at me, scanning my face.

"The way you fly, you might be in danger. I did not think you would come out of that last spin. You were almost aground before you finally decided to apply opposite rudder."

She raised her eyebrows in surprise. She sounded stern but looked ready to smile. "Evidently, there are no gardeners where you come from, but there are aircraft. And evidently you have opinions about my safety in the air as well as on the ground."

I had those opinions, indeed—such as about the risk of her blacking out from the dizzying maneuvers she performed—but I thought it best to keep those views to myself. I studied her face as she stared at mine. The steady gaze of her translucent brown eyes looked like that of an adult, while the splatter of freckles on her nose made her look a bit childlike.

"Want to go up with me, Alexander?"

I looked at Kristin's sleek, red craft shining in the morning sun. "Oh, yes."

"I promise I'll fly easy, so I won't shock you."

"Nothing can shock me." More correctly, my only shock was that I was still breathing.

"Why don't you come back? I'm usually playing with my plane early in the morning or late in the day before sunset."

"What did you call what you were doing?" I asked astonished.

"Playing."

How odd it seemed to use that word. On Asteron only small children played, and only up to an age when they could perform useful work for the people. But that word . . . *playing* . . . seemed to describe perfectly what I was doing when I flew my plane beyond my commander's protocol.

"Kristin, may I trespass again on this . . . you called it . . . property?"

"You have my permission, so it won't be trespassing." She glanced at her watch. "I've got to run now."

As she turned away to walk toward her quarters, words I had just spoken became a lie, because something indeed could and did shock me about this alien pilot who lived in a world where her life was not threatened and who flew a plane for no other reason than playing. Across the back of her jacket, in slanting black print inside a silver rocket, exactly as I had seen them on Feran's folder, notepad, and pen, were the letters *MAS*.

CHAPTER 9

I saw no one as I crossed the road and returned to my field. A few birds in the shrubs scattered when I climbed up to my spacecraft and slipped through the unlocked door. The branches outside the windows provided a dark curtain around the flight deck.

In the dim light I stared at the ship's radio recorder, dreading the task I had to perform. I turned the instrument on, and its dormant black screen lit up to a pale blue. I had to tap an icon marked *messages* to know if anyone had sent the ship a communication. As I reached for the icon, I hesitated, afraid to know. But more afraid *not* to know, I finally pressed the button. The screen remained blue, with the words "no messages" appearing. I sank back in my chair, the tightness around my shoulders easing. Feran had not contacted the spacecraft. I wondered if my scheme had worked and he was headed for a body of water miles away to search for my ship.

The sun was higher in the sky and the air was warmer when I climbed out of the craft. I jumped to the ground in time to spot Kristin's plane rising vertically. The little red ship headed in the opposite direction from my field, flying straight and upright, a style that seemed too tame for the talent and inclination of its pilot. Kristin was going to work this time, not playing.

While I watched the red object recede in the distance, more questions about Planet Earth sprouted in my mind than there were flowers in Kristin's garden. I wanted to visit the Center for Alien Orientation to learn about this strange planet. But with Feran searching for me, I thought it best to avoid places where refugees gathered.

Instead, I cautiously walked around the area, and the sights I saw were amazing. I passed many buildings even smaller than Kristin's quarters, which could house only a few citizens. Each residence was different from the others and had its own garden, which in turn had its own distinctive mix of blooms, shrubs, and trees. I saw people dressed in fantastically colorful clothing in countless styles, textures, and patterns. There apparently did not exist a single gray worker's uniform on this planet. I wondered if my eyes would burn from the assault of colors. Maybe Earthlings had superior vision that allowed them to absorb the brightness that marked their world.

Everywhere I looked I saw sights unprecedented: people who were not moving in mass unity; people who were remarkably unequal and distinct from one another in their appearance; people who were . . . unafraid.

I spotted a male and female walking hand in hand. To my surprise, they threw their arms around each other and kissed when they paused at a corner. I feared for their safety after such shocking behavior, but no one came to arrest them. An adult male hugged a child, then lifted her high in the air, making the little girl laugh. Young boys in a park tried to hurl a large round ball through a hoop while they leaped and shouted excitedly. A cosmic artist seemed to have transformed the gray existence I knew across the galaxy into a lively palette of life here.

The modes of transportation seemed as varied as the users. Small ground autos and froglike car-planes moved around the roads and in the air. Some people had vehicles new to me, including battery-operated platforms that looked like flying harnesses, which moved just above the buildings. After descending, the riders secured these flying platforms on special racks along the street, similar to the way Asteronians parked bicycles. Others used small aircraft like Kristin's, with powerful engines that flew at higher altitudes. Still others operated planes I had never seen before, quiet ships that ran, I assumed, on an advanced form of electric battery unknown on Asteron. These vehicles traveled at an altitude between the power planes and the platforms. In addition, there were underground roads for buses and trucks. Because of the different layers of traffic, the vehicles moved quickly, free of congestion. There did not seem to be a central mode of transportation, but rather a variety of inventive avenues left to the individual tastes of the travelers.

Food apparently had immense importance to Earthlings. I saw that instead of having a regulated ration, people obtained a wide range of different foods from robotic carts on the street. The carts had multiple arms that grilled, prepared, and dispensed the food, then accepted coins in payment. People indicated their food selections by talking to computer monitors, some of which were designed to look like human faces. Much of the food was unrecognizable to me, and like everything else, it was spectacularly varied. I suddenly became aware of a sensation I had ignored throughout my trip—and my life—a hollow, aching feeling in my stomach. I walked over to an open trash bin in a nearby park. It contained enough food to incite an entire Asteronian village to riot. Furtively, I reached into the bin to grab a half-loaf of bread filled with meat, but I quickly withdrew my hand. Despite my hunger, I could not take anything from the garbage. I somehow did not want to soil this amazing place with an act unworthy of it.

Despite trying to remain unnoticed, I found it impossible to do so because the Earthlings looked directly at me, smiled, and said, "Hi." Every time a passerby looked at me, my body tensed in fear: *Is this one a spy?* I wondered. However, I did not recognize any of the people as spies from Asteron. I tried to imagine how it would feel to be free of my suspicions. On this walk that seemed like a scene from a child's imagination, could I not perhaps set aside for a few minutes the load I carried?

But just when I tried to relax, something startled me. A male in a blue uniform with a badge and weapon got out of a vehicle marked "Police." The man came directly toward me, then raised his hand and touched my shoulder. For a chilling second I felt like a trapped animal too stunned to flee. However, the officer did not seize me, but simply brushed by me to stop at a robotic food cart, where he bought a monstrous item called a "jumbo hot dog with cheese sauce." As he took a giant bite, I forgot all caution and stared at him, aghast. He noticed my stare and held the gruesome object up to me, smiled, and exclaimed with great satisfaction, "Best dog in town!" To my astonishment, the officer intended not to arrest me but merely to lavish praise on his food.

Despite my desire to ease my fears, I found it impossible to be calm. A gray fog clouded the rainbow of sights before me. In that fog floated Kristin and Feran, the two people I did not want to collide. Why did Feran's folder, pen, and pad have the letters *MAS* in common with Kristin's jacket? I did not want Feran to have even one letter of the alphabet in common with her. Why was he coming to Planet Earth? Would his plans here somehow touch a young pilot who danced through the skies in her plane?

Later that afternoon, as the Earth's sun arched across the ocean, I returned to Kristin's street. Walking to her quarters, I saw grassy hills with winding, flowered paths that led to one- and two-story domiciles like hers, partially hidden from the road by trees. I glimpsed large sheets of windows, slanted roofs, and porches with hanging plants in the serene landscape. I heard the buzz of an engine as Kristin flew her bright red craft above the empty field. She was already in the air, and this time there was another person in the plane with her.

I walked up the hill to her garden. There the entangling arms of the ground robots were motionless and their commander, Jack, was out of sight. Many of the little blossoms had made their way into the moist black soil. Trowels, shears, and other tools were now stowed in the robots' midsections. I was relieved that the machines and human gardener had evidently completed their shift, so I would not have to encounter the alien Jack again.

Sitting on the grass alongside the robots, I watched Kristin's plane floating through the sky in thrilling maneuvers. Soon the little craft was hovering above its landing spot near me, stirring the grass as it descended. The door opened, then Kristin and a male companion jumped to the ground. She waved her hand at me, and her companion said, "Hi." After a day of hearing this word, I sensed that I was expected to reply, so I too said, "Hi." I leaned back on my elbows, watching the two of them by the craft.

"You did real well today, Kris. You've mastered all the advanced techniques for the air show," said the tall young male with alert eyes who I realized was Kristin's teacher.

"I'm ready!" Kristin replied.

"I scheduled a meeting tomorrow at five in the west conference room to go over the group formations for the show."

"Okay, I'll be there."

"I'd like to ask Roy Gilmore to join the group. With an extra flier, we can use the eight-pilot formations and you can have a partner for the opposing solos."

"Oh no, Jeff. Please don't do that."

I sat up straight, suddenly concerned.

"What do you mean?" asked the instructor.

"I mean I don't want to fly in formation with Roy."

I rose to my feet. Kristin was refusing to cooperate with her superior.

"Why not, Kris? Roy's an excellent pilot. He's ready for the show."

"I don't think so," she said.

Kristin was contradicting her teacher. Such behavior was unthinkable! I wanted to shout *no* to warn Kristin, but it was too late. I watched the instructor. His smile had vanished.

"Jeff, the last time I flew with Roy, he made some mistakes that showed poor judgment. I told him about them. I'll explain to you, him, and the group, if you'd like, but Roy's not ready yet. I don't feel comfortable flying at high speed with his wingtips close to mine in the formation."

"So you're refusing to fly with him?" the instructor said.

"I am."

As I watched the two pilots, I had a vision of a slim female standing on a wooden stage with her hands tied. A robed man declared that she had refused to obey an order. I heard the vicious jeering of people in the crowd who thirsted for human blood. I saw a platform with a rope—

Kristin's instructor turned to the plane and reached in to get something. I saw the loops of a rope fall out of the door. In the next instant I was standing beside Kristin, with shears from the garden raised high in my hand like a knife ready to strike. I saw Kristin's look of horror and felt her struggle to lower my arm and grab the shears, but I would not budge. Then I saw an object attached to the ropes, which the instructor was pulling from the plane—a parachute that was coming out of its packing, its ropes exposed. Instantly, the biting fear left me. I lowered my arm and the shears fell to the ground. All of this occurred before the instructor's head emerged from the plane and he turned to face us.

"Okay, Kris, I won't invite Roy Gilmore to the meeting. If you don't feel comfortable flying with him, then of course he can't join the group."

"Thanks, Jeff," said Kristin, her voice unsteady, her eyes darting nervously to me, her nails cutting into my arm to hold it down. "Oh, and this is Alexander. He's new around here."

"Hi, Alexander," said the instructor, extending a hand to me. Kristin placed my hand into his, and this alien stranger, whom I had been about to . . . harm, squeezed my hand firmly while he smiled so broadly that lines formed around his eyes like rays from the sun.

"Hi, Jeff," I managed to utter, returning the hand-squeeze.

After repacking the chute and putting it back in the plane, the instructor said good-bye to us and left. As he walked down the hill to a vehicle parked on the road, Kristin turned to me. "You were going to *stab* Jeff! You could have—" She covered her face with her hands, as if to block out a fact too horrible to see.

"I was mistaken."

"I'll say you were mistaken! Whatever were you thinking?"

I was silent.

"Explain to me why you did that, Alex, and why I shouldn't think you're crazy."

"I am crazy."

"I can't fly with you if I think you're . . . disturbed."

"I am disturbed."

"Tell me why, Alexander, or you'll have to go away and never come back."

I paused. I sighed. Kristin waited. Finally I spoke. "You contradicted your teacher and refused to obey. When your teacher reached into the plane, and I saw the rope, I . . . I thought it was something else. I expected you to be punished."

Kristin stared at me in bewilderment. "You mean because I disagreed with Jeff, you expected him to . . ."—she suppressed a laugh—"to *beat* me with a rope? Or no, maybe you thought Jeff would *strangle* me?" Kristin threw her head back and laughed. "Or wait, I've got it—you thought he'd fling the rope around a tree and *hang* me, didn't you?"

I remembered a lively spark of gold hair against a dead sky. I wanted to reach out, but my wrists were tied. I wanted to cry out, but my mouth was gagged. I had to stop an unspeakable act, but I—

Then I felt two warm hands covering mine. "Alex, you're shaking. Your hands are so cold." Her rising laughter had vanished. Her untroubled face had creased with lines. "You really thought . . . something horrible. . . . You tried to *rescue* me . . . again."

I wanted to erase the dark lines I had marked on that face. "Laugh at me, Kristin. I want to feel ridiculous, to know that what I thought would not happen here."

Kristin did not laugh. "I don't know much about those planets where the refugees come from. But I probably will someday, when I become a space pilot. I know only that here on Earth no one can hurt me. I'm in no danger, believe me. But *you* are."

"What do you mean?" I asked, startled. *Does she know I am being pursued?*

"There's one thing you're *not* allowed to do here, and it's the thing you seem intent on doing," she said sternly. "You're not allowed to go around assaulting people. The police will arrest you if you do."

"But is it not the *police* who do most of the assaulting?"

Kristin shook her head at me wearily.

My tension eased the moment we rose above the trees and floated through the clear sky in Kristin's plane. With superb precision, she traced patterns in the air over the ocean. She made circles with perfect curves and squares with sharp corners. We rolled and spun in every direction until the empty stretch of clear sky apparently became too tame for the keen reflexes of my daring pilot. She took me to a deserted mountain range a distance from the city. There she dived into canyons and climbed over cliffs, with ground and streams below me, then sky below me, then all of it spinning together in a stunning swirl of river, rock, and sky. I wondered if it was the light-headedness from racing through negative and positive *g*-forces that made me want to fly forever, never to touch the ground again, never to hear anything but the steady buzz of the engine and the eager laugh of my pilot.

After Kristin left the mountains and flew upright for a stretch, I asked a few of the questions stirring in my mind.

"Kristin, how is it that you speak my language?"

She laughed. "*Your* language, as you call it, originated here on Earth. English is spoken on other planets that trade with us and send people here, but it's *our* native language."

Remarkable! The tongue my teachers called Asteronian was a language from Earth called English.

"But you don't use contractions," said Kristin, "like the word *don't* for *do not*. We contract our words all the time. You speak more properly."

I had another theory. "Just less frequently. Where I come from, we do not need to condense words because we have so little to say. Maybe contractions have been lost in our speech because we talk so seldom."

"Maybe on Earth we talk too much. I know I'm guilty." With one hand on the controls, Kristin raised her other hand to cover her mouth.

My mind raced back to a scene in which I had to speak out, to shout, but— "Do not gag your mouth!" I pushed her hand down with a jerk that surprised the both of us.

"Alex, what's wrong?" she asked quietly, her eyes searching my face for a response I did not offer.

I realized my hand was squeezing hers tightly. To make up for my awkward behavior, I eased my grip, stroked her hand softly for a moment, and then released it.

"Do you have a military on Earth, Kristin?"

"Of course. Just about every country has its own military. There's also an alliance that most of Earth's nations belong to, which was formed to defend our planet against an alien attack, but we've never had one."

"Does the military not stop alien spacecraft that are entering Earth's atmosphere?"

"Only if they're armed. Our sensors can detect all known military weapons. If the ship has none of them, it's free to come and go as it pleases. If aliens come in, they're processed at the centers we have for that, and we help them find work."

"What if the alien craft has no weapons but perhaps has spies? Would Earth's military not want to stop it?"

"We haven't had any wars in a hundred years, not since the Reckoning. Besides, we have the best forces in the galaxy. Nobody's going to attack us." Kristin waved her hand to dismiss the notion. "No one here worries about that."

"What is the Reckoning?"

"Well"—she pursed her lips as she formed her answer—"it was a time in history when Earth took account of its ways. It marked the end of an old order and the beginning of a new one. We have an air show to celebrate it every year. I'm flying in this year's show."

Kristin turned her craft back toward the ocean, where the fireball that was the Earth's sun hung near the horizon, with thin bands of gold-tinted clouds layering the sky.

"What does *MAS* mean?"

"How do you know about that?"

"This morning I saw those letters on your jacket."

"Oh." She smiled. "*MAS* stands for 'Merrett Aerospace Systems.' That's the name of the company I work for. See?" she pointed to a sealed plastic water bottle fastened to the side of the plane that also had the letters *MAS* printed within the silver rocket.

"What do companies do here on Earth?"

"They provide useful things, like a certain kind of product or a service that they sell to others. That's how they make money. We call that 'doing business.' "

"How did MAS get permission to perform business on Earth?"

"Nobody needs permission."

"Oh?"

"There are a lot of companies on Earth. MAS is a big company with different divisions. I work in Space Travel. We transport people and equipment to places beyond Earth. We take crews to space stations, or workers to industrial installations on other planets. Our group also deploys satellites and conducts space exploration. We also run a weekly shuttle to the lunar cities. I'm in training to become a space pilot." Kristin spoke about being a pilot with an excitement that I could understand.

"Why does your company place its name on your jacket?"

"MAS puts its name on lots of things—shirts, jackets, hats, pens, you name it. Its logo is the initials in the silver rocket, which means its name is written in a way that's unique to it and stands out. It's like a signature, a special way of signing your name."

As our bodies hung inverted at the top of Kristin's perfect loop, I thought of how everyone on Asteron was forced to dress in gray to blend in equally with everyone else. Here it was not only the people that were unique but also the companies they formed. The companies also tried *not* to blend in but to stand out and be different.

"We give a lot of this stuff out to the public and to the people we do business with, our customers. They don't have to deal with us, you know; they can go to other companies that do what we do. So it helps to get our name out. It's good for business. That's called 'marketing.' "

Why would Feran curl his disgusting hand around a pen from this company? I wondered. "Does MAS do its business with other planets?"

"Yes."

"Which ones?"

"A lot of them—most of them." An angry edge suddenly sharpened her voice. "But not Asteron, of course."

"Why not Asteron?"

"Most of Earth's companies don't trade with Asteron."

"Why not?"

"We don't approve of Asteron."

"Why not?"

"It's a long story, but they're not like us."

Why, I wondered, did the name Asteron drain the smile from Kristin's face? "Do you know the ruler of Asteron?"

"No."

"Do you know his name?"

"No."

"Does he come here?"

"No."

"Does anyone from Asteron come here?"

"No. They're very secretive. They don't let any refugees out, and very few escape, so we don't know much about what goes on there."

"Do you know anyone from there?"

"No, and I don't want to. Well, only Mykroni, my boss, who escaped from there. But he's been on Earth and working for our company for twenty-five years, and he's my father's close friend, so I don't hate him."

"But you hate Asteron? Why?"

Her smile vanished and her face tightened into a solemn look at what I thought could be a memory that disturbed her. "They do terrible things."

"To you? Did Asteron do something to you, Kristin?"

"Hey, I thought we were having fun." Her voice told me that this topic was finished. Her face held a sadness that I did not understand and that she would not explain.

"So how do you like this plane?" she asked, changing the subject.

"I like it indeed. Is it made by an Earthling company?"

"Yup. The company's name is Taylor, see?"

She pointed to a name on the side of the instrument panel, a name I had seen before. I had flown crafts like Kristin's in Asteron, although they were less sophisticated models that I was sure she would consider outdated. *How does Feran get these planes?*

"Kristin, could Asteron get Earth's products anyway, even though you do not trade with them?"

"I suppose they could buy our stuff from other planets that we do trade with, sure, or else from the few companies here that deal with them." She looked at me suspiciously. "Say, why do you ask? You said you were from Cosmona, didn't you?"

I did not reply.

"But you couldn't be from Asteron. You'd have no way to get here. I mean . . . Alexander, are you keeping something from me?"

I looked into light brown eyes that had the shadings of the Earth's fertile soil, eyes that announced her feelings. I did not want to lie to such eyes, but I could not give out information about my past while Feran was pursuing me.

"Yes, Kristin, I am keeping something from you."

"Hey, just what do you mean?" she asked suspiciously.

"I mean . . . I can fly."

"Can you?" Her face brightened again.

"And I can fly this plane."

"Really?"

"And I indeed would like to fly this plane."

"Are you serious?"

"You will see that for yourself."

"Go ahead, captain." The plane had dual controls, so I began using mine as she released her hold on hers.

So Feran somehow managed to obtain planes and possibly other things manufactured by Earth's companies, even though they did not want to deal with him. He probably was trying to buy something from MAS. Maybe he was *at* MAS, trying to convince someone to do what Kristin called business with him. Maybe he got one of the company's pens and a folder and notepad. That was all. Surely he could not try to harm a company from a planet with a stronger military. Even he was not that stupid, I assured myself. And surely none of this posed any threat to Kristin. But then, what reason did she have for . . .

I could not think of such matters anymore, because I was feeling the superb sensitivity of a stick that seemed to move at the moment of a change in my intention, before it reached the nerves in my wrist. I performed a few simple maneuvers, and then as I got used to the plane, I traced more complicated patterns. I did many of Kristin's maneuvers, adding extra rolls and spins, increasing the speeds, pushing the maneuvers to the limits of my own imagination. When I was ready, I headed back to the mountains. I liked the landscape, especially as it became a liquid smear of climbs and dives, of stalls and spins, of cliffs and streams when I engaged in what Kristin had called playing. Somewhere on the edge of consciousness, I could feel her looking at me, stunned. I glanced at my speechless companion to be sure she was not blacking out from the maneuvers.

"Are you okay?"

She nodded, staring at me, her eyes now unblinking.

Then I forgot Kristin, the Earth, and the universe, itself. I had no room in my awareness for anything more than the superb feel of the plane racing through the air with the life and will that I gave it.

My hands almost touched each other around Kristin's slim waist as I helped her out of the cockpit and onto the grounds near her garden. When we sat on the grass, she spoke for the first time since I had taken the controls:

"Alex, my gosh! When you started flying, I tried to put your technique into words. I mean you were skillful, very skillful, but there was more to it. You have a style to your flying. When you performed my own maneuvers, I saw your style more clearly. Where I did one slow roll, you did two quick ones. Where I made a smooth turn, you made a sudden one. Where I pushed the stick easy, you pushed it hard. Where I descended smoothly, you dived faster and steeper. When I fly, it feels like dancing. But when you fly, it feels thrilling, aggressive, almost violent."

"Your flying has superb rhythm and grace," I said.

"And yours has . . . anger. Do you feel angry, Alex?"

"Yes."

She waited, but I volunteered nothing further.

"Is that why you don't smile or laugh?"

"I am not like Earthlings."

"What do you mean? I know there are different species of humans that evolved on other planets, but they look different. You look like us. You're *Homo sapiens* like us, aren't you?"

I shrugged my shoulders in ignorance of what I was. I wondered about the knowledge Feran withheld from us, knowledge about our nature and that of other humanoids. Why was it that only certain Asteronians, like spies or doctors, received biological information, and only in secret? The rest of us were told merely that aliens differed from us in every fundamental way.

"But you *feel* things," Kristin said, perplexed.

"Not the way you do."

"In your flying there's . . . passion."

I thought of the untroubled smiles and easy laughter of the humans here. Their manner was completely foreign to me. "I do not have the same . . . mental . . . abilities . . . as Earthlings."

"But you have incredible *flying* ability! Have you tried to find work through the Center for Alien Orientation?"

"No."

"Good. Don't!"

"Why not?"

"Because they'll grab you up in a minute. Do you realize how *valuable* your skills are and how much *money* you can make? There are companies working with the alien center that'll offer you a job as a domestic pilot to fly around Earth, which I think is kind of dull. My company is the only one around here that trains pilots for interplanetary travel. There you get to fly amazing spacecraft and go to exotic places. You encounter all kinds of terrain, atmosphere, weather, gravity, and other alien conditions. And there's also the fun of maneuvering through zero *g*'s in space. Skillful pilots are in big demand at MAS."

"And you said people here are paid for their work?"

"Oh, absolutely. MAS pays in gold, which you can use here as well as on the other planets you'll travel to. You'd probably start with five dollars a week. That's enough to get your own apartment and, after a while, a little house for yourself, something like the one my father and I live in, only smaller." She pointed to her domicile.

"You and your father live in quarters without other citizens?" I asked incredulously.

"Of course."

"And . . . and you live without guards watching you?"

"Of course, Alex."

"I see. I think I see."

"You'll need to start off more modestly, but in a short time you'll be able to buy or lease your own plane. You don't understand how things work here, so I'll tell you that all the things you buy will be *yours*, the way this plane is mine and this land is my father's, and nobody can take your stuff away. You'll like it here. You'll be able to fly like crazy all the time. I don't want another company to get you, Alexander. I want to speak to my manager, Mykroni, about giving you a job with us," she said excitedly, her words tumbling into one another. "Right now *I'm* the best flier among the trainees, but if you join us, then *you'll* be the best!" The thought pleased her.

Then she frowned. "MAS has been having financial problems recently. Our Product Development Division pulled out of a big project it was working on for two and a half years. The pullout was unexpected. The company had to let workers go. But the Space Travel Division is doing fine. We've got lots of contracts, so I think you have a good chance of getting hired. That is, if you want to come to work for us. Do you, Alex?"

Do I? Do I want to smell the flowers of many gardens, including my own? Do I want to see people consume an incredible abundance of food, no matter how grotesque what they eat may be? Do I want to live in a place where strangers grip my hand in theirs not to harm me but to welcome me? Do I want to do work that I have always yearned to do and be paid for it? Do I want to live in my own dwelling where I can sleep alone, without the unkempt bodies of three hundred others? Do I want to have things that no one can take away . . . including my own life? Do I want to join a primitive society corrupted with money, and obtain as much of it as I can to buy things for my own satisfaction?

It took a moment to steady my voice enough to reply: "Oh, yes."

"There's one more thing, Alex."

"Yes?"

"MAS has had a policy for almost three years that's strictly enforced and that I have no power to break, even if I wanted to. So before I can recommend you, I need to be sure I heard you right. You said you're *not* from Asteron, right? MAS doesn't hire anyone from Asteron."

CHAPTER 10

An ocean breeze boosted my steps as I walked to meet Kristin at a place I had never been to before, a place that on Asteron was frequented by the rulers and aliens but was a luxury to most of the people: a restaurant. My spirit also felt lifted by the gust of activity that was moving my new life forward.

I had again checked my spaceship's radio for messages and found none. Moreover, I had learned from Kristin that the field across the road from her residence was lying dormant while its owner, called a land developer, was building a village on Earth's moon. This gave me hope that my ship's hiding spot would remain undisturbed.

I also had another reason for feeling hopeful. After I had flown Kristin's plane yesterday, she called her boss, Mykroni, and arranged for him to interview me for a space pilot's job. Today I was to meet Kristin during her lunch break; then she was going to take me to see a native Asteronian who was supposed to believe I was a Cosmonan.

Can I get away with this? I wondered. With the ship's remarkable alien medicine rapidly healing my wounds and with Feran's Earthling-style clothes, I dared to believe that my appearance was unsuspicious—except for the scars on my neck from the iron chain I had worn so often on Asteron. I had applied the new medicine to these old scars, but without success. The neck marks were older and unresponsive to the ointment that had healed my fresh wounds so well. Would Kristin's boss suspect the origin of these scars? How many planets put humans on a leash? To be safe, I had selected a shirt that best concealed the markings and buttoned it snugly at the top.

Earlier this morning, to prepare for my job interview, I had set aside my fears of meeting Feran's spies and had gone to the Center for Alien Orientation. From outside I saw a rack of printed materials labeled "Free pamphlets—help yourself," and on it stood a booklet about Cosmona. I waited until the orientation center's attendant was occupied, and then in a silent, catlike motion, I entered, took a copy, and left without speaking to anyone. In a section aimed at introducing Earthlings to Cosmonans, the booklet described how that planet was inhabited by humans of different species, with the educated speaking English. Some of the immigrants pictured in the pamphlet looked similar to me, so I figured I could pass for a Cosmonan.

I thought I had a chance of getting away with this, as I followed Kristin's directions to a place called Big Eats. But I felt something dragging me down as well. As I observed the tidy little domiciles along my path, the children and pets playing, the colorful windows of the Earthlings' businesses, the quiet contentment—and openness—of their lives, a pang of guilt gripped me. I did not want to deceive Kristin, but I reminded myself of the sleepless night I had just spent, excited at the prospect of having a job filled with space travel, discovery, and adventure. When Feran became convinced of my death and had gone on to new diversions, I would no longer have to hide my past. Then I would look into the eyes that had poured more understanding over me than I knew existed, and I would tell Kristin the truth about my origin, whatever the consequences might be. But right then, I had to pretend that I was a Cosmonan because I yearned to pilot a spacecraft and explore the shiny dots that sprinkled the black sky, dots that had lit my imagination in my childhood with visions of bright new worlds beyond the dim one that bound me.

I reached a building with a large sign in front that read "BIG EATS." Earthlings engaged in lively conversations entered and left this busy institution, with a variety of food aromas escaping each time the door opened. With Kristin's instructions to guide me, I entered and got a table. While I waited for her, I watched the incredible spectacle of Earthlings having their midday feeding.

A computer screen at my table displayed the word *menu*. I understood this word to mean options on a computer. But at Big Eats it meant something quite different. The restaurant's menu described an astonishing array of foods of massive portions, displayed in colorful images. When I tapped on an item named *hamburger*, I saw three-dimensional flames dancing around the item on a grill, I heard sizzling noises, and I thought I detected a pleasing charcoal aroma emanating from the monitor. I tapped the screen repeatedly, and image after image of seemingly endless choices flashed before me.

I stared in disbelief at menu selections that contained more meat in one portion than I had been allowed in a year. I saw people around me eating steak, an item almost unheard of among the common people on Asteron. Our leaders told us that if they could not provide a particular food, like steak, to everyone, then it was only fair that no one should have it. Asteronians left the table with illusions of virtue, but the customers of Big Eats left with full stomachs.

Robots shaped like metallic humans with large heads and monitors on their chests attended the tables. A few actual human supervisors observed the goings-on and also interacted with the customers. The robots had long arms, each with two elbows, that reached into compartments in their backs and aided in serving the tables. Their mouths consisted of electronic screens displaying a range of emotions, with the default setting being a smile. Red aprons were painted on their metal torsos, with pockets containing bottles labeled *mustard, mayo, steak sauce.* These nimble devices wore name badges: *Whiz Kid, Big Head, Brain Man.* People spoke to them, and they replied.

I heard a female say to one of them, "Hey, Genius, this soup is cold."

The device replied, "You're unhappy with your soup? Is that correct?"

"Yes," the female confirmed.

The screen display that formed the robot's smiling mouth drooped downward into a frown, as the electronic creature replied, "I'm sorry. I'll get you another one right away."

A mass of circuitry named Genius was sorry for cold soup, I thought, astonished, while I remembered how live humans across the galaxy showed no such frowns at causing far greater . . . discomforts. Were they really living? I asked myself, wondering what ingredient on a planet's menu made human life possible.

People dropped money into slots on the robots, and to my amazement, the devices *thanked* them—just as the male alien in the crate had thanked me when I brought him water! My thoughts raced back to that odd incident across the galaxy when I had received a gold coin. Had Feran's boxed humanoid come from Earth? I had barely glanced at the coin when the alien gave it to me, and I was in darkness when I later hid it in my shoe. A chronic fear of its being discovered had made me obsessed with concealing, rather than studying, the coin, so it had remained hidden under my inner sole. Now, I reached down into my shoe and retrieved it. To my amazement, imprinted on the sparkling gold piece was a sphere with swirling patterns of land and sea, and above it the word *Earth.* I realized why the name of my new planet sounded familiar to me. I ran my fingers contentedly over the coin and could not wait to show Kristin my Earth money!

While music played, people talked, dishes clanged, and a monitor near my table broadcasted a news program, I struggled to absorb this symphony of sound. The news described a war in Cosmona, with refugees fleeing to Earth. A newscaster interviewed a few of them, confirming what I had read in the pamphlet. The Cosmonans were humanoid, although some of them were too small-limbed, large-faced, and hairy to be what Kristin called *Homo sapiens.* Then I saw other Cosmonan refugees who looked more like Earthlings. All of them spoke, in English, of oppressive conditions on their planet. *Surely I could have come from that kind of place,* I thought.

My fascination with this new setting was interrupted when two males in uniform sat down at the table next to me. My eyes gravitated to the word on their badges: *police*. I tensed at the sight of the weapons protruding from their holsters. I wanted to change my table, but I dared not get up for fear of attracting the guards' attention. I mentally rehearsed an exit plan should I need to leave suddenly.

Using one of its elongated hands with pronged fingers, a robot named Doc reached into a compartment behind his back for a basket of bread and served it to the guards.

The next news segment showed the mayor of Rising Tide making an announcement about an upcoming election and encouraging people to vote. Kristin had explained Earthlings' voting to me when we spoke about our ages. She was twenty and had voted in recent years. Although we ignored birth dates on Asteron, I estimated that I was twenty-one in Earth years. I could also vote, she informed me, when I became a citizen.

Just then I spotted Kristin at the entrance. Her shiny redwood hair tumbled about her face as she looked around, located me, and walked toward my table. She waved to people wearing MAS emblems like hers on their shirts. Kristin glanced across the guards' table to the one beyond it where her co-workers were eating and said a few words to them. She was about to join me but paused when she noticed the mayor on the monitor.

"After careful thought, I have made my decision. I will run for reelection as the mayor of Rising Tide!"

"I don't think he should be mayor again," Kristin shouted to her co-workers, her voice carrying over the police officers.

"Kristin!" I whispered. I reached out to grab her arm, but she had already raised it and was gesturing in the air. Instead I grabbed a tall glass bottle on the table labeled "chili sauce."

"I ask the citizens of Rising Tide for their vote," the mayor added.

"I'm *not* voting for him!" declared Kristin to her co-workers, almost hitting the officers' heads with her gestures. "He spends too much money."

I saw the policemen looking straight at Kristin, but what I felt were the menacing eyes on the prowling bodies that always watched me, waiting . . . hoping. I saw a robed male on a stage speak to a man standing beside his coffin, charging him with expressing ideas that contradicted those of established authority. The crime was treason. The man was young.

"Have you been inside the new city hall yet?" Kristin persisted. "You'd think it was a palace. I don't think it's right for a public servant to work in such luxury with the people's money."

While the officers were distracted looking at Kristin, I concealed the bottle of chili sauce behind me, gripping it tightly by the neck. But I must calm down! *This matter cannot be as it appears to me*, I tried to reassure myself. But my fears cried out louder. Kristin might have a voice when dealing with civilians, like her flower manager or flying instructor, but the two armed men here were the law! This was different. Kristin was spouting subversive remarks against an official that these guards were armed to protect. My eyes moved nervously from one officer to the other. I was ready to leap, strike them, and then grab Kristin and run out the door.

"I think the mayor should be replaced!" declared Kristin. Then, satisfied with having shared her traitorous viewpoint, she turned to me, smiled, and was about to sit. Suddenly one of the officers rose and stepped toward her. In a flash I was on my feet, my body wedged between hers and his. My wild eyes faced the guard, while my right hand, clutching the bottle behind me, faced Kristin. I felt her nails dig into my hand, trying to take the bottle from me, but my fingers refused to budge.

"Oh, uh . . . hi . . . Officer Hodges." My behavior had removed the steadiness from her voice. "This is Alex. He's new around here."

He smiled broadly, crinkle lines appearing around his eyes, and he raised an open hand to grip mine. I released the bottle into Kristin's clutch because I had to free my hand for grasping the officer's. I struggled to find my voice so I could offer a greeting.

"Hello, Alex. Nice to meet you." The guard grasped my hand firmly, and then he turned to Kristin. "I just wanted to tell you how sorry we are that Dr. Merrett is too busy to attend this year's Reckoning Day air show. I don't want to disturb him, seeing as he's busy, so I wonder if you could give him a message from all of us on the force. Tell him that if he finds time at the last minute, he shouldn't hesitate to call us. We'll be happy to reserve a place for him in the pavilion."

"I sure will. I'll let him know you said that."

"Thanks." The smiling guard then returned to his table, his weapon looking dusty from lack of use.

I sat, or rather Kristin gripped my shoulders and pushed me down. "Alexander! You're . . . you're . . ." She stood over me, speechless.

"Crazy," I said, assisting her in finding the right word.

"That goes without saying! And you're . . . I don't like to say it, but you're . . ."

"Disturbed."

"Without a doubt! But what I mean is I was wrong to tell you about a job with MAS. You're not ready to go to work. You're *dangerous*."

"No! I admit to being crazy and disturbed, but Kristin, believe me—I am not dangerous. I did not strike anyone."

"Not yet."

"Kristin, I want to be a space pilot more than anything. If you insist, I will be forced to agree not to intervene, even if you should be flogged right in front of me."

She looked disappointed. "Could you really watch me being—what word did you use?—flogged?"

"I could try to."

"Without rescuing me?" She frowned.

"Maybe it is unlikely," I had to admit.

Her expressive face brightened again with a smile, but Kristin tried to suppress it. Sitting down next to me, she searched my face with eyes that held real fear, if not real anger. "Tell me, please, why you were about to hit Officer Hodges with a bottle. Tell me, so maybe I can understand what you saw that was frightening in a room full of people eating and having a good time."

I thought of the publisher of seditious material standing tall on a wooden stage, with eyes whose flames would be extinguished in an instant to stare coldly for all of eternity. I rubbed my hands over my own eyes to wipe away that sight. "Kristin, I was afraid that the officer with the gun would . . . hurt you."

"Why?" She asked incredulously.

"You wanted to overthrow the government."

"Huh?"

"You wanted to replace the mayor. You expressed views that threaten his rule. I have seen people punished . . . severely . . . for that. You made your traitorous remarks in full, brazen hearing of the police. Indeed, you nearly leaned into their food."

She shook her head at me. "That's not how things work here."

"But you cannot criticize a public official. Kristin, you cannot refuse to obey your mayor."

"But I don't obey him." She waved her hand, dismissing the notion. "I mean we're the citizens. *He* works for *us*."

I stared at her, trying to understand.

"I realize you just got here, and you have a lot of new things to get used to. It's not fair to expect you to handle a complex job—"

"Expect me to, Kristin. Expect it."

"But I can't recommend you to my boss, and then have you be a loose cannon."

"Then I will be a tied cannon, a very well-fastened one!"

"Look, why don't we put this job interview off for a few weeks . . . or months? That'll give you time—"

"Kristin, I swear I will change my thoughts! I will alter them immediately. If I am hired and I become disturbed just once more, I will ask permission to leave the company, if I am allowed to do that."

"Of course you can leave! Do you think you're a—" Her hands covered her mouth in horror. Her voice whispered incredulously. "Is . . . that . . . what you were?"

"Kristin, if the matter of my interview is settled, then I have many questions to ask before your feeding time is over." I quickly changed the subject. "Who is Dr. Merrett, the man the officer referred to? Is he connected to Merrett Aerospace Systems?"

"Dr. Charles Merrett is the president of MAS. He owns the company."

"And how are those guards involved with your air show on the Reckoning Day?"

"The air show is a fund-raiser for the city. MAS helps the city by donating the pilots and planes for the show. Other companies donate the food. The police sell the tickets and run the show."

"Why should the officer ask *you* to convey his message to Dr. Merrett?"

"Because Charles Merrett is my father."

As I was absorbing this information, the computer terminal at our table asked for our order.

"I'll have the Ultimate Sub with the works, a chocolate milk shake, and French fries," Kristin replied.

The computer repeated the order and flashed images of the items on the screen.

"And make it the 300-calorie version today." She turned to me. "That costs extra. It cuts out a lot of calories to keep your weight down," she explained.

Then the computer asked for my order.

"Bread."

"Is that all?" Kristin asked.

"I do not eat your food."

"Bring him a piece of cheesecake too," Kristin told the computer, "and make *his* food with the *full* amount of calories."

The computer repeated the order and signed off.

"Kristin, do all Earthlings know their fathers?"

"Of course. Our parents have us and raise us. Then when we're old enough, we go out on our own."

"Why do parents raise their offspring?"

"Don't you know about families?" she asked, astonished.

"Not very much."

I waited while she looked at the ceiling, pondering her reply. "Our parents raise us because they enjoy watching us grow up and they care about what happens to us. You see, children are more than *offspring*, as you put it. Animals have offspring and walk away from them. But humans have *children*, who are a part of them, so the children are . . . special in some way."

I thought of a female with golden hair humming music by a lake, and of a fierce struggle to protect something that was special in some way.

"Alex, why do you stare so intensely?"

"Do you know your mother?"

Her eyes dropped. "I did," she said sadly. "I lived with my mom and dad at our house. We were so happy. But she died almost three years ago." Her eyes closed for a moment against a pain that suddenly surfaced. I placed a consoling hand over hers, because I knew how she felt about losing someone special.

A robot soon brought our food. Kristin described her Ultimate Sub, layer by layer. It was a precarious mountain of meat, cheese, and vegetables jammed between two thick slices of bread. I feared she would be permanently disfigured when her mouth stretched to take a bite out of this monstrous concoction.

"Why are Earthlings so fascinated with their feeding?"

"Take a bite and find out," she said, holding the frightful object out to me, but I recoiled. "And we don't call it *feeding*, unless we're talking about what birds do. People *eat* or *dine*, and we have *meals*, not *feeding times*."

Earthlings set their activities apart from the lower animals. I wondered why such distinctions were vanishing from the same language on Asteron.

I consumed the bread served to me. Then after some prodding by Kristin, I poked at the wedge on my plate called *cheesecake*. I placed a tiny piece of it on my fork, raised it to my mouth, studied it, then cautiously tasted it.

"Alex! Are you okay? Your eyes look wild and crazy!"

I took another, more ambitious bite. I thought of the fireworks exploding in the sky when the alien Alexander performed his home run, because I now felt as if similar sparks were exploding inside my mouth. A great upheaval was occurring, a bursting of taste sensations I had never known I could experience. I took another bite. I closed my eyes in deep contentment. I also realized that I was quite hungry.

"Do you like our food?"

"Yes, I definitely prefer dining to feeding."

So pleased was I with this cheesecake that I consumed the entire ration. Kristin ordered another for me, which I also dispatched with ease.

When the robot asked for payment, I showed Kristin my coin. "An Earthling . . . visitor . . . to my planet gave this to me after I got him a cup of water."

Kristin eyed the coin. "Wow, that's some tip! It's a five-dollar gold piece. You're almost rich, Alex." I dropped my coin into a slot in the robot's chest marked "payment." Then I picked up several smaller gold and silver coins that dropped into a tray labeled "change."

After we left Big Eats, I found myself irresistibly reaching into my pocket to shake the coins and to hear the jingle of my first real possessions. Kristin explained that the entrance to MAS was nearby, and we headed toward it. We had barely walked a block when I doubled over with a sudden, violent pain ripping my insides.

"Alex! What's wrong?"

"My stomach! I cannot digest Earthling food. I am going to die!"

With my arm draped around her shoulder, Kristin led me a short distance to a cylindrical steel booth on the street called Quick Fix. She explained that Quick Fix stations, common all around town, were well-equipped, portable medical-treatment facilities.

"You go inside, the instruments scan you, and then they tell you what's wrong and what to do. If you need a doctor fast, they call one to fly here and pick you up right away. Now go in, Alex. Be quick! I'll wait here," she said, guiding me into the booth.

Before she slid the curved door closed, I lifted her chin until her eyes met mine, and I whispered gravely, "Good-bye, Kristin."

Once locked inside the silver capsule, I heard buzzes and hums; I saw lights; I answered the questions of a computer that had a compassionate voice. Within minutes the door slid open. "Here's the diagnosis," Kristin said, grabbing the paper that had dropped into a slot outside. The document read: "stomachache." Quick Fix dispensed tablets, which I promptly swallowed with the water it provided, and I listened to its assurances that I would feel better in minutes.

"You see, Kristin, I am different from Earthlings, different inside. I knew this." My voice was heavy with disappointment.

"Hey, wait," she said, scanning the report. "According to this, you just went too fast. Quick Fix says you have to introduce foods slowly, because apparently, you haven't had much of them. But it says you're completely capable of digesting the food you ate."

I took the report from her, searching for something I did not find. Quick Fix said what Kristin had told me, but it did not indicate what human species I was.

"You see, Alexander, you're like us, inside and out."

"Quick Fix does not say that."

"I do. I think you can smile and laugh, and be happy just like us."

Laughter: a musical note rising from the throat and floating out of the lips, a natural sound for Kristin and other Earthlings. Was there any laughter inside me?

Quick Fix was worth the small coin I gave it, because my pain subsided by the time we reached the fenced complex of buildings, fields, and aircraft hangars called Merrett Aerospace Systems. There was a garden at the entrance, and in the center of it was a tall sculpture of the MAS logo, the soaring silver rocket with the letters *MAS* imprinted on the body.

After Kristin arranged for my clearance through various security points, we entered a building of glass and steel. The lobby contained a wall of miniature relics of Earth's early rockets, spotlighted in a glass display case, and over it the building's name imprinted in steel-gray block letters: SPACE TRAVEL DIVISION. We took an elevator and exited into a hallway where dense mazes of computers and spacecraft components were visible from every room. My eyes feasted on this amazing electronic universe.

We came to an office with a plaque on the door that read: DIRECTOR OF SPACE TRAVEL. Kristin introduced me to Mykroni Whitman, a tanned, light-haired man with a trim, youthful body and a face that looked a bit more than twice my age. His hand grasp was firm, and his eyes were direct and probing as they met mine. I recognized the first name, which was accented on the first syllable, as Asteronian, whereas the last name must have been Earthling. As if reading my thoughts, Kristin remarked that her father had given Mykroni his last name after he had arrived on Earth.

"Dr. Merrett gave it to me when I learned what the last syllable meant," Mykroni said.

I looked at him curiously, but he offered no further explanation. Kristin commented that I had just arrived from Cosmona, and to my great relief, Mykroni showed no reaction. He seemed uninterested in my origin.

He took me to a room in which a large computer screen resting on a small glass table seemed suspended in midair. He sat me down, tapped an option on the screen to begin my testing, and said, "Let's see what you can do." Then this Asteronian, who looked and spoke like an Earthling, vanished, leaving me alone with the keyboard and monitor.

The computer seemed determined to explore every facet of my mind. It posed mathematical problems. It wanted to know how well I comprehended English. It placed me in different hypothetical situations around the galaxy, giving me a problem to solve in each circumstance. It simulated a spacecraft's controls, gave me instructions on how they worked, then tested how well I grasped the information.

After placing me in command of a spacecraft, it blew out a computer onboard, sprung a leak in an engine, and otherwise caused my craft to malfunction, in each case asking me how I would solve the problem. I finished with time to spare and began to review my answers when a sudden fear gripped me. I remembered the test I had failed long ago when I tried to become a pilot. I failed because I had gotten all of the answers right. I could not be trusted to follow instructions because my performance was too good. *That cannot happen here*, I assured myself. *Why not?* a cold terror replied. *The boss is from* Asteron! In the time remaining, I changed some of my answers to responses I knew were wrong.

Uttering not a word, Mykroni returned, sat opposite me, and swung the computer screen around to face him. The room, darkened for viewing the monitor, formed a gray background around his face, which was dappled with light from the screen. I watched his eyes scanning my work while he pressed icons to turn the electronic pages. He paused a moment, resting his chin on his hand, saying, "Hmmm." He glanced at me and cocked his head, as if considering a laboratory specimen. Then his eyes returned to the screen to read the rest of my test answers.

Finally, he leaned back in his chair, folded his hands, and looked at me. "I'm disappointed."

"Oh?"

"Because you could have gotten a perfect score—you would have been the *first one* ever to get a perfect score!—but you made some stupid mistakes that I can't understand. If you know what this test shows you know, you couldn't have made the mistakes you did."

"But . . . but do you not want people who are sometimes unsure, people who can follow instructions and . . . obey?"

He raised his eyebrows and moved his eyes around my face suspiciously. "Say, what if I told you that you needed to get a perfect score on this test in order to be a space pilot? Would you have done anything differently?"

I did not know how to answer. Should I admit to being dishonest or stupid?

"Well, would you?"

"I . . . uh . . ."

"Show me." He swung the screen around to me.

I changed the mistakes back to my original answers, then rotated the screen to face Mykroni, who had been watching me the entire time. He examined the results.

"That's better. A perfect score! You took out the errors and left the intelligence. The only mistake you made here today was in thinking I don't want intelligence. If you think that, I can't put you in a spacecraft." He stared at me to stress his point.

I tried to quiet the dark voice that lived inside me, warning me of dangers. I thought of Kristin's speaking against the mayor and contradicting her flight instructor. Earthlings were not driven by obedience. "I will correct my mistake."

"Can you?"

"Yes." I was trying to convince myself as much as Mykroni.

With suspicion lingering on his face, he got up. "Let's see if you can fly."

Mykroni took me to a room that contained a large flight simulator, along with a small control panel near it. Our slim bodies formed two long gray shadows on the solid white exterior of the device as we walked up to it. He sealed me inside, where I sat in a life-sized cockpit with a full array of flight controls. He sat at the console outside, setting parameters for the device. First he had me perform a variety of basic maneuvers. The simulator moved in all degrees of flight motion, corresponding to the controls I engaged, and the scenery on monitors imitated what I would expect to see out the windows in an actual flight. Then the cockpit bounced and the scenery whirled as

Mykroni killed an engine, shook me with severe turbulence, set fire to my craft, and put me inside a meteor shower. In each crisis, I scrambled to resolve the problem. The enactments were so vivid that my pulse raced and muscles tensed as if the disasters were real. After I had managed to rescue the craft and crew during a string of these calamities, Mykroni finally stopped the simulator and let me leave the cockpit. I emerged with my legs weak and my mind spent from the nightmarish experience, only to find Mykroni smiling for the first time, a wide grin across his face.

"Let's go up now," he said simply.

He took me to the company's airfield, where to my amazement I saw several of the aircraft I had flown on Asteron, or rather I saw advanced models of planes I had flown. I went up with Mykroni in one of them. I took off and landed several times. I flew upright and inverted, high to the ground and low to the ground. I performed turns, loops, rolls, and spins of every kind. Mykroni called instructions to me, and I executed them. In several cases he had me climb at a certain distance per second to a specific altitude, then level off. When I finished, he checked my performance to see if I had met the requirements without overshooting or falling short.

Mykroni explained that although a plane could fly itself in automated systems, the intelligence and skill of a human pilot remained irreplaceable. Under MAS policy, humans were active in flying, as well as in overseeing, supplementing, and overriding automatic flight when necessary, especially in difficult or unexpected situations. "That's why we teach you to do everything," he said. I nodded, eager to learn all I could.

He talked about how precision flying was important for docking and rendezvousing in space. Because I had learned this kind of flying on Asteron, I could execute precision maneuvers in a whole host of situations. Mykroni posed many questions for me to answer, dazzled me with his own superb flying skills, and taught me new ways to harness the tremendous power of my ship to serve my will. We talked constantly, my words spilling together to keep pace with the many insights and questions that this master teacher stirred in me. I resolved to learn the Earthlings' speech contractions, because I was impatient to talk faster and say more.

When we finished, Mykroni jumped down from the plane, the sun catching strands of his yellow-brown hair, his face smiling, his lean body looking much younger than his years. He stroked the fuselage as though it were a prized animal.

"She makes you want to kiss her sometimes, doesn't she?" he said.

I remembered a superior with vicious eyes who had seen me kiss my aircraft, and then had ordered a punishment that almost killed me.

As Mykroni brushed one hand along the plane, he pointed to me with the other, his eyes sparkling with excitement. "You're the one who made her look so good. You're a crazy kid, and I hope to hell you don't kill yourself, but you did one fine job up there, Alexander. You're going to do damn well in a spacecraft."

I stared at him incredulously, realizing for the first time how much I wanted . . . needed . . . to hear the note of encouragement in a teacher's voice.

To clear me for space travel Mykroni arranged for a physical exam and fitness test, which I easily passed. I had an anxious moment when I was brought to the Human Resources Department for a background check on arriving aliens. Kristin had neglected to mention this! But because Cosmona was at war and there was confusion about who made passage on the refugee ships and how to locate their records, a check of my background could not be made at the time. I was told that Mykroni was alerted to this matter and that he waived the requirement.

When I was taken back to his office, I sat facing the man who could offer me a life. The wooden desk between us was bare of any papers or other objects, as if his sole concern was with me.

"Alex, we start space pilots at five dollars a week in gold. That'll get you a nice place to live, plus a fair amount of extra cash. I've got a contract to service a mining operation in the asteroid belt between two planets in our solar system, Mars and Jupiter, then to transport the materials to colonies on Mars. It's too expensive to keep mining and shipping materials from Earth when we can readily obtain them from the mineral-rich asteroids and extract them more economically in the environment of minimal gravity. Mining from space makes it so much easier to set up colonies there, so this project is very important to the future of space exploration. And it's important in establishing a completely new business operation for MAS in asteroid mining."

I looked at Mykroni intently, following every word.

"You'll need to learn all the systems on the spacecraft and to work through all the simulators, and then I'll send you out with our spaceships for field training. This training program would normally take a year, but the mining contract has to start in half that time. If you can be ready in six months, there'll be a bonus of twenty-five dollars, and you can be my pilot on the first ship out to the asteroids."

I nodded eagerly at the prospect.

He leaned across the desk, lowering his head so that he peered at me from under his eyebrows. "There's one condition. You must promise me you'll never again make an intentional mistake. You'll never again do something you know is wrong for the sake of what you think will please me. You'll never again think I'm so base as to want to be surrounded by inferiors. You'll never again try to hide your intelligence. As a space pilot, you'll have many lives and a fortune in equipment in your hands. For that, I need a man who thinks, not a robot who obeys. Which will you be, Alex?"

He paused for my answer.

"I will be a man, for I do prefer that option."

"I believe you on your preference, but can you promise to act on it?"

"Yes. . . . Now I can. Yes."

He studied my face, weighing my response. "Okay, Alex, the job's yours. I'll have Kristin give you a tour of the department. A quick one, mind you, so don't dillydally. I want you back here to discuss your training schedule before the day's over. Then first thing tomorrow you'll—oh, excuse me, I'm jumping ahead. I forgot to ask if you accept the offer."

I thought of the man in the crate and the words he had uttered when I gave him water. At the time, I thought those words were useless, but now I knew I had been wrong about them.

"Well, Alex, what do you say?"

"I say . . . thank you."

"Then we have a deal?"

"Oh, yes." The words seemed too small in exchange for my life. I felt a need to say more, to do more, to give expression to the most noteworthy moment I had ever lived. But how? I extended my hand. "Should we grip hands?"

"We definitely should, son."

The last word astonished me! Meanwhile, I squeezed Mykroni's hand with a force that could crush, were it not balanced by his own strong clasp.

I left my new boss and walked down the brightly lit hallway. Stretching my neck to glance inside any doors that were open, I saw the pleasing sights of the Space Travel Division's workers—a series of bowed heads so absorbed in tasks that they neglected to look up when I passed by. I reached an office with a display of flowers on the desk and a worker eager to see me. Kristin sprang from her chair, and when I told her I was hired, she clapped and jumped around with a child's excitement.

As she took me on my tour, a stab of pain dragged down what were otherwise the lightest steps of my life. On Asteron, despite the constant refrains I had heard about the duty I owed to all the people, such a thing never weighed on my conscience. But here on Earth I felt the pull of an obligation owed not to all but merely to two. How could two Earthlings tug at me more powerfully than all Asteronians? Why did I understand only now what it meant to have an obligation?

The thing I owed these two Earthlings was something that had never weighed me down before, because its opposite had been a way of life for me. *Can I be honest?* I asked myself. *Yes*, I thought, *unless I was something else, and that was desperate.* I knew that I would have to tell the two people who gave me a life that I had lied to them. But if I told them, I would not have a life. Feran's world required constant sneaking, hiding, and lying to survive, but my new world demanded a different code. When I got rid of Feran—with his vile threats of torture and death—I would be rid of deceit, I vowed. Then I could look at Mykroni and Kristin in the same open way they looked at me, tell them the truth about my origin, and face whatever penalty I must.

I could not think about that now because Kristin was showing me the superb training facilities that MAS had developed to produce what she called the best space pilots in the galaxy. She commented on a series of classrooms we passed: "Our pilots take courses in mathematics, physics, astronomy, computers, guidance and navigation, and other subjects."

We stopped at a laboratory where scientists were using high-powered microscopes to analyze rocks from space. In another area I saw large water tanks containing submerged mock-ups of spacecraft equipment, where astronauts were working in neutral buoyancy to imitate weightlessness and practice working in spacesuits. We passed simulators of spacecraft computers and flight decks, where pilots were studying the many onboard systems. I also saw replicas of complete ships, duplicated with the finest accuracy, down to the celestial views outside the windows.

I was disappointed when Kristin told me the tour was finished. I wanted to linger in the hallways, peer into the rooms, and never leave the building. As we headed toward an elevator bank, my guide turned to me. "So what do you think of MAS?"

I paused to face the slender female who was also an ace pilot. My hands softly squeezed her shoulders. "I think you saved my life by bringing me here."

"But it's you who tried to save my life—three times."

"But your life was not in danger."

"Was yours, Alex?" The many hues of her liquid eyes swept across my face.

"I will not be in danger at MAS. I am exceedingly pleased to be here."

"That means you're happy."

I looked at her curiously. She was using a word we did not think of on Asteron, a word I had never applied to myself.

"I mean that when you say you're exceedingly pleased, here we call that being happy," she explained.

I realized my hands still rested on her shoulders. I removed them . . . reluctantly.

"I will have to consider that word, especially when I meet the person who created this superb company, the smartest and noblest man in the universe—your father." *And when I expunge from my life the dumbest and vilest*, I thought. "Mykroni told me that Dr. Merrett likes to meet the new pilots."

"He does—usually," she replied as we resumed our walk. "But right now he's busy with other matters. I think he's looking for new projects. He's been preoccupied with business problems since he pulled out of a contract to deliver a product to a customer. It was a project he started two and a half years ago. The sudden cancellation of this work has caused a financial dilemma for the company."

I had questions about what she meant, but Kristin patiently explained the unfamiliar terms to me.

"Since the project's cancellation, my father hasn't been himself. Right now he has no time for the space pilots, or for flying with me, for our gardening, our walks, the dinners we've always enjoyed." She gazed flatly at the floor.

I thought of the man I had seen on my walk the previous day, who threw a child high in the air to make her laugh. "You mean he has no time to be happy with you?"

She nodded sadly.

We stopped at the elevator bank at the end of the hallway. Off to the side, I noticed a long corridor. It was an indoor walkway to a separate building. Something at the end of that corridor caught my attention.

I wandered through the walkway until I came to the other building. There I stood before an anteroom resembling an airlock that a person had to pass through to enter the facility, with security doors on either side of it. I walked up to the glass window of this anteroom because I saw something inside that made me gasp.

"Alex, what are you doing?" asked Kristin, following me through the passageway up to the anteroom.

"Kristin! What are those spacesuits used for?" I asked tensely, pointing to a clothing rack where three curious suits hung.

"They're not spacesuits. They're protective gear made with a new, impenetrable substance called flexite. Those suits are worn on Earth for dealing with harmful material."

"What harmful material?"

"I don't know. Some kind of hazardous substance that you could breathe or that could permeate your skin, I guess."

"What substance?"

"I don't know."

"What projects are those suits used for?"

"Only one, Project Z. This is the building for that project, and the anteroom is the only part of it that an outsider can see." She pointed to the small chamber where the suits hung. "That's the project I just mentioned, the one my father canceled. Everyone has to wear a flexite suit to go inside, and the whole area is lined with flexite. It insulates the walls, floors, and ceilings. That's the only thing I know about this area."

What is Project Z?"

"No one outside the project knows."

"Why is that?"

"It was a secret project. People had to pass the highest level of security to work on it. They were handpicked veteran employees who had been with

MAS for many years. And most of them, I'm sure, knew only about the one part they worked on."

"Who knows about the whole thing?"

"Just my father and a small inner circle of scientists and engineers. My dad managed the project personally. Why do you ask, Alex?"

"Does Mykroni know?"

She shook her head.

"Do you know?"

"No. Are you getting crazy again, Alex?"

"Just curious. Who are the scientists and engineers who knew about Project Z?"

"A very small group that my father knew personally for a long time and had worked with on other projects through the years. They're all gone now. Two months ago, when the project was canceled, they were out of work. My father usually can get new projects pretty easily, but this time he wasn't successful. With no new work for the people in the group, they all quit or were laid off."

"What does Z stand for?"

"No one outside the project knows."

"Who is the customer for this project?"

"No one outside the project knows."

"Why did your father cancel the project?"

"No one outside the project knows."

I tapped my finger insistently against the window. "Kristin, can we go into the area for Project Z?"

"Are you kidding? You need a special clearance to get in, and I don't have it. The project's been dismantled anyway, so there wouldn't be anything to see." She looked at me suspiciously. "That's enough now. I've got to get you back to Mykroni."

Kristin tugged at my arm, but the flexite suits had a stronger pull.

"Come on, Alex."

Finally, I turned away from the garments. It was the shiny sleeve of one of them that had caught my eye from the other building and lured me here. The suits that hung on the rack in the anteroom for Project Z were bright purple and looked identical to the suit that was hanging in Feran's spacecraft.

CHAPTER 11

Data streamed across a series of electronic screens, all vying for attention from Mykroni and me as we sat on a flight deck. My boss would sometimes step in to give me personal instruction on matters of special importance, as he had on this particular afternoon, and I eagerly looked forward to our sessions. Today we were in a replica of the spacecraft I was learning to pilot. Having been at my various lessons since dawn, I was pleased to get a break when Mykroni paused, reached for the thin strip of metal that was his phone, and made a call.

"I'll go through section five with him now, Tom. Then you can take over. Here's what I'd like you to do . . ." Mykroni was talking to one of my instructors about my training schedule.

He hovered over me like an Earth tiger with a new cub, I thought, reflecting on the first superior I had ever had who did not fire orders at me like bullets or intermittently throw a fist in my face. I leaned back and closed my eyes, content to listen to Mykroni's calm, even voice as if it were a favorite song.

Each day I found odd things like this that pleased me. Kristin said I was becoming more *relaxed*. What did that word mean? Was it the state of mind that occurred when no weapon was pointed at one's head? Of the many remarkable things I had experienced on Planet Earth, the most amazing surprise of all was never once having my life threatened.

I was becoming so relaxed that I had not attempted to rescue Kristin from any imagined dangers since the incident with Officer Hodges at Big Eats. When I mentioned this to her, wanting to receive full credit for my reform, she praised me, but with a tinge of disappointment.

"What if you're getting *too* relaxed, Alex? What if I were really in danger? Would you be too relaxed to save me?"

In my calmer state I was growing more aware of her full lips, her pointed nose with a slight upward arc, and her eyes of light brown glass that seemed to draw me through them to the spirit that lived inside. Kristin, I might not yet have mentioned, was exceedingly ugly. Her features were carved with delicacy and precision, a blending of the exciting female and the keen pilot in a stunning face that pleased me.

She seemed content to leave me alone in my new life, which filled immediately with work assignments, as well as the details of establishing my living arrangements. Kristin seemed to sense my preoccupation, waiting to be called for any help I needed. Although she was absorbed with her own busy life, she was openly pleased whenever I did seek her. I found myself wanting to see her often, not merely because she helped me, which indeed she did, but because she somehow, like the Earth itself, had a vitality that excited me.

After two weeks and two days on Earth, I concluded that everything here was the opposite of what I had known before, as if a cosmic architect had demolished one civilization to build something completely different. With my first paycheck plus the five-dollar gold piece from the man in the crate, I was able to buy the things I needed to start my new life. In the world I had left, everything had been provided for free, but none of it was mine. I had been told that everything was mine because I was the people, but I could not buy, sell, or control any of the things that were supposed to be mine. On Earth nothing was provided, and I had to pay for everything. In the world I had left, I had been taught that such a situation was cruel, but on Earth I did not find cruelty. Instead, I found ownership. I had acquired a growing collection of things that were mine and could not be taken away.

I felt as if I owned more than just the things I bought. When I had rented a furnished apartment with a small garden near MAS, I discovered that the lock on the door was not to keep me in but to keep others out.

Under Kristin's supervision, I had gotten my hair styled and acquired the beginnings of a wardrobe. "This red shirt goes great with your black hair, Alex. And this blue one is the same color as your eyes," she had said on one of our shopping trips. I added an item of my own, a silver neck chain, bought with my wages, which my Asteronian teachers would have considered a symbol of enslavement to my employer. The silver chain camouflaged the scars left by my neckwear from their world.

On one evening with Kristin, when I wore the clothes she had selected for me, she studied her handiwork and exclaimed, imitating my speech: "I indeed do think you look exceedingly . . ."—she lowered her head shyly, and I raised it, my finger on her chin—". . . handsome," she finished, which, I figured, meant I was ugly.

I liked picking out my clothes, styling my hair, and looking at myself in a mirror. I told Kristin that this new grooming made me conscious of my appearance for the first time. I had never before given myself such attention, and I felt . . . I could not find the word.

"Pampered," she suggested.

"Kristin," I asked on one occasion, "why do Earthlings have so much concern for everything that touches their lives, from the work they do to where they live, what they eat, how they dress, and what they grow in their gardens?"

"We're *living*," she replied.

"Yes, but living requires only that you consume nutrients, not cheesecake. And dressing requires only that you cover your body with a basic garment, not outfits of different colors and styles. And sleeping requires only a mattress, not an entire bedroom suite. And growing flowers, well, that is not necessary at all for living."

"Living to us means pleasure," she said simply.

While I closed my eyes and listened to Mykroni talking on the phone, I thought of Kristin's words. I was feeling pleasure from hearing my boss's voice, from my grooming, from eating Earth food, from planning my garden, from seeing Kristin, from spending time in my apartment. I was aware of pleasure as if it were a new companion, accompanying me everywhere, as pervasive as the air I breathed and even more life-giving. Earth was a place where I could feel pleasure, and that one fact was coloring my every activity.

But did I dare allow myself to relax and to feel pleasure?

Every night I slipped into my spacecraft in the dark field. Every night I performed the same ritual of checking for messages. Every night I found none, and my worry drained until the next time. *Do I dare miss a night?* I wondered. *Do I dare not go to the spacecraft tonight?* I had my work to complete. After that I needed to see my gardener about flowers for the planting bed outside my apartment. Then I had an appointment with my tailor, a robot that would record my measurements and make my clothes fit as perfectly as a second skin. I no longer had time for Feran. I had seen none of his spies, and I had not heard of any inquiries about me. I could learn nothing more about Project Z or the flexite suits. I had drawn a picture of Feran's cargo for Kristin and asked if she had ever seen such an object, but she had not. Could I dare forget that Feran possessed something called a flexite suit that belonged to MAS? Could I dare forget the cruelty he was capable of? What was Feran's business on a planet where the people filled their lives with pleasure?

Suddenly, the door to the flight deck slid open, and a tall young male with sandy hair, bearing a striking resemblance to my boss, came in.

Mykroni interrupted his phone call to glare at the visitor. "How dare you barge in here?"

"You didn't answer my messages."

"Get out."

"I have to speak to you, and it can't wait!"

Mykroni sighed as he ended his phone call and stood up. "Alex, start working through the next section. I'll be right with you."

A sensor by the door opened it, and the two of them left. The door slid closed behind them, but their muffled voices outside still reached me.

"How much, Chuck?" Mykroni asked curtly.

"There you go!" The man called Chuck sounded offended. "Putting me down already, when I came here to confide a problem to you?"

"How much will your *confiding* cost me this time?"

"Something came up . . . a bill I didn't expect."

"What bill?"

"Why would it matter what bill it was? I shouldn't have to account to you for everything."

"Don't ask me for money, and I won't ask for any accounting."

I heard a new tension in Mykroni's voice. I felt uncomfortable overhearing his affairs and tried to concentrate on my work, but I found myself bothered because something was upsetting him.

His visitor was also agitated. "Just this once, could you do me a favor without making me feel like a child?"

"Break the umbilical cord to my wallet, and you won't feel like a child."

"Look, I need nine dollars, but it's just until payday."

Mykroni seemed unmoved. "Did Teddy's call you on your gambling debts?"

"No."

"Did you buy more high-tech gadgets that even *I* can't afford, like that fancy phone you carry?"

"When I was considering a job in the lunar cities, how'd you expect me to communicate with them—by smoke signals?"

"Did you get drunk again and find yourself on a cruise with a girl whose name you can't remember?"

"Please don't bring those things up again!" Chuck sounded both pleading and demanding. "This is important. This bill has to be paid in three days, or I'm in a real fix!"

"A bill you never expected, yet it's due in three days? What is it?"

There was an awkward silence. Then Chuck replied, "An eviction notice."

"Eviction?"

"Please don't lecture me. If you can just spare nine, it's to pay the rent, not to gamble at Teddy's."

"How much rent do you owe?"

"Three months' worth."

"You mean you haven't paid it since the last time I lent you money? And not a dime back to me either."

"Look, man, what's done is done."

"But you just got a raise. Tell me, Chuck. I'd like to understand. Why did Charles Merrett give you a promotion?"

"You're seriously asking me that? After I automated the whole office-cleaning system as housekeeping manager and saved Uncle Charles a bundle?"

"I've wondered how you pulled that off."

"Why can't you admit that I did pretty well for myself after I left your department? After you *fired* me!"

"When you were in charge of food service, and you neglected to load enough provisions onto a craft, did you expect *not* to get fired?"

"In your perfect life, haven't you ever made a mistake?"

I tried to focus on the instruments before me, but I could feel my own anger building at the way my boss was being addressed.

"That spacecraft was on an extended voyage. If we hadn't caught your mistake before launch—"

"I made a mistake, but it could happen to anybody."

Mykroni sighed again. "Look, I believed you when you swore you'd reformed and begged me to get you another job. Now, over three years after I got you the housekeeping job, tell me: How have you changed?"

"How? I did a great job in housekeeping and got a *promotion*."

"Then why can't you pay your rent?"

"It's just a small loan—"

"When will you pay it back? And pay back my other loans?"

"Come on, now, really. You'll never spend the money you have in your lifetime!"

"But why would *you* be entitled to it? You act as if I'm still supposed to support you."

"Is that all you care about? Money?"

"My own. All you seem to care about is somebody else's."

"Look, I'm going to be *kicked out on the street in three days!* I have no one else to turn to!" Chuck cried in desperation.

Weariness seemed to replace some of Mykroni's anger. "If you must harass me, then do it in my office. I'll be there in an hour."

"I can't come in an hour. I'm on my way out."

"In the middle of the afternoon? Charles just got back from his trip. Don't you have work to do?"

"Why are you always looking over my shoulder?"

"You somehow talked Charles into making you his special assistant," Mykroni said sharply. "Whatever that means, it must require work. So why do I see your plane disappear during the day?"

"Why are you so nosy?"

"When you park in the executive lot right outside my window, I see these things. I don't like to think you're goofing off on company time. I don't want my friend to get taken."

"Uncle Charles can take care of himself! We were talking about my loan."

"I'm afraid Charles has had a soft spot for you for twenty-three years, since I named you after him."

"Uncle Charles isn't complaining about me, so why should you? Look, in three days, I'll be evicted! Won't you do something?"

"Why yes, I *will* do something," Mykroni answered, his voice hot with anger. "I'll *evict* you from this module right now!"

I heard a scuffle.

"Don't push me around!" Chuck warned.

Then I heard the thump of someone being shoved into a wall. That must have triggered the sensor, because the door slid open and the two men tumbled onto the flight deck.

Chuck was clutching Mykroni by the collar and about to land a punch. I leaped up, grabbed Chuck's arm, and twisted it behind his back.

"Ow!"

"You will not strike my boss!"

"Stay out of it! He's my *father*."

"Then you will certainly not strike him."

"Ouch! Let me go. You're breaking my arm!"

I thought of the robot at Big Eats named Genius, who said he was sorry for serving cold soup. Was not Chuck's behavior far worse than not keeping soup warm? "You need to make an apology, Chuck," I demanded.

"Let him go, Alex," said Mykroni. He tried to release my grip on Chuck, but I resisted.

"Make your apology, Chuck, and I will let you go." I twisted the arm tighter. A lifetime spent primed for violence gave me the edge over Chuck.

"Okay . . . *okay!*" He shouted.

I finally released him.

He moaned, rubbing his arm. "Who the hell are you?" He scanned me with bitter eyes.

I made a move to grab him again, but he stepped back and held up his hands to stop me.

"Enough!" he said. The boldness he had shown in attacking his father was tempered now that he was facing a male his own age—and one who cared nothing about his well-being.

As Chuck's glance moved from me to Mykroni, his face looked cunning, as though he was surveying the situation and calculating his next move. He then dropped his head and put his hands over his face.

"Dad, I'm in trouble, and it's all my own fault. I have no one to turn to except *you*." He looked up at Mykroni. "It's not because this guy butted in"—

he glanced disapprovingly at me—"but actually, I *am* sorry for the way I acted . . . really sorry."

Chuck's sudden change of mood calmed Mykroni down. He turned to me and smiled. "Get back to work, Alex. I don't need any rescuing."

As I was about to return to my seat, Chuck offered me his hand for a shake. "No hard feelings," he said, as if it were *my* behavior that needed excusing.

I shook his hand warily. He smiled at me, but there were no crinkle lines around his eyes. Chuck was the first Earthling to shake my hand whose smile did not extend to his eyes. Was his apology sincere? I glanced at Mykroni, who seemed taken in by the gesture.

The two men stepped outside. I could still hear muffled voices through the closed door, but they were calmer now.

"What do you say, Dad?"

"Why do I always give in?"

"I'll come by the house for it later."

"Come with a *payment* schedule, one you can stick to this time."

"Of course. Say, I really appreciate this!"

"A day will come when you push me too far."

From a window on the flight deck, I watched Chuck leaving. I noticed that Mykroni did not call him *son*.

On my first day at MAS, after my job interview, I had asked Kristin why Mykroni addressed me by that word. "It's a term of *fondness*," she explained, then added: "Mykroni has a real son who works at MAS. You're bound to bump into him."

Indeed I had.

I was invited to join a meeting later that day. When I arrived at the conference room, Kristin's flight instructor, Jeff, greeted me at the door. Jeff was also a pilot at MAS and captain of the flying team Kristin belonged to, called the Gold Streaks. The team's name reflected the curved gold stripe on the graphite body of their planes, which ran from the tapered nose, across the fuselage, to the tip of the tail.

"Thanks for coming, Alex," Jeff said. "Come in."

I sat at an oval table with Jeff, Kristin, and the other five MAS pilots performing in the upcoming air show. On the wall was a large, high-resolution photograph of six sleek planes flying in a triangular formation with the sun glistening off their fuselage and their wing tips almost touching.

During the past two weeks I had flown with each of these pilots in a similar configuration. On Asteron I had learned the high-performance, high-speed flying in tight formation that they were trained to do. The superb technical advancement of their crafts made it possible for me to learn their flying patterns in a short time.

After we all exchanged greetings, Jeff told me why they had asked me to come: "Alex, we've been looking for an eighth pilot to join the Gold Streaks. We fly in air shows around the area, and our biggest event is the show that Rising Tide has every year on Reckoning Day. Our team is completely voluntary. None of us has to fly in this show to be a pilot at MAS, although the company helps our team out. It gives us time off from work to practice and lets us use its planes—and it likes the publicity it gets from our performances.

"Anyone who joins the Gold Streaks must be approved by every one of the other fliers. Since the nature of the work is inherently unforgiving of any mistakes, every pilot on the team has to have the highest trust in all the others. We had a meeting in which your name was nominated as the eighth flier. We voted, and it was unanimous. We all want to have you on the team. No one so new to MAS has ever been offered a place in the formation before. So this is a compliment to your flying, Alex. It's the highest compliment we can pay, because we trust you with our lives." Jeff paused while the others nodded in agreement. "So what do you think, Alex? Would you like to join the Gold Streaks?"

I looked at Jeff, Kristin, and the others as they smiled at me. For the first time, I was being rewarded for the thing that made me unequal, made me stand out, made me different from others. I felt a bond with the people before me that went beyond flying and embraced life itself.

"I indeed would like to be on the Gold Streaks. *Thank you.* I accept!"

Then the most amazing thing happened. The pilots raised their hands to me and *clapped.* I thought of the other Alexander when he hit his home run. I remembered how his face had looked when the crowd cheered. I did not have a name for the high lift of his head, the contentment in his eyes, the glow on his face. I knew only that he acted the opposite of how I had been taught, which was to look down when others addressed me. At that moment, with the pilots clapping, I raised my head high like the nose of a plane on a climb.

When the meeting ended, I approached Kristin. "What is it called," I asked, "when a person is pleased with the things he can do, with his . . . abilities?"

Her big eyes swept across the ceiling as they did when they reached for answers to my questions. Then she smiled. "It's called *pride.* It's what you felt just now at the meeting. I know because it was all over your face, Alex. You looked so proud—of your flying and of yourself. And you deserve to be."

I thought of all the things Earthlings cared about—their food, their clothing, their gardens, their work. I realized that these things were important because the Earthlings prized something else above all. This something was not what I had been taught to appreciate. At the top of the mountain of an Earthling's cares was his own person, not as a small stone in a massive mound but as a separate peak of its own.

"Alex, do you realize you *smiled* at the meeting? That's the *first time* I ever saw you smile. And your eyes crinkled too, the way you say Earthlings' eyes do. For a minute, I thought you might even laugh. You looked as though you really could, you know."

Earth's only moon was a sliver in the sky that night, protecting me with darkness as I entered my spacecraft in the empty field. I glanced at my watch: It was midnight. There were no lights on along the winding lane of dwellings folded into the hillside, including Kristin's house, across the road. Lifting myself up to the craft, I thought of Kristin, my job, the Gold Streaks—all the things I now had to live for. Feran and his world were fading fast, like a nightmare exposed to the light of day. I was eager to get back to my apartment, sleep for a few hours, then wake up early to prepare for my classes on the solar system and my exercises in navigation. Later, there were rehearsals for the air show. I had so much to do in the rich new existence that was my life. I sat by the radio's serene blue monitor on the flight deck. It had remained dormant for two weeks. Perhaps Feran had returned to Asteron and found another amusement. I checked for messages, but I expected none. Suddenly, jagged vertical lines slashed the monitor, forming the rising and falling inflections of Feran's malevolent voice.

"Animal!" he raged, gashing the screen with sharp peaks of violent colors. "Did you expect me to drain the entire Gulf of California on your behalf? I have recovered enough sections of the camper to realize your vile traitor bones were not in it. I found the parachute, and it was *still stowed.*"

The camper had a parachute that could be deployed so that the vehicle would have a good chance of landing intact and staying afloat for a while to enable a rescue.

"If you were inside the camper, you would have deployed the chute. Even *you* would not be so stupid as to fail in that task."

I could have released the chute from the mother ship, but a parachute landing in which the camper remained intact would have made it easier to locate—and easier to discover I was not aboard. So instead I took my chances with the chute stowed. What were the odds that Feran would find that particular piece of equipment in the miles of sea and know for certain that I had not deployed it? Did his luck mark my doom?

"There was not a fragment in the water to suggest the spacecraft had hit, and no reports of any ship crashing over land either. Where are you, pig? You have no fuel and no password for navigation. You are trapped where you are."

The new blue shirt, which Kristin said matched the color of my eyes, was now stained with dark patches of sweat.

"You are an alien on a hostile planet. Do you think you can hide from the supreme ruler of Asteron? Oh, and by the way," he added mockingly, "Coquet has learned of your little trick, and she is quite displeased with you."

I listened in dismay.

"No doubt you are hiding somewhere, like a rat in a sewer." He laughed viciously. "So I am going to help you, traitor. You give me the metal box in the ship's bay, which is of no value to you, and I will give you your rotten life, which is of no value to me. You get rid of something you have no need for, and I will do the same. Call me."

He gave me his phone number.

"Call and tell me where the cargo is. That is all you have to do, and I will pick it up and have no further dealings with you."

I stared at the screen, waiting for him to finish.

"You have twenty-four hours to get me the cargo in exchange for your life. Of course, if you do not comply, Coquet will want to know. She will demand that I find you. She will want to play with you until she has her fill. Then, swine, you will die exquisitely."

The waves of Feran's voice disappeared into stillness. The monitor returned to a peaceful blue. And I dropped my head with a thud against the flight deck.

CHAPTER 12

After I had heard Feran's message on Friday, my sixteenth day on Earth, his threats pounded my mind like a headache I could not shake.

How long? I wondered, as I sat in a meeting room on the MAS airfield. I gazed at one of our team's planes parked outside. The exquisite flying machine looked like a painting framed within the large window. *How long?* I wondered the entire weekend, while I flew one of those awesome machines in rehearsals for the air show and met with the other Gold Streaks after each run to correct any near errors in a routine intolerant of any mistakes. Despite the safety I felt in the air, how long could I remain alive while on the ground?

This question continued to worry me when I returned to work on Monday morning to perform underwater maneuvers in a spacesuit, mimicking the buoyancy of space. Two divers were on duty for the sole purpose of rescuing me should a failure of my life-support system trap me underwater in the suit. Why the painstaking effort to protect my life? For the pleasure of Coquet?

How long would it take Feran to find me? There were almost a million people in the city of Rising Tide. What group would Feran be stalking—young males, pilots, aliens, or alien pilots? I shuddered at the thought of how small that last group might be.

And why was Feran holding a flexite suit that belonged to Merrett Aerospace Systems, a suit used solely for a secret project? How was Feran linked to Project Z? Did he have a spy at MAS? Because Feran nurtured a cadre of spies on Asteron as meticulously as the Earthlings tended their gardens, I figured he must have had someone gathering information for him on the now-canceled secret project. But with the security measures in place for MAS grounds and buildings, it would be difficult for someone from the outside to break in. Indeed, I had learned from Kristin that MAS had experienced no break-ins, or even attempted break-ins, for the duration of Project Z. Without evidence of any breach of security from the outside, I figured Feran's spy might more likely be someone *inside* MAS.

After completing my work in the tank that Monday, I joined Kristin for a soft drink during our break. Too worried to sit, I stood over her as she relaxed on a bench in a grassy area outside our building, with the soaring MAS rocket sculpture behind her in the distance.

At the risk of raising her suspicions, I leaned toward her, my foot on the bench near her legs, and once again I asked why she hated Asteron.

Her hand stopped with her cup midway to her mouth, as if she had lost her desire to drink. She placed the cup on the bench and paused a long while before answering. "They do things to us. Then they disappear like ghosts without a trace."

"What did they do to you, Kristin?"

Her mouth drew tight and her eyes became hard with hatred, an unyielding hatred that surprised me. Although she flew only unarmed craft, Kristin had the skill to be a military pilot. When I saw her face at that moment, I felt certain that she could drop a deadly payload without flinching. I knew how the name of my vile homeland could drive *me* to kill, but I had no idea why it seemed to evoke the same response in Kristin.

"Others say we can't prove a thing, but I think they come here and try to hurt us!" She stared fixedly into space at a disturbing vision of her own.

I raised her hands to my chest and squeezed them. "How did they hurt you, Kristin?"

"Why do you insist, Alex? And why do you stare so intensely?" She pulled her hands away and drew back from me. She did not seem to notice hitting the drink by her side, which spilled onto the grass. "How can this concern you?"

I righted the cup and leaned in closer. "Did Asteron have anything to do with Project Z?"

"No, not with Project Z."

"Are you sure?"

"Asteron had nothing at all to do with Project Z."

"Are you positive?"

"Yes."

"Why do you look so troubled at the mention of that planet, Kristin?"

"It's something I want to forget, something that happened *before* Project Z started, so, Alex, please don't pester me! And don't get crazy again over dangers that are only in your mind. You have this thing about Project Z, you know."

I continued to ponder this matter as I walked to my workplace after our break. The only direct link I had to both Asteron and MAS was Mykroni. But he had been here for twenty-five years and acted just like the Earthlings.

Besides, after a lifetime of suspecting everyone around me of being an agent—and many were agents—I could not bring myself to doubt the man who called me son and who presided over my training as though I were a rare gem he was cutting. I would have to find another link.

Kristin was troubled by Asteronians who seemed to sneak around like ghosts, upsetting her contentment. I too was haunted by those ghosts, especially the bristly presence inside the black cape that I could not escape. It seemed to accompany me when I arrived at my workspace, a narrow room containing the essentials of my new life: a desk at the end under a window, a computer, several monitors, and rows of shelves rapidly filling with notebooks and manuals from my studies. I sat at my desk and reviewed the things I knew about Project Z.

According to Kristin, the people involved with that secret project were a small group of accomplished scientists and engineers whom her father had worked with closely in the past. Others who performed more limited tasks on the project were, she said, handpicked veteran employees who had been with the company for many years. It seemed unlikely that a spy from Asteron could infiltrate such a carefully selected project team. Perhaps the spy was someone *inside* MAS but *outside* Project Z. How, then, could the spy learn about this secretive undertaking? To know about Project Z, I figured, was to read its computer files.

As a pilot in the Space Travel Division, I could access some of the MAS databases with security codes. Would not the Project Z team, including Dr. Merrett, use a similar protocol to access its databases? I pulled my keyboard toward me to conduct a small test. When I tried to search for entries containing the term *Project Z*, only one item came up. It was a memo that Charles Merrett had sent to his employees announcing the cancelation of the project. That memo, available to the entire staff at MAS, contained no information about the nature of the project. I continued searching, but I found no other documents on the project. As I suspected from common security protocols, the files from the secret project appeared to be unavailable on the company's general computer system. The records from the secret project were probably accessible only via specific computers in protected workspaces with their own separate systems.

I figured it would be difficult for someone outside the project to gain access to these restricted files. I restlessly tapped my fingers on the keyboard. Was there a simpler way?

Pondering the matter, I leaned back in my chair and gazed out the window. Outside my building was the executive parking lot, and across from it was the executive office building, where Dr. Merrett had an office. I had an idea. Could a spy somehow have read privileged information from Dr. Merrett's computer monitor? Could a spy have seen Dr. Merrett's screen with a telescope from a window in our building? Because Dr. Merrett managed the project personally, he would have been the one with access to *all* of its files—the perfect person to spy on. Surely a computer in his office would have access to those files.

Earthlings did not expect danger. Instead, they were *relaxed.* There had been no wars on the planet for a century and no break-ins at MAS for years. Despite the secret nature of Project Z, could Charles Merrett have been *relaxed?* I wondered if he could have overlooked a way in which a sinister mind might steal information from him. I decided to look for an opportunity to examine his office.

My chance came that afternoon. From my window I noticed Kristin's slim form as she walked toward the executive office building with flowers in her arms. Guessing what she was going to do with them, I raced out to meet her. Just as I thought, she was about to bring the flowers to her father's office. I asked if I could accompany her. At first she hesitated. "He's been so grouchy lately. I really don't want you to meet him until he's back to his cheerful self again." But when I prodded, she relented. "Well, okay. Come with me."

Dr. Merrett was not in when we arrived. However, his assistant, a nicely groomed older female, introduced to me as Margaret, looked up from her desk to greet us with a smile. She extended her hand to me for the handshake that I found typical of Earthlings. Eyeing Kristin's flowers, Margaret approached an electronic keypad by the closed door of Dr. Merrett's office in what seemed like a routine procedure for them. While Kristin and Margaret exchanged a few pleasant words, I positioned myself in a spot where I could see the numbers the assistant pressed. With neither of the females paying attention to me or showing the slightest suspicion, I committed the code to memory.

The door opened, and Kristin entered. She picked up a vase sitting on her father's desk, then proceeded down the hallway to a kitchen to prepare her arrangement.

With Margaret resuming work at her desk and Kristin occupied with the flowers, I had an opportunity to observe the inner office of my employer from a spot in the outer reception area. Located in a corner of the third and top floor of the building, Dr. Merrett's office contained a pleasing arrangement of bookcases, leather chairs, and large-leafed plants, with a desk and table for his work area. Included in the office arrangement was a small adjoining conference room, which could be entered either from his workspace or from the hallway. His desk area contained two large windows, one facing the side of the building and another facing the front. The window on the side looked out onto the parking lot and the five-story building of the Space Travel Division across the way, which housed many of our group's facilities, along with the offices of other departments in the company that rented space from our division. The window in the front faced the building entrance and gardens, as well as the mountains in the distance. Typical of Earthlings, Dr.

Merrett had his desk arranged so that it faced the entrance and the mountains rather than the parking lot. To Earthlings life meant pleasure, as I was learning, so I was not surprised that Dr. Merrett preferred looking out at the more scenic sight. The table on which he kept his computer screen, at a right angle to his desk, was set so that his back would be toward the parking lot. This meant that his monitor was visible from the window facing the Space Travel Division.

Apparently liking the natural light, Dr. Merrett kept his desk and worktable close to the windows. It seemed that from a window directly across on the third floor, Dr. Merrett's head would block the screen. However, a window one flight of stairs up, on the fourth floor of our building, seemed to be positioned at a good angle for looking down on Dr. Merrett's screen. Could a telescopic camera positioned there pick up and record the contents of Dr. Merrett's monitor?

Afterward, I learned who occupied the fourth-floor office in our building that seemed to be at a perfect vantage point. To my surprise, it was someone I had met from another department who was interested in transferring to our division. He liked the Gold Streaks and had come to watch us practice for the air show. I had an idea. With Mykroni's permission, I invited him for a ride with me in one of our aerobatic planes. We arranged to meet at dawn the following morning, Tuesday, before our shifts began. I suggested meeting him in his workplace so that I could see how Dr. Merrett's office looked from that location.

A break from my worries came later that afternoon when two gold-striped planes left the runway, their graceful lift forming a sharp contrast to the roar of their engines. Kristin and I rose high in the sky to practice our two-plane demonstration for the air show. Climbing steeply, our sleek crafts pierced the blue sky like two gray-black rockets. From her plane, Kristin called commands to me on the radio, which I had to execute with flawless precision because of our high speed and close proximity. Although our planes were equipped with automatic flight systems, the pilots in the show flew them manually, which gave us the greatest maneuverability and a thrill beyond imagining.

Kristin and I began miles apart, flying upright directly toward each other at a combined speed of over one thousand miles an hour. Within moments her plane grew from a speck to a ball to a large presence in my windshield. I held my path head-on toward her as the distance between us rapidly closed, because I would not change direction without her command. Finally it came: "Break now," said the soft voice through the receiver in my ear. On the *n* in *now*, as we had planned previously, I tugged at the stick, rolling exactly ninety degrees right, with my wing tip up before Kristin could pronounce the rest of the word. Kristin, I knew, had made the same rotation in her plane. I felt the thump of the sudden change in air flow and the blast of her engines as our planes passed belly to belly within a couple of feet of each other.

We flew out, turned, and then headed straight toward each other again. At scant seconds before impact, I again had not received Kristin's command. She seemed to be waiting as long as she dared, testing me to see if I would flinch first. I held my speed on a blinding course toward her, the distance between us shrinking rapidly, until there were no more miles—only yards—separating us. "Pull now," her voice finally whispered in my ear. Before she completed the second word, I pulled the nose of my craft directly vertical. She did the same with hers. Our planes rose together, their bodies almost touching, like a couple joined for a dance. With our planes forming mirror images, we looped away from each other and nose-dived in spirals toward the ground.

After ending the dive, I overtook her plane, flying inverted a scant few feet above her, so we were canopy to canopy. She was so close that I could feel her presence change the air currents around me. Then we maneuvered so that I flew upright, my plane remaining just above hers. Without being able to see her plane from my canopy, I rolled on her command and could only trust that she would roll with me. We ended our program by tumbling effortlessly through the sky together, our two planes so close they cast one whirling shadow on the ground.

After we landed on the runway, Kristin barely had time to lift her canopy and remove her helmet before I grabbed her by the waist and pulled her out of the cockpit, her hair bouncing in disorderly waves with the snap of my wrists.

"I thought that if *you* gave the commands, you would have more control to execute the maneuvers with a margin of safety, Kristin. You did *not* have my consent to fly crazy the way you did!" My hands remained tight around her waist, pulling her toward me. Her arms fell against my chest and she leaned back to look up at my face. "You were waiting too long to take us out of danger."

"But Alex, you fly like that all the time."

"But not when I fly with you. From now on *I* will give the commands, and *you* will follow them. And we will fly safely."

"Why are you so cautious when you fly with me? Don't you think I'm a good enough pilot—"

"You are a superb pilot. But I do not want to see you in danger. I want to keep you safe." *Perhaps you are the only thing in my life that I can keep safe,* I thought.

"But Alex, it was . . . exciting . . . to fly the way we did. If you didn't like it too, then why didn't you stop me? You had a radio."

She was right! I could have objected while we were flying, but I did not. Kristin had an odd power of knowing what I felt before I did. Despite my worries about her safety, I was indeed strangely excited by flying to the limit with her.

"What is it called, Kristin, when your eyes are filled with the presence of another and your thoughts are filled with how supremely well the other moves like one with you?"

"Closeness. It's called closeness," she whispered, her mouth just inches from mine.

I still pulled at her waist. She still arched back. Her words somehow struck me like another command, this one of warning. I released her abruptly and stepped back.

She smiled softly in acceptance. She seemed to sense my limits and did not push beyond them. "I'll see you tomorrow," she said, turning to go.

"Wait." I reached into my pocket and pulled out a paper. "Mykroni printed out this admission for two to an event of some kind. He said he had to work late tonight and was too busy to attend, so he gave the tickets to me."

Kristin looked at the paper, which contained a scanning code and the words *admit two* written beneath it. "Wow, these are tickets to the Lions' championship game!"

"Are they the large Earth cats shown in the billboard for the zoo?"

"These lions are much more predatory. People would *kill* to get these tickets!"

"Do you want to go?"

"Do I? Yes!"

"Then it is settled. We will go togeth—"

Suddenly a vision flashed before my mind like a warning signal I could not ignore. I was leaning into a window, helping a slim figure with golden hair to slip out. I heard a rustling sound. I grabbed a rock, ready to smash the source of the sound with all my might. Then I realized it was only a ground animal, and the terror drained for the moment, until the next panic.

"It is allowed, Kristin, for you and me to attend this function together? Are you absolutely sure it is allowed?"

"It's for *us* to decide, not for anyone else to decide for us. Don't you understand that yet, Alex?" she asked softly.

"There are still areas of Earthling life that I have little knowledge of and . . . and that I must not be mistaken about! I must be careful!"

"Alex," she said, lifting my cold hands in her warm ones, "what's wrong? Do you realize you're clenching your fists and crumpling the tickets?" She tried to loosen my grip on the paper. "It's just a game, Alex. Everyone goes. Do you know what a game is? We're going to have so much fun! You can't imagine! Didn't we go shopping together? And to Big Eats? And it was okay, wasn't it?"

With Kristin's reassurances, the terror inside me quieted. I did not know what this lions' game was, because only children had leisure time for games in

Asteron. But Kristin's excitement aroused my curiosity. We decided to work as late as possible to make up the time we had missed for our rehearsal, and then we would attend what I expected to be some kind of feline demonstration.

"Alex, are you okay? Did you eat too many cheese dogs?" As I sat dazed in my seat, Kristin was reaching over to me, fanning me with the evening's program. "Your eyes are scary when they bulge out like that! Do you realize you stopped blinking?"

That night I was indeed stunned to find myself in a great arena, watching men in white uniforms playing what Kristin described as the centuries-old Earthling game of baseball. Sitting behind first base, I scanned the sharp lines of the reddish-brown field and on to an expansive carpet of grass and then to stands packed with tens of thousands of screaming spectators. The tiny video I had seen in Feran's spacecraft had come to life, with sights and sounds that overwhelmed me.

"Kristin, if this event you call baseball has nothing to do with state functions, then why else would such a large crowd gather?"

"For fun."

After Kristin explained the procedures of the game, I began to understand the power it held for the crowd. "Kristin, the athletes on the field are good, no?"

"You bet. They're the best of the best."

"You mean the best—the most skillful—are permitted to play?"

"They're the only ones who make it in this game. They're hotly pursued by all the teams."

"You mean they are not . . . punished?"

"For what? For being the best?" She stared at me incredulously. "They get a pile of money for being the best, and the fans worship them."

"Kristin, is this game played often? Can we come back again soon?"

"This is the last game of the season. After tonight this place will be deserted until next spring."

A sudden roar swelled from the crowd, pulling Kristin's eyes back to the action. "Hey, Alex, if you want to see the best player our home team has, there he is coming up to bat!"

Walking to the home sack, brandishing a fearsome bat and provoking the fans to thunderous cheers, was the player with bold, black letters across his back: ALEXANDER.

"Kristin!" I did not recognize the incredulous cry as my own voice. "In a place far away, on another planet, a . . . a very bleak planet, I saw this man from your world! I saw a video scene of him engaged in this game, but I did not know what it was."

I grabbed her arms urgently. Seeing my agitation, she stared at me solemnly.

"The things I saw, the prodigious swing of Alexander's bat, the maneuver he performed called a home run, the cheering of the crowd, the whole scene was . . . it was so . . . so . . . incredibly . . ."

"Joyful. It was *joyful*."

"Yes, yes! And then Alexander jumped in the air and laughed, and fireworks showered the sky, and his joyful teammates ran to embrace him. It seemed that Alexander must have done something extraordinary, and so I figured he was . . . he was a . . . a . . ."

"A hero. Was Alexander your *hero*?"

"Yes, yes! And the way his face glowed when he threw his fists up to the crowd, not in a gesture of violence but in what was . . . it was unmistakably a . . . a . . ."

"A triumph. Alexander was *triumphant*." Her eyes rolled thoughtfully over my face the way they did when she interpreted her world for me. "Do you mean, Alex, that in a place where you were sad, our Alexander brought you the promise of a new world . . . a place where you could be happy?"

Just then I heard the thump of a ball making contact with Alexander's bat. I watched the spinning white sphere soar out of the park and perhaps out of the galaxy itself. The crowd shot to its feet in a burst of excitement. I saw vividly before me the spectacle from the small screen that had held a promise for me. As Kristin and I rose to our feet to clap and cheer with the bellowing crowd, a shower of fireworks burst across the sky and stirring music filled the arena. I watched Alexander's face fill with pride in his victory. I embraced the wildly cheering figure beside me who had named Alexander's promise of joy and triumph. I lifted her light form off the ground and buried my face in the soft tangles of her hair. Afterward, Kristin informed me that I was smiling.

The fragrance of her newly planted garden sweetened the night air when I accompanied Kristin to her home after the game. Walking toward her house, I wondered about something. "Your plane is the only one here. Does your father not have one too?"

"He does. He uses a new electric one. Have you seen them?"

"I have. Before coming here I had not heard of planes powered with electricity."

"They're powered with new, supercharged batteries that can store more energy than a fuel tank. Electric planes are pretty new. They were invented here, so they're probably not available yet on the other planets."

"And where is your father's electric plane?"

"Looks like he's not home," she said sadly. "Maybe he's out on business this evening, or still at the office. I think he's working extra hard to find new contracts to reverse the loss caused by Project Z."

With a click on the mobile device she carried, the door to her house opened. "He's not here. The house alarm is set just as I left it."

Inside I saw an entryway with paintings hanging on the walls.

She paused at the door, looking disappointed. "I'm worried about him. He seems so . . . preoccupied lately."

"Kristin, you have said that Earthlings feel pretty safe from dangers. So why do you have an alarm on your house?"

Her smile vanished and her eyes took on a distant look. "Something . . . bad . . . happened here once. After that, my dad had a security system installed."

"What happened, Kristin, to cause you such sadness?"

"I don't want to talk about it." She shook her head, dismissing the matter. "Not on the night when our team *won!*" Her childlike, freckled face regained its smile. "Say, Alex, when you came to Earth, you named yourself after Alexander the ballplayer, didn't you?"

"Yes."

"What's your real name?"

"It is not important."

"Is there a reason you want to hide it?"

"I would rather not talk about it."

"Why not?"

"Because I want to keep you safe. I want to keep us both safe if I can."

"Why wouldn't we be safe? What danger are we in? What danger are *you* in? You know, you frighten me, Alex!"

Against my will, I reached out to hold her supremely innocent face. "I do not think I frighten you, Kristin."

"Alex, I don't think I . . . understand . . . you."

As we stood at the door, I raised her face to mine. Her lips glistened in the evening light. My eyes danced over the short-sleeved red sweater that stressed the slenderness of her arms and the inviting fullness of her breasts, and then over the remarkable item of clothing called a short skirt, a black one that curved around her slim hips and yet would fall so readily to the ground with one small tug on its little zipper. Kristin was so ugly that to kiss her was to want her, and to want her was to unleash a dreaded voice inside my head, chiding me, warning me. *It is your fault— It is your fault that she—* The urgent voice blared until I dropped my hands from Kristin's face and stepped away.

"Alexander," she whispered, "are you imagining danger again? Is that what stops you when you want to . . . kiss me? . . . Like now?"

"I cannot kiss you, Kristin."

"Why not?"

"Because you are exceedingly ugly."

She laughed, astonished. "You must be mistaken, Alex. I sometimes forget you've been here less than three weeks. You're mixing up your words."

How could I be mistaken? To be ugly was to stand out, to stand above, and Kristin stood out to me above all Earthlings. Were her eyes not bigger, her hair not shinier, her smile not brighter? And was she not ugly inside too? Was her laughter not joyful like the Earth itself? Was her mind not quicker to know my feelings and reactions better than I knew them myself?

"Kristin, I am not mistaken about this."

"Are you saying you can't kiss me because I'm too *ugly*?"

"Well, yes."

"Well, I can't kiss you because you have no manners! You're rude, exceedingly rude, and I don't have to take your rudeness!"

"Kristin, wait!" I said to the door that shut in my face. Kristin was gone before I could better understand what she meant by *manners*, which I did not have, and *rudeness*, which I had too much of.

After leaving Kristin's house, I walked to the field across the road, then pushed through the tall bushes that hid Feran's spacecraft. That Monday night marked three days since Feran had demanded his cargo for my life. Of course, I had not delivered into Feran's bloody hands an object whose nature I did not understand. I knew Feran's nature too well. What was his business on a planet where people hit home runs? Why had Feran kept a video of something as clean as baseball? I slammed my fist against the wall as I entered the flight deck, vowing not to let Feran touch Alexander, my hero, or the promise he held for me.

I knew there would be a message, sparing me the agony of suspense. I turned on the communicator, wondering where Feran lurked and how close he was to finding me. I pressed the icon on the screen to retrieve messages. Colored, jagged waves formed a frenetic pattern of peaks and valleys across the monitor in cadence with Feran's words.

"Traitor! While you hold my cargo, your countrymen are dying in the streets from starvation! I command you to surrender. If you do not, Coquet will tease you until you beg to die, but eternity will come first! Phone me, you vile pig." The vicious laughter was gone, and in its place I detected a note of desperation. Then Feran's voice subsided, and a calm blue screen returned.

Only one thing was clear to me: I would not give Feran the cargo. I would not give him a mysterious object to play with on a planet that gave me a life. The rest was confusing. What did Feran's message mean? Why did he link the cargo I withheld from him to starvation on Asteron? If I had given him the cargo, would Asteronians *not* be dying in the streets? To unravel Feran's puzzle, I had two clues: the possible spy at MAS and the secret of Project Z. I would have to learn more about them. Quickly.

CHAPTER 13

"Hey, Alex, come on in."

Frank Brennan, the young assistant manager of Housekeeping, greeted me with a firm hand grip and a broad smile. His short dark hair and plain white shirt gave him the neat appearance of someone concerned more with work than with fashion. Entering Frank's office on the fourth floor of the Space Travel building, I was surprised by its spaciousness and executive look. Its massive wooden desk and bookcases seemed incongruent with the feather dusters, solvents, vacuum-cleaner parts, and other janitorial supplies in the room.

The executive parking lot outside Frank's window was still almost empty, and most of the lights were off in Dr. Merrett's building across the way, including the ones in his office. While I waited a moment for Frank, I slipped my jacket off and dropped it on a chair. Leaving it here would give me an excuse to return after our ride, when more people would have arrived for work—presumably Dr. Merrett among them—so I could observe his office across the way with the lights on.

With the sun rising over the mountains that Tuesday morning, Frank and I walked to the MAS airstrip. I took him to the plane I had chosen for doing what he called "fancy stuff," which also had side-by-side seats for easy conversation. As I performed the preflight inspection and assisted my passenger with his flight suit, I learned that Frank was eager to transfer out of Housekeeping and into another job at MAS, one with more opportunity for advancement. He liked robotics and thought Space Travel might provide him a chance to pursue his interest.

Then, for a breathless moment, there could be no words, because my plane was stretching high into a new blue sky, pulling the sunrise west with it toward the ocean. Over the water, I began my demonstration, confining my-self to basic maneuvers that gave some thrills while not risking a blackout for someone unaccustomed to aerobatics. After performing a variety of rolls, in-side loops, and horizontal spins, I flew level for a while so that Frank could get his bearings.

"Have you been in Housekeeping the whole time you worked for MAS?" I asked.

"Yeah, I have. Too long now. It's time for a change."

"If you are thinking of transferring to Space Travel, I must tell you that our offices are a lot smaller than yours, cramped in comparison."

"Oh, I don't need anything that showy. The office you saw was Chuck Whitman's. He was the last Housekeeping manager we had."

"And now Chuck has another job, no?"

Frank nodded. "When he was promoted two months ago, I moved in, but only temporarily. I'm just the acting manager until they hire somebody else."

"Do you not want to be the manager?"

"I wasn't recommended for the job," he said, with a shortness I suspected was anger.

"And how long did Chuck have that office?"

"For at least the three years that I've been with MAS. Chuck interviewed me in that office."

"So Chuck hired you?"

"Right."

"And what was Chuck like to work for?"

"The worst." Anger was now clearly sharpening his voice. "What's his fa-ther, Mykroni, like to work for?"

"The best."

"Really?" Frank seemed pleased with my comment.

He stretched his neck to look at the long, jagged coastline as we flew across it. "Wow, what a view! Say, Alex, how long are you gonna fly this straight-and-narrow path? When do I get more tricks?"

In a split second, I inverted the plane with a 180-degree roll. "Does this please you more?" I asked him, as we hung suspended from our harnesses. He grinned.

Streaks of sun painted a few wispy clouds a light pink for a pleasing morning sky. I decided to smear the canvas for Frank. We tumbled through the air in a succession of more spectacular patterns. I explained the aircraft's controls, answered Frank's questions, and let him get a feel for the stick and rudder, because the plane could also be operated from his seat. Then I crossed the shoreline back to the gray blocks of buildings dotted with trees and ribboned with roads in the sunny mix of colors and shapes that was the city of Rising Tide.

"Why did you not like working for Chuck Whitman?"

Perhaps it was my interest in the subject, his anger at Chuck, or a combination of both that spurred Frank to talk.

"Well, for one thing, Chuck, who knew nothing about robotics, hired me, and I knew a lot. Although MAS had some janitorial automation, it was nothing compared to what I installed. I bought used robots dirt cheap at an auction. I refurbished them and programmed them for office cleaning. I dramatically increased productivity and slashed payroll. When robots work with eight arms and built-in vacuum cleaners, and without lunch breaks or paid vacations, you'd be amazed at how economically the job can be done. I called my mechanical staff the Clean Team, gave them human faces and name badges, and programmed them to greet people when they cleaned their offices. And the Clean Team responded—that is, *I* responded—to special requests. So if Mary Jones wanted Dreamboat to water her plants every Wednesday or if Bill Rogers wanted Speedy to dust knickknacks every Tuesday, I wrote the code for Dreamboat and Speedy to comply. The project was a big success."

"So this is very good for you, no?"

"You'd think so. But although Chuck wasn't too swift with robotics, there was one thing he excelled at, and that was in keeping me as far in the background as he could. He presented my ideas at meetings that he never invited me to attend. He had me working night shifts and weekends, so none of the brass would see me. When the employee newsletter did a story on what they called 'Chuck's Clean Team,' my name was never mentioned. I figured all of this was okay because Chuck was probably setting himself up for a promotion. Then I'd get to be manager, so the sooner I got rid of him, the better."

"And he got his promotion. So what about yours?"

"That's the thing that eats at me. Chuck gets a promotion out of sheer dumb luck, because he happens to be in the right place at the right time and because he has my program to ride on. Then he doesn't even recommend me as his replacement. Instead of griping to management, which I hate to do, I decided to transfer to another department. Human Resources is on the lookout for a job that would be right for me, but having an inside connection is always more helpful. That's why I wanted to get to know you and the other folks in Space Travel."

"Why did Chuck not recommend you to replace him?"

"You know, Alex, I can understand why he wanted to keep me down when he was my boss, because maybe he figured I could steal his job. But now, when I can't possibly affect him, and when he knows damn well I can do the job, why did he recommend to Human Resources that they get somebody else for Housekeeping manager? When I asked him, he walked away without answering."

I had no reply, except to mirror the puzzled look on Frank's face with my own. "What do you mean that Chuck was in the right place at the right time to get his promotion?"

"Hardly anyone's around on Sundays, so it's a big cleaning day for us. Now, I was the one who worked every Sunday, and Chuck was off. But on a Sunday two months ago, Chuck decided that he'd work instead of me, because he wanted to reorganize the supply closet. Wouldn't you know it, that was the day that Dr. Merrett came in to dismantle this special project he was working on in the adjacent building. No one knew Dr. Merrett would be here. His memo to the staff about the project's cancellation wasn't released until the next morning. That's what I mean by dumb luck."

"So what happened with Chuck and Dr. Merrett?"

"Everyone thinks that particular Sunday was a dismal day for Dr. Merrett because canceling the project caused problems for the company. Now, who was here to help the top boss on the one day of the week when the place is pretty empty, almost a ghost town, and at a very trying moment, perhaps the worst moment of Dr. Merrett's career? None other than our corporate superstar, Chuck." Frank looked at me uneasily. "Say, Alex, how can you fly this thing when you're staring at me like that?"

I softened my look and tried to make my voice sound casual. "How did Chuck help Dr. Merrett on the day he dismantled his special project?"

"According to my friend, who was the security guard on duty at the Project Z building, Dr. Merrett allowed Chuck to come in to help him. Then later, they carried the pieces of Project Z to the compactor just outside the building."

"You mean Chuck was in contact with Project Z?"

"Well, yes and no. According to my friend, the project was in pieces inside a couple of large cartons, and Chuck helped Dr. Merrett carry them out for trash compacting. No doubt Chuck lent a sympathetic ear, as well as his assistance, because right after that, he was promoted to be special assistant to the president for new project development."

While I pondered the matter, Frank pointed out the window. "Hey, Alex, those fields we're flying over now are MAS property, aren't they? Is the ride over so soon?"

"Not before I give you something to remember." Although we had been flying well over an hour, I had the impression that an entire day would be too short for Frank. To be sure he got the exciting ride he wanted, I decided to do a stall spin. I pulled up to zero air speed over an empty field, then fell into a stall. The high-performance plane I was flying did not recover easily, because in order to turn as superbly as it did, the craft was designed to be somewhat unstable. This meant that we would have to drop thousands of feet before I could stabilize. In the meantime, the view from the windshield was a whirling green field that seemed to be crashing in on us.

"Do you feel fulfilled now?" I said to the flushed face and shaking knees beside me, after I finally stabilized the aircraft.

Frank swallowed hard and made a few attempts to find his voice. "If fulfilled means dizzy and queasy . . . and scared . . . I'm very fulfilled, thank you!"

On landing, my efforts to apply subtle adjustments were rewarded when the wheels of my craft met the runway in a touch as soft as a kiss. As I headed back to Frank's office to pick up my jacket, he went on about how thrilling the ride was, while my mind drifted to other thoughts. Did Chuck Whitman know what Project Z was all about? When Dr. Merrett dismantled the project, was Chuck's unexpected appearance not an accident at all? Did Chuck know that Dr. Merrett intended to disassemble Project Z before anyone else knew it? My thoughts balanced precariously on one fulcrum: Could Chuck read Dr. Merrett's computer screen? In a moment I would know.

When we returned to Frank's office, and I looked out the window, I could see people and objects in many offices in the building across the way. However, in the room directly aligned with Frank's and one floor down—Dr. Merrett's office—I saw nothing but the reflection of the sky and our building, as if those particular windows were a mirrored surface.

"Is that Dr. Merrett's office?" I asked, pointing.

"It is," Frank replied.

"Why are his windows different from the others?"

"They're one-way mirrors. Dr. Merrett can look out, but no one can look in. That way no one can see his computer screen or his papers. It's a security screen."

"Do you know when these special windows were installed?"

"Not too long after I started working here. Why?"

"Because . . . well, security interests me."

"What? You mean *you're* thinking of transferring departments too? But you *can't* give up flying!"

"We shall see. Now, were the special windows installed before or after Project Z was started?"

"Does that matter to you, Alex?"

"I am curious."

"Okay, let's check it out." Frank sat at his desk, alternately talking to his computer and tapping icons on the monitor. Standing behind him, I saw a calendar appear on the screen. "Chuck hired me in October, so this month makes three years that I'm here. Now, the robot that cleans Dr. Merrett's office, Dustin, was the first one I launched, so Chuck could impress the brass. Dustin started . . . let's see . . . the following January." Frank turned to me. "I revised Dustin's code to reflect a change in cleaning procedures when the new windows were installed. You see, they're cleaned on the inside with a special solvent." He tapped his monitor again. "That was the following month in February. Now, Project Z began in . . . let me check. . . . I was planning to provide a robot for cleaning that facility, but the group decided to do its own cleaning. Here it is. My notes say April. Project Z started two-and-a-half years ago, in April, two months *after* Dr. Merrett's windows went up."

"Have the security windows been up the entire time of Project Z, without interruption?"

"That's right." He looked at me curiously, then smiled. "Oh, I see what you're getting at. You thought Chuck knew Dr. Merrett was coming in that Sunday to ax Project Z because Chuck snooped. So he arranged to be here to help, to bend the boss's ear, and to con Dr. Merrett into giving him a fancy title for drumming up new projects to fill the gap left by Project Z. It would have been a perfect way to hustle Dr. Merrett for a promotion."

"A . . . related thought . . . had occurred to me."

"Maybe you *do* have a knack for security, Alex. Except that no one could snoop through those windows. They went up two months before Project Z ever started and have remained up ever since."

"I see. And have you or your robots ever been inside the Project Z area?"

"Never."

I took a note pad and pen from my pocket and drew a picture of Feran's cargo. "Have you ever seen a metal box like this, about two feet high, closed on all sides, with no visible controls except for a large pin on the side near the top?"

"No."

"Do you have any idea what such an object might be?"

"None at all."

I slipped the pad back in my pocket, then put my jacket on. Frank thanked me for the ride, and I thanked him for the information.

Before I left, I asked him about another matter that confused me: "I am unfamiliar with some of the words you use here. Could you tell me what term you would use to describe a female who looked, say, like Kristin Merrett?"

He smiled. "Kristin's *beautiful*. Definitely beautiful."

When I asked what *ugly* referred to, his reply made me realize why Kristin was angry. So many things seemed upside down on Earth, or were they inverted on Asteron? Good and evil, beautiful and ugly. Why had the meaning of words from the same language been flipped over on Asteron, like a plane rotated 180 degrees?

"And we call only *animals* males and females, not *people*, unless we're in a biology class," Frank added. "Humans are women and men, or ladies and gentlemen. And the ladies are more touchy about that than we are."

Again I saw that Earthlings distinguished themselves from the animals in the names they reserved for humans only. Their beings went beyond the mere physical references of a biology class to deserve new titles, ones that were fading from the same language spoken across the galaxy.

"What would you do, Frank, if you mistakenly told a woman that she was ugly when you really meant the opposite?"

"Apologize. Apologize *profusely*. Ask for her forgiveness, and hope you get it."

"I see."

"Oh, and by the way, Alex, if you've got any designs on Kristin, don't be too disappointed if they don't pan out. Every guy here tries to date her, but she ignores all of us."

A few more inquiries that day taught me something about the thing Kristin told me I lacked—*manners*. I found that when Earthlings dealt with one another, they used manners as a sign of respect. Animals growled and clawed, but men and women said *please* and *thank you*. Animals devoured each other, but men and women apologized for so much as stepping on someone's toe. There was little use for manners on Asteron. The guards there never said *please* or *thank you* when they shoved us around. Their violence seemed as jarringly out of tune with life on Earth as manners were with life on Asteron. But the way of the Earthlings was supposed to be the rule of the jungle, whereas the way of Asteron, I was taught, was supposed to be humane. Why, then, were the guards without manners over there?

I had an opportunity later that Tuesday to use some of my new information. With Reckoning Day fast approaching on Friday, Kristin and I had scheduled another practice session to rehearse our two-plane demonstration. As we performed our preflight checks, with our crafts facing each other on the airstrip, she did not wave to me, as was her habit. After strapping my harness and putting on my helmet, I looked at her in the cockpit across from mine.

"Hello, Kristin," I called to her through the radio transmitter at my mouth.

A flat voice I hardly recognized came over the receiver. "Hi."

"You are angry with me."

"I'm not angry. I just don't want to see you any more outside of work. I want you to stay away from me."

"Oh, really?"

"I indeed do not want to see you," she replied, imitating my speech.

"Kristin, I will not fly with you while you are in such a state."

"If I couldn't fly perfectly well in what you call my state, I wouldn't be in this plane."

"I still will not fly with you until you give me what is called forgiveness."

"Why should I?"

"Because I apologize. You were right when you said I was rude, but I did not mean to be. And you were right when you said I was mixing up my words—"

"You were?" A note of hope lifted her voice.

"Yes. But you are wrong when you say you want me to stay away."

"Am I?"

"You do not want me to stay away, Kristin."

"Did you say you were mixing up your words?"

"Yes, and I apologize *profusely*."

"You mean you don't really think I'm ugly?"

I looked across the field at a dainty figure with a helmet inside a large, powerful plane. "I think you are beautiful, Kristin. Amazingly beautiful." I paused but heard no response, leaving my words to linger in the space between us. "Now let us fly together, so we can feel the thing you call *closeness*."

From my distance I could not perceive any expression beneath Kristin's helmet. Then I heard her engines start.

"I forgive you," a soft voice whispered in my ear.

CHAPTER 14

I walked quickly through the corridors of Space Travel, holding the new item that was now always with me, a well-worn paper that went back and forth between my pocket and my hand numerous times a day: Mykroni's checklist. I had to rush to complete the week's tasks that he had assigned. With Friday being a day off for the Earth holiday of Reckoning Day, I had only two days left to finish my work. As I was about to enter one of the simulators, a hand from behind me squeezed my shoulder. From long-standing habit, my body froze in dread.

"Hey, Alex, I want to tell you something."

I turned, relieved to see Mykroni, his warm smile instantly melting my fear.

"Since you and Kristin seem to be friends, I thought you'd want to know that today's her birthday."

I looked at him blankly.

"Here we *celebrate* a person's birthday," he explained.

On Asteron we celebrated only events important to the rulers, like military victories. "You mean Earthlings celebrate their birth anniversaries as if they were state holidays?"

"No. As if they were more important than state holidays."

"Really?"

"You see, if a person is special, then the day the person was born is important. We acknowledge it."

"How?"

"By buying the person something, a present."

"What kind of present?"

"Something we think the person will like."

114

Following this advice, I gave Kristin a present. But the results were *not* as Mykroni had led me to believe, which I told him later that day. Forgetting my new manners, I anxiously entered his office and sat down before being invited. "I gave Kristin a birthday present as you recommended, and it has gotten me into trouble."

"Oh? What did you get her?"

"You said to get her something I thought she would like. Not only did I think she would like the thing I got her, but I knew for sure that she would like it tremendously."

"And?"

"And she did not like it at all."

Mykroni smiled. "What's 'it'? What did you get Kristin for her birthday?"

"An Ultimate Sub from Big Eats."

"You didn't?" Mykroni's smile widened.

"My affairs seem to amuse you."

The smile turned to laughter. I waited patiently.

Finally, he spoke. "I'm sorry for laughing, Alex. I guess I forgot to mention one key thing about a birthday present." He leaned forward across his desk, as if trying to touch me with his words. "A present has to have value, which doesn't mean it has to cost a lot, but it has to be something prized, something more interesting than a common sandwich you can get anytime. Do you know why, son?"

I thought of the other differences I already had discovered—between bread and cheesecake, between rags and a wardrobe, between weeds and a garden, between life as cheap and life as . . . prized. "Kristin is special, so her present should be too."

Mykroni nodded the way he did when I completed an item on his checklist. "You got it, pal."

I arranged to take Kristin to what was called a *good* restaurant, and I got her a better present, perfume—a luxury item that women with only the highest connections could obtain on Asteron. Tonight we would celebrate an event more special than a home run by Alexander: Kristin's twenty-first birthday.

That evening Kristin let me fly her plane on our outing. As we headed for the restaurant I had chosen, a site I recognized caught my attention. It was the baseball stadium. It looked calm and peaceful now, a massive, hollow oblong with many rows of seats encircling the dormant field and with vacant parking lots stretching outside of it. The empty arena was a stark contrast to the packed, noisy scene the other night when we were there.

"The stadium is deserted now," I commented.

"With the season over, there won't be any sign of life down there till next spring."

"Even though we are close to the ground, I see no guards. Is the stadium not protected by guards or security systems in the off-season?"

"The stadium is an old landmark building—baseball's been around for quite some time—so it wouldn't surprise me if it was never updated with modern security systems, at least not in the open field. There's really nothing down there to steal." She stretched her slender neck to observe the arena below. "The seats are bolted down, and the concessions look like they're boarded up."

"Are there any property break-ins in Rising Tide?"

"Rarely. We don't worry much about that, unless it's a company like MAS, which of course has lots of security."

"Did your father worry about break-ins?"

I detected an edge to her voice. "Not in recent years, and I certainly don't worry about them on my birthday. Alex, you ask the strangest questions!"

Although her tone told me that our discussion of the topic I obsessed about was finished, my thoughts lingered on it as we flew to a secluded restaurant a distance away, where I hoped no one was likely to look for me.

Having left my evening's attire to my selection, Kristin was pleased with the outfit I had picked: dark silk slacks, a jacket, and a bright-colored shirt. These were clothes from the wardrobe she had helped me to choose—soft, well-fitting fabrics that moved and breathed with me in the utmost comfort.

"Because you're tall and slim, those clothes fall just right on you," she said flatly, like a tailor assessing her work. "And with your looks, you could model clothes, Alex." Upon seeing the question on my face, she elaborated. "A model is someone a seller hires to wear clothes so that potential buyers can see how they look. But on second thought, you wouldn't make a good model at all. Your eyes are too . . . penetrating. No one would notice the clothes."

From the sky, the restaurant looked as if it were carved from the Earth itself, a piece of jagged stone hanging over a mountain cliff east of Rising Tide, with sharp, angular lines defining the walls and roof. I carefully adjusted the controls to lower the plane gently, so that it sank vertically to the ground like a red blossom falling from a tree on a windless evening. In the twilight we walked toward the expansive quadrangles of glass that were the windows. I peered inside to see a large fireplace cast flickering gold lights against the walls and ceiling.

"Kristin, is there a word for the pleasing way the restaurant looks, the way it seems to invite us to come in?" I looked into eyes that danced with the same fiery sparks as the hearth.

"Enchanting. It's called *enchanting*."

When I opened the wooden entrance door, the shocking sights beyond it carried me to a distant clearing by a lake where a sweet voice was humming music. Removing Kristin's coat, I saw clothing of a thousand shimmering circles that seemed to have been poured over her body. The dress was a thin sheet of white metal that ended well above her knees, covering the pleasing landscape of her body with sparkles, which she called sequins, from her neck to her wrists. The back of the dress was another matter, because there was none, only a spread of suntanned skin from shoulders to waist, smooth, supple skin that felt warm against the cool, hard strip of dress that framed it.

As we were seated at a table by the fireplace, I saw the rest of the scene described to me in another age: the crisp, white linen, called a tablecloth; the glasses with the long handles, called crystal; the flowers, special ones called orchids, prized for their beauty; the shiny wooden floor where couples danced together to music—the whole of the scene painted for me in a time that seemed so long ago!

I stared incredulously at Kristin in the golden glow of the room. "Is there a man named Honey on this planet?"

"What?"

I knew the answer already, as well as the dark conclusion it implied: The images Reevah had seen in the spies' quarters meant that Feran's agents were studying the Earth! Why?

"Kristin, somewhere far away, someone described a place just like this to me, where a woman wore a garment that sparkled just like yours, a dress that was enchanting, and—"

"You think my dress is enchanting?"

"Indeed. And the woman with the sparkling dress danced very close to a man, so their bodies touched and swayed to the rhythm of music in a way that was . . . it was . . . is there a word . . ."

"Romantic. It was *romantic*. Through the dancing they showed how they cared for each other."

"Yes, yes! And the man's name was *Honey*."

She smiled. "Lots of people are called honey by folks who care about them. It's a term of fondness and affection, even love."

"But, Kristin, how can a sticky substance oozing from an insect be used to express love?"

"Have you ever tasted honey?"

"No."

On Asteron, there were bees in the rulers' fields, but the people were not given honey in their rations. It was one of the many foods cultivated for our leaders, with their protruding bellies, who kept their eating habits a secret from the citizens, with their protruding ribs.

Kristin ordered honey, and I was surprised to see it served by a human, not a robot. "Being served by a live person is a more pampering experience; that's why you pay more," Kristin explained. *Pampering*. The word intrigued me because that night I felt as if I was indulging my every whim more than any ruler on Asteron. But what I would have considered a disgusting display by them had the most sublime meaning to me. Was it paying for my pampering with my own money and leashing no one's neck to provide it that made all the difference?

I learned so many new things that night, such as the remarkable taste of different foods, including honey. I learned about the savoring of a prized wine, and the clinking of the glasses in a kiss that Kristin called a toast.

"Because a toast, you say, is to honor someone, and today is your birthday, should I give a toast to you?" Her face was radiant in the flickering light of the fireplace, somehow reflecting my own excitement toward the whole of my new universe. I held up my glass: "To the most beautiful pilot in the galaxy."

Our glasses touched in a chime of resonating crystal, which seemed to be the most civilized sound in the universe. Then I blinked at her with one eye, and she laughed like the woman in the story from another age.

"What does the blink with one eye mean, Kristin?"

"It's a wink. It's a way for two people to give a secret signal to each other. Were you giving me a secret signal, Alex?"

When we rose to dance, we stared at each other for a long moment, then our bodies touched with a sudden urgency that also seemed to be a secret signal.

From the grassy spot on a mountainside where we later sat, the distant towns below were reduced to dots of light shimmering in the night like the sequins on Kristin's dress. After we had left the restaurant, I brought the plane down on this secluded spot to catch its remarkable view. We sat on a blanket, gazing at the countryside, which was in sharp focus on that cloudless night. Could the fog obscuring my own existence be lifted too? I wondered. We sat awhile in silent contentment, and then Kristin turned to me. The white sparkle of her dress formed a stunning contrast to the red-brown hair that shone like the polished wood the Earthlings called mahogany.

"Alex, thank you for making my birthday . . . enchanting."

She drew near me, her hand curving my face. I felt her mouth on mine in a touch too soft to be a kiss, a touch that was merely the promise of one. As she withdrew, my mouth followed hers, deciding without me to fulfill the promise right away. Within moments she was in my arms, the intoxicating scent of the perfume soaking into my lungs, my hands memorizing the rhythm of hills and valleys in the soft skin of her back, my mouth locked on hers. I was calm, I was safe, I was on Earth, I told myself. I pulled her down on the blanket, my hands stroking her breasts, my head buried in her hair, my body pressing against hers. I felt her body answer me, her arms embracing me, her head arching back.

Suddenly, I sat up, my resolute face meeting her astonished one. "Kristin, I know this is rude, but we need to go." I began to rise, but her arm on mine stopped me.

"Alex," she said softly, "aren't you going to ask me what it's called when one part of you wants something, but another part says no, and you go back and forth with these two parts tugging at you?"

I waited quietly for the answer.

"It's called a problem. What do you do if you have a problem on a space-craft, when one computer tells you to go one way and the other tells you to do the opposite?"

I stretched across the blanket, listening, staring at the sky, weary from the thing Kristin called my problem.

"The things you like, Alex, things that are enchanting and roman-tic . . . and closeness. . . . Well, to have those things, you have to talk to the other person."

I rolled on my stomach, searching for a way to explain something I could not talk about.

"Tell me what's wrong. Will you, Alex?" she asked softly.

I sighed. She waited. I propped myself up on my elbows. "Kristin, where I come from, women are punished—punished *severely*—for choosing their own men."

"Was there a woman? Did you have someone you were close to?"

"Yes."

"Did you go out with her?"

"We were not permitted to go out as you do here, but I saw her secretly."

"Did you like her?"

"Yes. She was the one who told me of the scene between the Earthling woman in the sparkling dress and the man she danced with."

"So you had a girlfriend and you saw her secretly. Then what happened?"

"She . . . became . . . pregnant."

Grimly, I met her puzzled glance. "Was that why she was punished?"

"Yes."

"How was she punished? Did her employer fire her?"

"We had no employers."

"Did her friends shun her?"

"We had no friends."

"Did her family abandon her?"

"We had no families."

"Then how was she punished?"

My hands covered my face. I grimaced against the lash of a whip burning on my back.

"How was she punished, Alex?"

The voice I hated screamed inside me until I could feel my fingernails dig-ging into my hair: *It is your fault— It is your fault that she—*

I felt Kristin's arms around me, her sweet breath blowing against my hair. "You're shaking, Alex. Tell me . . . how was she punished?"

119

"She . . . was . . . hanged."

Somewhere on the edge of my mind, I heard Kristin gasp. I saw her translucent eyes blacken in horror. At first she was speechless. Then a look of clarity formed on her face, as if she was understanding a matter that had puzzled her. "The rope . . . Jeff, with the rope. . . . You thought . . . and I laughed at you!"

Kristin's presence was fading. I could smell the rotting wood of a platform I leaped onto. I could feel the vicious eyes of the guards around me. "I knew our acts were a crime against the people, but she told me she had taken a tablet and she was safe. I believed her. I was too quick to believe her. I wanted too much to believe her."

My fists clenched against an enemy I could not hit. "I tried to save her, but I could not. My hands were tied; my mouth was gagged. I was being beaten."

I slammed my fist on the blanket with a thump, but what I heard was the thump of a trapdoor giving way. "I could do nothing . . . but . . . watch . . ."

My mind could no longer contain the private torment of a coarse rope encircling a fragile neck with golden hair flowing along it. The anguished cry that I had heard only in the secret vault of my mind now exploded into the air. I bellowed it into the soft folds of Kristin's hair. *"I caused her to die! I caused her to die! I caused her to—"* Suddenly I choked and my throat burned.

"Go ahead and cry, Alex." I felt the whisper of Kristin's mouth just above my head as she held me.

"I never cry."

"Go ahead."

"I am not like the Earthlings. I cannot laugh or cr—"

The burning liquid spilled from my eyes just as I was denying its existence. I could feel the tiny sequins moisten where my head lay against Kristin's dress. I heard my own tortured cries as the raw wounds still blistered my memory, until finally there were no cries left. Then, feeling spent, I lay down on the blanket, astonished at my outburst and suddenly feeling strangely calm.

For a long, quiet moment, Kristin held my hand. Then she whispered, her voice deep with sorrow, "Nothing like that can ever happen here."

"What do you mean?"

"I mean here we can have babies or not, and it's nobody's business. It's simple. You go to Quick Fix. If you don't want to have babies, you get a pill, and its effect lasts for years. If you decide later that you want a baby, you go back to Quick Fix and ask for another pill to reverse the previous one's effects. There are pills for men and women. So you never have to be afraid of this again."

"How do you know about these pills?"

"Because I went to Quick Fix and got one, so I . . . wouldn't . . ."

"When did you do this, Kristin?"

She lowered her head shyly. I lifted it so that her eyes were level with mine. "When I met you," she whispered. Her face reddened as I somehow had the life left in me to stare at her . . . rudely. "But I don't want you to believe me." She moved away. "Don't believe any woman. Go to Quick Fix and get your own pill."

"But does the state not regulate baby production?"

"Of course not."

"But do you not have genetics?"

"Of course. We live until we're 150 years old. Part of that's due to our doctors, who can fix anything. They have techniques to repair and replace body parts. And they can even fix those scars on your neck because cosmetic surgery is incredibly advanced. But a lot of our long lifespan is due to the diseases we can eliminate through gene research."

"But who plans for the children that are produced?"

"Everyone. People decide for themselves."

"But if people are left to decide for themselves, what if their children are undesirable to the public?"

"We don't produce children for the public. In fact, somebody's kids are none of anybody else's business."

"But if this matter is important, then it has to be controlled, no?"

"Do you want the important things in your life decided by somebody else? Alex, don't you see, it's not any one thing? It's not as if I'm free only to fly my plane, or to disagree with my instructor, or to contradict the mayor, or to choose my own boyfriend. You don't have to keep asking the same question every time a new issue comes up. You don't have to worry about me. I'm free, period. And so are you. Alex, you're free of Cosmona forever."

I looked away, suddenly feeling . . . guilty.

"I never imagined what a . . . horrible . . . place that is!" She reached over to me, her long, silky fingers stroking my face. "Now I understand why you keep wanting to rescue me. And I like being rescued by you, but Alex, there's no real danger. You don't have to torture yourself."

I was beginning to understand, I thought, as I placed my arms around Kristin. I listened for the terrible voice inside me, but, incredibly, it was gone. It seemed to have been washed away with my tears, because I felt somehow free of it. I felt somehow . . . free. I kissed Kristin's mouth, her eyes, her hair. She flung her head back loosely, her neck losing its tension, her body moving with only the pressure of my mouth, inviting me to do more.

Then she pushed away. "No." Her voice was weak, but her arms were strong as they resisted me. "Go to Quick Fix and find out for yourself. Then you won't have to depend on anybody's word."

"But Quick Fix is not here. And you are."

"Alex, you're smiling."

I felt somehow lighter, as if a heavy weight had been lifted from my life. "I will go to Quick Fix later, Kristin. Now, I will be what is called your boy-friend."

I drew her close to me and wrapped the blanket around us. With a tiny tug on the scant supports of the dress, which I had studied over dinner, there were no more sparkling sequins, but only soft, warm skin in the darkness. Then, for the first time since I came to Earth, it was I who taught Kristin about a matter she did not yet know, and this fact seemed strangely exciting to both of us.

I raised myself to gaze at her face, to caress it, to kiss it softly. "Kristin, what is it called when you savor wine, when you drink it slowly to feel all the pleasing sensations that warm you, except it is not wine you want to savor, but a person you want to drink slowly?"

"Tenderness. It's called *tenderness*."

"And what is it called when every feature about another becomes some-thing you want to prize, like a voice so pleasing it makes you want to dance to it, or laughter so sweet it makes you want to taste the mouth that made its sound?"

"Caring. It's called *caring*."

"And what is it called when your thoughts fix obsessively on little things that make you ache inside, like a sweater you want to slide your hands under, or a zipper you want to tug at?"

"Desire. It's called *desire*."

"And did you call this *making love*?"

"Oh yes, honey, yes."

Then there were no more words, only two bodies wrapped together on a mountain, with the lights of the world below as the backdrop for an act that was, to use my new word, joyful.

After leaving Kristin that evening, I stopped at a Quick Fix booth to find, unsurprisingly, that everything she had told me was true. Here on Earth, I thought, Kristin and I could move about in the open because our goal was to fulfill our lives and all roads were paved to take us there. But what if we lived in a place where we found only roadblocks on our path? I tried to understand what drove Reevah to lie to me, causing her to skid off a cliff—and what drove me to believe her.

As I swallowed a tiny pill with the power to kill a monstrous voice that paralyzed me, I read the paper that Quick Fix emitted when it scanned me. The report said that the pill would be effective in my body and I would func-tion normally, but it did not mention my species. I apparently belonged to a humanoid group capable of crying. Babies cried on Asteron, but only until they reached the state of mental numbness that marked maturity. That was true, I thought, except in Reevah's case. I wondered if she had been an alien, because Reevah could laugh and cry easily like the Earthlings.

With the great sense of relief that the little pill gave me, I walked toward my apartment complex, a group of detached units set along a courtyard off a main street. I felt an unusual calm as I passed the Earthlings' well-kept houses with fragrant gardens, lighted windows with tidy furnishings inside, children's toys stowed on the porches, and colorful and varied vehicles on the road. Every sight was one of contentment. At that moment, I was held by the serenity of Earthling life. I felt oddly unconcerned with danger and ready to believe Kristin's assurance that the vast territory of freedom also reached the ground where I stood.

Tired of fearing people, I thought that maybe, just this one special night, I might return home through the front entrance of the complex, instead of sneaking around the back as I normally did. Perhaps I would even wave to the person I always avoided, the clerk in the management office. His small building, which stood on the street in front of the courtyard of dwellings, was open all hours to rent furnished units. I reminded myself to give him another month's rent on payday. When I had first arrived, the possibility of staying alive longer than one month had not occurred to me. But this evening, especially, made me feel hopeful. The activity called making love seemed to agree with me, and with Kristin too, I thought, remembering our exciting moments and already aching for her again. Somehow, I was not surprised that the Earthlings had given the most beastlike of activities the most spiritual of names when performed by humans.

Suddenly, all thoughts of relaxing my guard vanished. In the lamplight forty feet ahead, I saw two police officers heading toward the rental office. These men did not have the same kind face with smiling eyes as Officer Hodges at Big Eats. I knew these two, and they knew me. Dressed as Earthling officials with their badges flashing on their shirts, the men opening the office door were Feran's spies!

I ducked into the bushes that surrounded the apartment complex and moved silently in the night toward the small office building. I crouched down to hide in the shrubbery underneath the side window of the office. It was opened a few inches, sufficient for me to hear. The men who had barked orders and shoved me around when I delivered supplies to their quarters on Asteron had different voices now, friendly tones that I had never heard from their vicious mouths, and they abundantly used Earthling contractions and expressions. They had learned their lessons well! They introduced themselves with phony names and asked the clerk's name. They engaged briefly in what the Earthlings called small talk, a striking change from the big fists that spoke for them in their homeland.

"Say, Joe, we're looking for a young man for questioning, and we think he might be staying in this area," said one of the spies.

"Oh? Do you think he might be *here*?" I got a look at the clerk. He was the one who had rented me my apartment.

"It's possible," said the other spy. "We're questioning everyone in the area. He's twenty-one years old, six-foot-two, black hair, blue eyes. He's slim and athletic-looking."

"Gee, I've got twenty-five units. A lot of guys come and go all the time, officer."

"This kid's an alien, but he looks like one of us. His name's Arial, although he probably changed it. He arrived here just three weeks ago. Did you happen to see a spacecraft in the sky about that time, one that looked like it was disoriented?"

"I see crafts all the time, but I don't remember anything out of the ordinary, no."

"Do you know of any abandoned spacecraft, or any crashes that maybe weren't reported to us?"

"No."

"The kid's a pilot, but he could be working in any job. Here's a picture of him."

The spies no doubt had my photo identification from Asteron. I wondered if the desperate creature I had been back then resembled me today, with my new hair styling, wardrobe, and ample diet.

"Wow, this straggly kid looks like he's starving. I haven't seen anyone like that here," said the clerk.

I felt relieved that Kristin had insisted I get a new look. This also gave me hope that the spies would be unable to match my photo via face-recognition programs to that of any new hires at MAS, should they suspect I might be there. The spies would give up now, at least with the clerk, I hoped. But that was not to be.

One of them was persistent. "He speaks English. But in a stilted way, without contractions. And he's got markings around his neck—scars."

"Oh, *yes*. I did rent to someone like that. A few weeks ago, yes. He's still here."

I closed my eyes and missed a breath.

"Could you look up his records for us, Joe, if you please?" said one of the spies, who seemed to know his manners, although he had never wasted them on me.

"Let's see," the clerk said. I heard the light taps of his fingertips on a screen. "He's in unit 11, the one near the end of the cul-de-sac. J. White. That's his name."

I had decided to rent without Kristin's help, so I could give a phony Earthling name. I had chosen a common one that I had found in an electronic directory of Rising Tide's residents, which I had looked through in the rental office while waiting to check in. There were dozens of people in the area with the surname White whose first names began with *J*.

"What does the *J* stand for?" One of the spies asked.

"Don't know. He didn't say."

"And what other information do you have on him?"

"Hmmm. None."

"None?"

"As I recall, when he rented, he said he was in a hurry and he would come back later to fill out the rest of the information, but I guess we both forgot about it. He put a month down in cash, so I didn't complain."

"Do you have another address on him?"

"No."

"An employer's name?"

"Nope."

"Anybody else in that room?"

"Nope."

"Any visitors or callers?"

"Not that I know of. Say, is this guy dangerous?"

One of the spies laughed. "Now, don't go getting alarmed, Joe. We just want to talk to him."

"Well, I don't know if he's home," said the clerk, "but I'll call the apartment for you."

"Oh, don't trouble yourself," said the other spy. "We'll just walk down there and see if he's around. Hey, got a key for us, Joe?"

"Not without a search warrant, of course," replied the clerk, surprised.

"Of course," said the spy, laughing the matter off. "If we need one, we'll come back tomorrow with it."

Of course, I thought, hunched in the foliage, *Feran's spies will be back with some kind of permission—a warrant—to search my apartment.* That would happen just as soon as I gave Feran kisses! I knew the spies would be inside my door within minutes. But I would not be there, nor would any piece of information that could link me to the name *Alexander* or to MAS. After I had received Feran's first message, I removed from my apartment anything having to do with my Earthling identity and job. And I had never worn my work clothes, with their MAS emblems, outside of the company. Kristin had never been here, because out of caution, I had not invited her.

I was *safe*. I would wait until the spies headed toward my apartment, and then I would disappear from this complex forever. The spies would get a new wardrobe—*my* wardrobe, the animals!—but they would not get me, I thought.

"We'd appreciate it if you didn't mention us to Mr. J. White, if you happen to see him. Do you think you can do that for us, Joe?"

"Sure, guys. Anything I can do to cooperate. But what's this kid done?"

"We don't know. ES wants to locate him, that's all."

"*Earth Security*? You mean this isn't a local matter?" The clerk's voice sounded grave. "Does it involve a threat to the . . . *planet*?"

"Hey, take it easy, Joe."

"Is this guy a . . . spy?"

"Like we said, we just want to talk to him."

As I huddled in the bushes outside the window, I suddenly realized I would *not* be safe at all! I would not be able to vanish into the night and never come back. I *had to* get into my apartment. Before we left work that day, Kristin had given me a small bundle of flowers. When I came home to dress for dinner, I dropped the flowers in a glass of water in the kitchen. There was a card with the blossoms, a handwritten note from Kristin, that in my haste *I had left there unread.* The tension that curled like a snake around my stomach now squeezed it into a knot. Surely that note would contain her name!

Before these thoughts were fully formed, I was racing along the backyards of the row of dwellings on one side of the courtyard. As I peered out to the street between two of the units near where I lived, I could see the spies reach the entrance of my home. I would have to destroy Kristin's card because her name must not appear before Feran and Coquet! I would have to get to the card before they did, but they were already at my unit.

I quickly arrived at my back door, where I heard the stealthy movements of the spies at the front. Rather than break in, they were being careful to pick the door lock silently to avoid arousing the guard and to take me by surprise, if I were inside. This kept them stalled outside for a few moments as I pressed my remote electronic key to open the back door and slipped soundlessly into the kitchen. In the darkness I grabbed Kristin's card just as the spies entered through the front door. I thought I could feel the air whisk as they moved swiftly through the living room and bedroom.

I heard one of them whisper gruffly in his real voice, "He is not here."

Before they reached the kitchen, I slipped out the back and ran, with Kristin's card torn into pieces inside my mouth, ready to swallow if they seized me. I glanced back and saw the spies exit the kitchen and begin searching the yard. When I was a safe distance from them, I removed the soggy papers from my mouth and pieced them together:

"To the Alexander from another world who brings a promise to me. Kristin."

CHAPTER 15

The hum of the train's engine sounded too soft for the powerful vehicle I was riding. The train's speed melted rows of buildings outside my window into one brown smear. I was on the local commuter line called the Cheetah, a caravan of cars painted tawny in color with round black patches to match the coat of the Earth feline that provided inspiration for the train's name. After eluding the spies, I had raced to the Cheetah station and hopped on the first train leaving Rising Tide in order to find new lodging elsewhere. As I sat in my seat, my fascination with this feat of Earthling engineering gave me a brief reprieve from my worries.

Because it had no wheels and did not touch a track as it ran, the Cheetah looked more like a plane than a train. Propelled at the brisk clip of five hundred miles per hour, this bullet of a train enabled rural dwellers to commute to city jobs quickly. Disembarking passengers moved into a compartment called a cub, which was a small, rapidly accelerating and decelerating car that attached to the side of the main train, then separated from the Cheetah as it approached a station. This allowed people to exit from the cub without the Cheetah ever having to slow down for station stops. After the Cheetah passed a station, another cub that had picked up passengers gained speed and attached to the main train, bringing the new people onboard and collecting others for exit at the next stop. Like everything on Earth, the ride was coated with pleasure and convenience. For an extra coin, I had my choice of food, movies, music, and more.

I reached into my pocket for my new electronic device, a recent purchase that Kristin had selected for me and insisted I get. "It's a phone," she explained as she programmed her phone number into it, "but it's much more than that. Everything you ever wanted to know about anything is accessible through this thing." I had no idea what she meant about the object's greater capabilities, because where I came from, everything I ever wanted to know about anything was *in*accessible. With my days jammed with activities, I had not yet explored my new purchase. Now was a good time to begin.

I turned it on and called up a feature that gave me a trove of information about the cities and towns in the area where I was traveling. I was able to learn about furnished apartments available for rent along my route. I quickly selected a place for my new lodging in a secluded town one hundred miles from Rising Tide, which was a mere 12-minute ride on the Cheetah. I counted the money I had carried with me that evening. Thanks to the affluence of my new life on Earth, I had enough funds to rent a small furnished apartment and to buy a few articles of clothing and food until my next payday. When my stop was the next one, I walked through the train to the place where the cub was attached. I stepped in and watched it disengage from the Cheetah and, seconds later, pull into the station and come to a stop.

Despite my new town being far from a large city, I found abundant choices in restaurants, shops, and lodging. Why, I wondered, in a place where nothing was provided for free, was everything so readily available? And why, in a place where everything had been provided for free, had nothing been available? I wondered, but I had no time to discover the answer.

After renting a furnished apartment, I slept for a couple of hours. Then, too unsettled to sleep longer, I took the Cheetah back to my workplace.

The rocket sculpture was still bathed in its nighttime spotlight when I reached the quiet grounds of MAS. At four-thirty in the morning, the buildings were sparsely lit, and only a few vehicles dotted the parking lots.

A notice posted at the entrance announced the closing of the plant tomorrow, Friday, for the holiday of Reckoning Day. Tomorrow also marked a week since Feran began hunting for me in Rising Tide, as well as my twenty-third day on Earth. And because Kristin had insisted that I must have a birth celebration, she used my estimate of my age in Earth time to declare Reckoning Day as my twenty-second birthday. With Kristin planning my birthday and Feran my funeral, I figured I would have some type of ceremony in either case.

As my mind whirled with the problem that consumed me, I opened the door to my office and entered the narrow canyon of bookshelves that held the colorful manuals and electronic devices of my new life.

At my desk, I called up on my computer the memo that Dr. Merrett had sent to his employees announcing the cancellation of Project Z. I had already read this document, which was accessible to everyone at MAS. Now I reread it, wondering if there was a clue I had missed. The legend at the top noted that Dr. Merrett wrote the memo two months ago, on a Sunday in late August, and the computer sent it to all electronic mailboxes at MAS the next morning.

It read:

> Today I decided to cancel Project Z. There will be no delivery
> of its product tomorrow as scheduled, or at any other time, because
> I have just dismantled it. Because MAS has spent considerable time,
> effort, and resources on developing Project Z, I know that my sud-
> den and unexpected action calls for an explanation. I can say only
> that a grave problem, which plagued me from the beginning, and
> which I had confidence would be solved by the time of product de-
> livery, remains unsolved. In light of this, I have decided that I can-
> not release to the world a new invention with far-reaching and
> irrevocable consequences.
>
> Because MAS is now in breach of its contract, we are required
> to return all payments received for our work on Project Z and to
> pay a significant cancellation penalty. This means MAS will suffer a
> temporary, but quite serious, financial setback. I deeply regret any
> layoffs that will result. I will diligently be seeking new ventures to
> replenish our revenue stream, and those of you whose departments
> are affected by the slowdown will be given first priority when we
> are hiring again.

I stared at the memo on my screen. From the little I knew of Dr. Merrett, the communication seemed typical of him. It was in plain text, with no fancy formatting, images, or videos. I was struck by the difference between the simple memo before me and the mode of communication of my former leader. Whereas Feran coated his messages with honey to hide their true meaning, Dr. Merrett spoke directly, absent any sweet words to soften the truth. Whereas Feran's fiendish portrait was stamped on all directives and hung in every room of every Asteronian building—with penalties for people who did not dust and maintain the images—I had seen Dr. Merrett in only two pictures, both with him busy at work and unaware of being photo-graphed—one in which he wore a helmet and was coming out of a cockpit, and another with him on a ladder and with his head poking inside an aircraft's engine in a hangar. Whereas Feran was consumed with power, Dr. Merrett seemed consumed with work. Of all the contrasts between my homeland and my new planet, I wondered if the difference in its leaders was the most star-tling of all.

I leaned back, pondering the memo. What did it mean? What was devel-oped under Project Z? An invention. What kind of invention? One with *far-reaching* consequences. But many projects at MAS had far-reaching conse-quences. For example, my own project in the asteroid belt had consequences that would affect the future direction of space exploration and mining. Dr. Merrett's invention also had *irrevocable* consequences. But my going to the asteroid belt also had irrevocable consequences, because I could not undo my trip once I made it. It seemed as if another word should be added to Project Z's far-reaching and irrevocable consequences for them to disturb Dr. Merrett, a word he had neglected to mention: *dangerous*.

I sighed. What did I know? Feran had a protective suit in his spacecraft that linked him to Project Z. This project involved an invention whose effects were dangerous and irreversible. Could an Asteronian spy have found out about the invention? But how, if the plant and project were under tight security, and if no one could access the computer files or spy through his office windows on the one man who knew all the details of the project? Could Feran have wanted the invention? But why? Even if Feran had learned of the invention and wanted it, Dr. Merrett himself had dismantled and destroyed it. Was it not out of Feran's reach now?

I rubbed my eyes as if trying to make them focus more clearly on an answer to these riddles, but all I could picture were Feran's spies closing the distance between him and me. Did I dare tell Kristin my story? I remembered the look of hatred, so startlingly out of place in her eyes, when she spoke of Asteron. If I told her the truth about my origin, could she turn against me?

Did I dare tell Mykroni or Dr. Merrett my story? If spies masquerading as officers of Earth wanted me for questioning, whose side would my employers take? On Asteron everyone knew the officials were corrupt and no one trusted them. On Earth, however, people respected their officials, a view truly shocking to me. Because the power of Earth's civil authorities was tightly confined, their potential for corruption and cruelty also seemed limited. Why would anyone want to bribe the officials, when they controlled none of the citizens' businesses or personal affairs? What peaceable citizen would be afraid of an officer's cruelty when the police had no power even to search an apartment without a warrant? Even if Mykroni or Dr. Merrett believed I did nothing wrong, they could nevertheless turn me over to Feran's spies, thinking that those men were civilized Earthling officers who would release me when I explained my innocence. And besides, I thought guiltily, why would my employers side with me after I had lied to them about my homeland?

Did I dare go to the authorities? With Feran's spies impersonating Earth's officials, how could I? How far had his spies infiltrated their ranks? Because seeking help from Kristin, my employers, or the authorities was fraught with danger, I decided against it. I would first try to learn more on my own.

I rose from my chair and slipped into a port in my watch a small electronic cylinder called a pin drive, containing a program I needed. Then I left my office to commit my worst breach of the trust given me by the people who had welcomed me into their world.

Ever since I had seen the flexite suits at MAS and learned about Project Z, I knew it would come down to this, and I had prepared for it. A few days ago, I had feigned losing the personal password I used to access the computer terminal in my office. I called our systems administrator for help. Jill Thomas had arrived in my office to assist me. She spoke competently and had a cheerful face, which gave me hope that she would be helpful without also being suspicious.

After instructing me on the need to commit my password to memory and avoid this problem in the future, Jill installed a program on my computer to retrieve the code that would unlock it. On the screen flashed the words *Code Cracker*, introducing the program in an impressive graphic display that suggested the software was what the Earthlings called a commercial program, available to the public. Many such programs were used at MAS.

Code Cracker employed an incredible array of dictionaries and algorithms to search for the exact combination of letters, numbers, and special symbols that formed the password. It bypassed the computer's operating system and was able to test millions of password possibilities per second. As Code Cracker was running, I tried to gain information about it.

"Tell me, Jill, are there no security screens on my computer to resist such an attempt to unlock it?" I asked.

"Oh, absolutely," she replied. "There sure are safeguards on your computer against cracking a password, but the software to bypass them keeps getting more and more sophisticated. What I'm using here is the latest program, and it does the trick most of the time."

After Jill's various manipulations and attempts, the program did indeed come up with a code it presented on the screen. "Does that look about right to you, Alex?"

"I think that may be it!" I already knew that the result she had arrived at was indeed correct.

She tried the code and was able to unlock the computer and pull up my files. While working, she elaborated on what she had done. "Code Cracker doesn't let you see anything new. It just retrieves your password so you can see what you already were able to access."

"Okay."

"I should also mention that the program doesn't crack other codes you may use, only your password. For example, if you buy things from this computer, Code Cracker won't give you the separate codes you use to access your customer accounts. And if any directories or files require an additional log-in, you'll have to supply it."

"Do any of the systems here use biometrics?" The matter interested me more than my casual tone revealed.

"We use fingerprints, DNA, and retinal patterns in some cases. But they can be cracked too, and some people find it intrusive to have to give that kind of information, so we don't require it on their personal terminals."

With her work completed, Jill uninstalled the Code Cracker program. Before leaving she gave me pointers on picking a good password, and then commented: "Most people here are pretty relaxed about security—too relaxed, if you ask me."

After Jill had left, I visited a store in Rising Tide that sold these kinds of programs, and indeed I found Code Cracker on the rack. Here was a program of great power—and it was available to any person who wanted to buy it. Just as I marveled at the openness of Earth and the power and reach of the average person here, I felt a stab of pain at the thought of taking advantage of this wholesome environment by planning to do something . . . unwholesome. I bought the program and learned how to use it. Now, a few days later, I carried it on the pin drive in my watch.

I glanced at my watch as I walked across the parking lot to the executive office building. At five o'clock in the morning, I figured it was still early enough to perform my task without unwanted company. My security pass opened the entrance door. To remain unseen by anyone who might be in the building, I avoided the elevator and took a staircase up to Charles Merrett's office.

The door was locked that led to the outer reception area where his assistant, Margaret, worked. There was no keypad there to try the code I knew for the inner office, and I had no way of getting in. Then I remembered the conference room that was part of Dr. Merrett's inner office space. It also had a door to the hallway, the next one down the corridor. I glanced at it and saw that it did indeed have an electronic keypad, similar to the one on the other side of Dr. Merrett's inner office. Would the code I knew for the keypad entry through the reception area also work on this side of the inner office, through the conference room? I tried it, and the door opened. I walked in quietly and closed the door behind me.

In a moment I was sitting at Dr. Merrett's desk and starting his computer. Every sound reverberated in the stillness—from my chair swiveling to the computer starting to my pin drive sliding into a port on his terminal. I muted the computer so that it would communicate with me through written words, not speech. That way I could remain as silent as possible. I paused to listen but heard no sounds in the outer hallway. I glanced outside the window but saw no one entering the parking lot or walking toward the building at this early hour.

Soon the fancy graphic for Code Cracker came up on the monitor, announcing that the program was installing on Dr. Merrett's computer. I followed the prompts, activated functions, and set the program's powerful algorithms into motion scanning the hundreds of millions of possibilities to find the one combination of letters, numbers, and symbols that would allow me to discover the terminal's contents.

Like a safe cracker of old times, patiently turning the dial to find the right combination and release the tumbler, Code Cracker took time. While the program was engaged, I stared at the empty box on the screen labeled Password.

If the cracking was successful, a password would appear in that box. I waited. Every noise seemed magnified in the stillness. A car door slammed outside in the parking lot, and then two people walked across the front of the building. I heard a clamoring that startled me, but then I realized it was a robot moving through the hallway. I glanced at my watch. At five-thirty in the morning, I did not have much time left.

Finally, the small box on the monitor filled with a password. I committed it to memory and attempted entry. Success!

I did a search for Project Z, but nothing came up. Could the data I sought be intentionally hidden from a search? This meant I would have to probe the complex array of databases and files on the computer. I saw various directories and was able to enter them. There I found multiple layers of subdivisions. I dug deeper, opening some of the folders that looked promising. I encountered a wide range of information on the company's business—a prototype of a new plane, designs for a space station, financial reports, departmental reports, agreements to manufacture various types of products to customers—but I found nothing that resembled the project I sought.

With my hands perspiring onto the keyboard, I raced against time. Finally, in a remote folder buried several layers within a database innocuously labeled "Notes," there it was. I found a directory named, simply, Z.

My heart speeded in anticipation. I selected the database named Z and waited for it to open. Soon I would see before me the files of Project Z. At last I would be enlightened about the one thing I must understand.

But unlike the other directories, this one was not opening. Instead, a window appeared on my monitor, requiring that I enter an additional code word to access the folder. I knew there was no function in Code Cracker to find additional codes beyond the password into the computer. On the remote chance it might work, I tried Dr. Merrett's password, but it was, predictably, rejected. Remembering how close Kristin was to her father, I tried her birthday followed by her name as a code, then her name followed by her birthday—but these wild guesses were immediately rejected. After these rejections, as a security measure, I was prevented from making another try during this session.

Stymied, I pondered the matter but came up with no solution. I would *not* unlock the secret of Project Z after all! The mystery that enveloped my life and involved Kristin, her father, MAS, and—by his having one of the project's special suits—Feran would remain unsolved for me.

I had been at my task for two hours. By now, people were arriving for work. I saw several vehicles park in the lot. I heard doors opening and voices outside in the hallway. I nervously glanced out the front window to see someone walking toward the entrance. It was Margaret.

I quickly deleted all trace of the Code Cracker files and turned off Dr. Merrett's computer. Just as I heard the door to the reception area opening, I made a dash for the conference room door, and then slipped out into the hallway and down the stairwell.

CHAPTER 16

Later that morning I sat in a classroom, staring at a board filled with equations on the atmospheric science of planets. As I waited for class to begin, I tried to figure out how to rid my own mental atmosphere of the two pollutants poisoning it—Feran's spies. A reprieve came when the air suddenly filled with the scent of Kristin's perfume. She sat next to me, the whole of our special moments reflected on her expressive face. I had to strain to return a similar glance because my encounter with Feran's spies had drained me of all feeling that could be called romantic.

Kristin whispered excitedly that she had arranged for me to meet her father at five o'clock that afternoon. "I told my dad that I wanted him to meet my *boyfriend*. I figured that would get his attention," she explained.

At the scheduled time, I arrived at the executive office building to find Kristin holding a small bundle of blooms to take to her father. "You'll forgive him if he's preoccupied, won't you, Alex? He's been so upset since he canceled Project Z."

We arrived on the third floor and entered Dr. Merrett's reception area, where Margaret was working at her desk. "You just missed him, Kristin," she said regretfully, raising her head toward the open door of Dr. Merrett's inner office. "He just left."

"I'm sure he'll be right back, Alex," Kristin said hopefully. "He never misses an appointment with me."

The three of us turned toward the hallway door where the sound of a low, humming motor was approaching us. Gliding into the room on bristled feet that vacuumed the floor as they moved was a tall, slim, cylindrical robot with eight arms, large pockets containing cleaning supplies in the midsection, a head with a humanlike face of pliable material whose mouth curved up in a smile, and a name painted onto his chest: Dustin.

"Good afternoon, folks," Dustin said through moving lips, as he swiveled his head and shuffled into Dr. Merrett's inner office. The cheerful electronic janitor wore a baseball cap on his head that read: "Clean Team."

"Who called Dustin in?" asked Kristin.

"I did," Margaret replied.

"But I have an appointment with my dad."

"He said he was leaving for the day just five minutes ago," said Margaret.

"But he made an *appointment* with me. He never forgets that!"

Margaret pressed an icon on her monitor, and a calendar appeared on the screen. "I have no record of it, dear. If he made an appointment to see you, it didn't get on his calendar. I'm sorry, Kris, but I'm sure he's not coming back."

Kristin's face fell. "Alex, I apologize." Her voice was heavy with disappointment. "Maybe we can catch him at home. Over the weekend might be a good time."

"Okay," I said. *If I am still living by then,* I thought.

"While I'm here, I'd like to leave these flowers, Margaret."

"Sure, Kris."

"Alex, I'll just be a minute, if you'd like to wait."

I nodded that I would, as Kristin skirted around the industrious Dustin to remove the vase of flowers she had brought her father earlier that week. "I'll throw these out in the kitchen and get some fresh water," she explained.

With Margaret resuming her work and Kristin down the hall in the kitchen, I leaned against a windowsill in the reception area, watching Dustin plunge into his cleaning routine. One arm wiped the desk, another emptied the wastebasket into a shredder inside his chest, a third sprayed a cleaner on the window, and a fourth wiped it with a towel.

When Kristin returned, she sat in the reception area, arranging the flowers. She and Margaret conversed without engaging me, so I turned my attention back to Dr. Merrett's office. Dustin was gently wiping the computer screen with a cloth. Through a spigot on one of his arms, he watered a plant on a bookcase that faced the monitor. I noted that the plant, resting on a high shelf of the bookcase, seemed to have as good a view of the screen as the window beside it.

"Did something happen to distract my dad, Margaret?"

"I'm afraid so, dear. Right before you arrived, two men were here from Earth Security."

My eyes darted to Margaret.

"Oh? Why?" asked Kristin.

"They're looking for a suspicious person they think is somewhere in Rising Tide."

"Gee, if ES is involved, it must be serious," said Kristin. "It must be a . . . spy."

"I suppose."

"A spy from where?"

"They're looking for someone from Asteron."

"What!" gasped Kristin. "A spy from *there* . . . here?"

I moved away from the windowsill so abruptly that I bumped into Margaret's desk, shaking the items on it, because I had seen out the window two men leaving the building, two men dressed in business clothes who yesterday wore police uniforms when they broke into my apartment—Feran's spies! I steadied the desk, apologized, then placed my hands in my pockets, trying to act casual, until the two women who had suddenly turned to me looked away.

"I don't know much about it, just that ES is searching for a man they want to talk to, and your father gave them permission to look around and question the people here. He told me to alert all the divisions."

I heard a voice of such bitterness that I could not believe it was Kristin's: "I hope they get this guy fast. He should be punished for snooping on us and for working for those horrible people!"

In a flash of guilt, I looked away from Kristin. My eyes fell on Dustin—and what I saw next astonished me. One of his arms reached up to the small plant on the bookcase. Then his prong-like fingers closed, as if they were clutching something on the soil, but nothing was there. The arm moved to a small compartment that slid open in Dustin's shoulder, and the fingers dropped the imaginary object in the little bin, which closed again. The fingers then reached over to a similar compartment that slid open on the other shoulder, clutched at something that, again, was not there, and placed the imaginary object in the identical spot on the plant's soil.

"Hey, Alex, are you leaving us too?" asked Kristin.

Heading to the door, I paused to remember my manners. "I have to take care of something. Would you excuse me, please?" Then I raced out of the office, down the stairs, and out a side door of the building.

I whisked past the steely block letters that spelled SPACE TRAVEL on the lobby wall and the rocket replicas displayed under them. Avoiding the elevators, I took the stairs to the fourth floor. The building that had given me a life and that I favored above all other places was now fraught with dangers. Every voice, every footstep, every glimpse of a human being sent me hiding in doorways while I walked down what seemed like an interminable hallway to Frank Brennan's office. I felt my heart race in my chest, then calm momentarily, only to surge again at the next alarming item, such as a door opening or a person sneezing. I wondered how I had managed to spend my entire life in the state of a cornered rat. But that was before I had sipped wine from a crystal glass, when I had been forced to drink from Feran's stream.

Upon seeing me, Frank's eyes widened in a smile.

"May I shut this?" I asked, my hand on the door.

"Sure. Have a seat, Alex. Say, are you okay? You're whispering."

"I need to talk to you." I sat down, facing Frank at his desk.

"I'm glad you're here, Alex. I want to tell you something too. Mykroni called me to say he heard about my accomplishments in Housekeeping. He wants me to come to his office to talk about robotics. It sounds as if he might have a job in mind."

"Good."

"It was *you* who told him about me, wasn't it?"

"Yes."

"You know, Chuck's name never came up, and I hope it never will! I felt as if I could tell Mykroni what I really accomplished here, even if it does make a liar out of his son."

"I think you can tell him the truth and he will listen."

"Thanks, Alex. I owe you one."

"If you mean you would like to help me, I do have some questions for you."

"Shoot."

When I told Frank about the peculiar movement in Dustin's cleaning procedure, he pressed a control on his computer to summon the robot to his office. He gestured for me to follow him to an inner office, which contained a wall of instrumentation to rival my flight deck.

"This console controls the Clean Team," Frank explained, as we sat before the grid of buttons, lights, computer screens, and electronic panels.

Soon we heard the low humming sound of Dustin arriving, his vacuuming feet removing the dirt particles on the floor as he approached us. Frank sprang open a door on Dustin's back to access his control panel, then pressed a few keys. Projecting from Dustin's eyes into the space before us, a three-dimensional holographic image appeared of Dr. Merrett's office, with Dustin starting his janitorial routine.

"When did you see the weird move, Alex?"

"After Dustin watered the plant on the bookcase."

Frank sped the action up to that point, then played in slow motion the maneuver I had described, in which Dustin seemed to remove something from the plant and store it in one of his shoulders, then replace the item on the plant with something that he took from his other shoulder.

"Hmmm. I see what you mean," said Frank. "I never noticed that before. Let's see if it's on my master program."

Frank activated a function on his instrument panel, producing another hologram of Dustin at work in Dr. Merrett's office, exactly like the image we saw from the robot, but with one exception. On this master program, after

Dustin watered the plant, he completely skipped the maneuver I had questioned, advancing to the one that followed it.

"It looks as if someone added a few lines of code directly to Dustin, but never copied them onto my master program. That's against the rules!"

"Do other robots in the Clean Team have the program for Dr. Merrett's office?" I asked.

"No, only Dustin." Frank checked the compartments on Dustin's shoulders. "These storage bins are empty now, but I guess they once contained something to make sense out of the movements you saw. But what?"

"Do you have any security checks for the robots that clean the executive offices?"

"You know, because the bosses have office safes for their documents and passwords for their computer files, we haven't thought much about the robots gaining access to restricted information."

"Who could have changed Dustin's code? Could Chuck have done it?"

"Chuck is capable of writing a few lines of program. So are other people. The programming language I use for the Clean Team is also used by other departments at MAS. It's called QuikCode."

"I see."

"It's not as if we keep the Clean Team a secret. They roam the halls. They're on the elevators. They're in people's offices. They use a known programming language. Someone familiar with QuikCode could figure out the program and make changes, I suppose, although I never thought about that before."

"When was the change made?"

Frank punched keys in Dustin's back, setting his hologram in motion again, until we came to the image of the movement in question.

"Let me find out the date when this programming was done," said Frank, freezing Dustin's action at that point and pressing more keys in the robot's control panel. "It was in May, two and a half years ago. The maneuver you saw, with Dustin removing something from the plant's soil and placing something else on it, was programmed then."

"And the other day you said Project Z started in April of that same year, right?"

"That's right. Project Z started in April; Dustin's code was changed a few weeks later." Frank's worried eyes scanned mine. "What are you thinking, Alex?"

A camera. That was what I was thinking. A small, waterproof video camera—no doubt camouflaged to blend in with its setting. This device could have been disguised as a small rock, because the plant already had some shiny stones for decoration sitting on the soil. This camera would have been focused on Dr. Merrett's monitor, recording images but apparently not transmitting them. Maybe the thieves did not want to risk electronic transmission of the data, which could potentially be discovered and traced to them, so they had Dustin physically place and replace the camera regularly, thereby making the activity traceable only as far as the robot. Once Dustin left Dr Merrett's office with the used camera, someone could open the compartments manually, remove that device, and insert a new one to be planted on Dr. Merrett's shelves during Dustin's next scheduled cleaning time. This someone could be hard to find, because Dustin roamed the halls and came into contact with many people.

"Unless that plant eats some kind of special plant food that has to be taken away too, I can't explain what Dustin was doing," Frank added.

Dustin waited patiently for us to complete our examination, a benign smile on his face.

"Could someone on your staff have changed the code?" I asked.

"A few of them would be able to. But wait, no one from my staff was here two and a half years ago, so none of them could have programmed the sequence you saw in Dustin."

"You mean your staff does not remain employed for very long?"

"I mean *Chuck's* staff. Everybody had run-ins with Chuck at some point. When he got heavy-handed with them, they'd quit or get fired. And the best workers left the soonest. That is, until Chuck left Housekeeping two months ago for greener pastures. I don't know how his promotion is working out for Dr. Merrett, but it's allowing me to build a more stable department here."

"You had mentioned that Chuck and Dr. Merrett were carrying the pieces of the dismantled invention to the compactor when they were together at Project Z on the day before Dr. Merrett's memo came out. How do you know that?"

"That's what my friend Mike, the security guard at Project Z, said."

"Did they both go to the compactor, or did only one handle the matter?"

"I'll tell you what. I guess there's some valuable equipment remaining in that building, because Mike's still assigned there. He works weeknights and Sundays." Frank glanced at his watch. "It's after six, so he should be on duty. Let's go talk to him."

The lobby of the building that housed Project Z was stark. Glass entrance doors led us into a hollow space without adornments of any kind. A guard's desk and a security passage with a face scanner were the only objects it contained. Frank introduced me to his friend Mike, the security guard who sat at the desk.

"You're the pilot, aren't you?" Mike asked me as we shook hands. "Frank told me about the fantastic ride you gave him."

"I think we both enjoyed it."

"Say, Mike," said Frank, "an incident happened with one of the Clean Team that I'll have to report to Security for investigation. It's raised some questions we have about the Sunday Dr. Merrett dismantled Project Z."

"Oh?" Mike was an older man with a soft voice and an easy smile; however, an intensity in his eyes told me he took the matter seriously.

Frank began. "First of all, we were wondering how Chuck Whitman got inside this building that day."

"He and Dr. Merrett walked in here together. The boss asked me to let Chuck in. By the way, only Dr. Merrett could authorize someone outside the project to come in. So I let Chuck in through the locked door around the side of the lobby while Dr. Merrett came in the usual way, through the face-scanner entrance here."

"And the two of them came out with two big boxes, right?"

"That's right. I personally had to let Chuck out; otherwise, the alarms would have gone off. Anyway, they left with two big wooden boxes on a motorized dolly. I let Chuck and the boxes out through the locked door, and Dr. Merrett left the usual way, through the face-scanner entrance."

"How'd you know the pieces of Project Z were what was inside the boxes?" Frank continued.

"Dr. Merrett mentioned it on the way out. Come to think of it, that was odd, because he never commented on his business before; he was always tight-lipped about the project. But that day he said that he and Chuck were headed for the compactor to destroy the material from Project Z. I guess because his memo about the project's cancellation came out the next morning, he figured the whole thing was no longer a secret."

"Did both men go to the compactor with the boxes?" I asked.

"As far as I could see. They both stepped onto the motorized dolly with the boxes and rode around the building toward the compactor."

"Are there any records there that the materials were actually destroyed?" I continued.

"No. We don't keep records at that compactor."

"And was anyone else with them?" Frank asked.

"No."

"Have you ever been inside Project Z, Mike?" I asked.

"Not inside the flexite area, no."

"Would you say that the security systems at MAS are good?"

"They're good, Alex, yes."

"Impenetrable?"

"There could always be something we've overlooked, of course. When modern advances make possible better security, they also make possible new ways to breach it. Take fingerprints, for example. We used to employ them at security entry points and also for computer passwords. But the crooks found credible ways to duplicate them, so we had to find new ways. We've also used iris recognition, but that can be gotten around with high-resolution images of the eye. Then there's the matter of some of these methods being too intrusive, and we like to avoid having our staff and visitors grumbling. So, boys, that's why you've got *me* here—a live security guard is still pretty hard to beat," Mike said, pleased with the notion.

"Do the people here worry about security?" I prodded.

"They do. Maybe not as much as they should." He stroked his face thoughtfully. "I've read that in the old days, when Earth was filled with power-hungry rulers and wars, security was a huge concern. Now it's something we take care of, sure, but I suppose we're not as worried about it."

"How long have you worked for MAS?"

"Since before you were born," said Mike, smiling at me. "About thirty years now."

I decided to take a chance. I took out my pad and pencil to sketch Feran's cargo. "Have you ever seen an object that looked like this?"

"No, never."

Mike waited for more questions, but Frank and I were finally silent.

"Anything else, boys?" he asked. We shook our heads. "Then let me warn you. If you know something that's in the slightest way suspicious, you need to fill out a report, you hear?" We both nodded. "Don't go playing amateur detectives. Security has to know what's going on."

"Sure, Mike, of course," said Frank.

Another puzzle, I thought. First, many people had access to Dustin and could have changed his programming, leaving me with no clear suspect. Then the evidence showed that the components of Project Z never left Dr. Merrett's personal supervision, leaving me again with no suspect who could be Feran's spy.

We said good-bye to Mike and started walking toward the exit door.

"Oh, by the way, there was one odd thing that happened that day," he added.

We stopped and turned around to him.

"You see, Dr. Merrett checked in twice that day, but he checked out only once."

"What do you mean?" asked Frank.

"Our computer records the people who go in and out of this building. Well, Dr. Merrett went through the checkpoint once earlier that day, about nine in the morning, before I started my shift at noon. He came through a second time when he asked me to let Chuck in. Then I saw them leave with the boxes. That's the strange thing. We don't have any record of Dr. Merrett checking out the first time. We had our computer serviced, but the technicians found nothing wrong with it. Yet that kind of thing has never happened before or since. Now you're a computer whiz"—Mike turned to Frank—"so would you know how that could've happened?"

"Was there was an interruption in the power supply?"

"Not that I know of."

"Did the computer crash for a brief time?"

"Not that I know of."

"That's strange," Frank concluded.

"We thought so too."

Something is missing, I thought, as I walked with Frank back to Space Travel. First came Project Z, then shortly after it began, Dustin's code was changed. This alteration allowed Dustin to hide a sensor of some kind, a tiny camera camouflaged as a leaf, clump of soil, stone, or other item, and to remove and replace it regularly to spy on Dr. Merrett. That was cause and effect. But did Project Z really come first? The security windows in Dr. Merrett's office came before Project Z. What prompted them? There I had an effect without a cause. Dr. Merrett was concerned about security two months before his secret project started, when he installed the security windows. And I remembered Kristin saying she hated Asteron for something that happened before Project Z began. Did I need to reach further back? Was there a significant event that occurred earlier?

"Frank, did anything happen at MAS *before* Dr. Merrett got his security windows in February of the year that Project Z started? Something that would have prompted him to tighten security at that time?"

Frank looked up to the darkening sky, thinking. "Nothing that I can remember."

That evening, I stood with Kristin on her lawn. Although seeing her was reason enough to draw me there, I also asked to borrow her plane for a task I needed to perform.

"Sure. I keep the door to my plane unlocked. You can just go in and start it, Alex."

Before I left with the little red craft, I held Kristin in my arms and kissed her. For one enchanting moment the events on top of the mountain with Kristin were more real than Feran and his spies.

"I will bring it back without disturbing you, so you can get a good night's sleep. Then I will go home and do the same. Okay, honey?"

She raised her eyebrows, surprised by the last word, but not as surprised as I was. Something was happening to me inside. Like a plane worn by combat, I was ready for a refurbished engine, one that could lift me higher than I had ever climbed before.

"Okay," she said softly, tilting her head back for one last, lingering kiss.

When I returned Kristin's plane to her lawn, the evening sky shimmered with stars, promising fair weather for the air show tomorrow, I thought, as I walked across the road toward my hidden ship. There I would perform my final—and most dreaded—chore of the day.

"Good evening, Mr. White," said the message in my spacecraft, the mocking edges of Feran's voice palpable through the sharp peaks on the screen. "It seems we are closing the distance between us, and we shall soon meet. That much you know. But there is something else you do not know, Mr. White."

The voice paused. The peaks fell. I waited, too exhausted to guess.

"We know there is a *girl*."

I slapped my hands against my face as if to smash the words that stung me. The other voice, the one I thought had been silenced forever, was now back, stronger and more reproachful than before: *It is your fault— It is your fault that she—*

"Stop it! Stop it!" I ordered, but the voice shouted louder: *It is your fault that she died!*

"We know you have a girlfriend," said the outer voice. "Inquiries around Rising Tide place you in a shop buying clothes, with a female on your arm, doting over you." The voice pattern changed color on the screen as Feran laughed maliciously. "I should have known a female would be your demise—again!" The voice sneered. "Tell me—do you think Feran, the supreme ruler of Asteron, cannot find one little female on Planet Earth and remove her? What method of erasure would entertain you the most? Could it be . . . *hanging?*"

Feran paused, his final word echoing in the still night.

"Get that cargo to me by midnight, and I will give you the password to navigate my spacecraft. Then you and your cupcake can blast yourselves out of the galaxy. That is my offer: the cargo for the girl. If you refuse, prepare to watch another of your little diversions swinging by her sweet neck."

My hands covered my ears as two voices—the haunting one inside and the vile one outside—rattled through my mind.

CHAPTER 17

On a runway near the ocean, eight planes left the ground in quick succession. The powerful engines rumbled like an earthquake through the spectator stands at the airfield. Reckoning Day had arrived, and the Gold Streaks' air show was its main event.

In the midmorning sky, with me in the lead slot of one group, we formed two graphite diamonds, with a shiny gold streak across each fuselage. I flew inverted, moving hundreds of miles an hour, with the wing tips to each side of me and the nose behind almost touching my plane. Being in the first slot of our four-plane configuration, I felt the combined disturbance of the three other crafts in my air flow, which meant I constantly had to maintain just the right pull on the stick to hold me within the tight bounds of our formation.

We looped and rolled in close proximity and executed formation changes at high speeds. After performing in our group of four, we linked with our other teammates to create a series of geometric patterns in the sky, each one looking like a single speeding figure painted with eight bold strokes on a blue canvas. For our final maneuver, eight glossy fuselages, clustered like sticks of dynamite, stretched vertically into the sky. Then the cluster burst apart as if the dynamite were exploding.

After an intermission, I aligned my plane with Kristin's on a wide runway for our two-plane demonstration. "Happy birthday, Alex," she whispered over my radio. To the sound of the show's music transmitted into our cockpits, Kristin and I lifted off simultaneously, which felt as if we were rising for a dance. We did a figure-eight in broad loops that filled the sky. Then we rolled, stopping sharply every ninety degrees. Flying upright alongside Kristin and low to the ground, past the smear of color that was the spectators, I flipped my plane upside down in a clean, split-second motion. From my

145

headset I heard the crowd applauding. Their cheers intensified my own excitement, and I think Kristin would have said I was smiling.

With our noses to the vertical and our planes stacked together, we climbed, moving as one shiny needle threading through a cottony puff of thin white clouds. Maneuvering in such close proximity required of Kristin and me an almost hypnotic awareness of each other that was somehow part of our intimacy. We passed the stands in tight mirror formations—belly to belly, then canopy to canopy. We looped, rolled, and turned gracefully through the air to music made for dancing. For our finale, we separated, then flew toward each other in what seemed to be a high-speed collision course in full view of the gasping spectators, until we broke at the end, narrowly missing each other.

Was it the dizzying physical motion or the excitement it produced that made me feel light-headed? I wondered, as I had for years. Each time my plane brushed against the clouds, the thrill it gave me intensified. It was like being with an enchanting woman who grew more exciting with every new encounter. I felt the power of the plane and the control I had over it, and then the moment became joyful. It was my home run.

I thought of the two things that thrilled me—power and control. They were the very same things that Feran also craved. How could the things that made me triumphant be the same things that made him depraved? I knew that I did not belong with Feran. I belonged with the Earthlings in their world. My power and control were a personal matter between me and my plane, but Feran's power and control involved breaking people's spines. Feran and I were opposites. And in some way Asteron and Earth were opposites too. What was the meaning behind these two different powers in the universe? I wondered.

When Kristin and I landed, the wheels of our planes hit the broad runway at the same instant. Through my headset, I heard her cheer our performance. But my mood suddenly cooled, because being on the ground was fraught with danger for me. I quickly slipped away from the other fliers and avoided the crowds that packed the stands, clustered around the food tents, and walked along the field to view the many aircraft being exhibited as part of the show. People were everywhere, and Feran's spies could be among them. I walked past the procession of planes on display and over to an empty hangar just beyond the activities where I could observe the ceremonies unnoticed, concealed in the shade of the structure. I watched the events taking place on a flower-laden makeshift stage that held a band. As I stood in the distance, the chief of police stepped up to a podium, greeted the people, and introduced the mayor, who thanked the Gold Streaks for their performance and made several other remarks.

Then a senator named Robert Goodwin ascended the steps to the stage with a sprightly gait. As he took the podium, his white hair and trim, energetic body formed a pleasing blend of wisdom and youth.

Good morning, ladies and gentlemen. Today we pay tribute to our beloved Planet Earth, which we call the Home of the Individuals, and we salute the independent life that is our way. People of every human species from around the galaxy flock here above all other places. They choose to live on Earth, although our nations give them nothing by way of food, clothing, shelter, or other provisions. They come here because the one thing we do offer is that which makes human progress and happiness possible: *freedom*. I'd like to take a moment to explain the meaning of the celebration we call Reckoning Day, for those of you who are new to our planet and also for those of us born here, so we may rekindle our appreciation of our homeland.

For many centuries Earth was beset by the clash of two irreconcilable forces, two opposite approaches to life. This conflict was given many names over the ages in the numerous countries of Earth. Ultimately, it became known as the Great Clash Between the Meddlers and the Individuals.

These two antagonists disagreed over how a society should function and what role the state should play in a person's life. The Meddlers said that the state must direct people's lives for their own good, but the Individuals said that people's lives were theirs to live as they choose. The Meddlers thought the state should control and redistribute people's property to serve what they said was a greater good, but the Individuals thought that people's property was as sacred as their lives and must not be tampered with or taken away by anyone.

For many centuries, in one form or another, it was almost always the Meddlers who were in charge of Earth's various countries. They sought to use their power to manage the lives of their citizens. "We will provide for everyone's welfare" was the way they put it. Although they told the people what they allegedly would give them, the Meddlers never mentioned what they had to take away. If the people needed jobs, housing, food, or countless other things, the Meddlers sought to provide them. How did they do this? By making laws to control the people who produced them, and by taking away from the citizens the money they had earned and were going to spend the way each saw fit, so that the Meddlers could spend that money the way they saw fit. The result was that people were no longer captains of their own lives. The people worked at jobs that were regulated by the Meddlers, for wages that were approved by them, to earn money that was taxed by them, to support causes chosen by them. The schools were run by the Meddlers, medical care was arranged by them, and pensions were given out by them. Even when people died, they were still not free of the Meddlers, because their property would again be taxed by them before it ever reached their heirs.

If a person decided to run a business, the Meddlers would have rules on who to hire, where to build a plant, what permissions to get from which agencies in order to operate, and, of course, how much of the profits, if there were any, would be taken in taxes.

As you can imagine, the Meddlers needed lots of money to feed their many bureaucracies and agencies, so they helped themselves to repeated dips into citizens' wallets.

The Individuals were dismayed that the people could not decide things for themselves and choose their own actions. The Individuals said that this was all wrong. It was not the state's job to provide for the people, which meant to seize the citizens' wealth, intrude in their lives, and funnel their money to the rulers' favored groups and causes. The Individuals said that the state was their servant—not their master—and that its only job was to keep the peace, which meant to protect the citizens from criminals from within and without. But this was a very important job, because it defended each person's life, liberty, and property, and made a civilized society possible.

I looked out at the crowd. The movement in the field had ceased. The thousands of people there had become silent, and they seemed solemn as they listened attentively.

If you study history, you'll be amazed at the extent of the meddling that occurred. There was no aspect of life that was untouched by the state. It issued hundreds of thousands of pages of laws to control all the goods and services the people used. Then, as the Meddlers got even bolder, they issued laws to control how people could express their opinions and participate in political activities. You can imagine what that led to. And this happened in the countries that were considered to be the freest. I won't mention the open savagery reached in countries that even more fully smothered the individual's life.

Now, I'm a businessman. I serve as a senator just as a juror serves in a court case: for a limited time and purpose. My job in the senate is part time. Because the state we have today can't make any laws that interfere with commerce, I don't have a whole lot of committees to meet with or legislation to pass. No big shots or special groups take me out to lunch, invite me to parties, give me expensive gifts, or try to slip me money under the table, because I can wield no power over their lives. Who am I to tell any of you how to live? It's not my place to tell you what schools to send your kids to, what compensation to accept for your work, or how to spend your money. That's all your business, just as it's not your place to tell me what products to make in my plant, or how much to charge for them. You should not have to bail me out with your taxpayers' money if I fail, or be able to rob me of my profits if I succeed. And if any of us has problems or misfortunes, we seek private help that's given to us voluntarily. We don't think it's right to pick our neighbors' pockets to help us out, or to elect a representative to do that for us. That's the way things now run here on Earth.

But back then there were many wars between the two opposing forces because they could not coexist. Then a hundred years ago, there was one final struggle, called the Great Clash. This conflict had the highest stakes of all, because the winner was to claim the Earth and the loser was to be banished forever. It was the Individuals who prevailed in the Great Clash and thereby won the Earth. At that fateful time a century ago, which history calls the Reckoning, they banished the Meddlers. And the people of Earth took sides.

Many went with the Meddlers. Some were misguided, but others had different motives. Those with an appetite for wielding power over people knew where their bread was buttered. And those who dreamed of obtaining, in one way or another, a guarantee against life's risks—a way to avoid the responsibility of governing their own lives, a way to be taken care of, a way to further their own lives by controlling their fellow citizens—those people went with the Meddlers. However, those believing that people are the masters of their own lives stayed with the Individuals. Those believing it was their right—and glory—to run their own affairs, to deal with one another as free people not forced or compelled, and to keep what they had earned, remained with the Individuals.

Today the outcome of this great battle is obvious for everyone to see. Earth is thriving with the greatest level of production, advancement, and prosperity ever known. The Meddlers and their followers had their chance. They took with them the plants, animals, food, equipment, and supplies they needed to start life over on a newly discovered planet, a place that was the jewel of the galaxy, a fertile land with a mild climate and superb conditions for human life. But they purged our names and customs from their history. They tried to hide from their later generations any knowledge of the kind of society we offered. And they vilified us and blamed us for the problems they caused themselves. They did not heed our advice that in order to survive and thrive, people must be left free. The Meddlers have turned their jewel of a planet into a wound on the face of the galaxy, and we denounce them for their evil ways. Perhaps the most startling difference of all between the two clashing worlds is that the banished achieved only misery, but the people of the Earth achieved happiness. The great lesson we learned from the Reckoning is: *If your destination is happiness, freedom is the fuel to take you there.*

So, ladies and gentlemen, that is the story of Planet Earth. We celebrate the Reckoning because it is the birthday of Earth as a planet that truly supports human life.

He paused, smiling, as the audience applauded.

Let us now continue our program with a song we play each year in tribute to our ancestors, whom we have to thank for our way of life today. They had the courage to defend our freedom. They had the daring to fight for our liberty. And they had the prowess to banish the Meddlers forever to the planet of Asteron!

The senator's final word reverberated through my mind, leaving no room in my awareness for anything else. The band began to play a stirring melody, but I was only dimly conscious of it. I do not know how long I stood at that spot in the shade of the hangar, staring vacantly into space.

Finally, I felt someone shaking me by the shoulders.

"Alex. Hey, Alex," Frank Brennan was saying. "Are you okay? You look stunned, like you just got bopped on the head."

"I feel okay, Frank," I whispered, barely able to find my voice, astonished by the revelations I had just heard.

"What are you doing all the way out here by yourself? Everybody wants to shake hands with the Gold Streaks. And you missed all the publicity shots the media took of your team. Don't you know you're a celebrity, man? And all the food's down there. The hot dogs are going fast."

"I have no appetite right now."

"I'm glad I found you. I want to tell you something, Alex. Last night, after I left you, I went through everything again in my mind. There *was* something that happened just before Dr. Merrett had the security windows installed."

I stared at Frank intently.

"It made the news at the time but died down soon after. It was a private matter that Dr. Merrett was very quiet about, and he gave no statements to the media. It never got recorded on my calendar because it was something personal that happened to him. A few weeks before he changed his office windows, a thief broke into his house, a thief that I don't think was ever caught. I don't know if it connects at all with security at MAS, but something very bad happened. You see, during that robbery, Dr. Merrett's wife was killed."

CHAPTER 18

"Alex, what are you doing here? Is the sun too much for you?"

Kristin's perfume refreshed the stale air in the hangar where I stood. After Frank had left, I called her on my phone, asking that she come here.

"I'm sorry you didn't get to be in the team pictures, Alex. We looked all over for you. I called, but you didn't answer your phone."

"Kristin, I have to talk to you!"

She stretched her arms, and she pranced about like a fawn ready for play. "And I have to talk to you too! I have to tell you that I think your flying was terrific and our demo was thrilling!" She looked at me, her freckled face lit by both a childlike joy and a sensuous smile. "Will you let me take you out for your birthday? There's a restaurant on the beach where we can dance outside and watch the waves. Alex, it'll be enchanting!"

"Kristin, I cannot." How could I tell her that I must not see her as long as Feran was alive? If the Earthlings' medicine kept people going for 150 years, Feran had about a hundred left.

"I'll bet you're worried about Mykroni's checklist. It's a holiday, and besides, you can't work on the night of your birthday."

She paused for my agreement, but I could not give it.

"Were you planning to go to MAS tonight, Alex?"

"No." How could I tell her that I must not go back there until I could celebrate Feran's funeral?

"Oh, I know—you thought you could meet my dad tonight, because I told him I had a boyfriend."

I grabbed her arms and shook her urgently. "Kristin, do not tell anyone I am your boyfriend! Swear to me you will not!"

The smile vanished from her face. She whispered, crestfallen. "Don't you want to be my boyfriend?"

"No! I cannot be!"

She looked at me aghast. "I thought you were . . . my . . . boyfriend."

"You must not use that word anymore!"

She pushed me away sharply. "Maybe you really *are* what you say you are. Maybe you're some kind of creature that's not human like us at all, a creature that doesn't feel anything. Maybe you're just . . . empty . . . inside!"

I pulled her body against mine. Her arms flew up to punch my chest. But I easily restrained them behind her with one hand while I squeezed her tightly with the other, pressing my mouth hard on hers the entire time. Her futile cries were muffled by the force of my mouth, and her desperate resistance was reduced to a quiver by my grip. Finally, I lifted my head to look at her.

"Be quiet, Kristin, unless you want me to remind you, right here, that such capacities as I do have are enough to make *you* feel human!"

Her eyes flashed over me excitedly before she could stop herself, daring me to carry out my threat. Too distraught to consider the matter, I released her. She stood staring at me, her face no longer angry but injured. Her eyes became glistening ponds about to overflow.

"If you make love to me on Wednesday, then tell me you don't want to know me on Friday . . . it hurts. It makes me want to hurt you."

"Kristin, I am in danger, *real danger*! And as long as you have any dealings with me, you are in danger too! I will not have that!"

"Now, Alex, you must be imagining things again."

I remembered how much I had wanted to say certain things to someone, but our time had run out. "Kristin, if I have to go away . . . suddenly, I want you to know that I will come back. If I am . . . alive . . . I will come back for you, because you make my life so . . . joyful."

Her face softened. She curled her arms around my neck. "Alex, what are you saying? I can't imagine why you'd think you have to go away, and I can't imagine how crushed I'd be if you did. Tell me," she whispered, her hands holding my face. "Tell me what's bothering you. I helped you with the other problem, didn't I?" She smiled playfully. "Maybe I can help you again." Then her smile tightened to a look that was earnest, almost solemn. "I want to help you, because you're not . . . empty inside. You're as not-empty inside as anyone I know."

How could I reveal my situation, especially with my habit of imagining dangers and with her animosity toward my homeland? Even the senator's astonishing story of the Meddlers could not explain the personal antagonism Kristin felt toward Asteron. I could not trust something in her that I did not understand.

"Kristin, you *can* help me. You said that for two people to have closeness, they must talk to one another about important things. The other night I told you something upsetting to me. Now I have to ask you about something painful to you."

She looked at me, puzzled.

"Tell me about your mother's death."

"My mother?" Her eyebrows arched in astonishment. "What does she have to do with you being in danger?"

"Your mother's death has something to do with Project Z, does it not?"

"No, nothing. You know Project Z doesn't exist anymore, yet it's like a bogeyman—that's something unreal that scares people. It's what Project Z is: a bogeyman! First, my father has been upset ever since he canceled it. He didn't come to see me fly today. . . . For reasons I can't imagine, he missed my show. You know he taught me to fly when I was nine. I wanted him to see me—" Her voice broke. I drew her closer, and she rested her head on my chest. "I hardly ever see him anymore. Now for some strange reason, *you're* afraid of Project Z, and you say you're going to go away suddenly. My mother left me suddenly!" A few warm tears seeped through my shirt.

"Kristin, you and I are both in danger. Your father may be too."

She looked at me once again, not understanding. I ran my fingers over her cheeks to clear away the fallen drops.

"Now tell me what happened to your mother. There was a robbery of some kind? Was that what prompted your father to set up a security system for your home?"

"Alex, I can't imagine how any of this can be connected to you at all, but I'll tell you. It's not a secret." She looked at me earnestly. "Maybe the more you know, the more you'll understand, so you'll see you're not in any danger."

I led her to a bench inside the hangar. We sat in the shadow, concealed from the events outside, hand in hand.

"Next January will be three years since I lost my mother. I was eighteen when it happened. That night I went out with my parents and Mykroni and his wife to a dance performance, a ballet. The five of us liked the ballet, so every year my father got us season tickets—that means we go to all the different programs staged for the year.

"That afternoon my father called my mother to say he'd be late. A report he was waiting for had just arrived, so he planned to stay at the office, skip dinner, and read it. My mom reminded him of the ballet, which he had forgotten. He didn't want to miss it, so he decided to bring the report home to read.

"When he got home, he locked the report in his office safe. As we left for the theater, he programmed the fireplace in his office to start later, before we were to arrive home, so he'd come back to a warm fire. You see, he planned to read the report after the show, and that January night the weather was perfect for using the fireplace—a chilly Friday during a cold spell.

"Now, my mom's back was bothering her that night. Quick Fix told her she needed to see a doctor, which she was going to do. Anyway, the pills Quick Fix gave her wore off during the performance, and it was painful for her to sit up, so at the intermission, she decided to go home to bed. My father wanted to leave with her. I remember how troubled he was that she was in pain. But she made light of the matter, insisting that he stay. He had set aside his work specially to see the performance, she said, so she didn't want him to miss the rest of it. Finally he agreed, reluctantly. We both kissed her good-bye. We didn't know we'd never . . .

"We think that when she got home, Mother must have heard noises from Father's office, because she went in there." Kristin struggled to keep her voice steady. "We found that she had been . . . strangled . . . in a struggle with a thief who was stealing my father's report."

"What was in this report?"

"It was an investigation my father ordered into an accident that had occurred at MAS a few weeks earlier. My father had been studying unusual rocks from the planet of a star in our galaxy. During an experiment, a lab technician was exposed to the new material and suffered an odd injury. I don't know much about it, except that the technician was somehow incapacitated. My father was very upset—and tight-lipped—about the injury. He vowed he would search for an antidote for whatever substance had injured the worker."

I nodded, following Kristin's story.

"In addition to the insurance MAS carries for workers injured on the job, my father paid the employee's family a lot of money. He was fond of the technician, so maybe that's partly why he wanted to give them something extra, but there was another reason. In return for the money, he asked the family not to make any public statements about the matter."

"Why would your father want to keep the accident a secret?"

"I don't know. But in general, companies don't like bad publicity. My father surely wouldn't have wanted to have a big news splash about how MAS discovered a strange new substance that harmed someone."

"Did the injured employee die?"

"No. He's still alive. He lives with his wife in Clear Creek; that's a desert town a little over a hundred miles east of here."

"What kind of injury was it?"

"I don't know. He was found on the floor of the lab by his co-workers. I was in school and didn't work at MAS yet, so I didn't hear much about it."

"You told me that Earth's doctors can fix anything."

"This was something they couldn't fix."

"And did your father find an antidote?"

"Not that I know of."

"What is the technician's name?"

"Steve Caldwell."

"Did the thief get the report?"

The question provoked fresh pain for Kristin. I put an arm around her shoulders.

"Yes and no. There were signs that my mother . . . struggled . . . with the thief before she was strangled. He had already opened the safe and must have had the report in his hands when she caught him, because she apparently seized it from him and threw it into the fireplace. Charred pages from the report were found in the fire, so I don't think anyone ever knew how much the robber actually got and how much was burned."

"Why would someone want this information?"

"I don't know."

"Would your mother have known? Did your father tell her about his work? Did they have closeness?"

She nodded, her face wistful. "They spent many evenings talking in the garden. On Sundays they lingered after breakfast, talking on the patio. My father confided in my mother about everything and respected her advice. My mom acted as if the sun rose and set around that man; she was always interested in any matter than involved my dad. Mother might have known something about the report, because she apparently tried very hard . . . she fought . . . to destroy the papers. Maybe she'd be alive today . . . if she had just . . . run away."

I asked softly, "Who was the thief?"

"I don't know. He was never caught. The authorities launched a big investigation, but never arrested any suspects."

"What kind of investigation?"

"Earth Security got involved—that's the agency that investigates espionage that threatens the planet as a whole—but neither the authorities nor my dad said much about it. I know only that the man who killed my mother was never found."

"Was anything else stolen from your house?"

"Just the report."

"Shortly after the crime, your father tightened security, right?"

She nodded. "Losing my mother was devastating for him. He worried about my safety afterward. He put alarm systems in the house. We had never worried about security before; I used to go out and leave the door unlocked. But after the break-in, I felt . . . uneasy, so I was glad to have the alarms. My father had special windows installed in his office at MAS too, so no one could look in."

"Did he suspect someone of looking in?"

"Not that I know of. You see, when we had this . . . horrible experience, it made us feel a little paranoid. So I think he just beefed up security in general."

"And then, a few months after the robbery, Project Z began."

"Well, I guess so. But what would that have to do with my mother's death? Do you have any evidence that Project Z had anything to do with my mother's death?"

"No."

I wondered if I were imagining some connection, just because one matter occurred soon after the other and both involved extra security. That was not much of a link. However, I now knew that thieves—or spies—obtained information from Dr. Merrett's home just before Project Z began, and from his office, through Dustin, after Project Z started. I knew that Mrs. Merrett lost her life trying to protect some of this information. And I knew that the supreme meddler, Feran, possessed a flexite suit from Project Z and brought spies to Earth.

"As far as I know, Project Z was just another assignment for my dad; it had nothing to do with my mother's death."

"But why was Project Z a secret? It must mean that something was being produced that was dangerous."

"No, not at all, Alex."

"Could it have been something for the military? MAS does work for them."

"Sure, but we do work for a lot of other customers too. Even though we started as an aerospace company, we're diversified now. Project Z could have been anything. It could have been a hot new product, maybe a vehicle or computer, made for a company that wants to market it before a competitor steps in. Project Z could have been a new consumer gadget, costing a fortune to design. My father could have been bound to secrecy, without Project Z having anything to do with the military or dangerous inventions."

"Then why would your father say, in his memo to the staff, that he could not release Project Z to the world because it had 'far-reaching and irrevocable consequences'?"

"I don't know, Alex. But how could this possibly concern you?"

I grabbed her arms and turned her toward me. I said gravely, "If I tell you why, your life will be in danger. It already is. You must promise you will tell no one that you are my girlfriend. No one!"

She sighed in the same way she had on other days when I had thought she was in danger and I tried to attack the gardener, her instructor, and then Officer Hodges. She shook her head, her half smile of frustration softened by affection. "Alexander, this is ridiculous!"

"Kristin, please!"

"All right. I have no reason to tell anyone our personal business. No one at work knows I see you, and I like it that way. So okay, I promise. Now do you feel . . . calmer?"

"I have one more question."

"Oh?"

"Why do you hate Asteron?"

She stared into space in the icy way that she always did at the mention of my vile homeland. She stood up and walked a few steps from me, as if she were crossing back into the past.

"When we found my mother, she was clutching a piece of the robber's shirt pocket that had ripped off in the struggle. She was also holding a gold coin from the thief's pocket, an unusual coin I had never seen before. Now, other planets' coins, if they're hard currency like gold, are accepted in trade and circulated on Earth, just as ours are used elsewhere. So nothing could ever be proven, we were told, about the thief's origin just from the coin he had in his pocket." Bitterness sliced through her voice. "But I know what I think."

I rose from the bench to stand next to her. "What kind of coin was your mother holding?"

"One side of the coin had a picture of a farmer working in a field behind a mule, with a farm tool hitched between them that I've seen only in museums . . . a hand plow." Her voice rose in disbelief. "Can you imagine a place that keeps people sweating like slaves in a field, a place that's oblivious to the farming inventions and progress of centuries, and proud of it, boasting of this kind of life by honoring it on a coin? I think the thief came from a place that can't afford to buy a tractor, much less a robot, to make life easier, but spends its money sending someone on a spacecraft to *our* world to do us harm."

Her liquid eyes with their light, swirling hues seemed to become darker, almost black.

"On the other side of the coin was an imprint of a planet that looked like Earth, but it was no coin from here. There were words printed around the sphere, words that have haunted me ever since, along with the place they represent. You see, the coin said: *One People, One Will. Asteron.*"

CHAPTER 19

The sprawling carpet of lawn swept up to the flat-topped hedges and rounded shrubs in front of Steve Caldwell's home. I walked toward the attractive wood-and-stone house. It was tucked on a hillside in a small community that contained the only expanse of vegetation in the parched landscape around it. Built at the base of a mountain, the small town of Clear Creek was an oasis in the desert, just as Planet Earth was an oasis in the lifeless void of space surrounding it.

The Earth was my oasis, my refuge, my home. What business did Feran have on a planet that had already banished his blight a century before? Was control over all of Asteron not enough to satisfy Feran? Why did he prey on a people whose way of life he denounced? The Earthlings considered Feran's ways evil, so they sought nothing from him. Feran considered the Earthlings' ways evil, yet he and his spies were here. Was it possible that Feran could not survive without the things he denounced as evil?

Kristin had seen something unavailable to Feran's people: an Asteronian gold coin. Such coins were forbidden in my homeland because our leaders warned against what they called the idolatry of money. According to our rulers, money was evil. It drove us to accumulate more and more of it, and this led to wealth, which made some of us better off than others, which led to inequality, which everyone thought was immoral. Then why did Feran mint coins? And why did the things he considered good bring only starvation? I could clearly imagine his repulsive hand squeezing the life from Kristin's mother, for surely that monstrous deed was the work of his spies. I swung my hand at a fly with the force of Alexander the ballplayer swinging his bat to make a home run. Feran was not going to get Kristin! And was Dr. Merrett in danger too?

I now knew that Feran was linked not only to Project Z through the flexite suit in his spaceship but also to the death of Mrs. Merrett through the Asteronian coin in her hand. Was Project Z linked to the laboratory accident whose report Mrs. Merrett had died trying to rescue? That was the question I hoped Steve Caldwell could help me answer.

I now also knew that, incredibly, Asteron's ancestors were Earthlings. Did this mean that I was of their species? Did I possess the full range of their capacities? Was the Earthlings' bright laughter cocooned somewhere inside me, waiting for its wings to form?

I had obtained Steve's phone number and spoken to his wife, Kate, who was taking his calls. I explained that I was employed by MAS and asked if I could visit, because I wanted to ask Steve a few questions about his laboratory work. She eagerly invited me to their home, expressing her desire for Steve to have company. With a call to one of the pilots, who was heading east after the air show, I got a ride on his small plane, which dropped me off in Clear Creek early that Friday afternoon. My teammate also showed me where I could catch a branch of the Cheetah for my trip back.

A cheerful, young, blond-haired woman answered the door. She introduced herself as Kate Caldwell and promptly asked to see my MAS identification.

"We don't talk to the media, only to relatives, friends, and co-workers, so I was just checking," she explained, as she escorted me into a spacious living room with sun-dappled furniture and thriving plants the size of small trees. A leather couch and chairs along with a piano and a few tables were arranged on a shiny wooden floor, with a colorful rug defining the seating area. A normal, healthy-looking man about thirty years old smiled at me from the couch. Despite his handsome features, something about his smile seemed unusual.

"We have a visitor from MAS today, Steve. His name is Alexander," said Kate.

"Hello, Steve," I said.

"Hello, Alexander."

I extended my hand, and Steve shook it. I realized that his grin was odd because the skin around his eyes did not crinkle. I was used to Earthlings putting the whole of their faces into their smiles, but Steve's smile did not reach his eyes.

"It is kind of you to see me, Steve."

"Oh, Steve sees everybody," Kate said, gesturing for me to sit on a chair while she sat on the couch next to her husband. "You're not from around here, are you, Alexander? You speak differently."

"That is true, Kate."

"And you have only one name?"

"That is also true."

"So you work at MAS?"

"Yes."

"I'm always glad when someone from the company comes over. I know Steve's going to get better by seeing people he knew and talking about the work he did. Won't you, honey?" She tapped his hand, and he looked at her obligingly. "In fact, the other day Dr. John Gordon came over. How'd you like seeing John again, dear?"

"It was nice," said Steve indifferently.

"John was Steve's best friend in medical school. Now John's on the staff at the hospital near us."

"Did Steve study to be a doctor?"

"Oh, yes," said Kate.

I kept looking at Steve for a response, because it felt peculiar to discuss him in the third person with Kate, as if he were not there. But he seemed content to gaze at us blankly without volunteering to join our conversation.

"Steve was working his way through medical school. He used to work the night shift at MAS so that he could attend classes during the day."

"I see." I turned to Steve to engage him. "And do you work at the hospital too, like your friend John?"

"Yes," said Steve.

"So you have finished your training?"

"Yes."

"And you are a doctor?"

"I work in the laundry."

I tried to hide my surprise.

"Steve isn't ready to be a doctor, but he will be when he gets better," said Kate, with a strained cheerfulness. "Since he had spent years studying for his exams when the accident happened, we decided he should take them. He scored very high on the knowledge section—that part tests how much you know about medicine. You see, my husband knows medicine inside out. And he also passed the skills and techniques section. That's where the teachers direct you to perform certain tests and procedures on dummy patients that have elaborate computer mechanisms, so they react as if they're real people."

"So then Steve has passed his exams, no?"

"The section Steve failed was clinical judgment. There you get a set of conditions about a patient, and you have to decide how you'll treat."

"And could Steve not make the right decisions, based on his knowledge and skills?"

"No," Kate said, her voice now tinged with sadness. "You see, Steve couldn't decide."

"Why not, Steve?"

"I don't know," Steve replied, his eyes vacant, his tone colorless.

"You have the knowledge?" I continued.

"Yes," he said.

"And you have the skills and techniques, as you showed with the dummies?"

"Yes, I do."

"Then you can treat, right?"

"No."

"Right now Steve needs guidance," Kate explained. "If only he could have a kind of cookbook that told him which procedures to use and when, then he would be okay. He flounders when he has to decide for himself. But the skills are there. Just the other day he got to practice them, and he remembered everything. When Steve reported to the hospital for his part-time job, someone was needed to wheel a patient into a room, and Steve was told to do it. While he was wheeling her stretcher, her heart stopped beating. And what do you think Steve did?"

"Did you restart her heart, Steve?"

"Yes, I did."

"Then you *can* treat," I concluded.

"No," said Kate.

"How can that be?"

"It's hard to explain, Alexander, but when her heart stopped and no one else was around at that moment, Steve at first just continued to wheel her into the room, until one of the orderlies who knew him before the accident screamed at him to save her. Then Steve did save her. But he himself couldn't decide which was more important—to wheel her into the room or to save her life—until someone made the choice for him and ordered him to carry it out."

My thoughts suddenly crossed the universe to an engineer at the locked door of a spacecraft who also could not decide what to do in an unexpected circumstance but could only follow orders. Troubled, I stared incredulously at Steve's blank face.

"I keep hoping that being around the things he loved and the people he knew will help Steve get better. That's why I thought it was a good idea for him to work in the hospital."

"Do you like working in the hospital, Steve?" I asked.

"It's nice."

"Do you like medicine?"

"I used to."

"And now?"

"It doesn't matter."

"Do you still want to be a doctor, or do you prefer to work in the laundry?"

"Doesn't matter."

"This isn't my Steve talking! He had a passion for medicine, didn't you, dear? Now, tell Alexander the truth."

"All those ideas I had. How did I get them, anyway?" Steve replied tonelessly, looking at neither me nor Kate but gazing blankly out the window.

"Maybe you'll feel differently, honey, when you get better in other areas first. Maybe that's what needs to happen!" Kate said wishfully. "We have to work up to medicine with gradual improvements in other areas. You know, I think we should take that vacation abroad that we've always talked about."

She picked up a large book from the coffee table, one filled with colored pictures of distant places. She placed the book in Steve's hands, thumbing through the pages.

"Here's the cathedral you always wanted to see. And the art museum. And look at the statues in the old town square. And here's the ancient palace you mentioned so many times. Remember how you always wanted to visit it, dear, but we could never afford to go? Well, now we can. And look at the beaches." She paused on pages of interest to her, pointing them out to Steve. "When we get tired of sight-seeing, we can rent a house by the sea. We'll travel for my birthday. Remember how you always loved to take me to romantic places on my birthday? You'll have your chance again, honey, and it'll all come back to you. I know it will!" She turned to me. "Steve loves history and art. He always wanted to make a trip abroad to visit historic sites."

When Kate released the pages of the book, they fell to one side of the binder. Steve had looked at the pages when Kate pointed them out but showed no curiosity to explore the book on his own.

"Do you like history and art, Steve?" I asked.

"It's good," he said without inflection, as the book dropped to the side of the couch.

"And romance?"

"It's nice."

I pointed to the long, sleek piano in the room. "Do you like music?"

"It's okay."

"Steve plays the piano. It's always been a hobby of his since he was a kid. We have home movies of him playing."

"May I see one?"

"Why not? What do you say, honey? Shall we play a home movie for Alexander?"

"Why not?" echoed Steve.

Using a remote control on the coffee table, Kate drew the curtains, then activated a holographic image in the air before us. The lively scene she chose suddenly stirred the room with a whirl of music, voices, and laughter.

"This is from a party we gave just before Steve's accident."

The scene showed a more modest room with a smaller piano. A group of people flanked the instrument, singing and swaying to a robust song played by a lively man. His hands raced along the keyboard in a blur of motion. The tune was a vibrant melody that made me think of Earthlings I had seen leaping into the ocean and laughing as the waves broke against them because the people at the piano sang with the same elation. In the scene, Kate's bright hair swirled out from behind the piano player, and she placed a drink on the instrument for him. As she moved toward him, his face stretched up high to catch her mouth in a kiss as ardent as the music he played. Then he laughed as the others sang, throwing his head back in total surrender to the moment.

I gaped at the scene in amazement because the animated face at the piano belonged to a man with a mind that encompassed so much, from music to medicine, from art to science, from the mastery of a skill to the arousing execution of it. I could not believe that the energetic man in the hologram was the same as the subdued one before me, but the features were unmistakably Steve's. Then Kate tapped a button on the remote control, and the music stopped, the animated scene disappeared, the curtains reopened, and the room became still again. What force had removed the music and spirit from Steve Caldwell's life? I wondered.

"Steve, can you play that same joyful tune now?" I asked.

"Yes."

"Would you like to play music now, Steve?" Kate asked.

"Whatever you'd like."

"But what would *you* like?" I asked.

"Doesn't matter." Steve looked at Kate for guidance.

"Honey, why don't you play for Alexander?"

Steve sat at the piano and played the same tune from the home movie. That is, the notes were the same, but there was no variation in volume, no mood created, no vitality in the performance. What I heard was a normally rousing song played monotonously. Steve's music had notes but no spirit. It took me back across the galaxy to a place where people devoid of their own desires and intentions performed acts they were instructed to do.

After the one song, Kate seemed as eager to proceed with another activity as I was. She suggested that Steve return to the couch, which he did dutifully. Then she invited me to stay for lunch.

"That is kind of you, but I am not hungry, Kate."

"Steve, do you want lunch?"

"I am not hungry, Kate." Steve was looking at me and seemed to be echoing my words and inflection.

"But it's two o'clock, dear. You should eat now."

"All right."

"This morning I prepared something you love, poached salmon with fresh dill! And I made your favorite pâté."

"That's nice," said Steve in a tone that made me think he could just as easily have eaten the dried nutrient cakes from my previous diet.

"I like to cook," Kate explained to me. "And Steve was always an appreciative subject to cook for because he has such a discriminating taste for fine food and wine."

"I see."

"You might change your mind about lunch when you see my food, Alexander. Why don't I set places for all of us on the patio while you and Steve talk about MAS?"

When Kate left, I leaned forward in my chair toward Steve, my eyes staring into his, trying to reach him. "Steve, what happened to you the night of the accident?"

"I don't really know."

"There was an unusual rock, a new material from another planet in the galaxy?"

"That's right."

"And you were experimenting on it?"

"I did some routine analyses that I was instructed to do."

"And then what?"

"Then I knew I had something there."

"What did you have?"

"Something I'd never seen before. Something no one had ever seen before."

"What was it?"

"A new kind of matter."

"What kind of matter?"

"Something we don't have anywhere on Earth. Something that reacted in a new way."

"What way?"

"I never really found out. I only had a hunch."

"What did you do about your hunch?"

"I got excited about it."

"What do you mean you got excited, Steve?"

"I used to want to know about everything. I was curious."

"So what did you do?"

"More tests."

"What kind of tests?"

"Tests I did on my own."

"Did a supervisor have to authorize a technician's tests on an unknown material?"

"Oh, yeah. There were strict rules. But my boss worked days, so he had gone home for the night, and I felt too excited to wait until the next day to talk to him. I used to be that way, inquisitive about everything."

"Did you try to call your boss by phone?"

"No. I think I just forgot about him, about everything except the new matter. I did more tests, wondering what I had."

"And what did you have?"

"Matter that behaved in a new kind of way."

"What way?"

"When I accelerated a small amount of it, a new kind of energetic particle appeared, one I had never seen before."

"So what did you do, Steve?"

"I introduced matter from Earth. When I collided the new alien particles with Earth's matter, there was a further interaction. Then, a most amazing thing happened."

"What happened?"

"The particles annihilated each other completely. Not even a trace of ash remained, and no gas or liquid was formed, either. Nothing on Earth behaves like that."

"Then what happened?"

"I couldn't believe what I saw. So I took a larger microscopic sample of the alien matter and began to repeat the experiments."

"And?"

"That's all I remember."

"Did you black out?"

Steve nodded. "The other technicians found me on the floor. I woke up, feeling sleepy for a few days."

"Then what?"

"Then nothing."

"Then you became the way you are now?"

"Yes."

"Do you like the way you are now?"

"It's okay."

"Are you happy?"

"I don't know."

"Do you miss the way you used to be?"

"No. It seems strange to be the way I used to be."

"What is strange about it, Steve?"

"I don't know."

"You used to care about many things, no?"

"It all seems odd now, to care so much."

"What do you do here all day?"

"Sometimes nothing."

"And do you like that?"

"It's okay."

"Has Dr. Merrett found a cure, an antidote, for you?"

"He's tried, but no. He doesn't like us to talk about the accident."

"Does he pay for your house?"

"Yes. He gave us a lot of money."

"Why?"

"Just to be quiet while he tried to find a cure. Kate didn't want publicity anyway, so she didn't even need the money to be quiet."

"And you, what do you want?"

"Doesn't matter to me."

"Why did Dr. Merrett want you to be quiet?"

"I don't know."

"Do you want a cure? What do *you* want, Steve?"

"Whatever they want, Kate and Dr. Merrett."

Steve's eyes stared at me like two fading stars that had lost their energy, then he turned to Kate with the same stare as she called us to the patio.

Lunch was as artful as the images from the Caldwells' travel book: fresh foods served on colorful plates against a starched tablecloth, with a bouquet of flowers in the center of the table. The aromas of food and garden blended sweetly with the fresh air as we sat on a shaded patio that overlooked a green hillside. I picked up a delicate fork for an item Kate served, remembering to use my new Earthling table manners for lunch—and trying to forget that another creature stalked me for his dinner.

After the meal, Kate brought out a tray of home-baked cookies, along with a silver coffee pitcher and white porcelain cups.

"Steve, would you pour the coffee, please?" asked my hostess.

Steve lifted the pitcher. Just as he poured the hot liquid into the cup Kate held, the lid fell off, and the coffee scalded her hand.

"Ow!" Kate shrieked, but Steve kept pouring with a steady hand.

In an instant, she yanked her hand away, screaming for him to stop, which he did just a moment before I grabbed the pitcher from him. I poured ice water onto my napkin and placed it on Kate's reddened hand while Steve looked on passively.

"Steve, get something for the burn, quickly."

At her direction, Steve acted without hesitation. From a medical kit he brought in, he applied ointments and a bandage with the assurance of a doctor. Because of the remarkable Earthling medicines, Kate soon sighed in relief as the pain subsided.

"Steve," I said, trying to suppress my alarm and ask as calmly as I could, "did you not know that you were hurting Kate?"

"I was pouring coffee."

Kate smiled in understanding, but not before I saw the pain that shut her eyes and made her moan for an instant.

After the spills were cleaned up and we had taken a few sips of coffee, I thanked Kate for the outstanding lunch and expressed my need to depart, as well as my reluctance to leave them for fear they might need assistance.

"We're fine, Alexander. I have doctors I can call in a minute. And I have attendants who stay with us, or with Steve, when I need to . . . get away for a while. So don't be concerned, but do come back for another visit."

When I mentioned that I was going to catch the Cheetah, Kate insisted on their accompanying me to the station. "It's just a walk away. I know a shortcut through the back roads, and Steve needs the exercise. Sometimes he sits for hours doing nothing, and that's not good."

The afternoon sun in the desert was strong when we left the house. We strolled along a dirt road, with newly built houses placed on either side and more under construction ahead of us.

"The station's directly ahead, just past the construction. You can see this little town is adding some new homes," Kate said.

Steve walked silently with a neutral expression. "Steve, we're going to walk Alexander straight to the Cheetah station the short way, and then we'll walk back the long way, through town, so we can stop for ice cream. Okay?"

"Okay."

Along our path, we saw a neighbor collecting her mail. Kate greeted her, pausing to compliment her garden. While I waited for Kate, I noticed the meticulous care that the people of Clear Creek took with their landscapes. As the neighbor returned to her house and we were about to continue, suddenly Kate and I gasped. Twenty feet before us, Steve was heading straight past a warning sign and into a ditch in the road at the construction site.

I leaped toward him, yelling, "Stop! Steve, stop!"

He halted when he heard me, so curling my arm about his waist an instant later and pulling him back from the ten-foot drop was unnecessary.

"Steve, darling, what on Earth were you doing?" Kate's voice was barely a whisper.

"Walking straight to the Cheetah station the short way."

I turned away to spare Kate from seeing the wave of pity that washed across my face. I heard her sigh wearily. When I looked at her again, she was reaching into her purse for an object.

"Now I didn't want to do this, but I think it's best if I do, Steve. No one will notice it if we walk close together and you stay by my side. Okay, dear?"

"Okay."

Kate placed a harness over Steve's head, pulled his arms through it, and tightened it around his chest.

"And we'll take the back roads home again. We don't need ice cream to-day."

She clipped a strap to the back of the harness, holding the other end in her hand.

"Okay, Stevie?"

"Okay."

I was stunned into silence.

CHAPTER 20

While I waited for the Cheetah, I gazed at the town of Clear Creek lying beyond the station platform. Deep in thought, I barely noticed the sights of Earthling life that usually fascinated me: the attractive houses, the well-dressed people, the lively children, the green-velvet lawns, the abundant harvest of beauty and pleasure that could sprout only in the serenity of an untrampled field. Instead, I saw a destroyer.

Would Feran be interested in Steve Caldwell's injury? Would a mosquito be interested in a ready supply of its favorite beverage—human blood? Steve Caldwell's fate was exactly what Feran had planned for *me* when he sentenced me to undergo the calming probe, the vile brain surgery to sever the fibers of my sovereign will. Would Feran be interested in the ultimate calming probe, whose blade conveniently misses the brain's areas controlling knowledge and skills while it cuts away only the areas controlling self-direction? He surely would have a use for an injury that leaves a person unable to choose between lunch and no lunch, between a lifetime of practicing medicine and a lifetime of doing laundry, between harming human skin or protecting it, between reviving a heart or letting it die—until someone directs him. Such an injury would leave people unable to focus on work, romance, music, or travel—unable to act, even to protect their own lives—without direction from someone else.

On Asteron, injured Steve Caldwell would be seen as the ideal person. Feran taught that obedience was good. Who could be more obedient than a man who had no ideas or passions of his own? A man who took no action of his own? A man who moved by the direction of others and was paralyzed without it? I thought of Steve standing at the edge of the ditch and heard a senator at an airfield tell why the old ways were banished: *People were no longer*

169

captains of their own lives. Would Feran, the supreme meddler, be interested in a person ready and waiting to wear a leash?

I needed to know more about what happened to Steve, so I turned on my mobile device as I boarded the cub that took me to the Cheetah. Soon I was on the main train, feeling the smooth hum of an engine under my seat. I raised the device close to my face, gave it a few oral commands, and soon found local news stories that had occurred almost three years ago in the month of January. I located an article about Mrs. Merrett's death, but it contained fewer details than I had learned from Kristin.

The article described the theft of documents, with no mention of a specific report or a prior laboratory accident. The story quoted the police as saying the matter was under investigation, but no details were given. A few briefer mentions appeared in the following days, but officials named no suspects and gave no further information. Typical of the private manner that seemed characteristic of him, Dr. Merrett was reported as in seclusion, unavailable for interviews, and having no comment. His wife's funeral was a family affair with no media permitted and no photographs released. The only picture that appeared was one taken at the crime scene, with Mrs. Merrett's body covered by a sheet as it lay by the fireplace of her husband's home office. I searched further back in time but uncovered no stories of the laboratory accident or the injury to Steve Caldwell.

I kept returning to the picture taken at the crime scene. A few gold embers still burned in the fireplace amid a mass of black charred paper that looked as if it would crumble at the slightest touch. Among the residue were a few white spots that looked like small patches of paper that had escaped the flames. I saved a copy of the photo on my device. Then it was time to enter the cub that would take me to my destination—the one place where I could collide head-on with Feran's spies.

It was four o'clock in the afternoon when I arrived at MAS. I noticed several vehicles in the parking lots, a sign that some staff members were working on Reckoning Day. But surely Feran's spies would not choose a holiday, when the MAS plant was only sparsely populated, to interview employees in search of their prey. They would delay their arrival until the next workday, Monday—I hoped. Nevertheless, I must get in and out of here as quickly as possible.

I entered the building that to me was grander than any palace from the Caldwells' travel book. I walked across the lobby, past the relics of Earth's early rockets and the block of metallic letters that boldly announced the building's name and my own lifelong yearning: SPACE TRAVEL. As I bypassed the elevators for the stairway and climbed the steps three at a time, I hoped that the building where I had restarted my life would not be the place where I lost it.

I reached the second floor and headed toward a lab equipped with the software to magnify my crime-scene photograph to its best resolution. When the lab door automatically slid open to admit me, it grated against its track just as the dangers of going in grated against my nerves. Several computer workstations were laid out on a long counter, and I seated myself at the one closest to the window. I opened the window, then oriented my stool toward it for a quick jump out into the shrubbery below if necessary.

I loaded the crime-scene picture on my terminal and brought Dr. Merrett's home office into view on my screen. In the fireplace, I counted four white spots of uncharred paper, which appeared to be remnants of the laboratory report. I zoomed in on the first one. The resolution of the picture was not fine enough for me to decipher the words, even with the automatic adjustments that the software provided, so I tried to improve the image quality manually. I strained to identify letters that stubbornly remained hazy. Just then the lab door slid open, causing me to leap off my stool and almost out the window.

A lab technician from Space Travel entered and sat at another workstation. "Hi, Alex."

"Hi," I replied, pretending to adjust my stool, as if it were the reason for my sudden move.

After several more unsuccessful attempts to focus the text, I was forced to accept the limitations of the picture. However, I noticed letters in the white patch above the paragraph of text I was trying to read. It looked like the title of a section in the report, which might be decipherable because it had letters that were in bold and larger than the other text. I zoomed in on the heading and did find more clarity in those letters. But the part I could read was incomplete: "Symptoms of Exposure to Z—." The rest of the heading was charred, leaving me no clue as to what "Z" was. I searched for other titles, subtitles, or areas with readable print on the page fragment, but there were no more in the first patch of paper. I moved on to the second of the four white patches in the fireplace. It contained nothing I could read. Just then the sliding door jangled my nerves again. I leaned toward the window, my legs tensed to jump, when a second technician entered.

She sat at another workstation.

I moved to the third white patch.

"Did you read the memo that's going around?" the first technician asked the second.

"The one about Earth Security?" she replied.

"Yeah. They're looking for someone from Asteron. That means a spy, of course."

"I heard."

The third patch had a heading: "Composition of Za—." I saw nothing but black soot after the Za. I searched the entire third patch, but there was no other readable text. I examined the heading again, but all of my wishing would not clarify even one more missing letter.

"Have you spoken to the ES agents yet?" continued the first technician.

"Nope," replied the second.

I focused on the fourth and final page fragment. Scanning its area, I found one heading.

"Hey, Alex, have you spoken to the guys from ES?" asked the first technician.

"No. Are they coming today?"

"Don't know."

I zoomed in on the final heading. It read: "Energy Needed to Produce Zam—."

Now I had obtained one more letter from the unidentified word that began with Z, but the name of the substance was still incomplete. I had exhausted the patches of uncharred paper. I could conclude only that the substance Steve found, the thing being studied in the report, had a name that began with Z-*a-m*.

"I heard the ES agents were supposed to be around today," commented the second technician, "but it's after four now, and I haven't seen them."

I felt as if my clothes were stifling me. I pushed back wet strands of hair that were falling into my eyes. I changed the field to focus on the whole of the fireplace contents once again. I examined the image closely. Was there anything I could have missed? One of the embers looked peculiar. I magnified it. I found near the ember a sliver of paper I had missed, a yellowish strip that I had not noticed, similar in color to the gold ember. I zoomed in closer. The small strip of colored paper resembled a tab from a folder. Had Dr. Merrett placed the report in a folder? Had he labeled it?

The door slid open once more. I tensed like a cat ready to leap.

"Say, is that report ready yet?" someone called to one of the technicians.

"Not yet. Give me another half hour."

The door closed again. I returned to my image, adjusted more controls, then saw the strip of yellowish paper magnified on my screen. It indeed did look like an index tab to a file folder. I zoomed in further. Handwritten on it in ink was a complete word that I could read clearly. The word was *sunbeam*.

I stared at it. That meant something to me. . . . *Sunbeam* . . . meant something. But what? Had I heard that word used recently? Was it here on Earth? Or maybe— My thoughts wandered across the galaxy to another place and time. I used to think of someone's hair as the color of a sunbeam. Was I thinking of a young woman with golden hair and a sweet voice singing to me in a place where no one . . . *sings*?

Suddenly I knew! I recalled the last time I had loaded cargo onto a spacecraft on my final day in an intolerable place. After the cargo had been secured and all of the preparations for a long journey had been made, I remembered a malicious laugh and a voice saying:

"When the sunbeam stings, Asteron sings."

CHAPTER 21

While I pondered these new revelations, I removed all trace of the crime-scene photo from the computer and closed the program I had been using.

The substance that had injured Steve Caldwell apparently began with the letters *Z-a-m*. The three headings I could read contained fragments of the word: *Exposure to Z—*, *Composition of Za—*, and *Energy Needed to Produce Zam—*. Project Z, of course, began with the same first letter.

However, there was another name associated with this substance, a name that had been handwritten on Dr. Merrett's folder and used by Feran. What did this other name signify? Could *Zam* be the beginning of an official scientific name used in the report, and could *sunbeam* be a nickname, or code name, for the same material, written on a folder? Earthlings often used short names that pinpointed the essence of things, like *Quick Fix, Big Eats, Clean Team,* and *QuikCode*. *Sunbeam* had the same ring. What essence did it pinpoint?

I could not yet leave MAS because I had an idea—actually only a guess. But I had to test it. Quickly!

The lobby of the executive office building was empty when I arrived and entered with my security pass. I raced up the stairs and across the third-floor hallway. Walking past the kitchen, I paused, surprised to find a man and a woman in there eating sandwiches, apparently two staff members working late on the holiday and taking a meal break. I did not know these two employees, which was perhaps why they looked at me curiously.

"Hi," I said from the hallway as casually as I could.

"Hi," they said together, and smiled.

I continued toward Dr. Merrett's office, where the doors to both the reception area and the conference room were shut. Hearing no voices inside and ensuring that no one was in the hallway to see me, I entered the conference room, where I knew the keypad code to open the door. I quietly closed it behind me, and I checked to be sure that no one was inside the inner office or reception area. Then I sat at Dr. Merrett's desk and turned on the computer. Using the password I had previously lifted with Code Cracker, I unlocked his files. From my seat, I could look out the windows and keep an eye out for anyone approaching the building. A glance at my watch showed it was five o'clock in the afternoon. Surely Feran's spies would not arrive so late.

I knew where to look, and I made my way through the various databases and subdirectories until I came upon a folder called, simply, Z. When I tried to enter it, a security window appeared, asking for a further code word, as it had on my previous attempt at a time that seemed long ago but was only yesterday morning. Now I had a word to try for access—the word handwritten on Dr. Merrett's folder.

However, it was unclear from the writing on the folder whether *sunbeam* was spelled as one word or two, or which letters might be capitalized. I knew from my prior experience that I had only three chances before I would be locked out for this session by the security system. I made one attempt. It failed. Another attempt. It too failed. I had one more chance left before the computer would shut me out. I tried to imagine how a busy, direct person, as Charles Merrett seemed to be, would write the code word. He would cut to the essence, I figured, so I gave the computer simply one word with no capitals: *sunbeam*. A new electronic hum and change of color greeted this last attempt. To my astonishment, flashing on the screen before me was nothing less than a menu of files that were the secret documents of Project Z!

So the name appearing on the report folder for Steve Caldwell's injury was the password into Project Z. That was *proof* of the connection I had suspected. I skimmed the entire database, finding reports written by those who worked on the project, letters between Charles Merrett and his customer, and memos circulated among the small group of trusted insiders who knew the full nature of the undertaking. I studied the screen, mesmerized by the treasure trove I had unearthed. The mystery of Steve Caldwell's injury and the undertaking of Project Z were unfolding before me.

Somewhere on the edge of my mind, I noted that although Feran knew the name *sunbeam*, proved by the comment he had made on Asteron about the sunbeam's sting, the name alone would not have been enough to gain him access to the project's files. Computer access would have required Feran to know that *sunbeam* was a valid code for getting into the database, at least on Dr. Merrett's computer, and also to know a valid password for that terminal. Instead, Feran had resorted to a camera for reading the Project Z files from Dr. Merrett's computer screen. The supreme snooper somehow used the robot Dustin to plant the camera and replace it regularly while it cleaned Dr. Merrett's office, thereby providing him with ongoing data.

I located the laboratory notes that Steve Caldwell had recorded on the night of the accident and began my search there. He was testing a sample he had received from the MAS Space Research Center, a group studying materials collected from other stars and planets in the galaxy. That night Steve's sample was a rock taken from the dusty terrain of an uninhabited planet named . . . *Zamea*.

In studying the nuclear structure of the alien matter, Steve placed a sample of it in the beam of a particle accelerator. This produced a new kind of subatomic energetic particle with properties unknown to him. Steve then experimented with these particles to learn more about them. He collided them with matter from Earth. Then something truly extraordinary happened: The masses of the Zamean matter and Earth matter in the experiment *completely annihilated* each other, leaving no residue—no liquid, gas, or ash—of any kind. This did not happen with the fundamental particles naturally occurring in Earth's matter, Steve noted.

Was the Zamean mass *completely* convertible into energy? Steve asked in his notes. If so, this would make the Zamean rock the most powerful energy-producing substance ever discovered.

Steve commented that of all the energy that fueled the Earth, even from the planet's most powerful nuclear reactions, only a very small amount of mass was ever converted into energy. From this small conversion, the amount of energy produced was tremendous because it equaled the mass multiplied by the speed of light squared. Steve calculated that if the Zamean matter could be collided with Earth's matter to convert *completely* into energy, then the two-pound sample sitting on his lab counter could generate enough energy to power the entire Earth for one whole day! And according to the Space Research Center, he noted, there were millions of pounds of the same rock readily available on Planet Zamea—enough to power the Earth for millennia.

Reading these notes, I understood why Steve had gotten so excited.

He found the Zamean rock capable of generating particles that were totally different from the ones found in Earth's matter, particles that were *mirror images* of Earth's particles, which meant particles that had the same mass but opposite charge, just as positrons are mirror images of electrons.

Actually, something like what occurred with the Zamean matter did exist on Earth, Steve noted, but only in small experiments. Scientists knew that Earth's fundamental particles and their mirror images could be collided, and that they could completely annihilate each other, forming pure energy. However, the researchers were unable to produce mirror-image particles except in infinitesimal quantities and at great expense in experimental labs. Using Earth's matter, scientists could produce only a scant few million mirror-image particles yearly, an amount smaller than a grain of sand and insufficient to generate enough energy to power an Earthling home for five minutes. But the Zamean rock, Steve observed, seemed able to produce such mirror-image particles in abundance and on a monumental scale. The implications for a revolutionary new kind of energy production, he noted, were staggering.

Steve wanted to learn more, so he was going to repeat his tests, this time using a larger sample of the alien matter. I directed the computer to give me the next page of Steve's notes, but there was none. That was the last comment that Steve Caldwell ever made as a scientist.

Next, I located the report on Steve's injury, whose printed copy had been stolen from Dr. Merrett's home. It confirmed Steve's findings that when Zamean matter was accelerated, it produced a new energetic particle, and that this particle could be collided with Earth's matter, leading to the complete annihilation of mass and the creation of pure energy. The investigation, however, revealed a fact that Steve did not know: Before he had redirected the energetic particles to interact with Earth's matter, he had been exposed to them, and they were indeed harmful. Dr. Merrett and his team later isolated and studied these particles, which they named the Zamean beam.

Nowhere in the stolen report did I encounter the word *sunbeam*. At the time, it must have been merely Dr. Merrett's personal nickname for the Zamean beam, appearing only as a handwritten term on the charred folder landing in his fireplace. Later, when Project Z began, the nickname must have stuck, because I saw it used in print on project materials, and not only by Dr. Merrett but also by members of his inner circle in their private memos. Feran must have encountered this name in material photographed from Dr. Merrett's computer screen through the hidden camera in the plant.

In the report on Steve's injury, Dr. Merrett's scientists described their studies of the harmful new radiation emitted by the Zamean beam. Though it had no damaging effect on inanimate matter, this ray of subatomic energetic particles, they found, penetrated the human body and had a chilling effect on brain tissue. The Zamean beam blocked the proper functioning of nerve impulses in a way that impaired an exposed person's ability to make decisions, exercise judgment, and consciously choose among alternative actions. According to the report, a person's will, the seat of personal autonomy, was damaged by the Zamean beam.

After Steve's accident, others were exposed to the beam in secret experiments. Convicted murderers awaiting execution were offered a chance to volunteer to be exposed to the beam in exchange for having their death sentences commuted to life imprisonment and receiving an antidote to the radiation as soon as one became available. The judge who permitted the experiment said he was doing so in the name of science. However, he urged the murderers *not* to volunteer, because their execution, he believed, would be preferable to the effects of the radiation, which he described in detail to discourage them further. Nevertheless, doomed murderers did volunteer, and twelve were exposed to the Zamean beam.

The results described by the prison guards were extraordinary. The most disorderly and violent of the inmates, those constantly clashing with the guards, were reported to have become completely changed in personality. They became calm, docile, indifferent, lacking any initiative, much easier to manage, remarkably responsive to directions, and compliant. One prison guard said: "Even when I give orders remotely over the computer, the phone, or the loudspeaker, they're carried out without question or delay." So the Zamean beam, which Dr. Merrett called the sunbeam, produced model prisoners.

Before the robbery, Dr. Merrett wrote calmly of the implications of a "new and dangerous substance that must not get into the wrong hands," and therefore the "need to avoid publicity about Steve." Because Earth had experienced no wars for a century and it maintained the best military force in the galaxy, Dr. Merrett had no real cause for alarm.

However, after the robbery, he wrote in anguish: "Not only has my beloved wife been brutally attacked and taken from me and my daughter forever, but we have no assurance that she succeeded in protecting the secret she fought for with her life. The Zamean beam in the hands of Asteron—if they are the culprits—could be a real and horrifying threat to us all."

Dr. Merrett had contacted the highest government officials of Earth's various countries. Their intelligence agencies banded together to conduct a secret investigation of Asteron. Officials considered military action, but no hard evidence against my homeland emerged. For one thing, Earth's intelligence found no indication that Asteron was producing the sunbeam. Furthermore, no one was tapping the only known source of the rock on the planet of Zamea, which was being monitored by Earth. And officials believed that critical pages of the report on Steve Caldwell's injury were burned in the fire.

The Asteronian coin in the perpetrator's pocket was insufficient evidence to implicate Asteron in the crime because such alien coins did circulate on Earth. A high-level government official commented in a confidential memo: "We need more evidence than just a coin in someone's pocket to send our troops to that hostile place to risk their lives and to open up once again a long, bloody chapter of history that we closed a hundred years ago." Because no additional evidence appeared, Asteron was not invaded.

Earthling fringe groups sympathetic to Asteron were also investigated, but no evidence was found linking any of them to the crime at Charles Merrett's house. I wondered how thoroughly this investigation had been conducted. Even though Earth had the most advanced military in the galaxy, it might not have had the most robust human-intelligence network, I figured. With its peace and prosperity so complete and enduring—without any wars for a hundred years—the Earthlings seemed innocent, relaxed, and unwary of evil. Did they really have all the resources needed to seek out and infiltrate groups where Feran's spies could be active and recruiting cells to further their vile aims?

Despite the lack of hard evidence to justifiably blame Asteron for the crimes committed in Dr. Merrett's home, the possibility of the Zamean beam getting into the hands of my vile homeland still troubled Dr. Merrett and the officials. For that reason, they launched a project.

This led me to documents describing the formation of Project Z. I called them up on my screen and read feverishly.

Project Z's customer was Earth's military, a force formed from an alliance of nations to handle their mutual self-defense. The project's purpose was to create a compact device to generate the Zamean beam and then aim it at a target, producing a military weapon called a zametron. The official name for the undertaking, known to the insiders, was Project Zametron. The code name was Sunbeam.

I looked at a file describing the purple-colored protective suits used in the project, one of which sat in Feran's spacecraft. Experiments showed that the Zamean beam did not penetrate a material called flexite, a substance that, like lead, blocked harmful radiation. But unlike lead, flexite was lightweight, was flexible, and could be made into clothing. So the Project Z area was lined with this substance and everyone inside the area wore flexite suits.

Project Z had Dr. Merrett's full commitment. He said in a memo: "If there's any chance that Asteron is making this weapon, Earth, of course, will produce the first and best one. This is essential for our self-defense." But he had one great concern: "The sole purpose of the sunbeam is to disable the enemy, allowing us to capture its rulers and military without shots fired or lives lost. The purpose is *not* to create a population of zombies. Such a thought is more reprehensible than war itself. We must find an *antidote* that can be administered immediately after the perpetrators are captured, to free the innocent civilians from the sunbeam's grip. The sunbeam is not intended to induce a permanent subhuman state in a population but only a temporary anesthetizing effect to achieve military victory. Any other purpose would pose a threat to all human life. I will make this weapon only on the condition that an antidote also be developed, so the sunbeam can be used as I have specified." Because Earth's alliance of governments shared Dr. Merrett's concerns, they agreed to finance both the development of the zametron and its antidote.

The weapon that Dr. Merrett and his team produced surpassed his expectations. They designed a compact device capable of creating enough Zamean beams to irradiate the entire planet of Asteron. Incredulous, I read the sentence twice.

In the weapon, an accelerator would generate the Zamean beam. Then this beam would propagate through the air like radio waves. It would be sent to the electrically charged ionosphere and be reflected back down to the ground and up into the ionosphere again, back and forth, traveling at nearly the speed of light and propagating completely around Asteron within seconds. As the particles propagated, they would lose some of their energy, so that after forty-eight hours, the beam would dissipate completely and the threat of radiation would disappear. All of this would be accomplished using a small sample of Zamean matter contained in a weapon that was a miniature particle accelerator. As Charles Merrett concluded, "With no battles, no destruction of physical material, and the immediate surrender of the entire population, the lightweight, portable sunbeam is the ultimate military weapon of all time."

But I saw from his memos that a great concern troubled Dr. Merrett: "While we made the sunbeam to use against Asteron, that planet is so similar in size and atmosphere to Earth that with minor modifications, the very device we made, if it fell into their hands, could be used against us." His fears intensified when repeated attempts to find an antidote failed. In a memo to Earth's military alliance, Charles Merrett insisted on waiting for the antidote before he could in good conscience deliver the sunbeam. The reply from the military assured him of additional funding as needed to continue work on the antidote but sternly warned him that its interpretation of their contract required delivery of the weapon in the meantime. A dispute arose: The military demanded the weapon, and Dr. Merrett's lawyers confirmed that the contract he had signed supported the military's claim.

Then suddenly, just when the sunbeam was completed and ready for delivery, Dr. Merrett reneged. He wrote a memo to his inner circle announcing his decision to break the contract. This memo, containing the first mention of the cancellation, was written on the same Sunday two months ago when he dismantled the invention. So apparently, no one in the project's inner circle knew of his decision beforehand. The memo stated:

> As president of MAS, I have decided that I cannot deliver the sunbeam without a suitable antidote. Since I was overconfident of finding one, I didn't adequately address the contingency that we would fail and that I would be in violation of the contract. MAS will have to take quite a financial hit for my action, but nevertheless I am canceling the contract.
>
> Stunned by the tragic loss of my wife and the unthinkable implications of the report being stolen, I now believe that I acted too hastily in accepting the contract for Project Z. After all, there never has been any evidence that Asteron is producing the sunbeam. Our sensors on Planet Zamea tell us that no one has ventured there, and the supply of its rock remains untouched. Our surveillance of Asteron reports no signs of new weapon production. And I think that a regime such as the one heading up Asteron couldn't preserve

a mind capable of making the sunbeam from the fragments of the report it got, if it stole the document.

Charles Merrett told the inner circle of Project Z the same thing he told his employees, that he could not release his new invention to the world because it had "far-reaching and irrevocable consequences." But he added an extra phrase for the insiders: "dire consequences for the human race."

I leaned back in my chair and rubbed my eyes, releasing for a moment the hold that the monitor had had on them for the past half hour. I thought that I finally understood why Dr. Merrett had been reported to be so upset since he had canceled Project Z.

I leaned forward again, determined to learn more. I tried to access the technical data and mechanical drawings of the sunbeam. But they were off limits to me. Accessing them required an additional level of security that I did not have. I tried, nevertheless, to get a picture of the zametron. As I maneuvered through various files, searching for an image or sketch of the device, I thought of the things I urgently needed to tell Dr. Merrett, things that would intensify his worries, because Feran had stolen secret information from Project Z and was now here on Earth stalking me for a—something on the screen made me gasp.

Then a glance out the window gave me another start. Escorted by an MAS guard and about to enter the building were two men whose business suits looked too civilized for their sly faces. They were Feran's spies!

I could not delay my next task an instant. I knew I had become too engrossed and stayed too long. I could understand what had happened to Steve when he got too excited and forgot danger. Would I too suffer far-reaching and irrevocable consequences for my lack of caution? Would Earth suffer? I could not let that happen, so I got ready to leave immediately. By the time these thoughts formed in my mind, I had copied the Project Z files available to me onto my pin drive, being careful to encrypt the data and to protect it with a password only I knew. Then I turned off the computer. There was a lot more information I had not yet absorbed that I wanted to return to later—if I was still alive.

With the drive containing Project Z's files in my watch, I opened the conference door a sliver to peer out, hoping to find the hallway clear so I could exit. But just then the elevator door opened, depositing the guard and Feran's spies in the hallway!

They walked to the end of the hall where the kitchen was located, and they stopped to speak to the two people inside. I could not leave the building while the spies were in the hall. Instead, I kept the door opened a slit to observe them and listen.

I saw the spies flash badges as phony as their smiles. Their friendly Earthling voices seeped through the crack in my door as they greeted the staff members and then engaged in a bit of small talk. The employees remained in the kitchen, but I could hear them as they responded to questions. One of the spies explained his purpose there and gave them a description of me. The other held up a photo of me, probably the one they had shown the clerk at my apartment complex. I hoped the scrawny, half-starved creature I had been on Asteron was unrecognizable to the employees, as it had been to the clerk. But that was not the case.

From inside the kitchen, I heard one of the employees reply, "You know, he looks a bit like the guy who passed by here a little while ago."

"Oh? Which way did he go?" asked one of the spies.

"Toward Dr. Merrett's office."

"This way, officers," said the MAS guard.

I shut the door as he escorted the spies straight toward me.

Which door would they use to enter—Margaret's in the reception area or the conference-room door where I stood? I returned to Dr. Merrett's desk, positioned in between the two rooms with the doors, and I waited for what seemed like an eternity.

Then I heard an electronic beep coming from Margaret's area and the door unlocking there. I raced into the conference room and slipped silently out from there while the guard led Feran's spies into the reception area.

CHAPTER 22

I took the stairway on the opposite side of the hallway to avoid passing the kitchen, and I sped out the building and off the company grounds, rapidly putting distance between me and Feran's spies. I reached for my pocket phone to make the most important call of my life.

Kristin answered! "Hi, Alex."

"Where are you, Kristin?"

"Home. Say, it doesn't sound like you. . . . Alex, what's wrong—"

"Is your father there?"

"He's here."

I breathed the greatest sigh of my life as I heard the two most comforting words ever uttered. "I'll be *right* there. I *must* speak to him. The matter is of the greatest *urgency*. He is not about to go out, is he?"

"No, he's here, and he's not going out."

I walked rapidly along the side streets toward Kristin's house nearby. The people in vehicles driving by me, the pedestrians walking along, the man with his dog, the woman with a briefcase—every face I saw—looked like a spy from Asteron. I tried to calm myself. In a few minutes I would be safe. I would have help. The protective arms of Planet Earth would enfold me like a blanket. I would be relieved of the burden of concealing from a destroyer the most deadly weapon of destruction ever conceived.

I knew before I had seen its diagram that the cargo I had carried to Earth was the sunbeam. I wondered how Feran had gotten it, but that did not matter. The only thing that mattered now was getting Charles Merrett safely to the sunbeam so he could take possession of it. I imagined an armed escort of Earthling officers protecting us, an impenetrable force that Feran would not dare challenge. Then when the sunbeam was secured, I would give Feran's description to Earth Security and have him caught. After attending to these matters, I might even celebrate my birthday with Kristin after all!

I now understood the puzzling events that had occurred on Asteron on the day of my escape. I realized that the entire fleet of spacecraft being readied at Feran's Space Center was coming to Earth. Feran was transporting his troops for an invasion. When I loaded cargo on his spacecraft that day, the maps I saw on his computer screen were of Earth, pinpointing the strategic areas of interest to him: *food production, aircraft, power supply, communications, military headquarters.* The names of Asteron's military officers written under these facilities were those of the unit leaders assigned to them. As Feran released the sunbeam on Earth, the Asteronian officers would be en route. Because the prison experiments showed the beam's victims responding to instructions given remotely, Feran's officers would have been able to achieve control from their spaceships, commanding the irradiated populace to relinquish Earth's broadcasting networks, military command posts, and other facilities even before the troops landed.

With Earthlings drowsy and compliant because of the beam, Asteron's commanders could appear on computer screens and other receivers, giving directives to their obliging victims. All key leaders of Earth's countries and industries could be under the power of the Asteronian fleet before it ever hit the atmosphere. Feran could even orbit the Earth for two days, free of the beam, so he could remove the flexite suit while waiting for the radiation to dissipate. In a mere forty-eight hours after Feran activated the weapon, when the Zamean beam was no longer a danger, Asteron's troops would land.

I understood now why Feran connected his cargo to the starvation in Asteron. He was going to use the sunbeam to transform Planet Earth into a giant slave camp to serve Asteron. Feran was going to end starvation and poverty on Asteron by looting the Earth. He was going to ravage the human spirit.

That was his plan, I realized, as I reached the flower-lined walkway up the hill to Kristin's house. On the lawn I saw a sight more comforting than an Earthling mother's arms: two planes, representing the two people who would help me. The bright red plane with the customary fuel engine was Kristin's, and the new, gray-toned electrical one had to be her father's. My only assignment was to calmly explain the entire matter to the one man who could rescue us all from Feran's grip.

Kristin recoiled when she answered the door and saw my face. "Alex! What's wrong? You look . . . desperate."

"Kristin, I must see your father at once! Is he still here?"

"He's here."

I sighed in relief.

"But he's working in his office. I can't interrupt him. What's this all about?"

"I will tell you everything later, Kristin. But I *cannot delay* telling him. I assure you he will see me immediately. Tell him it concerns the *sunbeam*."

"Alex, what on Earth—"

I pushed past her. "Then I will tell him myself. Where is his office?"

"Wait, now. I'll tell him. Wait just a minute, okay?"

Kristin entered a room at the end of a hallway. Impatient beyond measure, I could not contain myself enough to manage courtesies. I sped down the hall and into the room myself.

There, sitting behind the desk, a man gasped incredulously at the same moment I did. It was Feran.

CHAPTER 23

Before he could recover from the shock of seeing me, I leaped over the desk, bent his neck back, and towered over him, a triumphant grin on my face. My reflexes were quick, and I had the advantage. I grabbed a crystal vase of flowers, no doubt placed on the desk by his loving daughter. I raised it high in the air, tumbling the flowers and splashing cold water into our faces. With a fierce new strength, I aimed the vase directly at his head. I curled my other hand like a claw around his throat. My mind was wild with visions of golden hair swaying on a scaffold and a strangled body under a sheet by a fireplace. I would now have *my own* theater of justice, and every muscle in my body burned for it!

But Kristin's reflexes were also quick. She threw herself over the stunned figure sprawled on the chair, covered his head with her own, and shrieked at me: "No! No! Alex, don't!"

I managed to stop the falling vase a mere inch above Kristin's head, and I dropped it on the desk. I grabbed Kristin roughly and sent her crashing against a bookcase, causing a shelf's worth of volumes to flap to the floor. I grabbed the vase and raised it again over Feran's head, but it was too late. He had already opened a desk drawer, and I was looking straight into the obscene mouth of his prized weapon, Coquet.

That mouth was a toothless cylinder of bluish metal, pursed at the end like lips stretched into a perpetual snarl. Coquet's tongue was a long strip of steel that jutted out viciously at the press of a button, spitting rays and beams of torture. Glowing buttons sparkled like jewels about Coquet's neck. Feran's hand caressed her throat lovingly while her circuitry purred and hummed, waiting impatiently for her prey.

I dropped my arm slowly, letting the vase fall to the carpet. I eased my grip on Feran's throat. I backed away from malicious eyes that were unmistakably Feran's, as I heard a soft voice with an Earthling accent that sounded nothing like the accent I knew, "Don't try anything."

While he pointed Coquet at me, he stood up, pressed a button on his pocket phone, and then spoke to someone who was no doubt one of his spies: "I'd like to inform you that our visitor from Asteron is my *daughter's boyfriend.*"

"Asteron!" Kristin screamed.

"Imbeciles!" barked Feran into the phone, with a telltale crack in the smooth voice, like a fissure in the ground just before a quake. "Kristin, dear," he said, his voice steadying, "you told me that your boyfriend is a fellow named Alex who just appeared one morning on our lawn, and that you got him a job at MAS. But you neglected to tell me he was an *alien.*"

Kristin stared from me to him. "But . . . but Daddy. You were too busy. You didn't give me a chance."

"I guess I have been busy lately, dear," he said apologetically. Then he returned to his phone call. "I think his spacecraft landed by my house. Search the vacant lot across the road, and call me back as soon as you locate the ship. I want to enter it *myself.*" Then his voice cracked again: "There's been enough bungling of this matter!"

As Kristin's eyes widened in confusion, mine narrowed in clarity. The moment I had seen Feran behind the desk, I had known the answers to the remaining questions that puzzled me.

"Alex . . . ? Daddy . . . ? What's this about?" Kristin asked incredulously.

While aiming Coquet at my head, Feran reached into the desk drawer for another object familiar to me.

"You call him *Daddy*?" I shouted. "This is *Feran*, the supreme ruler of Asteron, the planet of corpses. Did your daddy ever have a weapon like that, Kristin? Did he ever keep handcuffs in his desk? These things come from Asteron. I know them well, because I have encountered them many times."

"What? Alex, are you really from . . . *Asteron*?"

"I am from the place where evil disguises itself as good, ugliness as beauty, and a demon as your father." I turned to the loathsome eyes that never left me. "You dare not kill me until you get the cargo, so I can speak the truth. You stole from Charles Merrett the zametron built for Earth's military as the ultimate weapon of all time, the weapon made to unleash the Zamean beam that injured Steve Caldwell's brain, the weapon Charles Merrett called the sunbeam and made under Project Z, but he decided he could not deliver it because he had found no antidote."

I could see Kristin's confused gaze moving back and forth between Feran and me. I had to get as much of the story out as possible, so she would know the truth and somehow foil his scheme.

Feran held out the cuffs. "Put these on him, Kristin."

"But . . . but Daddy, what's this all about? That can't be necessary. That . . . hideous . . . weapon can't be necessary!"

"He tried to *kill* me. You saw that yourself. He's the spy from Asteron, the man Earth Security is looking for. Oh, he changed his appearance, all right, but he didn't fool me. I recognized him from a picture ES showed me. Now we have to hold him until they get here. Okay, honey?"

Kristin did not reply.

"Look, this guy came to Earth. He took advantage of you to get a job at MAS. And he stole a weapon from me, a dangerous weapon I *must* retrieve!"

"Why would he come here today looking for you if he stole something from you and knew you'd report him to the authorities?"

"He wanted to . . . gain my confidence so he could steal more secrets." Feran hesitated, groping for a story to satisfy Kristin. "But when he . . . saw that I recognized him . . . he knew he had to kill me. I'm sorry, honey. I know you were taken in by him. I know he toyed with your feelings and hurt you. But he's working for the people who killed your mother! Now put these on him!" He rattled the cuffs impatiently.

Kristin seemed to be searching our faces for an answer, standing motionless as if unable to move toward her father or toward me.

"Oh, Kris! You don't see it, yet, do you?" Feran shook his head, sprinkling a little affection into his impatience, no doubt following a recipe he had learned. Then he told me to put my hands behind me. Pressing Coquet into my back with one hand, he used the other to snap the cuffs shut on my wrists.

While this task engaged him, I continued. "Now I understand why you had those bandages on your face in Asteron. That was over two Earthling years ago. We thought you had an accident that injured you, but when the bandages were removed, you had a new face. Your old face, with its grotesque nose, drooling lips, and feeble eyes, which we called beautiful, was replaced by the proportional features we called ugly. Then we thought you did not have an accident after all but intentionally changed your face to look more like the aliens you courted, so you could get more aid to feed us. But now I know the real reason for your transformation. After you discovered that Charles Merrett was making a weapon with the Zamean beam, you were making yourself into Charles Merrett. No doubt you two have a similar height and build, so that was your starting point. The rest, you manufactured. Kristin says Earth's cosmetic surgery is incredibly advanced. Well, Asteron's surgeons surely came to Earth secretly and were trained here, because there is no modern medicine there, and they replaced your vile face with Charles Merrett's good one. Unfortunately they could not replace your soul too." A sudden spurt of blood trickled into my eyes as he tapped my temple with Coquet.

"Daddy!" Kristin screamed in horror. But she remained frozen in place.

With my hands now locked in the cuffs and Coquet still aimed at me, Feran walked to a closet, looking for something on the shelf.

"You changed your face to match Charles Merrett's so you could get through the security system to Project Z." I remembered the words of Mike, the guard. "When modern advances make possible better security, they also make possible new ways to breach it. The remarkable surgery on your face may be Asteron's only contribution to the history of medicine, the perverse distinction of aiding your identity theft to destroy a free world."

"Preposterous!" barked Feran. He shot a nervous look to Kristin, wondering what she was thinking.

"Now I see why you had Dustin plant a camera to read Dr. Merrett's monitor. I thought you could not access Project Z's computer files directly, and that may be, but it was not the only reason. You were studying more than files with your camera. You were studying Charles Merrett—the way he moves, the tone of his voice, the clothes he wears, the hairstyle he sports, the people he talks to, the way he runs his business." I glanced at Kristin but could read nothing from her face. "The way he talks to his daughter."

Feran took a rope from the closet and approached me, swinging it gently in his hand, his vicious eyes belying the tame gesture, warning me of other moves he might make.

"Kristin, did your father really keep an alien weapon, handcuffs, and a rope in his office?"

"Daddy, where did you get these things?"

"Quiet, dear. He's a wanted man, a suspected spy!"

"You're not gonna tie him up, are you? Please, Daddy, no!"

My words spewed out, because I knew I did not have much time. "Feran has to play his part until he gets the sunbeam, Kristin. Then we will all be destroyed. You will not hear any 'dears' from him then. What you will see is a brutality—" Feran's punch cut me short and knocked me to the floor.

"Daddy, stop it!" Kristin moved toward me, her arms outstretched.

"Stay away from him, Kris." Feran blocked her from reaching me. "Tell *him* to stop it. You hear him taunting me with his lies. You saw him try to kill me. You heard him say he's from Asteron. What more do you want?"

She dropped her arms at his words. But I was determined to reach her with the truth, because she had to find a way to stop him. Feran stooped down, tucked Coquet into his belt, and tied the rope around my legs. He was being exceedingly careful because he realized that all I needed was one chance.

"Almost three Earthling years ago, you learned of the laboratory accident through your spy at MAS. There were no news stories about it, but the people at MAS knew. They found Steve Caldwell and talked among themselves. That was how you found out. Because MAS makes weapons and inventions, it is an Earthling company you would spy on to find out about just such an event as Steve's discovery. Then the following month one of your men broke into this home, stole the report on Steve's accident, and murdered Charles Merrett's wife. You must have retrieved enough information to know that the Zamean beam that injured Steve's mind had tremendous potential for evil in the hands of someone like you. But you did not retrieve enough data from the stolen report to produce the beam yourself. Besides, the source of the material to make the beam was being monitored on Planet Zamea, so you could not get at it. You knew about that because you read Charles Merrett's papers on his computer screen through the camera you had planted with his cleaning robot. And you knew from those papers that Earth's intelligence was surveying Asteron, so you had to watch your moves. You further knew that Asteron was suspected in the robbery and murder that took place in this house, and that with just one more provocation, Earth would invade. So you were helpless to make your own sunbeam."

"Shut up!" He muttered, as he squeezed the rope tightly around my ankles.

I propped myself up on one elbow and looked at him as I spoke. "Then your hidden camera informed you that Dr. Merrett was launching Project Z to make the very weapon you lusted for but could not produce. All you had to do was wait until he finished, then steal it. But to steal it, you had to have Charles Merrett's face to get into the Project Z area. You had to subdue your bristly stalks of hair and your savage expression to cultivate a more civilized appearance. You had to have lessons on how to speak and act like Charles Merrett. But a little surgery, grooming, and studying were surely worth the prize of total conquest of the Earth. Besides, why not adopt such a plan, because it enabled you to exchange your ugly face for a handsome one?"

He lost control and punched me again, and blood trickled from the corner of my mouth.

"Stop it!" Kristin screamed at him. She bent down to me and wiped the blood with a handkerchief.

"Get away from him, honey," Feran said in his calmest Daddy voice. He lifted her up gently and placed Coquet in his pocket now that my arms and legs were restrained. "I know he played with your feelings and deceived you, and I'm sorry. But he's a wanted man. He's dangerous. Nobody's gonna harm him. I just need to hold him here for ES."

Kristin stepped away from me again. As I wondered what she was thinking, Feran searched the closet for another item.

"You cannot kill me until you are sure you have the sunbeam intact. You still have to be civilized, at least for now, in your role as Charles Merrett, because you first have to find the device, and then you might need to call an engineer for a repair or get a replacement part if I damaged your cargo. That allows me to finish my story."

Feran bristled, but Kristin listened intently.

"You did not know that Dr. Merrett was going to dismantle the weapon. No one knew that. You were at MAS the Sunday he canceled the project, but you were here to *pick up* the sunbeam intact. By reading the documents from Dustin's camera, you knew that the weapon was finished and ready for delivery. You were going to deploy it outside the flexite area and thereby end the greatest chapter in the story of human life. You chose Sunday, when MAS is at its emptiest, when it is almost a . . . a . . ."—I searched for Frank Brennan's words—"a ghost town, so you could take the sunbeam when no one was around to question you. How inconvenient that Dr. Merrett had disassembled the weapon just before you arrived. You had to return to Asteron with the parts for your engineers to reassemble. That is how the sunbeam ended up on Asteron. This time your people had the complete instructions and diagrams, recorded by Dustin's camera, plus all the sunbeam's parts, so even *they* could not fail.

"While you were waiting for the sunbeam to be reassembled, you went back and forth to Earth, pretending to be Charles Merrett, no doubt intensifying your acting lessons for a bigger role than you had anticipated. For the past two months, you had to play Charles Merrett until the sunbeam was fully reassembled on Asteron. You might have needed help from the project team, or parts from MAS. Above all, you had to pretend you were Charles Merrett, because if Earth officials knew that he and his invention had vanished, you could have faced a full-scale invasion of Asteron to hunt for them. You had to live at Charles Merrett's home, deal with his daughter, conduct his business, and make his appointments so no one would suspect anything had happened to him.

"Now, you did not originally intend to continue your masquerade longer than it took to reach the secured area and pick up the sunbeam intact, so there has been seepage through your seams, signs that you are not really Charles Merrett, if Kristin cares to examine your behavior closely."

Kristin looked at him sharply.

"Kristin says she has seen little of you since Project Z's cancellation. Could that be because you did not want her to take closer notice of your appearance, your expressions, or your memory of family situations that only Charles Merrett would know? Has Kristin tested you?"

Kristin cocked her head in curiosity, studying the figure that had found what he was looking for in the closet, a scarf.

"Haven't you exploited my daughter enough?"

"Of course, you never got any new projects for MAS, because that was not your intention. And your business failure and unusual *grouchy* state, as Kristin called it, was blamed on Project Z, not on your being a different person, a completely opposite person, as black is opposite to white. Your odd behavior was not blamed on your being *Feran*! And of course most recently you have had more reasons to be grouchy, because I stole your spacecraft with the reassembled sunbeam inside just as you were ready to embark on your mission of destruction."

Feran walked toward me, unfolding the scarf.

"No!" Kristin blocked his path. "You can't gag him."

"Oh, can't I?"

"You don't understand, Daddy. It makes him feel helpless. Something terrible once happened to him—"

"Oh, did it, now? Isn't that too bad?"

I knew my time was up as Feran spread the cloth out in his hands and bent down to me. Kristin fell to her knees by my side, struggling to stop him, so I had a final moment. "Kristin, you must find a way to stop his scheme. If he activates the sunbeam, we are all doom—"

Fresh blood dripped down my throat as the gag cut into the gashes his punches had made on my mouth.

"Now Kris, dear, we need to keep him quiet until we can give him to ES. You trust them, don't you? They'll treat him fairly."

The gag was in place.

Then his phone rang. "Yes? . . . You did? Good! I'll be there in a minute." He placed his hands on Kristin's arms, lifting her up with him. "Earth Security found his spacecraft hidden in the empty lot across the road. That's where we think we'll find the weapon he stole from me. He's right, you know. Project Z *is* a weapon, a very dangerous one that we can't let fall into the hands of his government. Now come with me, honey. I don't want to worry about you being here with him. I can't take any chances with your safety, you know. When I lost your mother, it was . . . devastating."

With superb acting, Feran lowered his head and seemed to let fall a little tear.

"I didn't mean to be rough with him, Kris. I know what you must be going through, but every time I think of the way we found your mother—"

He threw his arms around Kristin. She permitted the hug but did not return it. I lay on the floor, my hands and legs bound, my mouth finally silenced, my body propped up on one elbow. I stared at Kristin's distressed face as I wondered about her thoughts.

"Come with me, please, Kris," said Daddy.

Kristin's eyes lingered on mine. Just as in a time that seemed long ago, I was gagged and a most beautiful female was staring at me in bewilderment and fear. I wanted to reach out to her, but I could not. I wanted to cry out to her, but I could not. I thought of the only thing I could do. This time I knew it was a most inappropriate gesture for a desperate occasion. But was it not the acknowledgment of a secret shared by two? A salute of some kind? An expression of . . . closeness? I blinked at Kristin with one eye.

Her eyes swept over my body in a soft caress. Then slowly, painfully, she closed them.

"Come on, baby, let's go." Feran gently took her hand.

With obvious effort, she opened her eyes and turned to the door, and then she walked toward it. She paused to look back at me once more. With Feran holding the door for her in a display of good manners, she left the room to accompany him in retrieving the invention that would end the human epoch on Earth.

Before joining her in the hallway, Feran paused a moment. Out of her view, he gripped the drooling mouth of Coquet, her lights blinking. He fondled the tiny band of buttons he knew intimately, until he found the one he wanted. A mocking metal tongue jutted out at me.

There was a sudden flash of light, a whoosh of air, and a burning sting to my forehead. I convulsed in agony in a liquid room that whirled around me.

Then there was only darkness.

CHAPTER 24

A cool draft hit my face and brought me back to consciousness. As I lay curled on the floor, I felt blood dripping from my forehead. I was in the room for attitude adjustment, I thought. There was something important I must do. I tried to recall. . . . It was night, and I was never going to see another sunrise. . . . Slowly I opened my eyes to a blur of trees and blue sky from a window. I was confused. Was it night or day? . . . Was I to end my life or to begin it?

Then I saw the carpet, the desk, and the whole setting of my new world as I felt the restraints of my old one cutting into my limbs and mouth. I realized I was in Dr. Merrett's office. No, in the office of Feran the executive.

As the fog from my blackout lifted, I felt a new sting, more horrible than a bite from Coquet. Feran would find the spacecraft and get the sunbeam! He would put on the flexite suit and release the deadly ray. A clock on the desk read: 6:05 P.M. I judged that I had been unconscious for about ten minutes, time enough for Feran to reach the ship. In a moment, the will I was struggling to summon would be lost forever.

But no, I realized, as more thoughts returned. I had borrowed Kristin's plane the previous night in order to move the sunbeam. Feran's spies were getting too close, so I had removed the cargo from my ship. We were safe. Or were we? Feran would know by now that his cargo was not in the spacecraft. He would be back any moment to torture me for the sunbeam! He would do something unbearable; he would use Krist— I had to hurry!

I inched my way to the desk and raised myself to my knees. With my head, I spilled a small dish of paper clips onto the floor. With my hands behind my back, I picked up one and began molding it into a shape that would unlock the handcuffs. Although out of practice, I was quite familiar with this task from my previous life.

Suddenly I heard engines overhead. I continued with my tedious task and finally bent the paper clip into the desired shape. I placed it in the key slot, gently . . . gently. I heard the tiny squeak that disengaged the lock. I was free! Within seconds I had untied myself and removed my gag. I sprang to my feet, jolted with a sudden surge of energy.

I sped to the front door and peered out. Near the garden, two planes were descending vertically and about to land. I could see the faces of the pilots—Feran's spies. Kristin's shiny red plane was just steps away from me. Fresh, cool air washed through my lungs as I opened the door and sped toward Kristin's cockpit. Moments later the spies were on the ground and running toward me, weapons in hand. Then I watched them dive into a thorny rose bush as I swept Kristin's plane over them, barely missing their heads.

I took the plane above a few scattered clouds into the late-afternoon sky, forming a plan. I loaded the files of Project Z onto the plane's computer so that I could search through them for information that would help me to safely dismantle the zametron.

My plan was to get the sunbeam from its hiding place before Feran got me, then take it to a remote spot in the mountains and remove its Zamean-matter fuel. Next, I would reassemble the machine with dirt inside in place of the fuel. Distraught over the thought of his torturing Kristin, which he would certainly threaten to do, I would contact Feran to make a deal. In exchange for the sunbeam, I would demand Kristin. I would also ask for the spacecraft because he knew I would not stay to be irradiated. I would let Feran think I was giving up Earth to him. Once Kristin and the Zamean matter were out of his grasp, she and I could get help. That was my plan. But first I had to lose the two speeding planes behind me.

I headed away from the coast toward an area of uninhabited mountains where I had flown with Kristin. Would the spies hit me? Surely they could not risk killing me until they had the cargo, but they could try to force me down and bring me to Feran.

I came dangerously close to a wall of red-brown rock and climbed vertically along it. After flying over the top of the wall, I suddenly flipped the plane over to reverse my course. Hanging inverted from my harness, I saw the spies climbing over the rocks just as I was diving back down the same rocks in the opposite direction. I disappeared into a deep, narrow canyon. The winds whipped through the canyon at high velocity, as sometimes occurs in that kind of terrain, creating turbulence. They shook my plane incessantly, swaying it toward the jagged stone walls, but I struggled to avoid the menacing ledges that jutted out close to my wing tips. After traveling some miles from where I had last seen the spies, I could no longer locate them. Certain that I had lost them, I climbed away from the V-shaped stone gorge to get out of the maze of mountains.

But just then the curved beaks of two metal vultures appeared overhead. How could Feran's spies have known exactly where to find for me? I descended back into the winding canyon, with the spies' planes on my tail.

The rocks flowed by in a liquid smear as I cut through the narrow rift. The winds ripped by incessantly, shaking the craft, changing my altitude in sudden spurts, vibrating the wings. I constantly tried to steady the plane, with the spies still in pursuit. I flew higher and then lower but found turbulence at every altitude. I meandered along the snakelike canyon until it narrowed too much for me to chance going any farther at low altitude in the high winds. I pulled back hard for a steep climb, just missing a protruding sandstone spire. When I looked back, only one hooked nose was behind me. The other had burst into a fireball of molten metal on the spire I had just missed.

I thought I was headed out, but found myself amid more high peaks. I dived under an arch of rocks spanning from cliff to cliff above my plane, all the time fighting nausea. I had to get out of the mountains and into the open sky, but I was losing my way. I was turning left, directly toward the rocks. I had to lower my right wing to correct. But no! My instruments told me my wings were level and I was not turning. I had to resist the urge to correct the wings, because I could no longer trust my senses. The turbulence was upsetting my equilibrium. I was in an exceedingly dangerous place to be afflicted with the condition I was now experiencing—vertigo.

I had to force my eyes to lock on the instruments that presented a true picture while I disregarded the illusions of my mind. I had to resist my distorted perceptions and concentrate. Just then a wall of rock appeared directly in front of me. I had to climb above it, but I was diving instead. I had to adjust quickly. No, the instruments said I was not diving; I was climbing. I had better not adjust or I would stall! I was hesitating too much, and the mountain was coming at me. Suddenly, I rolled sideways through a sliver of blue space between the jagged peaks I did not quite manage to climb over. Then I turned to see a blinding explosion that was the second of the spies' planes splattered on one of the peaks behind me.

After traveling out of the turbulence, I continued to battle dizziness for a while. I set the craft's instruments to automatically fly me to my destination, and then I tried to regain my orientation.

I felt better by the time I reached my target. Detecting no one following me, I descended softly into the quiet crescent that was the baseball stadium. I landed in foul territory in front of the dugout between home plate and first base. Because the stadium was empty during the off-season, I thought it would make a good place to conceal the sunbeam. As Kristin had surmised, there were no security guards or systems monitoring the open field. I had confirmed that the previous night when I had come down here with her plane to deposit the cargo in a new place. I figured that Feran would think a giant, open arena too preposterous a hiding spot ever to consider.

I left the engine of Kristin's plane running while I jumped out. Wobbly, I fought the lingering spatial disorientation as I walked into the stands near the dugout. There I found lodged under the seats, where I had left it, the gray box that was Feran's cargo. Carefully I slid it out, its cool metal solidly in my grip.

The sunbeam was mine! Feran would never get it now. Presently it would be nothing more than a harmless metal box full of dirt, and the Zamean fuel would be a mere clump of matter without a mechanism to generate its deadly rays. There would be no fireworks tonight. The peaceful arena of Earth would remain undisturbed for the enduring season of the human epoch. There would be no noxious beam released but only a deadly demon captured. I lifted the sunbeam into my arms gingerly, as if it were a baby. I turned to head back to my craft. Then I stopped.

On the field in front of my plane I saw three mouths gaping at me: one in innocence, one in malice, and one in drooling excitement of impending violence. I saw Kristin, Feran, and Coquet.

"I'll take that, please," said Feran pleasantly.

CHAPTER 25

Kristin's father's plane had quietly descended into the infield and landed at the foul line behind where I had parked her red plane. Because I had left the noisy fuel engine of her plane running, I had not heard the nearly silent electric plane approaching. While I was reaching under the seats to retrieve the sunbeam, I had not seen the two passengers get out and walk in front of my plane to watch me.

As I stood speechless at this sudden change of events, I noticed a small electronic object stuck to the red fuselage.

"Did your spies shoot a sensor onto Kristin's plane while I was flying? Was that how they tailed me and how you knew where to find me?"

Feran smiled smugly, saying in his gentle Earthling voice, "It's one of the things our security forces have here on Earth that you don't see on Asteron."

"We do not need to see things on Asteron. We have a ruler who sees for us."

The smile vanished. "Move slowly and don't try anything. Bring that box to me here on the field. Oh, Kristin, dear?"

"Yes, Daddy?"

"Bring me the flexite suit we took from his spacecraft, will you, honey? I need to make a quick adjustment on the . . . object, so it'll be quite harmless. Then I'll bring it to the Project Z area to disassemble and destroy once and for all, with no renegade from Asteron stealing it this time."

"Kristin, as soon as Feran gets the sunbeam and the suit, he will either kill us, which I am hoping for, or make us into robots, along with the rest of the people on Earth." I studied her face, its expression revealing nothing.

"Shut up and move—now! This game is over," Feran said to me.

"I'll get the suit, Daddy." From where she stood with Feran in front of her red plane, she walked back toward the electric plane behind it.

As I reached the field, I looked at Kristin. What would she do? Would she make a catastrophic mistake with far-reaching and irrevocable consequences for us all?

"Kristin! You *must not*—" I began, but a beam from Coquet's mouth tore my sleeve, barely missing my skin and threatening to blow off my arm the next time.

"Be quiet, Alex!" she said sternly. "Just put that thing down in front of my father and keep still."

"Thank you, darling," said Daddy, gloating at me.

Kristin could act, but I could only stare at Coquet. I would have to trust my girlfriend. I followed Kristin's instructions and dropped the sunbeam gently at Feran's feet.

There it stood, a metal box, about two feet high, two feet wide, and one foot deep, resting on feet of the same metal. I now understood its assembly. All of the metal sheets were lined with flexite. The top of the box had a circular piece of metal, about six inches in diameter, which was sealed to the same metal surrounding its rim. On the side near the top was a large ring-shaped steel pin. Over the pin, protecting it, was a plastic covering. Inside the box was a miniature particle accelerator and a sample of Zamean matter. Pulling the pin, I now knew, would start the accelerator, producing the harmful Zamean beam. The metal circle would unseal and slide open, leaving a hole on top. Then the powerful beam would shoot out of this opening, travel to the ionosphere, and from there propagate around the world like a rippling ray.

"Let's see. I hope you weren't foolish enough to tamper with something you knew nothing about." Keeping Coquet poised at me, Feran bent to inspect the sunbeam. "Well, now, it looks just fine to me." He smiled. The more pleased he looked, the closer I was to death.

Kristin reached into the electric plane for the purple flexite suit. "Here it is, Daddy."

Walking toward Feran, she stopped as she passed her plane, its engine humming steadily. With Feran's eyes on me, and mine on her, Kristin did something that summoned me to high alert: She blinked at me with one eye.

In a flash, she raised her arms and shoved the flexite suit into the engine at the rear of the fuselage. With a whoosh, the suit was sucked into the running blades of her plane and chopped to bits. The engine made a piercing screech as it expelled the last remains of the suit in a puff of purple vapor. In utter astonishment, Feran turned to see what had happened. Instantly, I lunged at him, snapping Coquet out of his hand. Then *I* was pointing the weapon at *Feran's* head!

"Imbecile female!" snapped Feran in his true voice of pure hatred. "And I was going to spare your life so you could be my servant!"

The suit had jammed the engine, leaving the three of us in dead silence. I winked back at Kristin, who was now smiling broadly. Then I turned to Feran.

"Back off," I demanded. Feran moved a few feet away from the sunbeam. "Now which of Coquet's buttons did you use on me? I will activate that same one until I figure out which of the others will kill you."

Coquet, now securely in my control, buzzed impatiently, drooling to attack him. This was surely the first time anyone had ever held the upper hand over Feran, and I wondered how brave he would be in meeting the fate he had so cruelly inflicted on countless victims. I remembered how Reevah and others had met their end, with their heads high, with the quality the Earthlings called pride stamped indelibly on their faces to the end. How would Feran meet his demise?

He fell to his knees, trembling pathetically before me, unable to conceal the stark terror that gripped him.

"Wait! Do not shoot!" he squealed. "You cannot destroy me! If you kill me, you kill the people of Asteron. The deed I came here to perform is for my people!"

"Even if your deed saved Asteron from starvation, it would still be evil if it produced just one Steve Caldwell—if it destroyed the mind of just one person." I turned Coquet's little throat until the button I wanted sat directly under my finger.

"But wait! Wait! You must listen to the truth!" On his knees, he locked his hands together, pleading for his vile life. "It is unfair for one planet to have all the food and wealth. The rich Earthlings must help the poor Asteronians." He pointed a finger to the sky as if issuing a proclamation, while still begging on his knees. "I am a *liberator*, not a killer!"

"Slavery is liberation. Plunder is justice. The ugly is the beautiful. The bad is the good," I said. "Just as you hid your hideous face behind Dr. Merrett's handsome one, you hide your depraved soul behind a mask you call the greater good. But I will pull it down before I end your foul life. You cannot be content to plant your own garden and leave others to do the same, because then they would be free of your intrusion and you would be of no importance. Your perverse standing comes from trampling the gardens of others. But you will not crush the most prized of all orchids, the human will!" Impatient to end the matter and feeling no thrill at the prospect of torturing him, I reached for the button on Coquet's throat that I thought would kill swiftly. "Good-bye, Feran." I aimed the petulant mouth of Coquet at the head of her master. I pressed—

"Look out, Alex!" Kristin screamed.

I did not get to push the button, because at that moment someone shot the weapon out of my hand, splattering the innards of the prized Coquet into a jumble of circuitry at my feet!

CHAPTER 26

Kristin gasped in shock, but I showed no surprise, only a greater under-standing of the whole vile scheme, when I saw the man with the gun in the stands behind first base: Chuck Whitman.

"Imbecile!" shouted Feran to the person who had just saved his life. "You were supposed to shoot the man, not the weapon. Not *my Coquet*!"

"I shot exactly what I aimed to shoot. Why hit a guy who'll make a great servant when the new order's established?" Chuck carried a large shoulder bag, opened at the top, with a shiny purple material visible inside. "One of our men called to tell me everything." Chuck spoke with great self-im-portance, as if he were in charge of the operation. "Then I got a signal from the sensor that he landed here," he said, looking at me contemptuously. "I landed my plane in the parking lot, jumped a fence into the stadium, and went to check things out. I brought some flexite suits with me too."

"Bring them down here at once, and we will proceed with our business!" barked Feran. He had shed Dr. Merrett's kind voice and now spoke in his real voice of anger and malice.

Waving his gun in my direction, Chuck slowly walked down the steps to the field from about two dozen rows up in the stands. Feran inched closer to the sunbeam.

"Chuck!" Kristin was aghast, her voice barely audible. "You mean you're on *his* side?" She pointed to Feran.

"Whose side should I be on? On the side of privilege when I don't have any privileges? On the side of the landlords who own all the land and demand rent from the rest of us poor slobs? On the side of the companies that con-trol all the jobs and fire anybody they please? On the side of my father, who has lots of money but won't shell it out to help his own son? Or should I be on this guy's side?" He pointed to me with the barrel of his gun. "The new pilot my father brags about. A guy who comes here from nowhere and gets a sweetheart job that's gonna launch a whole new business. My father picks *him* for the maiden voyage, which'll get all the publicity and make his career for him in six stupid months! And he gets the girl everybody wants, a girl with great looks and a direct line to the top boss. Should I be on *his* side, when he gets things handed to him that others only dream about?"

"Alex didn't just *dream* about being a pilot, and then sit around and do nothing," said Kristin. "My father didn't just wish for a business, and then whine for somebody to give him one. Your landlord didn't just want land, and then wait for somebody to drop a building in his lap. How do you think people get to be what you call *privileged?*"

"Spoken just like my father," replied Chuck, looking down at us on the field.

"Commander Whitman, why do you stop to chat with these insurgents? We have the sunbeam, so we can eliminate them at once. Shoot them and bring me the weapon and suit—now!" screamed Feran.

Anyone on Asteron would have instantly complied with a command from Feran. But the supreme ruler's directive to an Earthling, even one who was a loyal supporter, carried nothing like the same force. Chuck did not move swiftly as Feran commanded. His eyes flashed with a strange excitation. He slowly took a step down, then another, and then paused, as if he was savoring the moment like a rare wine, lingering on it, intoxicated with it. The chatting pleased me too. It was the only tool we had for stalling Feran. I decided to engage Chuck in further discussion.

"At least three years ago you knew of Feran, perhaps through his spies or the groups who support him on Earth. You were sympathetic to his ideas, to his wanting an inroad to Earth to establish an order that he no doubt promised would provide you with everything you dreamed about. You gave Feran that inroad. Angered by being fired from Space Travel and knowing that MAS built new inventions and weapons, you spied on Dr. Merrett from your new office in Housekeeping to see if you could get back at a company where you had suffered a humiliating failure. You seem to like hurting others. You kept Frank Brennan from getting a promotion he deserved, and you provoked your staff, causing the best workers to quit. Would you not also want to hurt your father, Dr. Merrett, and all of us whose success stirs resentment in you?"

Far from looking ashamed, Chuck grinned brazenly, as if I were presenting him with a medal.

"I was sore, all right, when my own father canned me. And Uncle Charles wouldn't override him, either. Yeah, I looked around for some compassion, which I sure enough didn't get from my own kind. I found a group that sympathized with me, a group that wanted to right the wrongs here, to knock down the high-and-mighty and put everybody on an equal footing."

I knew Feran trained spies. Now, listening to Chuck, I knew where he sent them and why. "So you joined this group, Chuck?"

"I went to a few meetings. When I mentioned where I worked and my father's job in top management, they took a huge interest in me. They treated me like I was really somebody. They approached me to do a job for them, a super-important job. For the first time, I was sought out. I was needed. I was a kind of . . . hero . . . to them. And I discovered I was damn good at the assignment they gave me. It was easy to spy on a fool—to look through a window, to plant a camera. Uncle Charles never suspected anything. What a dupe!"

Kristin bristled.

"I got a real charge out of that. You could say I found my calling—and, man, did I hit on a mother lode for them."

"Commander Whitman!"

"Hold on." Chuck moved his wrist and the gun now pointed at an outraged Feran.

"So it was *you*," I said, hoping to keep Chuck talking while I tried to figure out what to do next. "Before Dr. Merrett installed the security windows, you read files off his computer screen from your office across the way. You learned of Steve Caldwell's accident and its implications. You told Feran about the report Charles Merrett was expecting on the cause of Steve's injury. But when the report arrived, you saw Dr. Merrett print a copy and leave the office with it, instead of reading it on his screen. You knew the Merretts were going out that evening because they had tickets with your parents for the ballet. You told Feran that a printed copy of the report could be found in Dr. Merrett's home office. That fancy phone you bought, which I heard you tell your father was for contacting the lunar cities about a job, probably makes calls to Asteron too."

Chuck's grin widened and he laughed outright, raising his head arrogantly. Although he shifted his weapon back to aim at me, Chuck was in no hurry to kill someone who was acknowledging his perverted feats. Indeed he was eager to brag about the only job he had ever excelled at. He slowly strutted down the steps as if the seats about him were filled and the crowd was cheering. He looked as if he wanted to take a bow.

"So you did not care that your action led to Mrs. Merrett's murder?" I asked.

"She complained about her back before. Why didn't she see a doctor like she was supposed to? Why didn't she let go of Uncle Charles's report instead of fighting for it? Nobody told her to foil our plans. That was *her* choice, not mine!"

"You bastard!" Kristin's face reddened with contempt.

"Eliminate the enemy!" ordered Feran. "Shoot them!"

"Cool your heels," answered Chuck. He again pointed his weapon toward Feran, and the supreme ruler was silenced.

"After Dr. Merrett installed the security windows in his office, you altered Dustin's programming so you could plant a camera to snoop," I said. "It was *you* who found out the nature of Project Z. *You* were the only one outside the inner circle who knew that Project Z was undertaken to build a weapon from the substance that harmed Steve Caldwell's brain. *You* provided the way for Feran to steal a device he could not produce himself."

Chuck beamed as if I were toasting his prowess.

"You told Feran the delivery date of the completed sunbeam. You arranged to meet him the Sunday before delivery to help him as he impersonated Charles Merrett. You were to help him find his way around MAS. You did not come in that Sunday to reorganize a supply closet, as you told Frank Brennan you would. You came to meet Feran so you could steal the sunbeam. It was Feran, posing as Charles Merrett, who let you into the Project Z area.

"But you did not get the sunbeam in one piece. You did not know it in advance, but Charles Merrett had just disassembled the invention. So you had to take the pieces out in boxes, which you said you were bringing to the compactor, but which you really managed to take to Feran's spacecraft for reassembly back on Asteron. By then you knew the project had been canceled, so it was plausible to say you were destroying the parts; that way no one would wonder what had become of them.

"Would the real Charles Merrett have left a secured area with the pieces of a top-secret weapon, without a security escort, to go to a compactor? And would the real Charles Merrett have shared his intentions with a guard? Mike, the security guard, told me that such behavior was unusual for Charles Merrett. Mike did not know that it was Feran who brought those pieces out of the Project Z area with you. And it was Feran who promoted you to special assistant to the president for new project development, because Feran needed you close by to instruct him on how to impersonate Charles Merrett. And besides, the time had come to collect more money for the services you were performing on Feran's behalf, so why not get a raise and have MAS pay for your espionage?"

"You're damn right. He owed me plenty!" Chuck shot an angry look at Feran.

"But apparently you had not collected enough money to support your habits. You still needed to borrow more from your father."

"He got maxed out too." Chuck gestured to Feran with his weapon. "Said I had to complete my assignment first, and then I'd get more."

"Enough!" Feran demanded. "Commander Whitman, eliminate the traitor and come to me at once!" With Chuck's weapon oscillating between him and me as its target, Feran seemed hesitant to jump him.

"Relax," said Chuck. He was now on the field and strolling toward us.

Then Feran tried a new tack, in a calmer voice. "Now, you just bring me the suits, and stay clear of the traitor as you walk."

"Stay away from him, Chuck. You will certainly be zapped too," I warned, but Chuck did not listen.

"Chuck, what are you doing?!" cried Kristin.

I turned to watch Chuck as he walked toward Feran.

Once Chuck was near him, Feran made his move. His eyes bulging, he scowled and stormed Chuck, pulling the bag from his shoulder. He also grabbed for the weapon, but he backed away when Chuck aimed it at him.

"You insisted that I make you president of MAS, give you Charles Merrett's home, and give you your father and the traitor"—he pointed to me—"and Frank Brennan as your personal servants, and you demanded an allowance that could run an entire Asteronian city, and you tell me to *relax*? Do you think there is no price? If I am to provide you with all the things you want, then *I* am the one who calls the plays! Now, shoot the insurrectionist!"

While he was speaking, Feran had removed one of the flexite suits from the bag. He had worked it over his feet and legs when he paused to point to me, in case Chuck was uncertain who it was he should shoot. I stood, my back now to the dugout, eying the sunbeam, a mere few feet from Feran.

"Chuck! The suit—" I warned.

"Shut up!" Chuck replied. He turned to Feran. "You didn't say anything about *killing* people." He complained. "We were just supposed to zap them with the beam, so they get . . . agreeable, that's all."

"Imbecile!" barked Feran. "You are like all the other useful idiots before you who claimed to support my ancestors. 'We never meant to do *that*,' they would stammer when one troublesome group or another had to be eliminated," he exclaimed. His hands and arms were now inside the protective suit, with the hood hanging at the shoulders. He reached for the garment's zipper.

"Once that suit is sealed, you too will be zapped!" I cried to Chuck.

"Hold it." Chuck cocked his gun at Feran. "Hold it right there."

Feran dropped his hands to his side.

"There are two worlds, Commander Whitman. Choose—mine or theirs! Choose a world in which you are a supreme commander, where you have subjects to do your bidding, where everything is provided to you for free and you are protected, or choose a world in which you have to stumble about alone and afraid, a world in which you are *nothing*. If you choose *my* world—if *I* am the one who provides for your sorry life—then you must do what I require. Choose!"

Chuck wavered, moving the gun barrel back and forth from Feran to me. Finally, the weapon fixed on one target: me.

"Wait, Chuck!" screamed Kristin. "What'll be left of *you* after you destroy MAS and the people who keep it going?"

"The zapping won't affect me—just them. I'll take their place and be what they were before."

Kristin tried to reason with him. "But don't you realize that if you tear down the people who give you work and loan you money, then *you're* going down too?"

Feran tried to entice him. "Would you like to rule all of Rising Tide? All of California? That can be arranged."

Though Chuck aimed the gun at me, he hesitated to pull the trigger. Unlike Asteronians, who saw executions as routinely as day turned to night, Earthlings were unaccustomed to acts of open violence. Would Chuck shoot? The fate of the entire human race now rested on a man who could not pay his rent. I was through with the matter! I would have my own say on that fate. I prepared to lunge at Chuck and take my chances seizing his weapon—

Just then Chuck's gun fired, but not at me. He fired at a target by the dugout behind me. Then I heard another shot and saw Chuck fall, blood oozing from his chest, his gun dropping to the ground. I turned to see a man gripping a gun, blood dripping from the side of his head. He was leaning over the roof of the dugout from the first row of seats. It was Mykroni.

I reached for Chuck's gun. When the weapon had fallen to the ground, a small object rolled out of an electronic panel on the handle, startling me. It was a black metal cone. Suddenly I remembered Feran's remark that Earth has things not seen on Asteron. I had never seen the black cone before. Or had I? Quickly, I put the object back into its groove in the gun and reassembled the weapon. Then I aimed it at Feran and Chuck. I knew that the protective presence by the dugout was also holding my enemies at bay.

Kristin ran to assist Mykroni. She grabbed a handkerchief from her pocket and pressed it against his head wound to stop the bleeding. "Mykroni, this man is *not* my—" she began, but Mykroni motioned for her to be quiet.

Feran switched to his Earthling voice. "Mykroni! I'm so glad you're here, my good friend. But you shot the wrong man! Your son tried to save my life just now. You see, the new guy you hired is the spy ES is looking for. He's from Asteron."

"Of course Alex is from Asteron. I knew that when I hired him. I saw the scars on his neck. I recognized the accent in his speech. I could tell he was a military pilot, a skill he couldn't have learned on Cosmona because it doesn't have an air force."

"Then I should be angry at you for breaching our company rules. Regardless, I'm still relieved you're here. Now, if you'll make the spy drop his weapon"—Feran gestured to the sunbeam—"I'll retrieve the property he stole."

"Not so fast," said Mykroni, pointing his gun at Feran. "Since you got back from your trip, I've been trying to tell you why I broke the rules for Alex, but you've been too busy to see me. When I found out ES was looking for Alex, I told you I had to discuss an urgent matter that could involve someone's life, but you were still too busy to see me. Now, that didn't compute. Charles Merrett would have made time for a matter that involved a person's life. A minute ago you were speaking with a different voice, one I remember from a time long past. It was the voice of a ruler's son and second-in-command, a young man of great cruelty, a man I fled from."

Chuck was lying on the ground. His drooping eyelids sprung open as he realized the score had changed. "Hey, Dad, I thought this was Uncle Charles. You mean—"

"I overheard enough, so save your lies. When you grudgingly came to my office today after I once again demanded a payment schedule for my loan, then you suddenly got a phone call and left, I began to feel as if I'd been had again. I saw you get in your plane with the suits from Charles's secret project and a weapon sticking out of your pocket. I wondered what you were up to, so I followed you here. I brought this weapon that I keep in my plane. It's one I've never used. You know, I bought it when you were a kid, when there'd been a rash of kidnappings in Rising Tide. I bought it to . . . protect you. . . ."

Mykroni's head fell onto the dugout. Kristin pressed her handkerchief, now blood-soaked, against the wound more tightly. He struggled to raise his head, intent on having his say.

I gestured to Feran to move away from the sunbeam. As he backed off, I moved toward it and stood like a guard at its side. I held Chuck's gun on Feran, ready to pull the trigger, waiting only for Mykroni to finish releasing the last of the words that seemed to have been bottled up under pressure for a long time.

"When you made a mess of your life, I shielded you from the results of your own chosen actions. I gave you a job servicing a spacecraft, which you didn't deserve, and you almost . . . caused . . . a crisis."

Mykroni's eyelids were shutting.

"I'll get an ambulance!" Kristin reached for her pocket phone, but he grabbed the device from her hand. She tried to grab it back, but he would not let go.

"I need to make a call first," he said, turning back to Chuck.

"I bailed you out again with a job in Housekeeping, where I see now that your motives crossed the line from laziness and resentment to something . . . very different. I knew it was wrong to pander to your vices. That was my big mistake. It wasn't healthy for you to be needy . . . and helpless. It wasn't right for you to act recklessly and expect me to save you from the consequences. Now, for the first time, you'll lie in the bed you made, traitor! *I* will be the one who turns you in. *I* will be the one who has you arrested for *high treason!*"

Mykroni tried to place a call on Kristin's phone, but his hand fell limply and the device slipped to the ground. His head dropped as Chuck's eyes again closed. They were both unconscious.

I released a string of bullets at Feran as he zippered the flexite suit and threw on the hood in one furious motion. I shot him in the head, in the heart, in the chest, in the stomach—but he did not fall. Within one startling second, he walked into the bullets and grabbed the gun from me. He was gloating. Feran knew something I had not: Bullets bounce off flexite.

Laughing wildly, convulsively, his crazed eyes bulging, Feran slipped his finger into the trigger. I plunged to the ground. His gun blasted, and I felt a burning sensation as blood spurted from my arm. Then he whirled to face Kristin, who was now behind him, shooting at him with Mykroni's gun. I yelled for Kristin to get down. She dived to the ground, but not before Feran grazed her shoulder. Her blouse reddened with blood.

Throughout everything, we heard fits of diabolical laughter muffled by the flexite visor. Feran was too excited to shoot more accurately and too absorbed with another task he relished more than dealing with us. Kristin and I remained motionless on the ground, pretending to be more seriously wounded, so he would not shoot again.

Sealed in the flexite suit, Feran approached the sunbeam. He pulled off the protective plastic covering from the pin. With his flexite-gloved hand curled like a claw, his fingers encircled the ring-shaped pin that activated the device. He yanked the pin out of the machine, throwing it high in the air, crying madly, his voice reverberating through the stands:

"One people, one will! Planet Earth!"

CHAPTER 27

The sunbeam hummed. The aperture on top opened. An electronic display panel slid out from the slot where the pin had been removed, flashing in red lights: STARTING.

The pleasant electronic voice of a female informed us: "Ten seconds to emission."

The sunbeam stood in front of Feran, while I lay a few feet to his side and Kristin lay behind him. Her face lit up with an idea. She crawled on her stomach, inching closer to him.

"Six seconds to emission."

Gesturing, Kristin described her plan to me. I nodded my agreement. As she crawled closer to the purple-suited legs, I readied my body for what was to come.

"Two seconds to emission."

Feran laughed wildly, waving his arms high in the air in victory.

From behind him, in one swift move, Kristin wrapped her arms around his feet and pulled them off the ground. Feran fell over the sunbeam just as I flew on top of him. I pulled up his flexite visor and pressed his face into the hole in the machine. The hood around his face had a rim that adhered to the visor with a sticky strip of purple metal. I now used that flexite rim to make a tight seal between the visor and the zametron, with Feran's unprotected face in the hole. I pressed down with the full force of my strength to keep him in this position.

"Emission of Zamean beam will begin," said the electronic voice. The word EMISSION now flashed in red on the screen.

"How will we stop this thing, Kristin? It will explode if the beam is trapped!"

Just then the machine started shaking, and its soft voice said: "Pressure buildup. Aperture blocked." The display panel changed to flash the word DANGER at us.

"I put files from Project Z on your plane's computer." I told her my password to unscramble the encrypted data and read the documents.

"I'll search the files for how to stop this thing!" Kristin cried, as she ran to her plane. "The engine's jammed, but the computer will work on battery."

I gasped at Kristin's last word, suddenly remembering something of immense importance.

"Danger. Countdown to explosion. Ten . . . nine . . ." The voice of the zametron continued.

Still pressing Feran's face tightly on the machine, I reached one hand under it. The metal feet raised the box just enough for me to grope for something in a slot on the bottom.

"Eight . . . seven . . ."

I found it! I curled my fingers around the object.

"Six . . . five . . ."

I tugged at it.

"Four . . . three . . ."

I yanked it out.

The sunbeam became still, the humming and shaking stopped, the electronic display went dark, and the voice inside no longer spoke to us. Then the aperture closed shut. Feran's face receded into the flexite headpiece, whose rim I still pressed tightly on the machine. Then in a flash, I slammed Feran's face visor down, sealing him in the suit.

I stood up to shake the tension from my arms, to note that Kristin and I had only surface wounds, to see Mykroni stirring and Chuck breathing. Kristin phoned for an ambulance. Then she and I looked at each other.

Her shoulder bled, but she smiled. Her face held no awareness of her pain, only eagerness for joy. "Alex, are you okay? I don't think I'm zapped. Are you?"

By my sudden need to feel the lushness of her body against me, I knew the answer. "I am not zapped," I said, smiling.

"What happened? What did you do?"

"There are many new things made on Earth that I never saw on Asteron. I noticed an object in the handle of Chuck's electronic gun, a black metal cone. I thought it looked familiar, but I did not know what it was. Then when you said the word *battery*, I remembered I had seen a similar cone-shaped object, only larger, underneath the sunbeam." I held my hand out to show her a three-inch-long shiny black cone. "Is this the new Earthling battery strong enough to run your electric planes—and to trigger the reaction inside this weapon?"

She threw her head back and laughed. "That definitely is one of our new batteries! You pulled out the battery and stopped the reaction before the beam could get out and hurt any—"

We both looked at Feran. He was lying on the ground in his flexite suit, sleeping.

"Feran," I said, propping him up and shaking his shoulders to arouse him.

His eyes opened slowly. He looked at us dazedly, a little grin curling his lips.

"Yes?" he said, his eyes still drowsy.

"Stand up."

With the glazed face and sagging body of a sleepwalker, he slowly rose to his feet.

"How do you feel?"

"Sleepy."

"Do you remember what you were before you became sleepy?"

"The supreme ruler of Asteron."

"Do you still want to be a supreme ruler?"

"Does not matter."

"Would you like to try a new way of life for the people of Asteron?"

"If you wish."

"I would like you to tear down the Theater of Justice. Will you do it?"

"Okay."

"Were you going to invade Earth, Feran?"

"Yes."

"Do you still want to conquer Earth?"

"Does not matter."

"Get Chuck's phone."

With the gloves of the flexite suit thin enough for him to grasp it, Feran took the phone in Chuck's pocket and docilely brought it to me.

"Can this phone call your planet?" I asked.

Feran examined it. "Yes."

"I want you to phone your generals and call off the invasion of Earth, Feran."

"Okay."

"Tell them you are coming home with your Earthling advisors to bring new ways to Asteron."

"Okay."

"And keep your visor down and your suit on. Stay sealed inside until we can quarantine you in the flexite area."

"Okay."

While Feran called his generals, Kristin beamed at me triumphantly. "Alexander, you hit a *home run!*"

I smiled until I could feel the crinkle lines radiating from my eyes. Then, for the first time, I felt as if a wave were propagating within me, loosening my face and tightening my stomach.

"Alex, you're *laughing!*"

I threw my head back and listened to the strange new sound spouting from my throat and rising into the air like Alexander's baseball. My laughter grew louder, until it hit the stands and echoed back at me. Then it curved around the higher notes of Kristin's laughter to form a single song. The pain in my bleeding arm seemed too unimportant to concern me. Like the fading remnant of a bad dream, all of the pain I had ever experienced suddenly seemed unreal. I grabbed Kristin in my arms and lifted her high in the air, all the time laughing fiercely until my mouth ached, my eyes teared, and my chest burned. I had found the world of Alexander's promise. At that moment of my first laughter I knew that every color on the Earthlings' bright rainbow of expression glowed within me. I knew that I was what Kristin called a *Homo sapiens*, and that there was nothing more glorious I could ever hope to be.

CHAPTER 28

A few moments later, while we were still on the field, Mykroni regained consciousness—and he *did* get to make the call to the authorities that led to his son's arrest.

Earth Security began compiling mounds of evidence for the trial of Chuck Whitman for high treason. With Feran's sudden cooperation, his remaining spies, including the one who murdered Mrs. Merrett, were also captured. Feran would meet the same end, but only after he completed his new assignment.

Under the guidance of his Earthling "advisors," Feran returned to Asteron to save his planet. He parceled land to the people and established private property. He signed a constitution and created a republic. In an address prepared by his new speechwriters, Feran declared that he was abdicating his power and that all people were now masters of their own lives. No longer could any ruler stifle the speech or peaceful actions of citizens. No longer could any ruler force the will of citizens or seize the fruits of their labors.

Once they were free to operate, farms and businesses of every kind started to sprout up, creating the first buds of opportunity for the people. With its shackles removed, the human spirit began its reawakening. For the first time in the history of Asteron, flowers started to bloom there and the people began to sing.

Immediately after our showdown with Feran at the stadium, when Mykroni was being treated in the hospital, I explained to him why I had to make an urgent trip to Asteron. He insisted on coming with me. Disregarding his doctor's orders, he checked himself out of the hospital and embarked on a space mission with his head injury still fresh.

214

Before leaving for Asteron, I told Kristin and Mykroni how much I regretted having to lie to them about my homeland.

"In this case, we're glad you did!" said Mykroni.

"You won't have to lie anymore to stay alive, Alex," said Kristin, affectionately.

On my journey with Mykroni, that master astronaut let me fly our ship while giving me a memorable lesson in space travel.

When we arrived on Asteron, I set about doing the things I had come to accomplish. I brought with me a large display of Earth's flowers, dozens of loose blossoms tumbling over each other in a violent explosion of color and fragrance. I placed them on the stage of the Theater of Justice. "These are for you, Reevah," I said to the radiant vision in my memory. "I found the place with the flowers. It is a place where you belonged, and a place that lived within me from the first night I held you." As I spoke, I saw Feran step onstage with his Earthling advisors. On their suggestion, before a gathering crowd, he raised an ax and split the scaffold in two. As it fell, the people cheered.

I also walked through the dusty halls of the Center of Records to learn the truth about a matter that had long disturbed me. I wanted to know if I was conceived with Feran's revolting genes. But when I reached the Department of Birth Documents, I realized that I no longer cared. I had shaped my own self through the thing inside me called my free will. I left the building without ever opening my file.

The most important reason for our visit involved a precious cargo that Mykroni and I were relieved to find intact in the underground cavern of Feran's mansion. We brought it to our spacecraft for the journey home.

When the lush green of Earth with its blue-and-white swirls grew large in the window of our spacecraft, I commented to Mykroni: "You said that Charles Merrett gave you the last name *Whitman* when you understood the meaning of its last syllable. I think I'm ready for a last name too." I noted with pride the Earthling contractions that newly sprinkled my words.

"What name would you like to pick, Alex?"

"I'd like my teacher to pick my name, because he seems like something more . . . something I never had and never knew how much I missed." Our eyes met in mutual affection.

He threw an arm around my shoulder, squeezing me fondly. "I'd say you learned the meaning of the very word I did, so you deserve a last name which reflects that." And so it was, after a brief discussion, that I became Alexander Manning of Planet Earth.

After I lowered the craft gently onto Charles Merrett's lawn, Mykroni and I jumped down to see Kristin's eager face. Then our "extra cargo" alighted from the ship, weak from his confinement in a dark room with little food, but otherwise healthy. I had remembered unloading two large boxes from Feran's spacecraft at about the time he would have brought the sunbeam to Asteron. One box contained equipment. The other, a crate with wooden slats, held the man whose face I couldn't see in the darkness, the man who gave me the gold coin as my tip for bringing him water and who said to me: "Thank you, son." Mykroni and I helped down from our spacecraft the man from the crate.

"Daddy!" Kristin screamed.

She almost knocked down the man from the crate as she leaped into his arms. While they clung to each other in a tender outcry of laughter and tears, I wanted to look away to give them privacy, but I was unable to do that because I knew that I was part of the moment. As if thinking the same thing, Charles Merrett stretched an arm around my shoulder to pull me into their embrace.

On the Sunday when Feran had stolen the sunbeam, the records showed that Dr. Merrett had checked *into* the Project Z area twice but checked out only *once*. Feran, of course, had checked in and out once as Charles Merrett. That meant that the real Charles Merrett had only checked in. My suspicion proved true: Feran had carried Dr. Merrett out in one of the cargo boxes after drugging him with a shot from Coquet. Then Feran had taken him back to Asteron to get him out of the way and take his place. But Feran had not killed him, in case he needed Dr. Merrett's skill in reassembling the sunbeam. He would no doubt have tortured Dr. Merrett for that information, but fortunately, the Asteronian engineers were able to reconstruct the device themselves, thereby saving their prisoner from undergoing any more cruelty beyond squalid confinement and mental anguish.

After welcoming her father, Kristin turned to me. As I held her close, drinking in the sweet fragrance of her skin and tasting her mouth, the two men were apparently analyzing the matter.

"I see what Alex meant when he said that he and my daughter have *closeness*."

"Now I've got to juggle the schedules around to try to get those two in space together," grumbled my teacher. "Separating them is harder than pulling apart two attracting poles in a magnetic field."

When I released Kristin, I saw the man from the crate smiling approvingly.

"Daddy, even though the company's finances need fixing, I hope you're not going to bury yourself in work so we'll never get to see you."

"I intend to spend lots of time with you, honey, beginning with dinner tonight—since we're all alive to have dinner together." His smile vanished as his mind seemed to drop back into the damp dungeon where he had lived for two months with the terrifying dread that Feran would irradiate Earth. Then his eyes met mine, and his face took on a solemn look. "We have someone to honor tonight. We have a special toast to make to an extraordinary courage that saved us all."

In a silent pause that felt like a tribute, the three of them—my new family—looked at me admiringly.

Then Dr. Merrett turned to Kristin. "And Alex tells me we also have *your* cunning and bravery to thank for defeating Feran."

I nodded, adding: "In the end, it was Kristin who tripped Feran and made him fall onto the sunbeam—and her plan worked, as you Earthlings say, like a charm."

Kristin beamed proudly. With her father's return, her spirit had lifted. In fact, she looked more radiant and desirable than ever to me.

"And over dinner I'm going to tell the three of you about my plans to not just rescue MAS's finances but to also expand the company tremendously." The same face I despised on Feran underwent the most appealing transformation when it graced the person of Charles Merrett. His vibrant eyes and broad smile seemed to dance with excitement. "And my plans for MAS are called *Zamean matter.*"

"What do you mean, Daddy? We don't need the sunbeam anymore, do we?"

"We don't need the *weapon*. But we sure can use Zamean matter. It's a revolutionary, clean, untapped, and abundant source of energy that we can produce cheaper than anything preceding it! The particle that injured Steve's brain can be immediately redirected to interact with Earth's matter. That way, we'll get the energy without any of the harmful radiation escaping. You see, there's nothing bad about any scientific discovery when we harness and control it for good purposes. What's bad is Feran, or what he used to be before Alex zapped him."

He turned to me. "You're smiling, son." His eyes seemed to hold a special sparkle when they glanced at me.

"In Feran's hand even a stone was dangerous," I said.

The others nodded in agreement.

"And during my confinement, I came up with an idea for an antidote to the sunbeam that I believe will work. I want Steve Caldwell's mind functioning when I chew him out for taking unnecessary risks with a life as valuable as his." Dr. Merrett put his arm around Mykroni. "You know, we need to talk about an operation to collect the Zamean matter and to transport it safely. . . ." The two of them walked arm-in-arm toward the house. "We'll fix dinner for you kids," Charles Merrett called back to us, but we weren't listening.

My fingers were tangled in Kristin's chestnut hair that was the color of Earth tree bark dappled with sunshine. I swam in her brown orbs with silver sparkles that were the color of Earth's loam sprinkled with bits of white sand.

"Kristin, what does it mean when you feel another's presence with such closeness that when you're away from that person, you can do nothing but ache inside for her?"

"And what does it mean, Alex, when the sight of someone so completely excites your eyes that they have no vision left to see anything but him?"

"It means you love me, Kristin."

"And you love me, Alex."

With Earth under my feet and Kristin in my arms, I laughed—easily, freely, lavishly, the way we Earthlings do.

IF YOU ENJOYED THIS BOOK

Independently published books like *Fugitive From Asteron* depend on word-of-mouth recommendations in order to succeed. Please take a moment to leave a few comments on Amazon's Customer Reviews and on your social media. *Thank you!*

And enjoy a copy of Gen LaGreca's other acclaimed novels, available in print and ebook editions.

ABOUT THE AUTHOR

Genevieve (Gen) LaGreca writes novels with innovative plots, strong romance, and themes that glorify individual freedom and independence.

Gen's debut novel is *Noble Vision*. This romantic medical thriller won two important national literary awards. It was a *Foreword* magazine Book of the Year Finalist. It was also a finalist in the *Writer's Digest* International Book Awards contest—one of only six picks honoring general fiction published by independent presses. *Noble Vision* garnered praise from magazine magnate Steve Forbes, Nobel laureate Milton Friedman, syndicated columnist Walter E. Williams, and other influential thinkers. Gen also wrote the screenplay for *Noble Vision*.

Showing her virtuosity across genre lines, Gen's second offering is the historical novel *A Dream of Daring*. This antebellum murder mystery took five book awards, including the celebrated *Foreword* Book of the Year.

In addition to fiction, Gen also writes social and political commentaries, which have appeared in *Forbes*, *The Orange County Register*, *The Daily Caller*, *Real Clear Markets*, *Mises Daily*, *The Gainesville Sun*, and other publications.

Prior to fiction writing, Gen worked as a pharmaceutical chemist, business consultant, and corporate writer. She holds an undergraduate degree in chemistry from Polytechnic Institute of New York and a graduate degree in philosophy from Columbia University.

Her variety of life experiences—in science and business, as well as in philosophy and writing—brings vibrant characters, urgent issues, thematic depth, and an outside-the-box approach to Gen's novels. Their sweeping themes of self-sovereignty and the triumph of the individual attract thoughtful readers across genre lines.

For more information, see: www.wingedvictorypress.com.
Gen may be reached at: genlagreca@hotmail.com.

Follow her on:
www.facebook.com/genlagreca
www.twitter.com/genlagreca

PRAISE FOR GEN LAGRECA'S FIRST NOVEL,
NOBLE VISION

"The novel deals with some of the most serious issues of the day, lending the story an immediacy and vibrancy. The author's prose is polished and professional."

—*Writer's Digest* magazine

". . . A well-researched . . . sensitively written . . . inherently captivating novel of suspense, *Noble Vision* is very highly recommended reading."

—*Midwest Book Review*

"This is a beautifully written book! . . . For a first novel, this is a marvelous achievement."

—Midwest Book Awards

"The mounting conflicts of this lovingly sculpted first novel will keep you turning pages late into the night."

—Laissez Faire Books

AWARDS FOR *NOBLE VISION*

Foreword magazine
Book of the Year Finalist in General Fiction

Writer's Digest 13th Annual International Book Awards
Honorable Mention in Mainstream Fiction

Midwest Book Awards
Finalist in General Fiction

Illinois Women's Press Association Fiction Contest
Second Place

PRAISE FOR GEN LAGRECA'S SECOND NOVEL,

A DREAM OF DARING

" . . . thought-provoking . . . [the tale] intrigues and should attract readers interested in historical fiction set in the antebellum South."

—Booklist

"Throughout the narrative, LaGreca masterfully creates metaphors to explore her key themes. . . . *A Dream of Daring* is suspenseful. The crime at the center of the narrative will keep the reader guessing until the final revelation. . . . LaGreca's exploration of how people respond to, and sometimes reject, change and progress is relevant for all generations."

—Foreword Reviews

"Old ways do not fade into the night quietly. *A Dream of Daring* is a novel set on the dawn of the industrial revolution. Tom Edmunton builds a proto-tractor, and tries to bring a world of change about Louisiana with his invention. But the whiplash is hard, as a loved one is killed and his invention is stolen. [As Tom is] faced with a crossroads and the charms of multiple women, *A Dream of Daring* is an enticing blend of mystery and romance, much recommended reading."

—Midwest Book Review

AWARDS FOR *A DREAM OF DARING*

Foreword magazine
Book of the Year Finalist in Romance

Midwest Book Awards
Finalist in Historical Fiction

Midwest Book Awards
Finalist in Romance

2013 Next Generation Indie Book Awards
Finalist in Regional Fiction

2013 Next Generation Indie Book Awards
Finalist in Multicultural Fiction